Birdwatching

FEB 2024

TO: Uncle Brian + cousins KATE + Alex

To Read prior to your trip to spectacular KASHMIR. ♥

xoLove to you 3, Meleni, Hands. ♥

Also by Stephen Alter

Birdwatching

A Novel

A BREATHTAKING STORY
ABOUT THE SECRET WAR
IN THE HIMALAYA

STEPHEN ALTER

ALEPH

ALEPH

ALEPH BOOK COMPANY
An independent publishing firm
promoted by *Rupa Publications India*

First published in India in 2022
by Aleph Book Company
7/16 Ansari Road, Daryaganj
New Delhi 110 002

ISBN: 978-93-91047-40-5

3 5 7 9 10 8 6 4 2

Printed in India

for
David Davidar
Editori sollertissimo

*I have become a queer mixture of the East and the West,
out of place everywhere, at home nowhere.*
—Jawaharlal Nehru

*I don't think the intelligence reports are all that hot.
Some days I get more out of the* New York Times.
—John F. Kennedy

*Communism is not love.
Communism is a hammer we use to crush the enemy.*
—Mao Zedong

Contents

Asian King Vulture

Sarcogyps Calvus

Also known as the red-headed vulture. Relatively common, though not as widespread as the white-backed vulture (Gyps bengalensis) and the Indian vulture (G. indicus). Approximately thirty inches in length, it has an average wingspan of seven and a half feet. Plumage is generally a dark brown with grey stripes on its wings. Adults have crimson heads, which are featherless with prominent flaps of skin on either side of their necks; juveniles have grey heads. Like all vultures their digestive tracts are highly acidic, allowing them to eat rotting flesh, which contains toxic bacteria and other pathogens.

March 11, 1962. Guy Fletcher discovered the body a day before Jackie Kennedy arrived in India. He had been standing on the rooftop terrace of a guesthouse on Malcha Marg, just after sunrise, watching a flock of rose-ringed parakeets and other birds beginning their day. Silhouetted against the sky, he noticed half a dozen vultures circling over a broad expanse of acacia forest immediately to the west of Chanakyapuri, New Delhi's diplomatic enclave. A wild, untended green belt, the forest marked the southern extremity of the Delhi Ridge, eroded remains of the ancient Aravalli Range that runs like an arthritic spine through India's capital. On earlier bird sorties, Fletcher had explored sections of the jungle and discovered an interesting mix of species in the understory, from babblers to pipits and peafowl.

Returning to his room and picking up his backpack, Fletcher headed downstairs and walked to the end of Malcha Marg, then dodged light traffic on Kitchener Road, before entering the jungle. Several weaverbird nests were hanging from the unpruned branches of ornamental shrubs bordering the road. A pair of grey partridges flushed in front of him as he headed down a dusty path between overgrown margins of acacia trees. The President's Bodyguard used trails through the forest for riding and there were a number of horses' graves amongst the trees, some of them with headstones:

SULTAN
1948–1957,
beloved horse of Major T. S. Khullar,
President's Bodyguard

The ruins of a fourteenth century hunting lodge, called the Malcha Mahal, lay within the scrub jungle, which covered more than 2,000 acres. This area seemed safe enough in daylight, though there was a sense of isolation despite the surrounding city, which made Fletcher alert to danger. It was the sort of place that attracted miscreants and loiterers, though nobody was about. At one spot, someone had dumped a pile of garbage in which rhesus monkeys were searching for edible scraps.

Through gaps in the trees overhead, Fletcher could see the vultures still circling. With his binoculars, he was able to identify their bald heads, which looked badly sunburnt. A number of kites and crows were also spinning a loose gyre above the urban forest. Slowing his pace, he kept an eye out on either side, feeling as if he was being watched.

Fletcher had arrived in Delhi a day ago, driving up from Bharatpur, where he had been conducting his fieldwork, observing flights of bar-headed geese departing for Tibet. It felt as if winter was over, though at this hour of the morning a slight chill lingered in the air. After three months in Bharatpur, he felt out of place in the city, even if New Delhi was more like a provincial town, with posh colonies attached, its streets laid out in a web of avenues, roundabouts, and ring roads. A decade ago, in the early fifties, Fletcher had grown up here as a boy, and he knew his way around the city, though it was rapidly expanding.

Treading as lightly as he could, he passed a ruined brick structure overgrown with a bougainvillea creeper that had gone wild, sprouting a few magenta blossoms. A magpie-robin was perched on its thorny tendrils. By now Fletcher could smell the odour of rotting flesh and he knew he was close to whatever carrion had attracted the vultures. Moments later, two jackals crossed in front of him, stopping briefly to glance in his direction before skulking away into the undergrowth.

About fifty feet ahead, in a dusty clearing, the vultures were squabbling amongst themselves, hunched and ravenous. A couple more of the big birds came swooping down and joined the feeding frenzy. Though he was close enough to identify them with the naked eye, Fletcher focused his binoculars on the birds. Definitely *Sarcogyps calvus*. He'd seen a few in Bharatpur, but not as close up as this.

Removing his Asahi Pentax from the backpack, Fletcher tried to take a couple of photographs, though the vultures were moving about restlessly and it was difficult to get a good shot. He paused, remembering that the roll of film had only a few exposures left on it. At the same moment, something caught his eye and made him reach for his binoculars again.

He had imagined the wake of vultures were feeding on the carcass of a tonga horse that had died from malnutrition and mistreatment, or a street dog run over by a car, maybe even a sacred cow that had succumbed to natural causes. But as he peered through the feathered scrum, Fletcher noticed a pair of walnut brown Oxford brogues. As soon as he moved in closer to get a better look, one of the vultures spotted him and let out a warning squawk. Within seconds the committee of raptors took to the air in a chaotic flurry of wings.

A couple of house crows remained on the ground for a few seconds longer. But they were wary of the human intruder and flew up onto a nearby tree, cawing loudly. Feeling suddenly alone and exposed, Fletcher approached the body with caution and unease. He could see where the birds had torn through the pinstripe trousers and disembowelled the corpse, starting from the soft tissues near the anus, as was their habit. The body lay facing upwards but was twisted at the waist, legs askew. The smell of decomposition seemed much stronger suddenly, as if Fletcher's senses had become more acute after he realized that the vultures were feeding on human remains. The sight of the man's entrails spilling into the dust and the white vulture shit on his suit, made Fletcher take a step back, though he could see that the torso and head had not been disturbed. A blue silk tie was neatly knotted at the man's throat and his pale features were remarkably calm.

Resisting an instinct to walk away, Fletcher circled the body. The dead man was not Indian but clearly of European descent, with thinning grey hair. Removing the lens cap on his camera again, Fletcher stepped closer and focused on the corpse's face, which was the colour of boiled cauliflower. There was no reason for him to take photographs but somehow it seemed as if it was his responsibility. From the right side, he could see a gunshot wound above the dead man's left eye, where a scab of dry blood marked the spot. Fletcher guessed that the bullet must have blown out the back of the skull but the exit wound was hidden, for the body lay facing up at the sky and both of the man's eyes, a grey-green colour, were staring at the clouds. After the second photograph, the film was finished, advancing no further. Fletcher closed the camera and stepped away from the corpse.

He had no idea what to do next, though he realized it was important to inform the police. Retracing his steps out of the jungle, Fletcher went back to the guesthouse, which was a private residence owned by Mrs Ruby Khanna, who rented out rooms to foreigners on a weekly basis. One of the administrators at the Fulbright office had recommended the place and Fletcher found it clean, convenient, and relatively cheap at twelve rupees a night, including breakfast. At 9 a.m., he decided that he would go to the American Embassy, which was a ten-minute walk from the guesthouse. Most of the diplomatic enclave was still being built and the surrounding area looked like a vast construction site with only a few trees. The US Chancery had just opened and the ambassador's residence was nearing completion. The Embassy was elegantly modern with straight, simple lines and a white facade of concrete grillwork that screened in the entire structure. Metal columns supported a broad, flat roof.

Fletcher carried his passport with him and showed it to the marine guard at the entrance, who waved him past. Inside was a sign for the consular section and he made his way through a labyrinth of bare corridors to a sparsely furnished office, where a US flag stood in one corner, along with an official portrait of JFK. The president stared out at him with a calm and confident demeanour. Fletcher had voted for Kennedy, though the rest of his family members were devout Republicans. The Chancery smelt of fresh paint. On the back wall, behind a chest-high counter was a poster listing 'Citizen Services.'

One of the junior consular officers, a young woman with an anxious frown, met him and, after he explained why he was there, asked him to wait. Several minutes later the Consul himself came out and questioned him. The man's impatient expression made it clear that he didn't have time to deal with trivial matters like a dead body, especially since everyone at the Embassy was preparing for Mrs Kennedy's visit.

'When did this happen?' he asked.

'About two hours ago,' said Fletcher.

'And you're here on a Fulbright?'

He nodded.

'Doing what?'

'I'm an ornithologist, studying migratory birds.'

'How did you find the body?'

'By accident,' Fletcher explained for the second time. 'I spotted some red-headed vultures and discovered they were feeding on a corpse.'

'Is the dead man an American?'

'I have no idea,' said Fletcher. 'He's definitely a foreigner. Maybe a diplomat.'

'So, what do you want us to do?' the Consul asked.

'I wasn't sure if I should go to the police on my own,' Fletcher explained. 'According to the instructions we were given during our Fulbright orientation, I was told to get help from the Embassy if I ever needed to contact the police.'

The Consul asked him to wait. After ten minutes, one of the Indian staff, a man named Ravi Jacob, was sent with him to the police station in Chanakyapuri. They drove across in an embassy car. Jacob seemed to know the station house officer, or SHO, who took down a First Information Report from Fletcher, which he signed. After that they went across to the green belt, so he could show them the body. Two jeeps accompanied them and six constables, as well as the SHO himself.

The corpse was exactly where Fletcher had left it, though the vultures had come back and eaten more of the man's flesh from his buttocks and thighs. Another few hours and they would have cleaned him to the bone. Ravi Jacob, who had been chatty and reassuring until then, fell silent as soon as they came in sight of the body. Moments later, he went off to one side and threw up. Fletcher's Hindi was good enough for him to answer questions from the police, who examined the site without much interest. It was obvious that the man had been killed somewhere else and his body dumped here.

As he looked down at the corpse again, Fletcher noticed something he'd missed seeing the first time around and it sent a current of fear and horror through every nerve in his body. On the dead man's right hand, three of his fingernails were missing. The blood had dried, but it was clear that the nails had been brutally ripped out and the fingers were bruised to the first knuckle.

One of the policemen gingerly checked the victim's trouser pockets and found they were empty. Both his wallet and watch were gone. The only thing they discovered, tucked into the inside pocket of his coat, was an invitation card embossed with a gilded emblem of the US Embassy. As the SHO examined it, Fletcher moved closer and was able to read what it said:

H. E. Ambassador John Kenneth Galbraith and Mrs Galbraith
request the pleasure of your company
at a reception for the First Lady of the United States
Mrs Jacqueline Bouvier Kennedy
on Tuesday, March 20, 1962
8 p.m.
US Embassy Chancery
Chanakyapuri, New Delhi

Glancing at the back of the card, the SHO casually pocketed the evidence and told two of his constables to remain with the corpse. As they retraced their steps to the vehicles, he questioned Fletcher more closely. After they returned to the police station, he wanted to take Fletcher's passport but Ravi Jacob was able to persuade him that the US Embassy would guarantee his availability for further questioning. Eventually, by three in the afternoon, they let Fletcher go and he went back to the guesthouse. Though he'd eaten nothing all day, he wasn't hungry, feeling a faint sense of nausea and exhaustion. Lying down for a while, he watched the fan spinning overhead like a whirling dervish hanging by his heels from the ceiling.

◆

By ten o'clock the next morning, Fletcher was at Palam Airport. He was allowed to enter the visitors' enclosure, just as an Air India Boeing 707 landed and taxied towards them. A crowd of embassy personnel and other expatriates had gathered, along with a large contingent of journalists. There were Indian officials and military officers too, airline employees, gawkers, and others, altogether about 500 people waiting on the tarmac. As soon as the jet manoeuvred into position and the engines shut down, a convoy of limousines and other vehicles drove across from the VIP terminal nearby. As the plane's doors opened, two staircases were wheeled up against the fuselage and the dignitaries were escorted forward. The prime minister had come to receive his distinguished guest. Jawaharlal Nehru looked spry and youthful for his age, in a white achkan, with a pink rose tucked into his buttonhole. On account of his presence, most of the cabinet was there, as well as a coterie of civil servants and ADCs in uniform. Fletcher recognized the US ambassador, John Kenneth Galbraith, towering above the others in a light tan suit. He looked like an adjutant stork. One of Galbraith's books, *The Affluent Society*, had been an assigned text in an economics class he had taken during his sophomore year at Wesleyan University.

It was a warm day and in the direct sunlight, everyone was perspiring. The ambassador and his wife went up the stairs to receive the first lady but before the guest of honour disembarked, the press corps travelling with her was herded off the rear exit, so they could witness Mrs Kennedy's arrival. Fletcher edged forward as he caught sight of Sage Carlyle coming down the stairs. She couldn't see him, though he waved as the reporters took up their positions directly opposite the VIPs. Sage had three cameras around her neck, two Leicas and a Hasselblad. Her brown hair was gathered in a loose knot at the back. She was wearing white pedal pushers with a paisley print blouse and her dark glasses were perched high on top of her head.

Following several minutes of anticipation, an enthusiastic round of applause broke out as Jackie Kennedy appeared in a radioactive pink summer suit, with a matching hat and white gloves. Coming down the stairs, she looked relaxed and smiling, as if she had just stepped out of a boutique on Fifth Avenue, rather than having flown halfway around the world. Nehru strode forward and greeted her, clasping Mrs Kennedy's outstretched hand in both of his. Sage was firing away— one camera after the other—jockeying for position amidst the squad of official photographers.

Within a few minutes, the first lady turned towards the crowd of admirers and waved. She was joined by her sister, Princess Lee Radziwill, along with a bevy of aides and secret service agents. Ushered into one of the Cadillacs, Mrs Kennedy was driven away. After the brief drama of her arrival, the crowd began to disperse, searching for shade. Fletcher could see that Sage had moved under one of the wings of the 707, which looked like a huge aluminium albatross, emblazoned with the Air India logo. Two stewardesses, in silk saris, stood at the top of the staircase.

The security detail had departed with the dignitaries and Fletcher was able to duck under the roped off enclosure.

'Hey, there!' he shouted. 'Sage!'

She turned halfway around, not sure where he was.

'Over here!' Fletcher cried, noticing one of the Air India officials beginning to make a show of stopping him, then changing his mind, as Sage spotted Guy.

'Gee!' she cried.

Sage was the only person who pronounced his name as if he were French. He collided with her cameras as they embraced and she kissed him hard on the mouth. 'I can't believe you're here.'

'I promised I'd meet you, didn't I?'

They kissed again, just as someone shouted for Sage. The press corps vehicles were about to leave for the hotel.

'Do you need a ride?' she asked.

'No. I've come on my bike,' said Fletcher.

'A bicycle?'

'Motorcycle,' he explained. 'I'll meet you at the hotel. You're staying at the Ashoka, aren't you?'

Flustered and distracted, she hurried off to join the others. As he watched her walk away, Fletcher noticed a pair of red-vented bulbuls perched on strands of barbed wire, which had been strung along the edge of the tarmac, to make sure that stray cattle didn't wander onto the runway.

2

Red-vented Bulbul

Pycnonotus cafer

*One of the most common garden birds in Delhi, with a lively, warbling
song, bulbuls have been celebrated for centuries by romantic Persian and
Urdu poets. This species has a black, crested head, mottled brown and grey
body, with a red patch under its tail. A similar bird, also found throughout
India, is the red-whiskered bulbul (Pycnonotus jocosus), which has
a more prominent crest, white cheek and throat, a black moustachial
stripe, and a flash of red behind each eye, as well as under its tail.
Bulbuls are extremely territorial and can scare off other species as well
as competitors of their own kind.*

Three and a half years ago, during the fall semester of his senior
year at Wesleyan, Fletcher had gone down to Sarah Lawrence for
a mixer, along with two of his classmates. It wasn't the kind of thing he
did ordinarily, though college was almost over and he still hadn't got
laid, which seemed an essential requirement for graduation. One of his
friends had a car, a rusty Oldsmobile, and they drove down to Bronxville
together. The leaves had just begun to turn colour and the days were
growing shorter, with a bite of autumn in the air, which made the whole
expedition feel like a lost cause. At the main gate, they were questioned
by security guards and showed their college IDs. The party had just
started in the common room of a dormitory. Roy Orbison was crooning
on the record player and scattered coveys of girls hovered in the shadows.
One or two couples were dancing but mostly people were sitting around,
smoking and looking self-consciously bored.

After an hour or so, things started to pick up—but by then Fletcher was ready to leave. His friends had met up with two girls that one of them knew and he was the odd man out. Wandering through a side exit of the common room, he headed out into a courtyard, where the moon had spilt its icy iridescence. Dry leaves rustled under his feet and he could hear hushed laughter beyond the trees nearby. Settling down on the grass under a shedding maple, he drew his shoulders in because of the cold. The shadowy profiles of the gothic buildings and the dark evergreens added to his loneliness as he wondered how he was going to get back to Connecticut. It was like being stranded on the island of Circe, with no sirens calling his name.

Moments later, however, an apparition appeared behind him and he saw the flare of a match, as someone lit a cigarette.

'Shitty party, right?' he heard a woman's voice. She was standing, looking down at him.

'I guess it's not my scene,' said Fletcher.

'Yeah, I saw you walking out...'

'Are you stalking me?' he asked, with a laugh.

'Maybe,' she replied. 'Yale?'

He shook his head. 'Wesleyan.'

'Hey!' she said. 'Cardinals. One of the Little Three.'

'I guess.'

'Can I join you?'

He nodded as she sat down cross-legged on the grass and he could see the winsome profile of her face silhouetted against the sheen of moonlight on the lawn. Her dark hair was pulled back in a ponytail.

'I'm Guy,' he said, putting out a hand.

Tucking the cigarette between her lips, she reached across and shook his hand, her fingers dry and smooth.

'Sage,' she whispered. 'Is Guy short for anything?'

He shook his head.

'So, I'll call you *Gee*,' she said. '*Français*. Is that all right?'

He shrugged.

'I'm glad you're not from Yale,' she said. 'They're all such dicks.'

'I don't know about that...' he said.

She offered him a drag from her cigarette but he shook his head.

'That's healthy of you,' she teased him, laughing.

'I run cross country,' Fletcher said.

'And what are you majoring in at Wes?' Sage asked.

'Biology,' he said.

'Pre-med?'

'No,' he replied. 'Why? Is this an interview?'

'Maybe,' she said, flicking the remains of her cigarette into the grass.

They sat for a while in silence. Fletcher leaned back and lay down on the lawn, looking up at the moon through the shaggy branches of a yew. He felt her finger trace the inside of his arm.

'I've got a bottle of vodka in my room,' she said. 'You want to join me…unless you don't drink.'

'Why not?' he said.

She got up with the agile grace of a gymnast, then reached out her hand. 'Viens avec moi, cher Guy!'

He let her pull him to his feet and brushed the leaves off the back of his head as Sage led him by the hand across the campus, along a brick path, to her dorm. Her roommate was away for the weekend.

They spent the next thirty-six hours having sex—a slippery, sweaty, sticky weekend in which she taught him all there was to know about a woman's body, and much about his own. Between bouts of lovemaking, they drank vodka and 7 Up, ate chocolate, and listened to Debussy and Ravel, particularly *Daphnis et Chloé,* which Sage said always turned her on. At her suggestion, they even timed a shared orgasm with the crescendo. By the end of it, Fletcher's nerves felt like the needle on the record player, tracing a pleasurable groove in a revolving disc of vinyl.

'This is my first time, you know…' he said in a hoarse whisper that stuck in his throat, after the LP had finished.

She looked at him, puzzled and amused.

'What?'

'I mean… You're the first girl I've ever made love with.'

Sage grinned at him, as if this piece of information pleased her more than all of their carnal contortions. 'No kidding?'

She was at least two years younger than him, a sophomore, but when it came to sex, she was far more experienced and it made him feel strangely content, letting Sage be his tutor.

She didn't tell him much about herself though he learnt that Sage was a photographer and planned to pursue it as a career. One of the walls in her dorm room was covered with posters from an exhibition of Henri Cartier-Bresson's work at the Museum of Modern Art in New York. Mostly, these were pictures of Paris—street scenes and a portrait of André Gide. But there was also a shot of Mahatma Gandhi with his spinning wheel.

Pointing at the picture, he told her that he'd lived in India for five years.

'Oh yeah?' she said. 'That's cool. What were you doing there?'

'My dad was a hydraulic engineer, working on an irrigation project funded by the US Embassy.'

Throwing aside the covers on her bed, Sage stood up and reached for a Leica that lay on top of a bookshelf. She turned and focused on Guy, who covered himself instinctively.

'Come on,' she said. 'Don't be such a prude.'

She herself was naked and the sight of her holding the camera made him laugh, as he moved his hands aside.

'You're going to blackmail me, I bet,' he said.

By Sunday afternoon, before the roommate returned, Fletcher showered in the bathroom at the end of the hall, put on his clothes, and headed out. Sage walked with him to the college gate and kissed him for a long time before letting him go.

'How are you going to get back to Wesleyan?' she asked, as an afterthought.

He held up a thumb and smiled.

Hitching out of Bronxville was the hardest part because it was a wealthy suburb and the drivers scowled at him with suspicion and hostility, accelerating past. Eventually, he got a ride to the Merritt Parkway. From there, a man in a pickup truck took him on to Interstate 91 and dropped him at the exit for Rte 9, after which a Wesleyan sophomore gave him a lift into Middletown.

Over the next two days, he wrote a long letter to Sage in which he told her that he would never forget their weekend and that he was still humming Ravel's music. He also told her things about himself, his family home in Colorado, and the years he'd spent in India, how he'd been devastated when they left and moved to Fort Collins, where his father took a job as a professor at Colorado State and his mother worked at a Buick dealership. He knew Sage wouldn't be interested in all this but he wrote it down anyway, as if it were some kind of confession of love or commitment, though he wasn't sure what he felt for her. They had met as strangers and, for the most part, that was what she remained, an all but anonymous lover. He wished he had a picture of Sage and wondered if she'd developed and printed the photograph of him in the nude. When he finished the letter, he didn't even know what address to use, though he found 'Sarah Lawrence' in a college directory. Fortunately, he had seen Sage's last name on a notebook in her room. The letter reached her and she took a couple of weeks to write back, a short, gushing note, telling him that he was her 'dream lover, etc., etc.'

They didn't meet again until spring, when he borrowed a friend's car and drove down to see her. The roommate was there, though she went out to the library long enough for them to have sex again. Sage seemed distracted this time, going through the motions without the same excitement. He went away mildly disappointed but they kept in touch. Fletcher now had a number for the hall phone in her dorm and he called a couple of times, though she was quick to hang up on both occasions, saying someone else needed to make a call.

That fall, he started graduate school at Cornell, where he met a girl from California. They hooked up for about a year, until she went back to San Diego. Though he realized that Sage must have moved on to other lovers, there was still a residual ache of longing whenever he thought of her, the intimacy of unknowing. Two years later, he realized that by now she must have graduated. In one of their phone calls, she'd mentioned moving to New York City, where she had an internship at *Cosmopolitan*.

Last August, before leaving the US to start his fieldwork in India, he had written to her on an impulse, just to tell her that he was going back to the place where he'd grown up. After flipping through a copy of *Cosmopolitan* at a newsagent, Fletcher found Sage's name on the masthead, near the bottom, listed as an assistant photographer. He sent the letter, care of the magazine, and was elated by her reply, an excited scrawl over three pages of notepaper, saying that she was so happy to hear from him and to know that he hadn't forgotten her. *Can you believe it? I'm coming to India in October. Covering Mrs Kennedy's visit for Cosmo. We've got to see each other. XXX Sage.* Her letter had gone to the Fulbright office in Delhi and was forwarded to him in Bharatpur, where it arrived at his one-room flat in the main bazaar, over a motor-mechanic's workshop. The letter made him whoop with excitement, as he read it that evening and he felt a jolt of anticipation like the bursts of white light from the welding torch beneath his window.

In the end, the first lady's visit to India was postponed until March but Sage had written to say that she would definitely be there, travelling with the press entourage. Her assignment was to capture the chic mystique of Jackie Kennedy's allure in an exotic setting. By this time, Fletcher had almost finished his first season in Bharatpur and his landlord, who owned the workshop downstairs, had persuaded him to invest in a battered 350cc BSA motorcycle, which he'd driven to Delhi.

◆

After kicking the bike more than a dozen times, he finally got it started. Heading out of Palam Airport he joined the two-lane highway that passed through fields and wasteland. There was a fair amount of traffic, mostly swarms of bicycles but also Tata trucks loaded with goods and spewing diesel fumes from their tailpipes. Black and yellow Ambassador taxis dodged between them, overtaking the trucks on either side and blowing their horns impatiently. A couple of bullock carts were crawling along a rutted country road, parallel to the highway. The last blossoms in the mustard fields added a bright yellow tinge to the tawny landscape. The air smelt of cow dung and dust, a sour-sweet odour that Fletcher remembered from childhood and always associated with the outskirts of Delhi.

The Ashoka Hotel had opened six years earlier, a sandstone edifice that symbolized the aspirations of India's tourism industry. It seemed to rival the Red Fort in size and grandeur with a marble-clad lobby stretching in all directions. Fletcher remembered watching it being built as a boy. The uniformed guards at the gate looked disapprovingly at his motorcycle, which had a loose muffler that belched smoke and sounded like a tractor. He was directed to park at the far edge of the lot, alongside a couple of other bikes and scooters.

The Sikh doorman saluted Fletcher as he entered. A few tourists were standing about at the reception counter but there was no sign of Sage. Fletcher asked one of the receptionists for her room number. He thought of calling her on the house phone, but impulsively took the lift up to the fourth floor. The hotel hallway reminded him of her dormitory, though on a much grander scale. When he came to the door, 436, he paused for a moment before knocking. There was no reply, so he knocked again and heard her call out from inside, asking him to wait.

When the door opened, she looked surprised to see him.

'Oh, Guy!' she said. 'It's you. I thought it was room service.'

He knew immediately that someone else was with her and felt like a fool for having blundered up instead of ringing ahead. She held the door open halfway, smiling awkwardly.

'Sorry. I can come back later,' he mumbled.

'No. I didn't realize....'

Just then, he saw a figure rise from one of the chairs inside and step behind her. He was an older man, maybe forty, with wisps of grey in his hair, a clipped moustache, and glasses with round tortoiseshell rims.

Sage glanced back over her shoulder, then looked at Fletcher with a helpless expression.

'Guy, this is Owen,' she said, as the man put out his hand. He had a confident grip and Fletcher was at a disadvantage.

'Owen Sidwell. Reuters,' said the man.

'Guy and I've known each other for ages, from college days,' said Sage. 'He's studying birds on a Fulbright.'

'Birds?' Owen said, as if he was genuinely interested. 'What kind?'

Fletcher retreated. 'Waterfowl,' he said.

Sage had her back to the man and made an apologetic face.

'So, you're an ornithologist, are you?' Owen persisted, as if there was no awkwardness at all.

'Yeah, okay, I'll see you later, maybe,' Fletcher said, turning back down the hall. 'You're here for a week....'

Sage nodded. 'Yes, but we're going to Benares day after tomorrow, then Agra and Udaipur and somewhere else, I can't remember. The whole tour. I'll be back on Sunday.'

'Monday,' Owen corrected her. 'We get back to Delhi from Jaipur on the nineteenth, late in the morning.'

She shook her head. 'Okay. Sorry. I'm in another time zone.'

'So long. See you later,' said Fletcher, trying to sound casual, though he felt as if his guts had been ripped out, like the dead man in the city forest. As he walked towards the lift, a room service trolley went past him, pushed by a waiter with an ingratiating smile. It had been too much to hope for, he thought, as he rode down in the lift, angry with himself for having been so stupid but also hurt that Sage hadn't warned him.

The doorman saluted again and the sweeping arc of his arm coming up and the fingers touching his turban seemed to mock Fletcher's humiliation. He squinted in the sun as he made his way across to the bike, which had leaked a puddle of oil on the asphalt, though for once it started on the first kick.

Driving back to his guesthouse on Malcha Marg, Fletcher gunned the engine and took the roundabout on Shanti Path faster than he should have, leaning into the turn and feeling the BSA begin to lose traction just as he straightened out. The left rear shock absorber was shot. He wished he could forget Sage completely and let her remain an anonymous lover, rather than trying to resurrect something he knew he could never retrieve.

As he headed up the stairs to his room, Fletcher remembered the face of the dead man from the day before and wondered if he should have seen the corpse as a warning that life never turns out as it should.

The fan was off when he entered, though he remembered leaving it on. He tossed the motorcycle keys on the desk and kicked off his sandals. Seeing himself in the mirror, his dusty blonde hair blown back from riding the bike and his sunburnt face, he began to laugh. There was nothing else he could do but recognize how ridiculous it had been to imagine that he would ever make love to Sage Carlyle again.

A moment later, he noticed that his camera was out of its case, lying upside down on the desk. The Asahi Pentax had been inside his backpack, along with his binoculars, but now he felt sure that someone had been in his room while he was away. He checked the drawer where he'd put his passport, which was still there, along with his notebooks and other papers. But the camera had certainly been moved. When he picked it up, he could see that the lever for rewinding the film was open. Turning it slowly, he felt no resistance and checked the counter, which was at zero. Before opening the camera, he already knew it was empty. Whoever had been in the room had taken the exposed roll of film.

3

Common Myna

Acridotheres tristis

Widespread resident of India, mostly a sooty brown colour with white flashes on the wings and a bright yellow eye patch that gives it an angry look. The bank myna (Acridotheres ginginianus) and the jungle myna (A. fuscus) are two related species, also commonly found in cities and rural areas, usually in gardens or near cultivation. A gregarious bird, mynas congregate at sunset, often filling a tree and chattering in unison, like a crowded cocktail party.

Through the glass doors that opened from the dining room of the guesthouse onto a small rectangle of lawn at the back, he could see two mynas hunting for grasshoppers and grubs in the flower bed. These were the first birds that Fletcher remembered identifying as a boy, looking them up in Salim Ali's *Birds of India* and trying to decide if they were common or jungle mynas. At that age, he had no aspirations of becoming an ornithologist, though looking back on his early years in India, Fletcher realized that it had been a formative period of his life.

Balbir, the head bearer at the guesthouse, brought his omelette and toast to the table, as he finished eating a slice of papaya. News of Jackie Kennedy's arrival filled the morning papers. There was a photograph of her on the front page of *The Statesman*, being greeted by Jawaharlal Nehru. The headlines were effusive, extolling her beauty and charm, as well as the naïve enthusiasm with which she spoke of India. 'I just can't wait to see the Taj Mahal! It's always been a dream....' After laying flowers at Mahatma Gandhi's Samadhi at Rajghat, she praised his 'message of freedom and peace'. The fact that she had come to

India without her husband did not diminish the excitement surrounding her visit. She and her sister, Princess Lee Radziwill, provided more than enough glamour and celebrity to propel journalists into raptures of hyperbole. 'American Apsara Enchants All India.' 'From the White House to Teen Murti Bhawan, a Fairy Tale Tour.' Reading the reports over breakfast, Fletcher couldn't help but be irritated by the overblown prose, as newspapers detailed everything from the couture fashions she wore to the deft elegance of her gestures and the entrancing qualities of her smile.

The first lady's visit seemed to have no significant purpose, except as a goodwill gesture between the two countries. A few grumpy editorials were tucked inside the inner pages of the papers, complaining that the principles of 'non-alignment have been forgotten in the frenzy of adulation that has greeted the American president's wife.' But these words sounded as churlish as Fletcher's own mood. He still felt the sting of humiliation after what had happened at Sage's hotel room and wished that he had stayed back in Bharatpur, counting ducks and geese, instead of coming to Delhi and making a fool of himself.

Fletcher flipped through the papers for any news about the dead man. Yesterday there had been nothing but this morning, in *The Statesman*, he found a short article on page six.

Remains of Unidentified Foreigner Found

Delhi. March 13. Police are trying to establish the identity of a dead foreigner, whose body was found in Chanakyapuri yesterday. The male victim is approximately 35 years of age. He was dressed in a light tan safari suit with leather sandals. According to the autopsy report, his death was caused by strangulation. All of the embassies in Delhi have been notified but none of them has reported a missing person, neither from amongst their diplomatic staff or any private citizens who might have been visiting India.

According to SHO Chanakyapuri, Inspector K. S. Yadav, it appears to be a case of murder, though until the body has been identified, it will be difficult to establish a motive. Yadav confirmed that the man's wallet and watch were missing, indicating that he

may have been robbed and then killed. No other items were found
on the body.

Reading the article several times, Fletcher realized that it described a
different victim altogether. This man was much younger than the corpse
he'd found and the clothes, as well as the cause of death, didn't match
at all. Confused and unsettled, he leafed through the *Times of India*
and found virtually the same report, supplied by PTI, the Press Trust
of India. The date given was also wrong and there was no mention of
who had discovered the body. Fletcher had found the dead man on the
eleventh of March but the newspapers said it was the twelfth.

When Balbir came to clear away his plate, Fletcher asked if anyone
had stopped by to see him yesterday but the bearer shook his head.

'Something is missing from my room,' he explained.

Balbir looked worried. 'Money?' he asked.

'No. A roll of film from my camera.'

'Your camera?' Balbir sounded even more alarmed, as if he were
being accused of the theft.

'Not the camera, just the reel of film.'

'Who would have taken that?' Balbir protested.

'I have no idea,' Fletcher said, looking him in the eye and seeing
only perplexity, not guilt. More troubling than the loss of the film was
the idea that someone must have known that he had photographed
the dead man. It was the only explanation for the theft. On the way
back from the police station with Ravi Jacob, Fletcher had mentioned
to the Embassy staffer that he'd taken a couple of photographs and
asked if the police would want them as evidence. Jacob had dismissed
the idea, saying that the police would take their own pictures. At the
time, the conversation hadn't seemed important, though now, thinking
back on it, he felt sure that Jacob must have told someone. Nobody
else would have known.

Later in the day, Fletcher went across to Fulbright House on Hailey
Road and checked in with the administrators who handled his grant.
The director was out of the office, attending a reception for the first lady
at Rashtrapati Bhavan hosted by the President of India. It seemed as if
everyone was caught up in the flurry of JBK's visit. Fletcher thought of

reporting the theft but it seemed a minor matter, nothing more than a 36-exposure roll of Kodak 200 ASA black and white film. He had a dozen other rolls, exactly like it, that he needed to get developed. After finishing at Hailey Road, he rode his BSA across to Mahatta's photo studio in Connaught Circus and left these for developing and printing contact sheets. Most of the pictures were from Bharatpur—shots of birds for his research, flocks of geese on the water, and storks roosting in the trees.

After leaving the film, he walked over to Kwality's for lunch. Sitting by himself in the artificial twilight of the restaurant, he wondered if he really wanted to hook up with Sage Carlyle again. Or was it just a futile impulse to try and reclaim the memory of that weekend in the fall of 1958, when he lost his virginity to a girl he'd met only an hour before? When he was a child, Fletcher's parents would treat him and his sister to ice cream at Kwality's on the weekends and it seemed to offer some slight consolation to be sitting here again, even if he was alone.

His family had moved to Delhi in 1949, when his father accepted a job with the US government's foreign assistance programme. Though Fletcher hadn't paid much attention to what his father did, he knew he was involved with a major irrigation project in the Punjab, something to do with canals and tube wells that supported 'the green revolution', helping India produce more wheat and rice.

New Delhi in the 1950s was an idyllic world for a teenaged boy. Within a year, he felt completely at home and picked up Hindi easily from friends and servants. The American School, where he and his sister studied, was housed in an annex of the Taj Hotel on Curzon Road, though it had now moved to a new campus in Chanakyapuri, behind the US Embassy. Living in Jor Bagh, Fletcher had free run of the city. His bicycle took him everywhere from the galis of Nizamuddin to the broad avenue of Rajpath. He knew all of the back roads and connecting lanes between the bungalows where diplomats and members of Parliament lived.

In those days, traffic was light and the city was relatively safe. He and his friends would dare each other to circle the roundabout in front of The Claridges hotel, without holding onto the handlebars. His Boy Scout troop would go camping to Tughlaqabad, a ruined fortress south of Delhi, where he tracked a mongoose to its lair and saw a snake—he was sure it was a cobra—disappearing into a crack in the crumbling walls. After dark, he and the other scouts played 'capture the flag' and 'flashlight beckon' amidst the crumbling remains of the ancient citadel.

Covert pleasures awaited him in different corners of the city: the sweet shops in Bengali Market, the Regal and Odeon cinemas where he watched English pictures, the zoo with its white tigers. If New Delhi offered leafy parks and lush flowerbeds in winter, Old Delhi was the opposite. Riding the old 'phut phatiyas'—WWII Harley-Davidson and Indian Chief motorcycles rebuilt as three wheeled rickshaws— from Connaught Circus to Chandni Chowk, he would enter chaotic, labyrinthine markets with a myriad tiny shops packed into twisting lanes, where he could buy everything from a gilt wedding turban to an army surplus gas mask. On the sidewalks photowallahs took people's portraits against painted backdrops, their antique cameras like boxes on tripods.

He had been heartbroken when his family left Delhi in 1955 and miserably homesick when they moved back to Colorado. America felt like a much more dangerous place where the threat of atomic Armageddon seemed imminent. In school they'd had emergency drills, crouching under desks at the sound of a siren or trooping into the basement, which had yellow and black signs that identified it as a fallout shelter. In India, he hadn't felt the pervasive paranoia of the Cold War and the constant threat of the Soviet Union's intercontinental ballistic missiles. In 1956, when Sputnik was launched, there was a fear that America was falling behind and the Russians would conquer not just the world but outer space as well.

After lunch, Fletcher went back to the guesthouse, which was deserted. Heading up to his room, he realized that anyone could slip in unnoticed at this hour of the afternoon, when the staff were napping in their quarters. From a bookcase downstairs, he had chosen a paperback copy of Hemingway's *Fiesta*, thinking it was a book he hadn't read. But after he flipped it open, he realized it was the British edition of *The Sun Also Rises*, with a different title. His recollection of the story, which he'd read in high school, was vague but he could remember how his father had always praised Hemingway's novels. 'Terse truths,' was the phrase Bill Fletcher used. Last year, his father had died of a coronary and it was still hard for Guy to think of him without feeling a vacant sense of grief somewhere beneath his ribs. Hemingway was also dead, having committed suicide last summer in Ketchum, Idaho, choosing for himself the kind of ending he might have written for one of his characters. When he'd heard the news, Fletcher immediately wondered what his father would have said about Hemingway's death, though he too was no longer alive, which made everything feel incomplete, disconnected, and unanswered.

His father had always been an enigma. The first time Guy remembered seeing him was at the age of seven, when Bill Fletcher returned home at the end of the war, like a stranger walking back into their lives. Though Guy had looked up to him with apprehension and awe, there was little acknowledgement from his father. They had gone through the motions of love but there had been few moments when they did the sorts of things that boys and men do together—fishing, or fixing a car, or going to a baseball game. His father always seemed distracted and distant, the absent presence at the centre of his life.

He now thought of him walking into the Engineering building at Colorado State on a Tuesday morning and ascending the stairs before stumbling forward as his heart cramped up. What had he felt in those few seconds of consciousness before his brain shut down, a searing white glare behind his eyes? And what would Hemingway have felt, putting the muzzle of a shotgun in his mouth? Had he hesitated, even for a second? Listening to house sparrows nesting in the desert cooler fitted into the window behind his bed, an undefined sense of dread and despair came over him, as if the world were about to end.

In Bharatpur, he had experienced the same feeling of loneliness and anxiety as he sat by the wetlands observing flocks of birds on the water, but there was a comforting stillness to the scene, especially in the mornings when mist hovered over the glassy surface and ducks were chuckling to themselves. Armed only with a pair of field glasses, he watched flights of geese, stitching the hem of the sky with their wings. The wetlands at Bharatpur had been the maharajah's traditional hunting grounds, infamous for the Viceroy's duck shoot in 1938, when Lord Linlithgow and his entourage shot 4,273 birds. Since then, the abundance of waterfowl had diminished though hunting was still permitted. For his research, Fletcher had been issued a permit to shoot ducks and geese. He drew blood samples from the birds he collected and was able to examine the contents of their crops and stomachs. Some of the specimens he skinned and preserved to take back to Cornell.

Though the main migration was finished, Fletcher planned to stay on in Bharatpur for two more months before returning to the US in May. He had brought some work with him to Delhi, several notebooks that he needed to read over and sort through for his thesis. At this moment, however, he couldn't be bothered, letting Hemingway take him back to the running of the bulls in Pamplona. The novel suited his depression. For a few minutes he dozed off but then opened his eyes again and rejoined Jake Barnes on his lonely, impotent quest for Brett Ashley's love.

Around five o'clock, there was a knock at his door. Fletcher sat up and set the book aside. Balbir was standing beyond the screen door. Along with a mug of tea, he handed him an envelope, his name written neatly in blue ink across the front. Inside was an invitation card to the ambassador's reception for Mrs Kennedy, identical to the one that was found in the pocket of the dead man's suit.

'Who brought this?' Fletcher asked.

'A man from the American Embassy, one of their drivers,' Balbir said.

'Did he say who sent it?'

Balbir shook his head.

Assuming that the invitation was Sage's way of making things up to him, Fletcher tossed the card aside, annoyed. He guessed she must have persuaded someone at the Embassy to add his name to the guest list. He had no interest in attending the reception and compounding his own sense of rejection by meeting the man from Reuters again. Though it was probably the most sought-after event on Delhi's social calendar this year, Fletcher assumed it would be one of those pompous, dull parties with long speeches, watery cocktails, and soggy canapés.

4

Green Bee-eater

Merops orientalis

A striking, aerobatic bird, between six to seven inches long, with sharply tapered wings and a tail that ends in two thin, wire-like strands. It is a bright bottle-green colour with a golden sheen on its head and the nape of its neck. The black gorget that extends from its neatly curved beak, across its eyes, gives it a masked appearance. Prevalent in open spaces, it is often seen chasing bees and other insects on the wing.

The next day, at five o'clock, Fletcher drove across to the Delhi Golf Club to meet Reggie Bhatia, a childhood friend. Soon after arriving in India last September, Fletcher had reconnected with Reggie, whose full name was Rajinder Pratap Bhatia. As boys, they had been close companions, though after Fletcher returned to the US they had lost touch with each other. Despite the gap of seven years, however, the two of them had picked up exactly where they'd left off and Fletcher was glad to renew their friendship.

Reggie had recently got his law degree, though his true ambition in life was to be a professional golfer and compete in The Open at St Andrews. His father, a Supreme Court advocate, was a longstanding member of the Delhi Golf Club. When they were boys, Guy and Reggie would tag along and take lessons from the caddies. Fletcher had never enjoyed the game, though he liked the golf course in Delhi, punctuated with sandstone ruins of Mughal tombs and plush green fairways lined with acacia and neem trees.

Two other young lawyers, colleagues of Reggie's, joined them to make up a foursome. Not having played for five or six years, Fletcher disgraced himself, hitting more than a dozen shots into the rough. Fortunately, there was an 'ageywallah' stationed ahead, who spotted the errant balls and helped avoid losing most of them. It was a warm afternoon, even as the sun slid out of sight. On the sixteenth hole, Fletcher noticed two bee-eaters chasing insects above the fairway, their emerald feathers gilded by the last rays of sunlight. Plenty of peacocks roamed the golf course and they took to the trees to roost with mournful, wailing cries.

After their game, Fletcher followed Reggie, in his Standard Herald, back to Jor Bagh. The Bhatia's home was directly across from the house where he had lived as a boy, on a quiet side street set back from Lodhi Road. Jor Bagh was a more modern, built-up colony than the spacious expanse of stately Lutyens bungalows that lay to the north, along broad tree-lined avenues. Fletcher wondered who was living in their old house these days—probably a diplomat or some other expatriate.

Reggie's grandmother was listening to All India Radio downstairs, full volume, in the living room. Fletcher greeted her with folded hands and she acknowledged him with a distracted smile. Stowing the golf clubs, they went upstairs to Reggie's room, which he had occupied since they were boys, with a balcony overlooking the walled garden at the back. Fletcher wondered what it must be like to still be living at home. He guessed that Reggie would probably stay here for the rest of his life, eventually sharing this room with a wife. In comparison, his own peripatetic existence seemed uprooted and disjointed, like something he could never piece together again, no matter how hard he tried. In a way, he envied the predictable stability of Reggie's future. The golf course would always have its eighteen holes—no more, no less. They would continue to serve fish fingers and chicken shashlik at the clubhouse. Eventually, inevitably, Reggie would follow in his father's footsteps, arguing arcane cases in the highest court of the land. Unlike many Punjabis who had moved here at the time of Partition, the Bhatias had lived in Delhi for several generations.

A servant appeared at the door and Reggie told him to bring up two Golden Eagle beers from the fridge and get some dinner ready. His parents were out for the evening, so they could relax and eat on the balcony.

After the beers had been opened and glasses poured, Fletcher recounted how he'd come upon the body in the jungle near Chanakyapuri. Reggie listened with interest, lighting one of his filtered Four Square cigarettes and letting the smoke trickle out of his nostrils. Fletcher described the bullet hole in the victim's head.

'I saw something in *The Statesman*,' Reggie said. 'Do you know who it was?'

'Not a clue,' said Fletcher. 'He was definitely European. But in the newspapers they had it all wrong, describing a younger man, wearing different clothes...and they said he'd been strangled instead of being shot.'

'You're sure it's the same person?' Reggie asked.

'How many dead foreigners show up in Chanakyapuri? There wasn't any other report in the papers.'

'It does seem strange,' Reggie said.

'But the really weird thing was,' Fletcher continued, 'three of his fingernails had been pulled out, as if he'd been tortured.'

Reggie grimaced, then drew in a lungful of smoke before stubbing out the cigarette in an ashtray, as Fletcher went on to explain how someone had stolen the film from his camera.

'Sounds like you've got yourself tangled up in a conspiracy, Guy Bhai,' he said, using the nickname he'd called him when they were boys.

'I may need a lawyer,' said Fletcher, half-joking.

'At your service,' Reggie replied. 'But one of the things you have to realize is that Delhi isn't the safe little town that you remember. It has changed a lot in the last few years. Property values have shot up and people are buying patches of wasteland as far south as the Qutab Minar for lakhs of rupees. With the new wealth, a lot of criminals have moved in from Bombay and other places. Murders have gone up, extortion. Delhi has lost its innocence.'

'It still seems like a pretty quiet place to me,' said Fletcher.

'Of course, it's not a full-fledged city like Bombay or Calcutta,' said Reggie, 'but there's an aggressive opportunism in the air. A lot of black money and dirty politics too.'

After they'd opened a second beer, Fletcher told his friend what had happened with Sage. Reggie shook his head, commiserating. 'That's why I've stayed clear of women. My mom keeps looking for a bride but I've told her I'm not marrying until I'm thirty, after that I'll let her choose a sweet, homely Punju bride and that will be the end of it, Bhai.'

He laughed when Fletcher made a face.

As the froth on his beer subsided, Reggie mentioned Jackie Kennedy's visit and how he'd heard she was staying nearby, in the Pan Am representative's bungalow at 12 Ratendon Road. It had been fixed up as a guesthouse for the first lady and her sister. The Galbraiths' residence was nearby. Reggie said that the prime minister had sent across two tiger cubs for her amusement. They were housed in a temporary enclosure at the back. A friend of his had gone to see them.

'I've got an invitation to the ambassador's reception but I'm not going...' Fletcher started to say.

'Why not?' Reggie protested. 'You need some socializing, Guy Bhai, after studying ducks and geese for the past six months.'

'I'm really not interested,' said Fletcher. 'Besides, I don't have any clothes.'

'You can borrow mine,' Reggie insisted. 'I've got a summer suit I've worn only once, to a cousin's wedding.'

The two of them were roughly the same size, both 5' 10" with lean, athletic builds. By the end of the evening, Reggie persuaded Fletcher to try on the suit, which fit him comfortably. Adding a shirt and tie, he packed it all in a garment bag that Fletcher carried with him on the bike, flapping behind him like a cape.

At this hour of the night, there was no traffic but after taking a left turn onto Safdarjung Road, he noticed a vehicle approaching behind him. It was picking up speed and the headlights were on high beam, bearing down on him as if the driver was intent on running him over. Fletcher slowed down and moved over as far to the left as he could, to let the vehicle overtake him but instead of accelerating past, it stayed a few feet behind the motorcycle. Though the lights in the rear-view mirror were blinding, he could just make out that it was a jeep station wagon with Delhi plates. Thirty seconds later, as he was about to turn off towards Chanakyapuri, the vehicle was still on his tail, its engine roaring. The garment bag made it awkward for him to drive, though he sped up as fast as he could and kept going straight, passing through a dark section of the road, without streetlights.

Ahead, on the left, was the main gate of the Gymkhana Club where a couple of guards were slouched in the shadows. Fletcher waited until the last minute before he swung his bike towards them. He could see the jeep begin to swerve behind him but then the vehicle turned back onto the road and drove away, leaving Fletcher behind. The guards shone a torch in his direction but said nothing. Easing the motorcycle into neutral, he stopped to catch his breath. Fletcher's hands were shaking and he repositioned the garment bag, folding it in front of him, on the fuel tank. He waited for several minutes, expecting the jeep to reappear but there was no sign of any vehicle and the streets were silent.

Slowly, he turned around and headed back in the other direction, driving on into Chanakyapuri. Though he kept anticipating that the headlights would appear behind him again, there was no sign of the jeep and he arrived at the guesthouse five minutes later, still shaken but convinced the driver must have been drunk.

◆

Reading the papers the next morning at breakfast, he began to have second thoughts about attending the reception. There was a picture of Jackie Kennedy and Princess Lee Radziwill on an elephant in Jaipur, their smooth, shapely legs demurely crossed at the ankles. Though he searched for more news on the unidentified body, there was nothing. Trying to put the mystery out of his mind, Fletcher spent the next two days sorting through his notebooks and cross-referencing hundreds of pages of notes he had collected. He also got his negatives and contact sheets back from Mahatta's and made a list of the pictures he wanted enlarged. Though he kept telling himself that he should go back to Bharatpur and finish his fieldwork, he decided to stay on in Delhi for a few more days, hoping the mystery surrounding the dead man would be resolved.

On 20 March, despite his misgivings, Fletcher asked Balbir to polish his shoes while he put on Reggie's suit. Armed with the invitation, he walked across to the Chancery, arriving a calculated ten minutes late. The marine guards were in their dress uniforms and he could hear music inside. It was a warm evening and there was still dust in the air from the construction sites nearby.

Entering the Chancery building, he saw a small orchestra set up in the atrium, near a shallow reflecting pool with stepping stones. A hundred or more people were milling about and he recognized no one at first, resisting an instinct to make a quick escape. Almost everybody was at least thirty years older than him. The collar of Reggie's shirt clutched at his throat and he felt a trickle of sweat slide down his spine. The music was soft and sultry, an Anglo-Indian crooner singing 'Bésame Mucho' in the style of Edmundo Ross. After finding his way to the bar, he was going to ask for a beer but changed his mind and got a Johnnie Walker on the rocks. Out of the corner of his eye, he spotted the man from Reuters, dressed in a seersucker suit and bow tie. Fletcher had forgotten his name already. Without trying to be obvious, he scanned the room for Sage but couldn't see her anywhere.

Just then, the conversations and music tapered off, replaced by the wheezing wail of bagpipes. Glancing around, he saw Mrs Kennedy enter on the ambassador's arm to the accompaniment of 'The Skye Boat Song'. She was wearing a long white gown, with gloves up to her elbows. The pipers, who looked as if they might be members of a Sikh regiment, played the highland tune at full volume. JBK looked as cool and composed as the first day he'd seen her, getting off the aeroplane. Everyone in the room pivoted in her direction. Fletcher had read an article that morning, which said she embodied the ideals of American femininity, elegantly sheathed in Oleg Cassini's fashions. Galbraith, who wore a dinner jacket and white tie, stopped at the corner of the reflecting pool, introducing her to a couple of guests. Before Fletcher knew it, they came towards him. His hand was still damp from the condensation on the whisky glass, but Mrs Kennedy shook it briefly as the ambassador tried to steer her aside.

'Good evening. Are you with the Peace Corps?' she asked, in a whispery voice, almost drowned out by the bagpipes.

'No, ma'am,' he heard himself say, as the ambassador eyed him with suspicion. 'I'm on a Fulbright, studying geese.'

'It's such a pleasure to meet you,' she said, her eyes already moving on, though he felt as if she had registered his words. Geese? Why had he said that? It was stupid to explain too much. Thankfully, the pipers fell silent. The fragrance of Mrs Kennedy's perfume lingered on as she proceeded to greet the other guests. A short while later, the prime minister arrived with his daughter, Indira Gandhi. Following a few minutes after them was the vice president, Dr Radhakrishnan, in his pleated white turban. Each of the dignitaries was accompanied by a cluster of aides. Once they had assembled, the ambassador led Jackie Kennedy across the stepping stones to the centre of the reflecting pool, where he offered a toast and made a short speech, thanking the first lady for travelling all the way to India and expressing his gratitude to everyone who had helped organize her visit. 'A terrific success,' he concluded. 'Just a perfect visit.'

She smiled and echoed his thanks, though her voice was so muted, nobody could hear what she said. Across the water, Fletcher recognized the Consul whom he'd met when he reported the dead body. He seemed more relaxed, a glass of champagne in one hand, sharing a joke with Lee Radziwill, who wore a yellow gown and sparkling tiara.

The ambassador waved to the orchestra, urging them to play on, and they drifted into a rendition of 'Mack the Knife'. As the party shifted back into a different rhythm, Fletcher heard someone humming along with the tune and felt an arm slide through his own.

'Hey, hello there,' said Sage. 'Didn't expect to find you here.'

She kissed his cheek, though he held back.

'I thought you were the one who got me this invitation,' he said.

Sage shook her head. 'No. But I'm glad to see you,' she said.

'Oh, yeah? How's it been?'

'Good…busy,' she said. He could see the make-up on her cheeks and mauve eye shadow, which made her look older and less attractive, though she was still one of the most beautiful women in the room. It was a different kind of American femininity, more southern belle than east coast elite.

'Listen, Guy, I'm sorry…' she started.

'Don't,' he said. 'I misunderstood. It's okay.'

He kept his cool, making up for his blunder the other day, acting as if he was mature enough to let things go. She kept her hand on his forearm.

'Are you having a good time in India?' he asked.

'It's work,' she said. 'But the country is amazing. Now I know why Cartier-Bresson loved this place.'

He shrugged and looked down at the remains of the ice cubes in his glass, wondering if he should get another drink. A waiter came by with a tray of cocktail sausages impaled on toothpicks with morsels of pineapple.

'You want one?' Fletcher asked.

'No thanks,' she said. 'My stomach's out. Delhi belly. It's better now but in Jaipur, I was really sick. They've given me Entero-Vioform, which makes everything taste like mud.'

He nodded. 'It happens. So, are you going to hang around, or do you go straight back to New York?'

'No. Mrs K is going on to Pakistan after this and we have to cover that too. Keep the generals happy. We leave tomorrow.'

He smiled at her again, as if he'd run out of things to say. She was carrying a pastel blue clutch that looked like a replica of the first lady's purse. Taking out a packet of Menthol Slims, Sage fumbled for a lighter. Fletcher reached into the pocket of Reggie's suit and, like a magician, found a box of matches. As he lit her cigarette, he heard a voice to his left.

'Mr Fletcher?'

Two men were standing a few feet away, both of them wearing dinner jackets that looked a size too small, straining to contain the bulk of their upper bodies. One of them was balding with pale blonde strands combed back from his forehead. The other had dark hair, a crew cut. One of the men raised a hand and gestured for him to follow, with a twitch of his trigger finger.

Sage eyed them through a haze of cigarette smoke and gave Fletcher a questioning look.

'What's going on?' he asked.

'We need a word with you,' said the crew cut man, whose voice was higher pitched than he'd expected.

'Right now?'

The other man nodded, then looked at Sage. 'Excuse us, please, ma'am.'

Fletcher thought of refusing but knew it was pointless. Waving at Sage, he followed the two men through the crowd, leaving his empty glass on a table as he went by. They led him to a stairwell that descended below the Chancery and he was surprised by the brightness of the lights and the windowless maze of passageways at the basement level of the building. These seemed to be offices and conference rooms. Nobody was around, though the lights were all on, a stark, florescent aura.

'What's this about?' Fletcher asked, trying to muffle the anxiety in his voice.

'Just a conversation,' said the blonde man, as they came to an unmarked door, which he opened. The smell of pipe smoke drifted out to meet them. Inside, two more men were seated behind a table. Neither of them was dressed for the party, wearing safari shirts and khakis. Both men were older than Fletcher's escorts, who pulled a chair forward so he could sit, then leaned against the wall.

Fletcher could tell the whole thing had been staged to intimidate him, though the pair behind the table were smiling, as if amused by his unease.

'I'm Jack Sullivan,' said the older of the two, putting out a weathered hand. He looked as if he was in his late fifties, a sandy-haired man with stooped shoulders but a trim build. His round, rimless glasses framed a pair of dark brown eyes that studied Fletcher with a sympathetic gaze.

'Mark,' the other man said, offering no surname. He seemed less friendly, stout, and sullen-looking, with a face that showed little emotion.

'Okay?' said Fletcher, after a brief silence.

'Enjoying the dog and pony show upstairs?' said Mark, as Sullivan relit his pipe.

'I guess,' said Fletcher, realizing now that it was these men who had arranged the invitation. Mark flipped open a manila folder and slid two photographs across the table. They were 5x7 prints of the photographs he had taken of the corpse.

'Do you know who this is?' Sullivan said.

'No idea,' said Fletcher.

'Why'd you take these pictures?' Mark asked, a note of inquisitive menace in his voice.

'I don't know. I wasn't sure what was going on,' said Fletcher. 'It seemed like something I should do, like gathering evidence....'

'Evidence of what?' Mark demanded.

'Hey, I'm not a detective. I don't find dead people very often, but I could see that he'd been murdered,' Fletcher protested. 'I explained all this to the Consul and the police.'

'Sure,' said Sullivan. 'You did the right thing. But we're still curious, why you happened to be wandering about in the forest that particular morning and then decided to take these photographs...for evidence?'

'Do *you* know who he is?' Fletcher asked.

Mark nodded. 'Joaquin Morales. First Secretary in the Cuban Embassy. Ring a bell?'

Fletcher shook his head.

'We're trying to figure out who might have killed him,' said Sullivan, leaning back in his chair. 'Anything more you can tell us would be really helpful.'

'Well, I'm pretty sure he was tortured before he died,' said Fletcher.

'What makes you say that?' Sullivan asked, with a look of concern.

'Three of his fingernails were missing and his knuckles were bruised.'

Mark and Sullivan exchanged a glance. 'Anything else?' Mark asked.

'That's it,' said Fletcher. 'But maybe you can tell me why the report in the newspapers described some other man. It was all wrong.'

'Journalists never get it right,' said Mark, with a dismissive wave.

'You're an ornithologist from Cornell, aren't you? Studying geese?' Sullivan spoke in a reassuring tone, as if they were exchanging pleasantries rather than conducting an interrogation. Fletcher wanted to laugh, as if for the second time this evening the subject of his research seemed absurd. They knew exactly who he was.

Switching to Hindi, Sullivan asked. 'You lived in Delhi as a child, didn't you?' He spoke the language fluently, a confident, colloquial tone to his voice.

After a moment's hesitation, Fletcher replied, 'Yes. Where did you learn Hindi?' The others in the room didn't seem to follow this exchange.

'Jamshedpur. My father worked at Tata Steel, forty years ago,' Sullivan explained, then asked, 'So, where in Delhi did you live?'

'236, Jor Bagh,' Fletcher replied.

'My place is right around the corner from there. 262,' said Sullivan switching back to English. 'You should come over sometime.'

Mark leaned forward across the desk and added, 'Maybe when you return that suit to your friend.'

Until then, Fletcher had accepted the intrusive questions. He didn't mind Sullivan that much, but Mark got on his nerves.

'What is this crap?' he snapped, his temper rising. 'You guys break into my room and steal my film. You seem to know all about me. And now you're spying on my friends. I'm an American citizen. I haven't done anything wrong.'

They kept their eyes on him, with calm, impassive expressions, as if waiting for him to explode, though he swallowed hard and sat up, trying to regain control.

'Listen, Guy,' said Mark, leaning forward. 'We've got a dead Cuban, who happens to be a person of some interest to us, and you're the only link we have to his death, so if you've got any more evidence than these...' he pushed the photographs forward. 'You need to tell us...now.'

'If he was a Cuban,' said Fletcher, 'What was he doing with an invitation to the party upstairs?'

'What do you mean?' said Mark.

'He had one of these,' said Fletcher, taking the card out of his pocket, and showing it to them. 'The police found it on him.'

For a moment both men seemed to hesitate, until Sullivan shook his head. 'The ambassador invites a lot of people from other embassies to these events,' he explained. 'It's a matter of protocol.'

'Even from hostile countries?' Fletcher said with scepticism.

'That's why it's called diplomacy,' Sullivan replied.

5

Pallid Harrier

Circus macrourus

An elegant, mid–sized raptor (fourteen to nineteen inches) that visits India during winter. Its pale grey colour, with flashes of black on the wingtips and tail, give it a distinctive, ghostly appearance, almost white when seen on the wing. It feeds on birds, rodents, and reptiles. Pallid harriers are a low–flying hawk that glides at a leisurely pace before surprising its prey on the ground and then striking with the accuracy of a guided missile.

The next day was Holi, the spring festival of colours. Before departing from India for Pakistan, Mrs Kennedy called on Prime Minister Nehru and applied a bright red tilak on his forehead with her gloved finger. A photograph of this was printed in every newspaper. When he was a boy, Fletcher had enjoyed playing Holi, roaming through Jor Bagh with a squirt gun and spraying anyone and everyone with coloured water. He and Reggie would fill water balloons with dye that they tossed from a balcony overlooking the street. These seldom hit their target but exploded like harmless grenades of yellow, blue, or green. This morning, from the rooftop terrace of the guesthouse, Fletcher had watched the neighbourhood children throwing colour at each other, resisting an urge to join them.

Around noon, Jack Sullivan dropped by unexpectedly. Someone had sprayed him with Holi colours. His white shirt and khakis were stained bright green, purple, and red, as if a rainbow had leaked onto his clothes. He also had streaks of yellow and blue powder smeared on his face and in his hair, though he didn't seem to mind.

'Looks like you got caught in the crossfire,' Fletcher said.

Sullivan shook his head and laughed. 'Yeah, there was a bunch of kids on the street outside who didn't realize I have diplomatic immunity.'

'So, what's up?' said Fletcher. 'I told you everything I know last night.'

'Sorry. No more questions. In fact, I came by to apologize,' Sullivan said. 'We didn't mean to grill you quite as hard as we did.'

'Yeah, it felt like I was getting the third degree,' Fletcher replied.

'Mark has a way of being a little too aggressive,' said Sullivan.

'And you're the good cop?' Fletcher said.

The older man didn't seem to take offence. 'I suppose so,' he said. 'Anyway, I hope there are no hard feelings.'

Fletcher shrugged and shook hands reluctantly. 'Okay. Would you like to come in?'

Sullivan looked around. 'Why don't we sit outside on the veranda? I don't want to get this colour on the furniture,' he said.

There were a couple of cane chairs facing the front garden. As they sat down, Balbir appeared and offered to make coffee but Sullivan declined.

'No, thanks. I won't stay long. I need to get back to the Embassy. With the first lady's visit everything has been on hold and there's a pile of work to catch up on,' said Sullivan, before looking at Fletcher intently, 'But, one of the things I wanted to tell you was that I knew your father, when he was working here in the fifties.'

'Oh yeah?' said Fletcher. 'Have you been in Delhi all this time?'

'Off and on,' Sullivan replied. 'Your Dad used to play poker with us, sometimes.'

'I didn't know he played poker,' Fletcher replied.

'He probably didn't want your mother to know,' said Sullivan with a smile. 'Bill was always a discreet sort of guy. How is he?'

'My father passed away last year,' said Fletcher.

'Oh, I'm sorry to hear that,' said Sullivan, with a sober expression. 'My condolences.'

'Yeah. Thanks,' said Fletcher.

They both fell silent for a minute before Sullivan spoke again.

'Listen, I want to hear more about your work. Why don't you come over for dinner tonight? Very informal. Just my wife and me. Our cook has the day off but Maryanne will rustle up something.'

Fletcher realized he was being played but he found Sullivan a likeable man, even if he was a spook. Covered in Holi colours, he looked much less threatening than he had the night before in the Chancery basement. His folksy, avuncular manner may have been superficial but Fletcher found himself being drawn in and he accepted the invitation.

◆

262 Jor Bagh lay two streets behind Reggie Bhatia's house. It was a smaller, two-storey building and the nameplate outside read D. S. Mittal, probably the landlord. Jack Sullivan welcomed Fletcher with a firm handshake and a pat on the shoulder then introduced his wife, Maryanne. She was an attractive middle-aged woman with bottle-blonde hair and the hint of a Southern accent. Fletcher also met Cocoa, their chocolate lab, who wagged her tail and licked his hand excitedly, until Sullivan told her to sit down.

While Maryanne went back to the kitchen, Sullivan got two bottles of Heineken from the refrigerator and they made themselves comfortable in the living room. Except for a few Indian artefacts, the interior of the house could have been anywhere in America. A La-Z-Boy recliner was positioned next to a three-foot brass statue of Ganesh and there was a Rajasthani mirror-work tapestry hanging beside a framed reproduction of a painting depicting the Battle of Gettysburg.

Seeing Fletcher studying the painting, Sullivan explained that both his and Maryanne's great grandfathers had died at Gettysburg. 'Her family were Confederates and mine fought for the Union. We keep that picture on the wall as a reminder of the truce between us,' he said, with a chuckle.

Cocoa nudged Fletcher's hand with her nose and he patted her head. 'She's a hell of a bird dog,' Sullivan said.

'Do you hunt?' Fletcher asked.

'Yeah, during the winter a few of us at the Embassy like to go out and shoot ducks at Sultanpur Jheel. Have you been there?'

Fletcher nodded. He had visited most of the wetlands near Delhi before deciding to focus his research on Bharatpur.

Sullivan continued: 'Around here the birds have pretty much disappeared but we're going to go up to Kashmir for a shoot this weekend, if you'd like to join us. Wular Lake is lousy with ducks and geese right now. You should come along.'

'Sounds interesting,' said Fletcher. 'But I was planning on heading back to Bharatpur tomorrow.'

'Come on, you can delay your departure by a couple of days, no big deal,' Sullivan said, switching over to Hindi. 'And I promise we won't ask you any more questions about your dead friend.'

The jocular insistence in his voice made Fletcher curious, wondering what Sullivan was after—he was pretty sure it wasn't just ducks—but the older man's easy-going manner made him drop his guard. Obviously, he had plenty to hide but there was an open, convincing way about him that was disarming.

'Okay, sure,' Fletcher said impulsively. 'Maybe I'll tag along.'

'Great!' said Sullivan. 'We'll be leaving Saturday morning early, at 5 a.m. You don't need to bring anything, except a change of clothes and maybe a jacket. It's still cold in Kashmir.'

Dinner was served and there was something comfortably familiar about the food that Maryanne put on the table, a macaroni and tuna casserole, coleslaw, and a green jello salad. It was the sort of meal his mother used to make in Colorado. Even the paper napkins had been brought from America.

As they ate, Sullivan spoke about growing up in India, from the age of three to eighteen. His father, who was from Pittsburgh, supervised the blast furnaces at the Tata Steel plant in Jamshedpur. A number of Americans had been hired as managers and engineers. In 1937, Sullivan had returned to America for college. He graduated from the University of Pittsburgh the summer before Pearl Harbor was bombed. As soon as war was declared, he'd enlisted in the army and was assigned to communications, a desk job in Washington, then transferred back to India once they realized he spoke Hindi and Bengali.

'Before I knew it, I was stationed in Bengal and Assam,' he explained, 'waiting for the Japanese to invade. We built a couple of airbases in India from where our pilots flew "over the hump" into China.'

'I've heard about that,' said Fletcher.

Sullivan nodded. 'You're too young to remember but it's hard to believe that we were fighting the Germans and Japs less than two decades ago. Nobody knew how the war would end. The Japanese made it all the way to Imphal through Burma and they probably would have just kept on coming. The Brits were hard pressed to hold them back after Singapore fell.'

He told war stories in a casual sort of way and Fletcher found himself being lured into the web. His own father had been stationed in Australia but never talked about the war and always seemed troubled by what had happened, though for Sullivan it was an adventure to be relished and remembered.

'Did you ever hear about "The Lake of No Return?"' he asked, as Maryanne put a cherry pie on the table for dessert.

When Fletcher whistled his approval she said, 'It's nothing. I got it from the commissary, frozen. All I did was heat it up.'

Turning his attention back to Sullivan, he waited for the rest of the story.

'We were flying C-47 Dakotas over the Himalayas. Those planes only had a limited range into Southeastern China, mainly Kunming, airlifting supplies to Chiang Kai-shek and his Nationalist army. If they iced up going over the hump or got hit with anti-aircraft fire, which often happened, or they used up all their fuel, the only option was to try and find a place for an emergency landing, but it's nothing but hills and jungle up there. On the Burma border, just this side of the mountains below the Pangsau Pass there's a fair-sized lake. It was the only place they could put a plane down and hope to survive. God knows how many Dakotas went into that lake. Only a few of the pilots escaped. It's a weird, spooky place, kind of makes your hair stand on end, knowing that all those flying coffins are lying at the bottom.'

'You've been there?' Fletcher asked.

'Once,' said Sullivan, 'After the war ended...'

'So, India's more like home for you than the States?' said Fletcher.

Sullivan gave a shrug.

'Yeah,' he said. 'I'm supposed to retire in a couple of years and I don't know what I'll do when I go back.'

Following dinner, Fletcher found himself being quizzed on his research. He explained that he was conducting a general survey of bar-headed geese at Bharatpur, observing the ways they interacted with other species, but also tagging them and gathering blood samples. Sullivan sounded genuinely interested in his project, both the objectives and the methods.

'How do you catch the geese to tag them?' Sullivan asked.

'It's not easy. There's a thing called a rocket net, which I've tried, but it's not too successful. Better than that, I've been able to set up snares at a couple of places, where the geese come in to land. Most ornithologists tag birds when they're young or moulting but we don't have access to their breeding grounds in Tibet and Central Asia, so I have to reverse the process. Of course, we don't know where they go exactly, but over the next couple of years, we'll find out if they come back to the same waterbodies.'

'Do you shoot any?' Sullivan asked.

'A few. I have a permit from the forest department to collect a limited number of specimens,' Fletcher said.

'And what are you looking for?' Sullivan asked.

'One of the things I'm doing is comparing the condition of the birds when they arrive in October–November, with their weight and other factors just before they get ready to fly north in March. I've been trying to get a measure of their subcutaneous fat levels, as well as comparisons between the number of blood platelets, which might give us some indication of how they adjust to high altitude crossings. It will take another couple of years of gathering data to put together a more complete picture.'

'Why bar-headed geese?' Sullivan had lit his pipe, exhaling a fog of blue smoke.

'They're one of the strongest fliers and we know they migrate up to some of the lakes far north in Tibet and Mongolia, where they breed.'

'Are you checking for diseases?'

'If possible. The blood samples are tested for pathogens but there's so little we know about these birds it's hard to predict what might come up.'

'And what purpose does all of this serve?' the older man asked, with an indulgent smile.

'I don't know,' Fletcher replied. 'Furthering knowledge. Science for the sake of science. Maybe we'll learn something about their physiology or behaviour that might be of some use, but more than likely it's just broadening our understanding of the way nature works.'

'And you're content with that?' Sullivan said.

'What do you mean?'

'I'm saying, you're going to spend the rest of your life studying these birds and then thirty-five years from now, when you get to my age, you'll ask yourself, "so, what was that all about?"'

'Sounds like you're asking yourself that question,' said Fletcher, with a laugh.

Sullivan didn't smile. 'I mean, don't you think it might be possible to direct your research to a higher purpose, something that saves people's lives for instance?'

'Maybe.' Fletcher eyed Sullivan with a sceptical expression, not sure what he was proposing.

'Let me give you a hypothetical situation,' said Sullivan. 'Let's say you collect blood and tissue samples from these birds that fly into Tibet and you could test them for radioactivity, which would confirm whether the Chinese are setting off atomic explosions. Wouldn't that be an added benefit?'

'Sure, but I don't know if it would work. Maybe, if the geese fly through a mushroom cloud or land on a contaminated lake, there could be traces.' He now understood where this was going. It was anything but hypothetical.

'But you could test for that?' Sullivan persisted.

'I'd have to find out what sort of analysis is possible.' Fletcher hesitated.

'Let's say you could identify the type of radioactivity in a goose's blood, indicating whether it was plutonium or uranium, wouldn't it tell us something significant about what the communists are doing at Lop Nur?'

'Lop Nur is a saline lake,' said Fletcher. 'It's not a breeding ground for waterfowl. Some of the geese probably fly that route but they nest along the shores of other wetlands that have plenty of aquatic plants to feed on.'

Understanding that he was being recruited, Fletcher felt an uneasy sense of indecision, but also some excitement and anticipation. In principle, he had no reservations about working for the US government.

After returning from India to Colorado, there had been a period of his life when he had thought about joining the army, though the regimentation and discipline didn't appeal to him. He had sometimes fantasized about being a spy, working behind enemy lines. The complexities and ambiguous terrain of the Cold War teased his imagination.

Later that evening, driving back from Jor Bagh to his guesthouse, Fletcher half expected the headlights of the jeep station wagon to appear in his rear-view mirror but the streets were silent and deserted. Unlike other big cities, Delhi shut down by nine o'clock.

◆

The Convair 880 sat on the tarmac, four turbofan jet engines weighing down the low, swept-back wings. Its streamlined fuselage was engineered to pierce the clouds. As he got down from the Embassy vehicle and helped Sullivan with the luggage and gun cases, Fletcher thought to himself how much the aircraft looked like a bird of prey. Cocoa followed at Sullivan's heels, her tail wagging with excitement.

'We're in luck. The ambassador authorized the Convair,' he said, 'otherwise we'd be using Cessnas.'

A couple more cars pulled up in front of the Indian Air Force hangar at Palam, not far from the VIP terminal, where Jackie Kennedy had disembarked a week ago. Fletcher recognized the pair of heavies who had yanked him from the Embassy reception, as well as the man named Mark. All of them were wearing Ray-Bans and white bush shirts, as if it were a uniform. Two Indian Army officers joined them, arriving in a jeep. It was six in the morning and the sun was just coming up, as they trooped aboard. Their pilot was the US Air Force attaché, Sullivan explained: 'He's happy for any excuse to fly this thing. It's the fastest passenger jet in the world, just barely subsonic, but a bitch to maintain.'

'Is it just for the Embassy?' Fletcher asked, noticing that the plane had no markings except for a sequence of numbers and an American flag on the tail.

Sullivan nodded, then pointed him to a window seat as they climbed aboard. Leaving a space between them, he sat next to the aisle, the dog at his feet. The Convair was configured with five seats across. Even after the doors closed, the roar from the engines made it difficult to have a conversation and Fletcher kept his thoughts to himself. As they taxied to the head of the runway, he saw a raptor circling in the distance. At first he thought it might be a black-shouldered kite, then realized it was a pallid harrier. The airport, with its expanse of open grassland, was the perfect hunting ground for the bird. Its chevron-like wings cut through the air like feathered shears.

As the jet took off, Fletcher knew he had made a choice that would probably change the rest of his life. Glancing across, he saw that Sullivan had closed his eyes, as if he'd fallen asleep. The Convair headed northwest from Delhi. After take-off, there was some turbulence but their flight smoothed off as the plains of the Punjab appeared below them, tufted with clouds. He could see the Himalayas, like a faint watermark upon the sky. Within thirty minutes they came in sight of the Pir Panjal Range. As the jet cruised over the forested hills, the air grew choppy again. Seeing the rugged terrain below, Fletcher thought of the pilots flying over the hump during the war. The snow peaks were much closer now. Minutes later, the Kashmir Valley opened up ahead of them. A lush green tapestry of fields and orchards slid past under the Convair's wings as they began to descend.

At Srinagar airport they were met by an Indian Army major and driven from there to a military camp near Baramulla. A line of tents had been set up, furnished with comfortable-looking beds and Kashmiri carpets. Each one had a washroom and toilet attached, outfitted with a thunderbox. Fletcher had a tent to himself, while Sullivan and Cocoa were next door. They were told that lunch would be served at one, when the corps commander would join them. Sullivan had explained that the visit was part of negotiations for technical assistance and surveillance equipment to be used along the ceasefire line with Pakistan.

Fletcher was surprised how openly the Americans mixed with their hosts. Everyone understood who was who and they didn't seem intent on hiding identities. When the corps commander, Maj. Gen. Rathore, arrived—a compact, jovial man with a furled moustache—he was accompanied by half-a-dozen staff officers. Sullivan introduced Fletcher as 'our technical expert. Doing his PhD on geese.' The general made a joke about a 'wild goose chase' and everyone laughed, as beer was served outdoors, under a spreading chinar tree.

Later that afternoon, when they got into jeeps for the drive to Wular Lake, Fletcher found himself seated next to a young Indian Army officer. He was in his late twenties, a few years older than Fletcher, with a thin, aquiline face and a trim moustache. At first he seemed standoffish, his manner aloof and humourless, but once they were on their way, he loosened up, talking about Kashmir. It turned out he was a mountaineer and had climbed several major Himalayan peaks.

'Captain Imtiaz Afridi,' he said, introducing himself.

6

Northern Pintail

Anas acuta

One of the most common migratory water birds in India, pintails congregate in large flocks, often with other species. The male has a ruddy brown head and white breast, with grey plumage on the wings and back. The female is a dull, mottled brown. Pintails breed in Europe, parts of Central Asia, and the Soviet Union, arriving and dispersing throughout the subcontinent in winter. Their name derives from the bird's sharp, pointed tail that can often be seen protruding above the surface of a pond, as it feeds upside down.

Wular Lake, the source of the Jhelum River, was situated at the northwestern end of the Srinagar Valley. A much larger body of water than Dal or Nagin Lake, where tourist houseboats lined the shore, it was surrounded by marshes that made access difficult. The army had arranged for the hunters to be ferried out to their blinds, which stood on a series of small islands a quarter of a mile from shore. A fleet of five shikaras were waiting when they arrived and the Kashmiri boatmen paddled their skiffs along channels cut through the weeds. Having departed immediately after lunch, the hunting party was in place by 4 p.m. Fletcher was paired with Jack Sullivan, who sat in the front of the shikara with Cocoa between his knees. When they reached the hide, he opened the gun case and assembled a Browning twelve-gauge over/under with a dark walnut stock. Fletcher had declined the offer of a gun, saying he would simply observe the slaughter.

Plenty of ducks and geese were on the water, though well out of range. The corps commander was positioned about 300 yards to their right and another general occupied a hide further off. Two of the Americans had been assigned positions on the other side of Sullivan, who seemed to have been given the prime location. The boatman, cloaked in a dark woollen pheran with a white skullcap, made himself comfortable in a patch of reeds, to one side of the small island.

The sun was descending towards the horizon and Fletcher could see the fretted profiles of snow-covered mountains to the northwest, beyond which lay the Indus River in Pakistan and the disputed Line of Control, established after the last border war. As they settled into the hide, Cocoa whimpered, quivering in anticipation. Facing the expanse of water, which reflected a shifting canopy of high cirrus, Fletcher felt as if they were huddled at the edge of the world. It was much colder than Delhi and Sullivan blew into his hands as he arranged boxes of ammunition beside him, loading the Browning with two cartridges of #4 birdshot. The hunters had agreed to hold their fire until flights of ducks began arriving before dusk.

They didn't have to wait long.

As Fletcher scanned the horizon with his binoculars, he saw a loose V of birds coming towards them, like a stray strand of smoke. Within minutes they were overhead, circling to see where they might settle. Sullivan had switched off the safety on his shotgun. It was a flock of pintails; Fletcher was able to identify them from their profiles. On the second turn, Sullivan put the gun to his shoulder and fired, one barrel after the other. Two birds dropped from the sky, one of them fluttering off at an angle, the other landing directly in front of the blind. Moments later, the corps commander discharged his weapon as the flight of ducks veered away to the north.

The gunshots were amplified by the stillness of the water and broke the evening silence with their brutal reports. Instantly, thousands of birds lifted off the lake, erupting in a maelstrom of wings. Many of them had been hidden amongst the reeds or lay far out on the water where the shadows of clouds merged with the dark reflections of surrounding hills. Like a tornado, the surface of the lake seemed to rise up and blot out the sun. Fletcher had never seen so many ducks, not even at Bharatpur. He couldn't begin to estimate their numbers as they clouded the sky, accompanied by honking cries of alarm. Sullivan had already reloaded as a flight of geese came directly at him. Again, he fired twice and this time one of the birds fell, landing in the marsh behind the blind.

'Go girl! Fetch!' he gave Cocoa her command and the Labrador shot out of the hide, straight into the water in front of them, catching a wounded pintail first, then following her master's gestures to retrieve the other dead bird. Returning to the hide each time, she shook herself, spraying Fletcher and dropping the ducks next to Sullivan. He now waved her into the reeds behind them while the spent cartridges popped out as he loaded again. All five hunters were firing from their hides, a sporadic cannonade that confused the ducks and geese, sending them wheeling in different directions.

Between salvos, Fletcher reached across and examined the male pintail, his fingers feeling its full crop through the soft layers of feathers. The bird was still warm, though its neck hung limply to one side and he could see blood beneath one wing, where the pellets had pierced its breast.

By the time the sun had set and twilight faded into darkness, Sullivan had killed twenty-two birds, mostly pintails and spotbills but also a couple of bar-headed geese. Duck hunting brought out another facet of his personality, a killer instinct hidden beneath his easy-going facade. Cocoa was exhausted though still ready for more when a whistle from the corps commander's blind signalled the end of the hunt. The boatman helped gather up the dead birds and laid them in the shikara as dog and master boarded the craft. Fletcher took his seat in the middle. They hadn't spoken until now, as Sullivan lit his pipe and the fragrant smoke trailed over his shoulder.

'Helluva good shoot,' he mumbled, glancing back at Fletcher. 'I told you there would be a lot of birds.'

'You can say that again,' said Fletcher.

When they gathered at the jeeps everyone counted their bag and the combined casualties totalled 110. General Rathore seemed pleased with the results.

'Tomorrow morning we'll have another go,' he said, as they boarded the jeeps.

After washing up in their tents, where buckets of hot water were delivered, they went across to the officers' mess, a prefab structure built in a willow grove at the heart of the military encampment. They were ushered into a brightly lit room with a ring of upholstered chairs along the walls and a bar at one end. A cast iron bukhari was burning in one corner and the smell of cedar smoke perfumed the air. Uniformed bearers served drinks. As Fletcher asked for a beer, he found Captain Afridi at his elbow.

'Beer, at this time of day?' he said. 'Nothing stronger?'

Fletcher laughed. 'Okay, maybe I'll have defence services rum instead.'

'Good choice,' said Afridi. 'How was the hunt?'

'My ears are still ringing,' said Fletcher, as they took their glasses and retreated to the far corner of the room.

'You're not with the Embassy, are you?' Afridi said. Something in the tone of his voice suggested that he already knew the answer.

'No, I'm a Fulbright scholar.'

'But you've lived in India before,' said Afridi, raising his glass.

'How did you know that?' Fletcher asked.

'I overheard you speaking to the driver,' Afridi replied without hesitation. 'Your Hindi is fluent and your accent is almost perfect.'

'Almost?' said Fletcher.

Afridi smiled and glanced across at Sullivan and the corps commander, who were seated together, deep in conversation. Fletcher guessed they must have been discussing surveillance devices and ways to eavesdrop on Pakistan. Cocoa lay on the floor between them, her head on her paws.

'Which part of India are you from?' Fletcher asked.

'Delhi, though my ancestors came from the Northwest Frontier Province, originally,' Afridi replied.

A bearer in a starched turban with a coxcomb and cummerbund brought around a plate of kebabs. Afridi declined but Fletcher helped himself. There was a ritual formality to the mess but also a casual, masculine air of regimental hospitality.

'It's duck!' said Fletcher, after tasting what he thought was chicken tikka.

'Yes, I've never liked the flavour,' said Afridi. 'Too gamey for me, though the Kashmiris have a way of cooking it that's not bad, as a shab deg, with turnips.'

Biting down on something hard, Fletcher removed a lead pellet from his mouth and showed it to Afridi.

'Do you hunt?' he asked, dropping the birdshot into an ashtray.

'No. Shikar never interested me,' Afridi answered. 'What about you? I've heard that every American owns a gun.'

'Not really, though I've killed birds for research,' said Fletcher.

'The pursuit of science rather than sport,' Afridi mused.

'I suppose,' Fletcher replied.

'You're studying migratory species only?'

Fletcher nodded, not wanting to have to explain once again.

'What about vultures?' Afridi asked, after a measured pause.

Meeting the steady gaze of Afridi's eyes, Fletcher realized there was more to this conversation than small talk.

'Why do you ask?' he countered, though his mouth was dry. Taking a sip of rum and water, he felt a soothing warmth at the back of his throat.

'I understand you were observing *Sarcogyps calvus* the other day,' Afridi replied. 'The king vulture. A noble bird. Very few people appreciate the services they perform, disposing of the dead.'

'Are you a birdwatcher?' Fletcher asked.

'An amateur,' said Afridi.

Swallowing most of his drink, Fletcher eyed the army captain with suspicion.

'Why do I feel you know much more about me than I do about you?' he said.

'Because you happened to stumble upon the body of a Cuban spy, working for the KGB,' said Afridi. 'Haven't the Americans told you?'

'What's there to tell?'

'He was selling secrets to your friends,' Afridi continued, glancing across at Mark and the other Americans, before lowering his voice. 'Though he was an unreliable source.'

'Was he selling secrets to you as well?' Fletcher asked.

Afridi shrugged. 'India is a non-aligned country. As you can see, we welcome both capitalists and communists. In fact, last week the Soviet ambassador was here shooting ducks on Wular Lake, though he had less success, only seventy-five birds.'

'Why are you telling me this?'

'I thought you might be interested,' Afridi murmured, then gestured to a bearer. 'Here, let's get another drink.'

'May I ask you something?' Fletcher said, as the bearer took their glasses.

'Of course.' Afridi nodded.

'How does this work? Here we are in a secure Indian military installation near the ceasefire line with Pakistan. But you've got four CIA agents having drinks and chatting with your officers as if there were no secrets between you. I thought spies operated under cover and never revealed their identities.'

'Are they with the CIA?' Afridi asked, with mock surprise. 'How do you know?'

'I guess I just made that assumption,' said Fletcher.

Afridi laughed. 'To begin with, this isn't a top-secret facility and shooting ducks doesn't endanger national security. People often think of secrets as being something like a light switch, either on or off. But the truth is it's all relative. There are varying degrees of knowledge and understanding. Intelligence gathering and analysis is all about the different shades of grey, not black and white.'

'Are you an intelligence officer?' Fletcher asked.

Afridi winced. 'Let's just say, I'm searching for the truth.'

'What kind of truth?' Fletcher demanded, irritated by the ambiguities.

'For instance, who killed Joaquin Morales and why?' Afridi replied. 'The Cuban?'

Afridi nodded as the bearer delivered Fletcher's rum and water along with the Captain's whisky soda.

'They told you his name, didn't they?' said Afridi.

'Yes, but why was he murdered?' Fletcher persisted.

'I'm asking you,' said Afridi.

'And I don't have the faintest idea....' Tasting the rum, he could tell it was stronger than his first drink.

'They didn't drop any hints?' Afridi's eyes shifted towards the Americans.

'Not really. No.'

'Maybe *they* killed him,' the Captain suggested. 'Perhaps he betrayed one of his handlers or tried to extort more money than he deserved. It could be that he gave them incorrect information about Castro's forces and they blame him for compromising the Bay of Pigs invasion, which justified his termination.' Seeing the doubtful look in Fletcher's eyes, he leaned closer. 'Even the Americans do that sort of thing. What's the expression? "Rubbing" someone out? Believe me, your compatriots don't just shoot ducks.'

'Are you warning me?' Fletcher asked.

'No. I don't think you're in any immediate danger. But be aware of the shades of grey. Morales was "bumped off", if you'll excuse another Americanism, because he had become a liability. He wanted to share information on his CIA contacts, the questions they asked, their modus operandi....'

'How do you know?'

'Because he approached our Intelligence Bureau with this offer. I'm sure he tried to sell information to others too, maybe the Chinese. He seemed desperate for money. The rumour is that he was having an affair with a Hungarian diplomat who demanded expensive gifts. On top of that, he was an alcoholic and drink is always the first step to debt.'

'If the CIA murdered him,' said Fletcher, 'Why would they interrogate me?'

'Is that what they did?' Afridi seemed amused. 'Interrogate you?'

Fletcher shrugged. 'In a manner of speaking. They certainly felt that I knew more than I was letting on.'

'But you were just an innocent witness who happened to discover a dead foreigner in the jungle. Isn't that correct?'

'Exactly,' Fletcher said emphatically.

Afridi paused for a moment, studying the patterns in the carpet at his feet.

'Would it surprise you,' he said, 'if I told you that the murdered man you found in the forest wasn't Joaquin Morales?'

This time Fletcher hesitated then nodded. 'You know, I wondered when I read the reports in the newspapers,' he said. 'The description didn't match.'

'The man you found was an American art broker named Emil Zorman. He's from New York and represents a number of exclusive clients,' said Afridi.

'Okay. But why didn't they tell me that?' said Fletcher, tilting his head in the direction of the others.

'Because they lied to you,' said Afridi, with a condescending expression.

'How do I know you're not lying?' he said.

Afridi raised his glass. 'I could be, of course. That's something you'll have to decide for yourself.'

'So, you're claiming that there are two separate victims,' said Fletcher, 'and their identities got mixed up.'

'Yes,' said Afridi. 'But more importantly, someone deliberately switched the two bodies and made Zorman's corpse disappear.'

'Who would have done that?' Fletcher asked.

'Perhaps your friends,' Afridi suggested.

7

Bar-headed Goose

Anser indicus

With light grey plumage, a yellow beak, and two unmistakable black bars across the nape of its neck, this goose is one of the highest-flying birds in the world and migrates over the Himalayas. In summer it nests on the shores of lakes in Tibet after spending the winter in wetlands throughout India. Flights of bar-headed geese have been spotted near the summit of Mt Everest and other major peaks, at altitudes above 27,000 feet.

The hunters were awake before dawn and reached their blinds just as the sky turned a pale rose. During the night, the temperature had dropped and layers of mist hovered over the water, hiding the birds from view. Fletcher scanned the lake and the reeds with his binoculars, spotting only a few ducks, though he could hear them on all sides. Eventually, as the sun began to rise, they started to take off and circle. Fletcher was paired with Sullivan again and the morning's shoot produced eighty-nine victims. They had agreed that he would collect all of the bar-headed geese, of which there were twelve, to be carried back to Delhi in a duffel bag, so that he could examine them and get blood samples.

The corps commander and his staff had arranged for breakfast on the lakeshore before they headed straight to the airport, accompanied by a military escort. Fletcher noticed that Captain Afridi was nowhere in sight. Instead of entering the main terminal, they were driven through a side gate, directly onto the tarmac, where two Cessnas were waiting. Sullivan muttered something about the Convair taking Galbraith to Madras.

Seating was cramped and Cocoa had to lie in the aisle. The smell of her wet fur filled the cabin as Fletcher scratched the dog's ears and patted her head.

'She's a real champion, isn't she?' he remarked.

Sullivan grinned as if the compliment had been directed at him.

'Nothing brings out her instincts more than ducks, though she's pretty good with partridges and quail too,' he said. 'By the way, I noticed you had a long conversation with one of the officers last night. What was his name?'

'Captain Imtiaz Afridi.'

'Never heard of him.'

'I thought you knew everybody.' Fletcher raised his voice as the Cessna took off, racing down the runway and lifting off on wavering wings. It was a much less comfortable flight and they hit several air pockets crossing the Pir Panjal. Fletcher wondered whether geese experienced turbulence.

'What was this guy, Afridi, talking about?' Sullivan asked, once they had levelled off.

'He asked me about the dead man in Delhi,' said Fletcher.

'Oh yeah?' said Sullivan.

'Other than waterfowl, it seems to be my main topic of conversation these days.'

'Did he offer any insights?' Sullivan took out his pipe and filled it with tobacco from a pouch in his pocket.

Fletcher knew that Afridi didn't expect him to keep any secrets. In fact, he probably wanted his observations passed on to the Americans.

'He suggested that you might have killed him,' Fletcher replied.

'Me?' said Sullivan, chewing on the stem of his unlit pipe.

'Not you, personally,' he said, 'but, you know…'

'Is that so?' Sullivan laughed, then lit a match and sucked on the pipe as it ignited, filling the small cabin of the Cessna with smoke. The pilot glanced over his shoulder from the cockpit.

'There's a fire extinguisher at the back!' he shouted.

'I'll keep that in mind,' Sullivan replied, then looked across at Fletcher and shrugged. 'Well, at least we can give your friend points for imagination.'

'So, the CIA didn't kill him?' Fletcher asked.

'Who said anything about the CIA?' Smoke trickled out of Sullivan's mouth with his words.

'Afridi did,' Fletcher replied.

'What else did he tell you?'

'He said the dead man I found wasn't a Cuban diplomat,' Fletcher explained. 'He was an American art dealer and the two corpses got switched.'

'That's an interesting theory,' said Sullivan.

'Is it true?' Fletcher demanded.

'I'd say your friend Afridi is a few sandwiches short of a picnic,' Sullivan answered. Drawing deeply on his pipe, he fell silent for the rest of the flight.

It took an hour and a half to reach Delhi, where they were met by embassy vehicles and taken straight to the Chancery. Fletcher had already been told that he could use one of the rooms in the Embassy's infirmary to carry out his autopsies. It was a cramped, windowless lab with a couple of steel tables and cupboards, as well as a small refrigerator. One of the nurses unlocked it for them and looked disapprovingly at the bloodstained duffel.

By noon he had opened up several of the geese, parting their breast feathers with his fingers and using a scalpel to make an incision from the wishbone down to the vent beneath their tails. The birds had already stiffened but he was able to weigh and measure them, then draw a blood sample from one of the veins on the inside of the thigh. Transferred to a vial and labelled, the sample went straight into the refrigerator. After that, he peeled the skin away from the breast meat and examined the layer of yellow fat. The bird looked healthy, no more than five years old and fully capable of flying across the mountains, if it weren't for the lead pellets that had broken its right wing.

Sullivan dropped by during the afternoon, with a couple of sandwiches and a Coke from the Embassy's canteen. By this time, half of the birds had been dissected and Fletcher's hands were covered in blood and goose down.

'Any surprises?' Sullivan asked.

'No, nothing so far. They've got plenty of fat to fuel their migration.'

Then he picked up the carcass of the first goose and showed Sullivan the broken bones on its wing. 'You can see here how lightweight its skeleton is but still strong enough to withstand the constant beating of its wings. When you have to fly above 20,000 feet and travel more than a thousand miles, every ounce matters. It's amazing how perfectly this bird's anatomy is adapted to those journeys, engineered by thousands of years of evolution. It's a masterpiece of nature when you realize that cartilage, bone, flesh, blood, and feathers are all calibrated and synchronized to carry it over the mountains to Tibet.'

'Sure,' said Sullivan, unimpressed. 'But I'll be more interested if you find traces of radioactivity.'

'Don't count on it,' said Fletcher, as he washed his hands in the sink, before opening the Coke and eating his lunch.

'How long do you think it will take to do the tests?' Sullivan asked.

'Should be pretty quick, once it reaches a lab. Again, I'm not familiar with the procedures but it can't be that complicated. The problem, of course, is that we don't know where these birds travelled and how many times they've been back and forth to Tibet, or wherever it is they breed. Even if we discover evidence of radioactivity, we wouldn't know where it came from, exactly.'

'What's the average lifespan of a goose?' Sullivan asked.

'Anywhere from ten to twenty-five years. Most of these are in their prime. I'd estimate they're four to five years old, ready to breed,' Fletcher replied.

'And when do you think you'll be done?'

'It's slow work. A dozen specimens.' Fletcher made a rough calculation in his mind. 'I should have all the samples finished by five this afternoon.'

'Sounds good,' said Sullivan. 'Mark will have the samples shipped back on the Pan Am flight tomorrow evening to New York and from there to Washington. We've arranged with a lab in Georgetown to do the tests. They say they can't detect radioactivity but there will be changes in the blood, something called a lymphocyte count, that indicates exposure.'

Fletcher nodded as he chewed the last of his sandwich.

'It's going to be a long shot,' he said.

'Well, no harm in trying, is there?' said Sullivan.

'How's Cocoa?' Fletcher asked.

'A little tired but happy. I dropped her home this morning. You should come over again for dinner tonight, after you're done. We need to talk some more about where we go from here.' Sullivan waved a hand in a vague sort of gesture.

◆

That evening, Cocoa greeted Fletcher as if he were a long-lost friend. He was beginning to feel like a member of the family at the Sullivans' home, though he couldn't quite reconcile himself to being co-opted by the CIA. After his conversation with Captain Afridi in Kashmir, he wondered if Sullivan had been lying to him or whether something else was going on. He had no reason to trust a young Indian Army officer he'd never met before, but at the same time it seemed as if he was tangled up in an elaborate game, the rules of which he didn't fully understand.

Over dinner, Sullivan talked more about his childhood in Jamshedpur and how he hadn't known much about America until he went back to college.

'My mother homeschooled me but we had textbooks from the States, which gave me a general sense of what it was like in America. There were ten or fifteen other Americans working at Tata Steel. The General Manager was a man named John Keenan. He was from Pittsburgh and recruited my father. They both used to work for Carnegie Steel but the Tatas gave them a better deal. When I went back to Pittsburgh, for a family visit in 1933, it was like being sent straight to hell. The air was so polluted, the smog shut out the sunlight and it was overcast all day. All of the houses were covered in soot. I remember a few days after we arrived, it snowed, which was exciting, but within an hour the ground turned from white to grey. Frankly, I hated America and couldn't wait to get back to India.'

Fletcher nodded. 'It was the same for me. One summer, when we went back on home leave, I couldn't stand it and I was miserably homesick for Delhi.'

After dinner, Sullivan got out a bottle of bourbon and they talked some more about the Chinese nuclear testing facility at Lop Nur. He explained how they'd been keeping an eye on the Chinese through aerial reconnaissance but last summer another U2 was shot down. The spy planes flew at altitudes of 70,000 feet but it was getting more and more dangerous because the Soviets had developed surface to air missiles that could reach that height. Sullivan's pipe created a smokescreen but Fletcher could see the older man's eyes watching him.

Taking a sip of bourbon Fletcher said, 'You know, I learned the pledge of allegiance here at the American School in Delhi, but I've never been sure where my loyalties lay. Of course, I'm not a fan of communism but when it comes to standing up for my country, I don't know how far I'm willing to go.'

'Yeah, I know what you mean,' said Sullivan. 'I work for the US government but that doesn't always mean I believe in everything it represents.'

'Really?' said Fletcher. 'I had you pegged as a flag-waving patriot.'

'The gung-ho soldiers are the ones who fight in the trenches. Those of us who keep to the shadows nurture our doubts,' Sullivan mused. 'Back in '41, I joined the army to fight the Japanese. After Pearl Harbor, they were the enemy, clear and simple. But when the war ended the lines got blurred. The Soviets and Chinese had fought with us against fascism. Now they were the threat we opposed.'

'I guess human beings always need an antagonist, to make us feel we're on the right side,' said Fletcher.

'Guy, this may come as a surprise,' Sullivan said, glancing down at his hands, 'but your father worked for the CIA and, before that, he was in the OSS, like me.'

Fletcher took a deep breath and leaned back against the cushions on the sofa, staring at the man across from him with a look of bewilderment and resignation.

'You didn't know?' Sullivan asked.

Shaking his head, Fletcher looked away for a moment.

'Sometimes I wondered,' he said, then shook his head again. 'But he never let on....'

'It's possible that your mother doesn't even know, though most of us, at some point, tell our wives.'

'Does Maryanne know what you do?'

'Only as much as she needs to know,' Sullivan replied.

'Son of a bitch!' Fletcher said, both angry and upset.

'Don't think of it as something your father kept hidden because he didn't trust you,' Sullivan said in a reassuring voice, 'but more as an inheritance that you can carry on. We're always happy to keep things within the family.'

Fletcher wondered what other secrets were concealed behind Sullivan's amiable facade. They were both silent for a couple of minutes before Fletcher got up to leave. Sullivan put a reassuring hand on his shoulder as they went outside where the BSA was parked in the driveway. After fiddling with the carburettor, he got it started on the fourth kick.

Heading out onto Lodhi Road, Fletcher passed a couple of cars going in the opposite direction. He still couldn't believe what Sullivan had told him, though he'd always suspected that his father was hiding something. As soon as he turned left onto Safdarjung Road, he noticed headlights in his rear-view mirror. The vehicle behind him accelerated to catch up, the same jeep station wagon that had nearly run him down last week. Again, the streets were deserted and there was nowhere to escape. Twisting the throttle on the motorcycle, Fletcher tried to outrun the vehicle but it kept gaining on him. The BSA had a top speed of fifty miles an hour. The driver of the jeep was now flashing his lights, as they turned onto the road past the Race Course and Polo Grounds. By this time the station wagon's front bumper was only a few feet from his rear tire. Then, without warning, the vehicle suddenly pulled out and overtook him. Fletcher immediately eased up on the throttle as the jeep hurtled past. For an instant, he felt a sense of relief but after another hundred yards, he saw the brake lights come on as the vehicle skidded to a stop, turning broadside to block the road. Pulling in the clutch, he geared down and stepped on the brake.

As the BSA began to fishtail, Fletcher had little time to react. Afraid that he was going to wipe out, he tried to regain control. The doors on the station wagon flew open and three men jumped out. When he squeezed the handbrake, the motorcycle swerved. The men waved their arms, signalling for him to stop.

Everything seemed to slow down for a few seconds as the bike started to slide out from under him. There was a grating sound as the foot peg dragged along the asphalt, spitting out a shower of sparks, and the BSA skidded wildly, veering towards the men, who saw that Fletcher had lost control. Leaping out of the way, one of them shouted a warning while the other took out a pistol. He began to aim at Fletcher just as the front wheel of the motorcycle connected with his shins, throwing him backwards against the jeep.

The impact was enough to swing the bike around. As it came to a stop, Fletcher was able to stay astride. Miraculously the engine didn't stall out and he hauled the motorcycle upright. When he let out the clutch and gunned the engine, the BSA roared off in the opposite direction. Now, he had a choice. Either he could take a left on Safdarjung Road, and go on past the entrance to the Gymkhana Club, or he could return to Sullivan's house in Jor Bagh. In the rear-view mirror, he could see his pursuers helping the injured man off the ground.

Taking a deep breath, Fletcher switched off the headlight and drove straight on, along Aurangzeb Road. Having bicycled through these streets as a boy, he knew every crossing and shortcut. At the next roundabout, he kept going straight but after another 200 yards, he turned into a side lane to the right that cut behind the line of bungalows. Glancing back, he saw the jeep's headlights in pursuit, but the station wagon hadn't yet reached the roundabout. They weren't likely to see him making the turn because there were no streetlights and the road was overshadowed with trees on either side.

Crossing Prithviraj Road he continued down another side lane on to Ratendon Road, keeping his lights off, just in case. Nobody seemed to be following him now. Heading back into Jor Bagh, he arrived at Sullivan's house and switched off the engine. The front gate was locked and the lights were all off, except for a single bulb burning over the front door. Searching for the bell switch, he kept glancing over his shoulder in case the jeep showed up. Finally, he found the switch and pressed it hard three times. Ten seconds passed before a light came on upstairs but within three minutes Sullivan appeared in his bathrobe, accompanied by Cocoa.

As Fletcher began to explain what had happened, Sullivan waved him inside and locked the gate behind them. When they entered the house, Fletcher could see Maryanne at the top of the stairs. He noticed Sullivan had a pistol in his hand, which he slipped into the pocket of his robe.

'Did you get a look at them?' Sullivan asked.

'Sort of,' said Fletcher. 'Two of them could have been oriental and one was definitely Indian.'

'They didn't say anything?'

'No, it all happened too quickly. I was lucky to get away,' said Fletcher. His hands were shaking and Sullivan poured him a stiff bourbon to steady his nerves.

'It's a good thing you came back here,' said Sullivan.

'They must have known I was having dinner with you,' Fletcher said, 'and followed me from here when I left.'

'Could be,' said Sullivan. 'In any case, you'll be safe in this house. There's a bed made up in our guest room. You can spend the night here.'

After Fletcher finished the whisky, Sullivan showed him his room, which was downstairs at the back of the house.

'Just take it easy and try to get some sleep,' he said. 'I need to make a couple of phone calls.'

Lying down, he could feel his whole body trembling, as if he was still on the bike with the engine running. It was impossible to fall asleep. The right pant leg on his jeans had been ripped and there was a scrape on his shin but other than that he wasn't hurt. Lying in bed, he kept replaying the scene in his head, seeing the glare of headlights even when he shut his eyes and the threatening pantomime of figures with their arms outstretched, trying to get him to stop. Finally, sometime around four in the morning, he finally dozed off and when he woke up, it was seven o'clock.

◆

Maryanne was in the kitchen and she offered him a cup of coffee, as if nothing had happened the night before. He wondered how much she'd been told. A short while later, Sullivan came downstairs, dressed for work in a coat and tie.

'Did you get some sleep?' he asked.

'A couple of hours.'

'Here, take a look at this. Page six,' said Sullivan, handing him the *Hindustan Times* and the *Times of India*. Both reports were short on details, though *The Times* gave it a larger headline:

CBI to Investigate Diplomat's Murder

New Delhi. March 28. The Central Bureau of Investigation (CBI) has taken over the case of a Cuban Embassy official whose body was found in the green belt to the west of Rashtrapati Bhawan and Chanakyapuri. The investigation, originally launched by the Delhi Police is ongoing and the motives and circumstances of the crime are still to be determined though it appears to have been a murder. The victim's name has not been released on account of diplomatic protocols.

When contacted, the Cuban Embassy refused to confirm or deny the death of one of its staff. The Ministry of Foreign Affairs has also declined to comment, except to say that they are aware of the police investigation and are awaiting a full report. News of the alleged murder has put New Delhi's diplomatic community on edge and several embassies have issued advisories to their citizens, suggesting they take precautions until the crime has been solved.

'Does this have something to do with what happened to me last night?' Fletcher asked, once he'd read the reports.

'I don't know,' said Sullivan, 'but it's an unusual coincidence.'

After breakfast, Sullivan drove Fletcher across to the guesthouse, so that he could wash up and change.

'Whatever's going on,' Sullivan said, as soon as they got in the car, 'you can't be on your own, or driving your bike. It isn't safe.'

'Who do you think they were?' Fletcher asked.

'Hard to say, but somebody wants to talk to you, or maybe they're trying to get you out of the way.' Sullivan's voice had a flat, matter-of-fact tone but he was obviously concerned. They drove the same route he'd taken the night before.

'This is where they started tailing me,' Fletcher said, as they turned onto Safdarjung Road. After another half mile, he pointed out the spot where the jeep had blocked the road. They could see skid marks on the asphalt, but other than that there was nothing there. Sullivan slowed down but didn't stop.

Five minutes later, they reached the guesthouse on Malcha Marg.

Sullivan went inside with Fletcher to make sure it was safe.

'Have a shower and get cleaned up, then pack your stuff and check out of this place. Sooner or later, they're bound to come looking for you here,' he said. 'I'll send someone across in an hour to pick you up and bring you over to the Embassy. Be ready with your luggage by 11.15.'

'Where am I going?' Fletcher asked.

'We'll talk about that when you come across. There are a couple of things I need to sort out.' Sullivan sounded impatient and on edge.

An embassy vehicle and driver arrived exactly at quarter past eleven and drove Fletcher into the Chancery, through the main gate. A few minutes later, he was in Sullivan's office.

'So, here's the plan,' said Sullivan. 'You need to get out of India tonight. We've got a ticket for you on this evening's Pan Am flight to New York.'

'Are you sure that's necessary?' said Fletcher.

'The CBI is planning to interrogate you,' Sullivan, explained. 'The whole thing could go south.'

'Are they the people that tried to get me last night?'

Sullivan shook his head, as he lit his pipe. 'No. That was someone else. You're a popular guy.'

'But I'm innocent. I've given the police a statement,' Fletcher protested. 'Besides, I can't just pick up and leave. I've got two more months of fieldwork to finish in Bharatpur.'

'Don't worry, we've cleared things up with the folks at Fulbright. I can send someone down to Bharatpur to empty your apartment and store your stuff until it's okay for you to come back.'

'But if I skip the country, who knows if they'll let me back in,' Fletcher said.

'We'll work that out. The CBI haven't issued a warrant yet and once you're out of India, it's more than likely they'll forget about you,' Sullivan reassured him.

'Why is the whole thing suddenly blowing up?' said Fletcher. 'I thought it was all over and done with.'

'So did I,' said Sullivan. 'But it seems there are…complications.'

'Is that all you can tell me? Complications?'

'Yeah. It's better you don't know the reasons. Ignorance is your best defence,' Sullivan's smile was more like a grimace. He glanced at his watch. 'We've got six hours before you leave for the airport. There's a lounge down the hall, where you can hang out.'

'Wait. Wait.' Fletcher put up both his hands. 'What if I don't want to go?'

'Then you'll be arrested by the CBI and spend the next two weeks in police custody,' said Sullivan. 'Either that, or your pals in the jeep station wagon might put a bullet through your head.'

'This is crazy,' Fletcher said. 'Why should I trust you?'

'Because, right now, I'm the only person who has your best interests at heart,' Sullivan replied. 'I know it's hard to accept but I wouldn't be doing this if I didn't think it was imperative.'

'What am I going to do in the US? I don't have a place to stay, unless I go back to Colorado and move in with my mother, which I'm not sure I want to do,' Fletcher said.

'We'll arrange temporary accommodation in Washington. You can check the lab work on the blood samples. After that, there are options…'

'What kind of options?' Fletcher asked.

'Well, there's a place called "The Farm".' Sullivan leaned forward, his hands folded over one knee. 'It's at Camp Peary, in rural Virginia, a couple hours' drive south of D.C. Have you heard of it?'

Fletcher shook his head.

'The Company runs a sort of a boot camp for prospective agents. If you're interested, we can arrange for you to join a course for two or three months. They teach you a lot of useful things, how to field strip an AK-47 or how to set up a wiretap. It's a rigorous programme, and not everyone passes, but at the end of it, we might even offer you a job.' Sullivan's voice seemed to have suddenly gone flat once again, without any inflection.

'I'm an ornithologist, not a secret agent,' said Fletcher.

'Don't worry. You'll be able to finish your PhD. We might even be able to chip in funds for your research,' said Sullivan. 'Studying birds is a good cover.'

'Sounds like you've got it all figured out,' said Fletcher without hiding his irritation. He had nothing more to say, as Sullivan reached over and put a hand on his shoulder before rising to his feet.

'Think about it, Guy. No commitments, I promise,' Sullivan insisted. 'But right now, we do need to ship you out of here before things get ugly.'

Fletcher hesitated and then stood up, realizing he had no choice.

8

Bald Eagle

Haliaeetus leucocephalus

America's national bird is a scavenger that feeds mostly on carrion, though it also kills small mammals and fish. It lives and breeds near waterbodies and coastal wetlands. Adult birds are easily recognizable from their prominent white head and tail, while juveniles are mostly dark brown until the age of four to five years. The yellow beak is proportionately larger than on most raptors. Its call is a muted, sniggering cry, punctuated with timid whistles.

Pan Am Flight 001 circled the globe from east to west. Departing Delhi, the Boeing 707 went on to Beirut, Istanbul, Frankfurt, London, and New York. With all of these stops it took close to thirty-six hours to reach the US. Last September, Fletcher had come to India on Flight 002, which flew around the world in the opposite direction. On his way over he had broken journey in Istanbul for two nights but this time he did the entire trip without stopping. He had a window seat and slept most of the way to Beirut, where the plane remained on the ground for a couple of hours as they refuelled. Permitted to disembark and stretch his legs in the transit lounge, he got a cup of coffee and a copy of the *Paris Herald Tribune*, a day old, dated 11 April 1962.

After reading the Indian papers for the past six months, it was interesting to see that there were other things happening in the rest of the world. US Steel had signed a new salary agreement with its workers. Police in Marseilles had recovered eight stolen paintings by Paul Cézanne. An American marine helicopter had landed in Saigon carrying military advisers. An army tribunal in Cuba had sentenced all

1,179 surviving members of the Bay of Pigs invasion to thirty years in prison and demanded $62 million from the US for their release.

When a voice over the loudspeaker called passengers to reboard Pan Am 001, Fletcher quickly flipped through the last few pages but stopped short when he came to the obituaries. Staring out at him was a photograph of the dead man in Delhi. He looked a bit younger and much more alive in the picture, but there was no mistaking who it was. As he queued up with the others to get back on the plane, Fletcher read the brief notice under the photograph.

Emil Zorman

Art Connoisseur

Born in Ljubljana, Yugoslavia, Dec. 3, 1920, Emil Zorman immigrated to the United States in 1938. He served in the US Army and OSS during WWII. Following the war, Mr Zorman opened an art gallery in New York, in partnership with Richard S. White. The gallery specialized in Asian art and he was a leading authority on Chinese and Tibetan antiquities. Following Mr White's death in 1953, Mr Zorman assumed full control of the gallery and opened a branch in Paris, where he represented a number of museums, including the Louvre. He travelled widely in Asia and was known to be an expert in 12th and 13th century Buddhist sculpture. Mr Zorman had returned recently from India and died suddenly of cardiac arrest in his New York apartment. A private burial service was held on April 7 at Forest Hills cemetery. Emil Zorman had no immediate family and leaves no survivors.

Once they were airborne, when the stewardess came around with breakfast, Fletcher asked for a Scotch.

◆

When he finally deplaned at Idlewild Airport on Long Island the following day, Fletcher was still trying to understand what was going on. It was obvious that Sullivan had lied to him but he couldn't figure out why, except that Emil Zorman must have been working for the CIA.

The OSS connection was obvious though it seemed to make no sense that an art dealer would be a spy, and why did they need to cover up his death and pretend it was a heart attack?

From Idlewild, he took a bus into Penn Station and caught the first train to Washington, as he'd been instructed, though Fletcher wasn't sure he wanted to be part of Sullivan's plan any more. Six hours later, he checked into a prepaid room at a cheap hotel on Reservoir Road in D.C., walking distance from the Smithsonian. Exhausted by the thoughts that kept running circles in his mind, he finally fell asleep and woke up twelve hours later. Taking the folded copy of the *Herald* out of his backpack, he read the obituary one more time, to make sure it wasn't a bad dream.

Later that morning, he dropped off the blood samples at the Georgetown Medical School lab, where a disgruntled-looking technician seemed to be expecting him. With an impatient expression, as if he was wasting her time, she said he could come back and collect the results in a couple of days.

Around noon, he used a payphone to call his adviser at Cornell. Professor Sergeant was surprised to hear that he was back in the US but seemed to believe the story that Fletcher had come down with a severe case of amoebic dysentery and been evacuated from India for medical reasons. Sullivan had come up with this alibi. Fletcher explained that he'd accomplished more than enough in the first season of fieldwork and he could pick up where he'd left off in the fall, when the geese and ducks returned to Bharatpur. His adviser didn't seem overly concerned and suggested he take a few months off to recover. He also explained that one of the other graduate students had moved into his office and there wasn't much point in returning to Cornell right away.

The following day, he went across to the Fulbright headquarters, where he was greeted with some scepticism. The grants officer, a man with a permanent scowl and pale blue eyes that peered through the thick lenses on his glasses, seemed to disapprove of his early departure from India. He informed Fletcher that since he had cut short his research, they would be holding back his monthly stipend for as long as he was in the US, though the money could be carried over into the fall, as necessary. He had to sign some papers and promised to submit a progress report.

A phone call to his mother in Colorado confirmed that he had no desire to go back home. He didn't bother to lie to her about the amoebic dysentery and she didn't seem to care that he'd returned from India earlier than expected. Dorothy Fletcher had always considered their time in Delhi an ordeal performed for the sake of her husband's career. She had never understood Guy's infatuation with India and often said she never wanted to leave America again. Fletcher was tempted to ask her if she'd known that his father had worked for the CIA but he decided to leave that question for another occasion. He also called his sister, Tracy, who was married to a Baptist minister and lived in Tacoma. They had little to talk about and he hung up after five or six minutes, on the excuse that he was running out of quarters.

Two days later, when he returned to the lab at Georgetown, the technician handed him a single page report that showed no signs of radiation. Sullivan had given him a number to call when he got the results and an anonymous male voice, presumably at Langley, promised to pass on the word to Delhi. Later that afternoon, with nothing more to do, he dropped by The Stable Door, a bar at the end of the block near his hotel. Only a couple of other customers were inside, as he ordered a Jack Daniel's on the rocks. The bartender said something about the baseball season, which was just starting, when Fletcher noticed the news on TV. There was a brief clip of the Kennedys leaving the White House and getting into a limousine. Sipping his drink, he remembered the gentle touch of the first lady's gloved hand.

Moments later, a red-haired woman, about thirty, took a seat on the stool next to his and ordered a grapefruit daquiri. She smiled as their eyes met but said nothing until the bartender delivered her drink.

Holding up her glass, she turned towards him and whispered, 'Cheers!'

Fletcher raised his glass cautiously.

'Have you recovered from jet lag?' she asked.

He nodded. 'How did you know I'd be here?'

She laughed. 'We keep our eyes peeled.'

Though he had been expecting someone to contact him, the woman's sudden appearance caught him off guard. She had an almost perfectly oval face, arched eyebrows, and a full mouth, accentuated by red lipstick, that made her look a little like Romy Schneider, an actress he didn't particularly like.

'Jack asked me to get in touch,' the woman said.

'All right,' said Fletcher. 'I'm listening.'

There was no subtlety or obfuscation to the offer. The woman spoke in a frank, even tone. The CIA was offering him a position as a Junior Officer Trainee, contingent on his successfully completing an orientation course at The Farm, a new session of which had just begun. They would start him on four thousand dollars a year, along with travel and other expenses. Whether he accepted their offer or not, he was expected to keep all of this strictly confidential and tell no one, not even family.

After she finished explaining the offer, the woman gestured for the bartender to bring them each another drink.

'What about my research?' said Fletcher. 'I'm in the middle of doing my PhD.... Will I have to give that up?'

She wet her lips, then shook her head. 'No. You should be able to finish your doctorate. In fact, your fieldwork can carry on concurrently with your agency assignment. Jack will sort all of that out.'

'He's an influential man,' said Fletcher.

The woman's face hardened into a humourless smile.

'You bet he is,' she said.

'What happens if I don't pass the training at The Farm?' he asked.

'Then, you'll be free to carry on with your fieldwork and finish your degree.'

Fletcher let the whisky singe his tongue then sucked on an ice cube, thinking for a while. He finally looked at her again with an uneasy, cornered expression.

'You've got nothing to lose,' the woman added.

◆

After filling out and signing what seemed like a hundred different forms, contracts, addenda, and non-disclosure agreements, as well as undergoing a physical exam and being fingerprinted, Fletcher was driven down to Camp Peary. Despite a lingering ambivalence, he felt strangely relaxed and content. The whole experience reminded him of when he'd been tapped for the Delta Tau Delta fraternity at Wesleyan, a secretive sense of being drawn into an exclusive circle and surrendering his autonomy. The Farm was located within the Armed Forces Experimental Training Facility, where JOTs were housed in a complex of Quonset huts. Nearby lay salt marshes bordering the Chesapeake Bay and there was a lot of birdlife, including ducks and geese, as well as a pair of bald eagles nesting in a tree near the main gate.

The majority of their classes were devoted to tradecraft, which included covert methods of communication and how to move about in a foreign country without arousing suspicion. Much of it seemed obvious like the dead drops they used to contact sources. Yet the procedures were elaborate with a litany of rules. Predictably, they were taught how to sweep a room for listening devices and what to look for if you were being tailed. There was even a workshop on playing poker and bridge. They were coached on how to win but also methods to ensure that they lost.

Each week, at least one or two visiting lecturers dropped by The Farm and gave a talk, followed by a Q & A, in an auditorium known as 'The Pit'. Most of the speakers were retired CIA officers who told stories about their glory days in the OSS, running agents behind German lines or sabotaging Japanese communications in the South Pacific. They used a lot of acronyms and abbreviations like ChiNats and ChiComs, for the nationalists and communists in China. Many of the speakers had a laconic, privileged manner about them, coming from Ivy League universities. Despite their cocksure, Yankee bravado, Fletcher could tell that most of them were lonely old men who wished they were still in the game.

During his fifth week, Fletcher attended a lecture by a man named Doug Pritchett, who began by admitting that this was his cover name. He looked as if he was in his mid-fifties, a grey-haired, garrulous man who gave the impression that he didn't take anything seriously. His talk was titled, 'An Anthropologist in Tibet', and he began by telling them that he had done his PhD in social anthropology and conducted ethnographic fieldwork in Nepal and Tibet, during the late forties and early fifties, 'before the Chinese intrusion.' He said that after he failed to find a tenured position at a university, he'd joined the agency because nobody else would give him a job and it was the only way he could use his expertise.

Moving on from his personal biography, he segued into a discussion about Tibetan refugees in exile and how some of them had become resistance fighters who were carrying on a guerrilla war against the communists. Many were Khampas, from Eastern Tibet, who were known to be warriors and bandits. He explained how they had a strong devotion to the Dalai Lama, even though they were culturally very different from most people in Lhasa. The Khampas referred to themselves as 'ten dzong ma mi' or 'guardians of the fortress of the faith'. Pritchett had conducted his ethnographic research amongst the Khampas and said they had a penchant for violence even though they were Buddhists. After this, he explained how some refugees in India had joined Chushi Gangdruk, an anti-communist insurgency that started in 1958. Chushi Gangdruk meant 'land of four rivers and six ranges' referring to the Amdo and Kham region in Eastern Tibet.

Pritchett went on to explain how the United States was supporting the Tibetan guerrillas, providing them with small arms, radios, and cash. Operating out of East Pakistan, the CIA was flying planes across the Himalayas and parachuting Tibetan insurgents into remote areas of Tibet. They had also established a training centre in Colorado, at Camp Hale, in conjunction with the US army's mountain warfare school. A number of Chushi Gangdruk fighters had been flown to the Rockies, where winter conditions were similar to Tibet. The emphasis was on infiltration and intelligence gathering but they were also trained in handling explosives and how to disrupt communications. He concluded his lecture by explaining how anthropology and intelligence gathering were similar pursuits.

'You need to gain an appreciation for the people you work with. Tibet is a unique and ancient culture with mostly pastoral communities as well as a strong monastic tradition. The lamas control Tibetan society and there is no separation between church and state, like we have in America. If you want to understand how Tibetans see the world, you have to accept Tantric Buddhism as a fundamental way of life. The guerrilla fighters we arm and assist are fighting for their faith as much as their freedom.'

At the end of the talk, Fletcher raised his hand.

'Do you really believe these fighters can overthrow the Chinese?' he asked.

Sensing his scepticism, Pritchett nodded.

'Of course, we don't have the numbers, at least not yet,' he said. 'Nevertheless, they're severely disrupting the occupation.'

Fletcher continued: 'But don't you think it could be a repeat of what happened at the Bay of Pigs?'

The speaker seemed taken aback for a moment but then, with a casual flick of his wrist, as if he were tossing something in the garbage, he replied. 'Remember that Doris Day song? "Que Sera Sera". Whatever will be, will be.'

◆

While some of the lessons at The Farm involved survival training and hand to hand combat, as well as firearms drills, most of it was classroom instruction, not too different from being back in college. Psychology was a big part of the curriculum, as were history and political science. The idea was to hone a trainee's critical faculties and help him learn to operate unnoticed within the shadows of society, anywhere in the world.

One of the instructors, who had worked in Venezuela until his cover was blown, emphasized the importance of engaging the enemy in a contest that had no fixed rules. 'You need to learn to deal with ambiguity,' he lectured Fletcher and the others. 'There isn't always going to be a clean line between right and wrong. You've got to work around the moral uncertainties that you'll face and recognize that ambivalence isn't necessarily a bad thing.'

The instructor didn't hesitate to let it be known that he was involved in the Bay of Pigs invasion. Though he admitted that Operation JMARK, also known as ZAPATA, had been a dismal failure, he defended the logic and planning behind it, claiming that there had been a high probability of success, even if, in the end, it was a catastrophe and most of the dissidents were killed or captured by Castro's fighters.

'We had a good chance of winning,' he said, 'but it wasn't our day.'

A lot of the discussions at The Farm, both formal and informal, centred around what had happened in Cuba, a year ago. Many of the instructors and visiting lecturers spoke about how 'the paradigm has shifted'. During the 1950s a lot of emphasis had been placed on technology, particularly the U2 flights, which produced large quantities of intelligence on Soviet military capabilities, through aerial surveillance. Some of the CIA leadership had even begun to suggest that human intelligence—moles, informers, and agents on the ground—were now obsolete. But then, after Francis Gary Powers was shot down by the Soviets in 1960, it created an international furore and the flights were scaled back. Only two months ago, in February, Powers had been released from jail in Moscow and exchanged for Rudolf Abel, a KGB agent.

Following the botched invasion of Cuba, those who promoted the idea of paramilitary operations and assassination as part of the agency's agenda, were being forced out of the leadership and 'a new way forward' was being promoted. Several of the speakers who came to The Farm emphasized the fact that the agency needed to 'go back to the basics', collecting information through sources whose cooperation was carefully cultivated and nurtured.

In their classes, a lot of emphasis was placed on identifying and recruiting assets, which was seen as the primary goal of every intelligence officer. The subtle psychology of gaining a source's trust was critical to ensuring that he or she would serve as a reliable conduit of information. Unlike the precise engineering and gadgetry that went into a U2 spy plane, the calculations and calibrations required on the ground were far less predictable.

Fletcher realized that he, himself, had been successfully recruited by Sullivan, using some of the same tradecraft they were teaching him now. Though, of course, he wasn't a foreign agent and the 'approach' involved fewer risks, it was still a confidence game. First of all, they were told that it was important to assess a potential target, and determine if he or she might be open to working for the CIA. After that it was essential to establish contact in a manner that exploited the individual's vulnerabilities.

The instructors at The Farm spent a lot of time talking about motivation and Fletcher wondered what was driving him now. He had never seen himself as a patriot. Nevertheless, he wasn't opposed to working for the government and believed in Kennedy's exhortation: 'Ask not what your country can do for you, but what you can do for your country.' At the same time, he felt some reluctance about becoming a spy because, as he already knew, it was a game of lies and subterfuge. Though he had no sympathies for the communists, Fletcher wondered whether he was willing to risk his life for the cause. He also thought about his father, knowing that he had agreed to join the CIA because, indirectly, it brought him closer to whatever motives Bill Fletcher might have felt. Perhaps it would help him uncover the secrets that stood between them when he was alive. As he went through the exercises and lectures at The Farm, the knowledge that he was being trained for clandestine missions and postings abroad, made him feel that he was part of a hidden, yet crucial, enterprise that could influence the future of the world.

9

Blue Rock Pigeon

Columba livia

*Probably the most ubiquitous bird on earth, blue rock pigeons are found
throughout the world, from the rooftops of London, Paris, and New York,
to the fields and farmland of India and China. This species is often bred in
captivity and a number of hybrids have been produced. The most common
colouration is a slate grey body with two black bands on the wings.
The head is darker with an iridescent green and purple collar.
Also called rock doves, they were introduced to the United States
from Europe in the early seventeenth century.*

One morning, soon after reveille, Fletcher stepped out of his room
in the Quonset hut and looked up at the sky, where a flock of
pigeons was wheeling overhead. He was surprised to see them this
far away from the free handouts in cities or towns, but the pigeons
immediately brought back memories of Delhi.

When he was a boy, Fletcher and his friend, Reggie Bhatia, would
hunt pigeons in Lodhi Gardens, which lay across the road from their
homes in Jor Bagh. Back then, in the early fifties, sections of Lodhi
Gardens were wild and untamed, with only a few dirt paths snaking
through a jungle of acacia trees. The sixteenth century tomb of Sikander
Lodhi and others of his dynasty were surrounded by flowerbeds and
ornamental palms but the rest of the gardens were mostly neglected.
Though some of the residents of New Delhi took their morning and
evening constitutionals along the winding paths, Lodhi Gardens was
mostly deserted—a perfect place for two young boys to explore and let
their imaginations run loose.

Occasionally, a disapproving adult, usually one of the gardeners, would scold them for hunting in the park, and shoo them off, but they knew every shortcut and goat path, quickly escaping out of earshot. Hunting pigeons was more of an excuse to wander about in the jungle than any form of serious sport, though Reggie was a crack shot with his .177 air rifle and, if they were lucky, they returned home with five or six birds. Guy's marksmanship improved over time and he killed his share of pigeons too. While Mrs Bhatia refused to let the boys bring the dead birds into her house, the Fletchers' elderly Muslim cook, Shaukat, would happily pluck the pigeons and make a kabootar biryani.

One of Fletcher's clearest memories of Lodhi Gardens was during his third year in Delhi. He and Reggie often crossed the park and headed over to Khan Market where they could buy ice cream. Sometime in early spring, they had noticed a strange man walking alone along the paths every evening with a string of prayer beads in one hand. He looked as if he might be Egyptian or Moroccan because he wore a red fez on his head with a black tassel. His round-rimmed glasses were tinted a dark shade of green that hid his eyes. The clothes he wore were European—a dark coat, with a white shirt and tie, striped trousers, and leather dress shoes. There was a dignified but shabby appearance to the man, who mumbled to himself as he shuffled along, absorbed in his thoughts.

Half-joking but half-serious, Guy and Reggie guessed he must be an Arab spy. Recently, at the Regal Cinema in Connaught Circus, they had watched a re-run of Alfred Hitchcock's *Secret Agent*, as well as *Diplomatic Courier* with Tyrone Power and Patricia Neal. They convinced themselves that the man in Lodhi Gardens must be in Delhi on a covert mission and decided to find out where he went after his walk.

Armed with the air rifle, they waited under the arches of Mohammed Shah's tomb until the man appeared. Following him on his circuit of the park, the boys tried to stay hidden in the shrubs and bushes along the path, though their target seemed so absorbed in meditation that he probably wouldn't have noticed them anyway. Circumambulating Lodhi Gardens, the old man passed a few other evening walkers, but did not exchange greetings or look up. A flight of pigeons landed in a neem tree along their route but Reggie and Guy resisted the temptation to fire. Two peacocks also crossed their path, as well as a mongoose.

Eventually, the man in the fez shuffled out of the gate, along Cornwallis Road, which led to Khan Market. Keeping to the pavement on the right side of the road, he continued to worry his beads, lost in thought. The boys now had no bushes or weeds to hide them, though they followed about thirty yards behind.

In whispers they speculated whether the man would catch a bus at Khan Market, or if he lived in one of the houses nearby. By now the sun had gone down and it was already growing dark. The shadowy bungalows they passed looked deserted though they had nameplates of members of parliament and army generals on the gates. Several of the residences were guarded by sentries, who eyed the boys and their pellet gun with suspicion. Guy knew he was supposed to be home by now and his parents would scold him for staying out after dark.

At the crossroads beyond Khan Market, the old man made his way to the other side of the street. He was still wearing dark glasses, as if he were blind, but seemed to have no trouble dodging bicycles and making his way across. As Guy and Reggie crossed over, a large car pulled up next to the man, who removed his hat before getting into the front passenger seat.

Stopped in their tracks, the two boys stared at the vehicle as it began to pull away from the kerb. The windows were rolled down and Guy could see the man clearly, still wearing his dark glasses, but he also noticed the driver seated beside him. At that moment, the headlights of another vehicle shone through the windscreen and Guy recognized his father behind the wheel. It was only a brief flash, but Bill Fletcher's features were unmistakable, leaning over to speak to the man he'd picked up.

Freezing, Guy looked across at Reggie but he could tell that his friend hadn't seen who it was. As they raced home to Jor Bagh, Reggie joked about tailing the Arab spy and Guy laughed along with him, though he felt a wrenching sense of confusion and couldn't understand why his father had been in the car.

Though the incident left him puzzled and suspicious, he never had the courage to ask his father what was going on. Soon afterwards, the old man with his fez and prayer beads disappeared. No matter how often Guy and Reggie searched for the stooped figure, shuffling along the paths, they could not find him—he had disappeared forever.

◆

Fletcher was three quarters of the way through the course and felt confident that he would pass without difficulty. At the same time, there was a nagging uncertainty about becoming a spy, as if he were selling his soul. He understood that once he joined the CIA it would be difficult for him to quit. Lying alone at night in his room, he argued with himself—maybe it would be better if he went back to being an ordinary graduate student, juggling grants and fellowships.

On the other hand, alongside the steady salary, there were other incentives to joining the intelligence services. As Sullivan had told him, during one of their conversations, 'There aren't many jobs that will bring you back to this part of the world.' At the same time, Fletcher worried that if it were ever revealed that he worked for the CIA, it would be impossible for him to return to India. All of these uncertainties weighed on his mind, along with his doubts about the lies he'd been told and Sullivan's motives.

'Why would you want to recruit me?' he'd asked, before leaving Delhi.

'Because you're a natural,' Sullivan had insisted. 'You know the language. You know the region.'

'But that doesn't make me a good spy,' said Fletcher.

'Yeah, but you've got the instincts too,' Sullivan had replied, 'the way you handled yourself when I first met you. I could tell you'd inherited your father's qualities, an ability to blend in and keep your eyes open. As a scientist you're trained to observe things with a critical eye and analyse the data. Not everybody is good at that kind of thing.'

A few days before the course ended one of the chief instructors pulled Fletcher aside and told him that he needed to go up to Washington the next day. He didn't explain anything further, except to say that there was a hotel room booked for him at The Willard and he was to meet someone for dinner at a restaurant nearby called The Rough Rider Bar & Grill on G Street.

'7 p.m. And you'll need to wear a coat and tie,' the instructor explained.

'I don't have one,' said Fletcher. 'What's this all about?'

'Then buy yourself one at Sears. A car will take you up in the morning. That's all you need to know.'

◆

The Rough Rider was a venerable Washington watering hole and feeding trough. Its decor centred around Teddy Roosevelt and the restaurant claimed to have opened in 1901, the first year of his presidency. Entering through a thick oak door into a shadowy foyer, Fletcher was confronted by a moose head on the wall above the entrance as well as a portrait of the twenty-sixth president. Beyond the foyer lay the bar, which was crowded with men in dark suits. A large number of pronghorn antelopes, deer, and big horned sheep looked down on them from the walls, as if it were a taxidermist's studio. Framed etchings from the Spanish-American War, of soldiers on horseback, were on display alongside photographs of Roosevelt and his sons on safari in Africa, as well as in Yellowstone National Park.

Fletcher was guided through the bar by a hostess with a blonde bouffant, wearing a tight black dress. She led him into one of three dining rooms, where Jack Sullivan was seated at the back, under a shoulder mount of a zebra.

'What are you doing here?' Fletcher exclaimed with surprise, as Sullivan shook his hand.

'I had some work in town,' he replied, gesturing for Fletcher to take a seat. 'Thought I'd check in on you and see how you're doing at The Farm?'

'It's been okay,' said Fletcher. 'A bit like summer camp, except more demanding.'

'Glad to hear it,' said Sullivan. 'From everything I've been told the instructors are impressed with your progress.'

'Have they sent you my report card?' Fletcher joked.

Sullivan shook his head.

'No. But I've got confidential sources, even at The Farm,' he replied.

'How's Maryanne?' Fletcher asked.

'She's good, thank you. We flew here together but she's gone down to Georgia to see her mother. Summer isn't her favourite season in Delhi.'

'Must be getting hot,' Fletcher said.

'You bet! When I left on Monday, it was 101 degrees. I don't think any of your geese are hanging around in Bharatpur. If I was them, I'd fly straight to Tibet.'

'It's too bad the blood samples came back negative,' said Fletcher.

'That's okay. We'll try again in October when the birds return,' Sullivan said with a shrug as a waiter arrived. 'I've ordered a highball. What'll you drink?'

'A beer would be great,' said Fletcher. 'Maybe a Budweiser.'

'Try the Rheingold, it's better,' Sullivan interjected.

A low roar of conversation was coming from the bar but the dining room was relatively quiet, though all of the tables were occupied. Fletcher could tell that Sullivan was a regular here, the way the hostess spoke to him and the comfortable manner in which he leaned back in his chair and filled his pipe. The room was dimly lit and the starched white tablecloths and gleaming cutlery contrasted with the dark wood panelling.

'This is a little bit different from our mess hall at The Farm,' said Fletcher.

'Yeah.' Sullivan laughed, firing up his pipe. 'Every JOT complains about the food but as the saying goes, "that which does not kill us, makes us stronger".'

Their drinks arrived, along with the leather-bound menus. A bison and an elk were studying Fletcher from the opposite wall as he glanced at the list of entrées.

'I guess this isn't a place for vegetarians,' he said.

Sullivan shook his head.

'The steaks are always good,' he said. 'The best prairie fed beef from Nebraska, where they don't believe in holy cows. My recommendation is that we both have the filet mignon, medium rare, with a side of asparagus and roast potatoes. But first we'll start with a dozen Chesapeake Bay oysters, in your honour.'

'What are we celebrating?' Fletcher asked.

Sullivan put his smouldering pipe in a crystal ashtray and smiled.

'I'll tell you in a minute,' he said, then raised his highball glass in a toast.

Despite its name, The Rough Rider had a discreet elegance that exuded an atmosphere of masculine power and authority. Only a couple of women were in the room and they looked out of place with detached smiles and inattentive eyes. Laying both hands on the table, Sullivan leaned forward.

'How would you like to go back to India?' he asked.

Fletcher swallowed a sip of beer and blinked. 'When?'

'Next week,' Sullivan answered. 'As soon as you're finished at The Farm.'

'What's the urgency?' Fletcher asked.

'Something's come up....' As if by instinct, Sullivan ran his eyes over the neighbouring tables, though they were out of earshot and all of the other diners seemed absorbed in their own conversations. Rubbing his palms together, Sullivan spoke softly but firmly: 'So, I'm going to tell you part of the story. The rest you'll learn in Delhi. But all of this is strictly confidential. Understand?'

Fletcher nodded as Sullivan continued:

'Several weeks ago, you had a speaker at The Farm named Pritchett. He must have explained some of the things we're doing in Tibet,' Sullivan said. 'It's a dynamic situation but we've parachuted more than two dozen operatives into eastern and central Tibet. Most of them have radios and we get reports on a regular basis about whatever the Chinese are doing—troop movements, road building, the killing of monks, and the closing of monasteries. We've also airdropped weapons, ammunition, and explosives. Some people, like Pritchett, for instance, believe that we can start an insurgency and if it gathers momentum the Tibetans will rise up against the communists.' He paused for a moment and ran his thumb across his lower lip. 'I'm not that naïve. We'll never be able to get enough fighters back across the mountains to take on the Chinese. But the men we've sent over there are providing us with a lot of valuable first-hand information, some of which we share with the Indians, some of which we keep to ourselves. A couple years ago, for example, a group of Khampa fighters ambushed a Chinese jeep carrying a PLA commander. They recovered 1,600 pages of documents, which revealed a great deal about their military presence in Tibet but also confirmed that there's a serious Sino–Soviet rift.'

The oysters arrived on a pewter tray loaded with crushed ice. Sullivan paused while the waiter set it down. 'I recommend the horseradish,' he said.

Fletcher wasn't a fan of raw shellfish but he ate a couple of oysters as Sullivan returned to the subject of Tibet.

'In 1959, soon after the Dalai Lama escaped, the Chinese overran a border post at Longju. The Indians have no roads up to the border in the Northeast Frontier Agency, NEFA, and only a small contingent of the Assam Rifles, a paramilitary frontier force. Over the past couple of months we've been getting news that the People's Liberation Army is moving more than 20,000 men up to the disputed border with India. They've disguised it as regular troop rotation but they're replacing every man they move out with five fresh soldiers. The Indians have confirmed this from their observation posts, though they haven't got much specific intelligence and don't seem particularly concerned. What we haven't told them is that most of the troops the Chinese are stationing in Tibet were deployed in Korea. The commanders are all veterans who fought against us along the 38th Parallel. Ever hear of the Chosin Reservoir or Hellfire Valley?'

Fletcher shook his head as Sullivan helped himself to the last of the oysters.

'December 1950. The PLA came over the mountains in mid-winter and outnumbered us three to one. Our marines and infantry weren't properly equipped for the weather or the terrain. It was a massacre and the US forces had to retreat. 2,500 killed. 5,000 wounded and 8,000 suffering frostbite and exposure.'

Sullivan fell silent as the waiter removed the tray of melting ice and the empty oyster shells.

'Anyway,' he continued, 'the troops that the Chinese are now sending to Tibet are trained and experienced in mountain warfare. Recently there have been a few incidents at some of the passes, where the PLA have challenged the Indians and tried to push them back from their positions.'

'Why is there a border dispute?' Fletcher asked.

'Because some Brit named McMahon—I suppose he's actually a Scotsman—drew an arbitrary boundary across the Himalayas to delineate the northern frontier of India. It was one of the things the British were obsessed with, marking out territory, though the truth of it was that nobody had really worried about Himalayan borders before. The main passes were controlled by one side or the other but the higher ranges and glaciers were a frozen no-man's-land. Anyway, in recent years, the Chinese have insisted that parts of the territory beyond the McMahon line belong to them. The Indians aren't treating it as seriously as they should.'

'Why not?' Fletcher asked.

'Because they don't know shit from Shinola!' said Sullivan. 'Nehru and his defence minister, Krishna Menon, want to cosy up to the Chinese. They believe that Mao and Chou En-lai are India's friends because of their policy of non-alignment. No matter how much we tell them, they don't realize that the communists plan to take over Asia. Korea was the beginning and now you can see what's happening in Laos and Indo-China. It's a concerted strategy to conquer the world!'

On that note, the steaks arrived.

'So, what does all of this have to do with me?' Fletcher asked, after they had been served.

Sullivan held a lethal-looking steak knife in his hand, pointing it at Fletcher.

'We need your help monitoring the situation, keeping an ear to the ground.'

'Don't you have enough people in Delhi?'

'You're not going to be posted to Delhi.' Sullivan cut into his steak, which bled onto his plate. Before he took a bite, he added, 'We're going to send you up to the mountains instead.'

The filet was perfect—tender and well-seasoned. Fletcher fell silent as he enjoyed the meat, though in his mind he was still trying to unravel everything Sullivan had told him so far.

'Where, exactly, am I going?' he asked.

'Kalimpong,' said Sullivan. 'And Sikkim. You'll be working on a bird survey sponsored by the Smithsonian and the Bombay Natural History Society.'

'Where is Kalimpong?' Fletcher asked. 'I've heard the name, but I don't think I could find it on a map.'

'It's a hill station near Darjeeling, overlooking the Teesta Valley, in a part of West Bengal they call the Chicken's Neck. Bhutan is on one

side, to the east. Nepal on the west. A little ways to the south is East
Pakistan and to the north, across the Nathu La pass, is the Chumbi
Valley, a little piece of Tibet that protrudes into India. The Brits used
to call it "the dagger pointed at the heart of India". It's a strategic area
with a complicated history,' said Sullivan, 'and some interesting birds.'

'What am I looking for?'

'Don't worry, you'll get a full briefing in Delhi. I'm flying back
tomorrow,' Sullivan had been concentrating on his food as he spoke
but now he looked up. 'How's your steak?'

'Terrific.'

'This is the one thing I miss in India.' Sullivan put down his knife
and wiped the corners of his mouth with a napkin. 'It's impossible to
get good beef.'

Fletcher realized that he wasn't going to glean much more
information but as they finished their meal he tried to coax a few more
details about his assignment out of Sullivan, who seemed to assume that
he had already agreed to go back to India, just as he'd complied with
his recommendations from the menu.

'By the way, what happened with the CBI investigation?'

'Don't worry about it,' said Sullivan. 'Everything's sorted out. Case
closed.'

Studying Sullivan's face, Fletcher had to wonder whether the whole
story about the CBI wanting to question him had just been a ruse to
bring him here to the US and get him started at The Farm. For the
first time it struck him that maybe Jack Sullivan was an alias and he
wondered whether he would ever learn his real name.

'Did they confirm the dead man's identity?' he asked.

Sullivan glanced up, a hint of caution in his eyes.

'He was Cuban, the first secretary at the Embassy. I don't know why
there was any confusion. CBI solved the case within a week. It turned
out that he was murdered by one of his girlfriends who discovered he
was having an affair with a Hungarian woman. Fucking bed-hopping
communists.'

'Did they arrest the murderer?' Fletcher asked, testing to see how
far Sullivan would carry on with the lie. He wanted to tell him that
he had seen Zorman's obituary in the *Herald* but as he'd been taught

at The Farm: 'If you know the truth it's worth a lot more if you don't give it away.'

'No, she'd already left the country and flown back to Havana.'

As they finished their meal, Sullivan changed the subject, talking about Darjeeling. When he was growing up in Jamshedpur, his mother would take him and his brother to the hills for a couple months every summer. Travelling by train to Siliguri, they switched to the narrow gauge railway that ran through the tea gardens.

'I've always loved Darjeeling. This was way back in the twenties, just after the war. My mother rented a cottage facing Kanchenjunga and every day we'd wake up to see if the mountains were visible through the clouds,' Sullivan explained. 'In those days, the Brits were just starting their Everest expeditions, going up into Tibet by way of Nathu La and the Chumbi Valley. It was a different time, a different world. In 1924, I remember just after we arrived up the hill, somebody pointed out a group of Englishmen strolling along the Chowrasta, near the bandstand. One of them was George Mallory. They were about to set off for the Rongbuk Glacier and the north face of Everest. Of course, Mallory and his climbing partner, Sandy Irvine, disappeared on that expedition. Nobody knows if they made it to the top.'

When it came to ordering dessert, Fletcher asserted his independence. Sullivan wanted him to try the chocolate mousse but he asked for pecan pie instead.

'Was India very different under the British?' Fletcher asked.

'Yes, in many ways. It was easier for us to do whatever we wanted, even if we weren't English. Being white gave us a licence to go almost anywhere we chose and at that age—I was twelve or thirteen—Darjeeling was our playground. My brother and I got into plenty of trouble but somehow we always got out of it too.'

Sullivan was a man of obvious contradictions and Fletcher could imagine him as an all-American boy running wild in India. Despite the lies he told there was something transparent about him. Seated here in this restaurant, surrounded by trophies and memorabilia from the Spanish-American War, it felt like a place where neither of them belonged. Pointing to an etching on the wall, of Teddy Roosevelt leading his volunteer cavalry against the Spanish forces in Cuba, Fletcher couldn't help but make a sarcastic remark.

'That's a little bit different from the Bay of Pigs, don't you think?' he said.

Glancing up at the picture, Sullivan frowned at the bespectacled hero on horseback with his sabre drawn.

'The rules have changed since Roosevelt and his Rough Riders charged up San Juan Hill,' he admitted. 'The agency shouldn't be in the business of organizing invasions. We're not a military force. Our primary job is to gather information and, sometimes, to sow the seeds of dissent. Occasionally, we can support opposition elements in a hostile country but believe me, there will always be yahoos from some glee club at Yale who think they can start a full-scale insurgency. That's what happened in the Bay of Pigs. We can't repeat those mistakes in Tibet.'

10

Coppersmith Barbet

Megalaima haemacephala

Also known as the crimson-breasted barbet, this small bird (six inches) is mostly green with a dull, striated underbelly, yellow throat, and bright red patches on its forehead and breast. Its common name is derived from the bird's rhythmic call, which sounds like a hammer striking a copper vessel with a steady, monotonous beat. Found in most parts of India, it prefers ficus trees, either banyan or peepul, making its nest in hollow cavities of the trunk.

Awakened by the roar of a tiger, Fletcher had no idea where he was for a minute or two. The deep-throated call, more of a moan than a growl, seemed close at hand, only a few hundred yards away. As his mind gradually came into focus, pale streaks of dawn shone through a gap in the curtains. He had fallen asleep with his clothes on, under the whirlwind of a ceiling fan. Fletcher felt drugged and struggled to keep his eyes open as his numbed senses emerged from sleep. The tiger called again, a deep, resonant sound that echoed inside his muddled brain, as he gradually began to remember how he had arrived in this room.

Despite the fan, the air was hot and suffocating. His clothes stuck to the sweat on his arms and legs, as he crawled off the bed. Drawing the curtains apart, Fletcher opened the door onto a balcony. It was a few degrees cooler outside but still oppressively hot. Above the line of kikar trees that bordered the Delhi Zoo, he could see the crenellated ruins of Purana Qila silhouetted against the sky. A second tiger was calling now, answering the first. As the sky brightened, a chorus of birdcalls arose from the direction of the zoo, mostly bulbuls and jungle babblers, but also a coppersmith barbet. The soft, persistent tapping sounded like a metronome marking time before the sun rose.

Sifting through a fog of recent memories, he recalled the crowd outside the Arrivals Hall at Palam Airport last night. Even at 2 a.m., when he had emerged from the terminal, the heat was oppressive. Anxious families jostled with taxi drivers and tour operators, all of whom were kept at bay by two police constables with bamboo canes that they waved threateningly as the impatient throng kept trying to surge forward. Fletcher was prepared for the onslaught. Three different taxi drivers grabbed his duffel bag and tried to wrestle it out of his hands until he shouted at them. Moments later, he spotted a man holding a sign that Sullivan had told him to look out for: Sunrise Tours.

As they headed out onto the highway there was hardly any traffic at this time of night. The fields and scrub jungle on either side of the road were cloaked in darkness. A couple of jackals ran across in front of the taxi, eyes glinting in the headlights. After twenty minutes they came to the outskirts of Chanakyapuri. Though he had been away for only two months, it seemed as if even more buildings had come up. Sullivan had given Fletcher the address for the safe house in Sundar Nagar, but the driver already knew where to go. Situated at the rear of the colony, facing the zoo, it was a large, cream-coloured building, two storeys high. Getting out of the car, Fletcher wiped sweat off his face with his sleeve.

After he rang the bell, a middle-aged man with bleary eyes opened the door. Nobody spoke as the driver carried the bag inside and up a flight of stairs. Fletcher was taken to his room, which had a large double bed and dark wooden furniture. The yellow aura from the light bulbs barely reached the corners of the room. As soon as Fletcher was alone, he threw himself flat on his back under the swirling air from the fan, turned up full blast.

Now, four hours later, he struggled to wake up, as he stood on the balcony. Realizing there were mosquitoes in the air, he withdrew back into the room and shut the windows. The tigers had fallen silent. Taking a cold shower, Fletcher shaved and changed into a fresh set of clothes before heading downstairs. The same man who had let him in the night before was in the kitchen and soon handed him a cup of tea.

The safe house was sparsely furnished, with no pictures on the walls and only two chairs and a sofa in the living room. It had a musty, abandoned smell. The curtains covering the main window were grey with dust and grime. When Fletcher pulled them aside, he could see a weedy garden at the back and heard the coppersmith again, each *took... took... took* of its persistent cry like water dripping into an empty bucket.

◆

An hour later, after he'd been given breakfast, the doorbell rang. Fletcher had been expecting Sullivan but it was Mark. He was carrying a suitcase and something that looked like an oversized hatbox, both of which he hauled upstairs.

To begin with, Mark asked to see Fletcher's passport. After studying the visa and entry stamps, he nodded and handed it back. The passport, which Sullivan had given him in D.C., was in the name of Allan Swift. 'Remember two "As" and two "Ls"' Sullivan had said. His year of birth was correct but the date had been changed, April 12 instead of December 18. His permanent address was in Fort Collins, Colorado.

'Make sure you memorize all that information,' said Mark. 'Your new research visa is valid for a year. And these are your credentials from the Smithsonian.'

He handed him an ID card and an envelope containing a letter explaining the purpose of his research: A Survey of the Birds of the Eastern Himalaya. A second letter, from the Bombay Natural History Society, indicated that he was a research fellow. It had an official stamp and was signed by the president of BNHS, Salim Ali.

Fletcher looked up in surprise. 'Is this actually his signature?'

'Yes,' said Mark, 'But of course he doesn't know why you're really here. Your research project has been approved by BNHS though we've kept the details a little vague. The main problem will be the police checkpoints on the road up to Gangtok. There's an inner line permit stamped in your passport, which should be enough to get you through. These documents are just for backup.'

'Got it,' said Fletcher.

'We're calling this Operation Staghorn,' Mark explained. 'Your codename is Icarus. Jack will be handling your mission himself. His codename is Merlin.'

'Like the magician or the bird?' Fletcher asked, wondering if Mark had any sense of humour.

Scowling at him for being a smartass, he asked, 'Does it matter?'

'I suppose not,' said Fletcher, pointing to the suitcase. 'What's all this?'

'We've got an anorak for you and a down mummy bag,' said Mark.

'That's exactly what I need right now,' said Fletcher, wiping the perspiration from his forehead.

Mark responded, 'Up in the mountains, you'll be glad you have this stuff. I'm also guessing you didn't bring any rain gear, as well as waterproof boots and gaiters. Hopefully, these are the right size. Eight and a half wide?'

'Correct,' said Fletcher.

'Did you bring the mist nets?' Mark asked.

'Yes, I've got those in my bag, along with the kits for blood samples,' Fletcher told him.

'Good,' said Mark, pointing to a rectangular cardboard carton, packed in with the clothes. 'That's the portable tape recorder you requested and here's the parabolic microphone.'

Unzipping the hatbox-like container, he showed him the convex aluminium dish, which was about two feet in diameter, with a pistol grip. After closing it up again, he took out a padded satchel that contained what looked like a spotting scope.

'This is a night vision monocular. You can use it for birds, maybe owls, but it can pick up the heat signature of a human being at a hundred yards.'

'Cool,' said Fletcher, starting to raise it to his eye.

'Hang on,' said Mark, 'Don't take off the lens cap unless it's completely dark. If you use it during daylight, it will burn a hole in your retina.'

Fletcher lowered the monocular cautiously, as Mark opened a small metal box. 'Here's a compass and an altimeter,' he said. Then, from one corner of the suitcase, he took out a manila envelope and handed it over.

'That's fifty thousand rupees in cash, mostly smaller notes. If you go up into the higher country in Sikkim, I suggest you change some of this into coins, because nobody uses paper money.'

'What if I need more?' said Fletcher.

Mark shrugged, as if that wasn't his problem. 'Merlin will explain those procedures. And, one last thing,' he said, reaching into the bottom of the suitcase and pulling out a pistol. 'Beretta 70s, .32 calibre. Nice little gun,' said Mark, exhibiting emotions for the first time as he admired the weapon before passing it to Fletcher. 'Of course, it's completely illegal and unlicensed.'

'Are you sure I need it?' Fletcher asked, turning it over in his hand.

'Yeah, I think so,' said Mark. 'Of course, if you don't have to use it that would be ideal. There's a special compartment in this suitcase where you can keep it. I've also included a hundred rounds of ammunition. To be honest, I don't think anyone's going to check your suitcase but it's better to be safe than sorry.'

Unzipping the fabric lining, he showed Fletcher where one side of the case had been extended with a sliding cover that was flush with the hard plastic shell. Slipping this open, he pointed out the extra ammunition then tucked the Beretta inside. Once the lining had been zipped shut the weapon was safely concealed.

◆

Sullivan showed up at noon accompanied by Cocoa, who twisted around Fletcher's knees with excitement as he scratched her ears. By this time Mark had got the desert cooler working in the living room and the temperature was almost bearable. The fragrance of wet khas khas straw reminded Fletcher of summers in Delhi when he was a boy. The coolers only worked in the dry months of April and May, before the monsoon arrived and the humidity rose.

Sullivan had brought lunch, a tiffin carrier full of biryani that he handed to the caretaker, instructing him to heat it up. He also had a bag of mangoes.

'Sorry this safe house is a bit makeshift but we don't use it very often,' Sullivan apologized.

'How secure is it?' Fletcher asked.

'Water tight. The Embassy used to rent this place for some of our consular staff. Now that the new residential units in Chanakyapuri are ready, we don't need it any more, though we still have a year on the lease. Raju, who looks after the place, is a hundred per cent loyal and discreet.'

A week had passed since they'd had dinner at The Rough Rider though Fletcher felt as if his sense of time had been warped, not only because of jet lag but on account of the sudden changes in his life.

'Has Mark set you up with your gear?' Sullivan asked.

'Yeah,' said Fletcher, 'Now I feel like a real secret agent.'

They sat down in the living room and Cocoa lay at her master's feet, tongue hanging out.

'Okay,' Sullivan said. 'We've got a train ticket for you on the Brahmputra Mail to Siliguri, first class, departing just before midnight tomorrow. It's about a thirty-six hour journey. From there you can hire a cab to take you up to Kalimpong, about two and a half hours' drive from the railhead.'

Sullivan went through the familiar ritual of filling and lighting his pipe, as he continued. 'Kalimpong is thirty miles east of Darjeeling, on the other side of the Teesta River, a nice little town but crawling with spies—Tibetans, Bhutanese, Nepalese, Brits, and Chinese. India's Intelligence Bureau has a number of agents stationed there. You never know who's who.'

'Anyone specific I need to look out for?' Fletcher asked.

'Yes,' said Sullivan, coughing as he exhaled. 'There's a man named Thupten Lepcha, an officer with the West Bengal forest department. He's an avid birder and your official liaison for the research project. Of course, he doesn't know anything about the other stuff. Thupten will handle all of the official paperwork and permissions for the survey.'

Reaching into a leather briefcase he'd brought with him, Sullivan took out a hardbound blue book. 'Here,' he said, 'I brought you a present. It was just published a couple weeks ago. Hot off the press.'

Turning it over in his hands Fletcher saw the title: *The Birds of Sikkim* by Salim Ali.

'Thanks,' he said, 'But if this just came out, why am I doing another survey?'

'Because there's much more fieldwork that needs to be done. There are significant gaps in the research,' Sullivan replied. 'Particularly pheasants.'

Though he had accepted the assignment, Fletcher still felt some uncertainty, even if it was now too late to turn back. For one thing, he was puzzled why he had been chosen for this mission. Other than his expertise in ornithology, he had little or no experience in the Himalayas. Though he spoke Hindi, the region where he was headed was populated by people who spoke mostly Bengali, Nepali, Sikkimese, and other Tibetan dialects. After Sullivan and Mark explained more of the details, Fletcher finally asked: 'Why aren't you sending a more experienced agent, somebody who knows that part of the mountains?'

'Well, for one thing,' said Sullivan. 'We don't have anyone else. Most of our resources in the past few years have been focused on the conflict between India and Pakistan, as well as Afghanistan and Iran. Our New Delhi Station is part of the Near East Division. However, the Tibetan programme is being run out of India by the Far East Division, so it's one of those bureaucratic anomalies.'

'But you must have people with contacts among the refugees.'

'Yes, but all of them are well known. If a guy like Doug Pritchett showed up in Kalimpong he might as well have CIA tattooed on his forehead,' said Sullivan.

'Am I going to be that inconspicuous?' Fletcher argued.

'No, but you're an unknown quantity and your cover story is legit,' Sullivan said. 'Listen, every American in India is under suspicion of working for the agency. Even the Crown Prince of Sikkim's fiancée, Hope Cooke, is accused of being a spy.'

'*Is* she working for you?' said Fletcher.

Sullivan laughed and shook his head. 'No way! She just graduated from Sarah Lawrence. Certainly not one of ours.'

'Sarah Lawrence?' said Fletcher. 'I didn't know that.'

'I guess you don't read the *New York Times*,' said Sullivan. 'There was an announcement of her engagement last year in the society pages. The wedding is going to be next March. Anyway, Miss Cooke is going to have enough problems on her hands without working for us. More than likely you'll meet her at some point. Gangtok is even smaller than Kalimpong. The current maharajah, or Chogyal, is an elderly recluse and spends most of his time meditating or painting pictures of the mountains. Though he rules by divine right, he's handed over running the kingdom to his son, Maharaj Kumar Palden Thondup Namgyal. He's a capable young man though his life hasn't been easy. His older brother was killed in an air crash. His first wife also died and he has three children from that marriage.'

Sullivan went on to explain that India had signed a treaty with Sikkim in 1950, allowing the Chogyal to retain his titles and throne but giving up control of foreign policy, trade, communications, and defence. Like Bhutan, it was seen as a 'buffer state'.

'The Indians are nervous about Sikkim because it's always had close ties with Lhasa. There's plenty of palace intrigue, which I'm sure you'll discover. The Maharaj Kumar's sister, Coocoola, married into one of the prominent Tibetan families and she's actively involved with rehabilitating refugees. Of course, the Chinese aren't happy about that and they keep making noises that Sikkim is part of Tibet. They could easily escalate the situation and use it as a pretence to push their way across the Nathu La pass.'

'How did a girl from Sarah Lawrence end up in the middle of all this?' Fletcher asked.

'They met in Darjeeling, a year ago. Hope Cooke was wandering around India and landed up at the Windemere Hotel while the Crown Prince was visiting his two sons who attend a boarding school in Darjeeling.'

'Sounds like that movie *The King and I*, with Yul Brynner and Deborah Kerr,' said Fletcher. 'I guess it helps our interests to have an American queen in Sikkim, even if she isn't a spy.'

'Maybe so,' Sullivan said. 'By the way, Maryanne loved that movie but I thought it was a load of crap.'

'So, what else am I supposed to be keeping an ear out for?' said Fletcher.

'Birdcalls,' said Sullivan. 'You're an ornithologist trying to catalogue what species are found in the eastern Himalayas, looking at distribution patterns, migration, and any distinctive behaviour. In particular, you're interested in pheasants, partridges, and snowcocks.'

'Sure, but...'

Sullivan raised his hand to fend off the question he knew was coming.

'We need you to learn whatever you can about what's happening along the border, both the Chinese troop build-up and the Indian response,' Sullivan explained. 'As I told you earlier, we know that the PLA has reinforced its presence at several places, particularly in the Chumbi Valley. If the Chinese are going to invade Sikkim, that's the logical route. The Indian Army has a battalion posted north of Gangtok, guarding the road leading up to the Nathu La pass.'

Later that evening, before he left for the railway station, Mark handed Fletcher a dossier full of background information. He told him to do his homework and then destroy the dossier after he got to Kalimpong. Mark also gave him a thermos of boiled drinking water for the journey.

11

Himalayan Whistling Thrush

Myophonus caeruleus

Larger than most thrushes, its dark indigo feathers are flecked with pale streaks. In direct sunlight it appears a brighter blue but in the shadows it looks almost black. Male and female are identical, with yellow beaks and black legs. The call is a distinctive whistle, interspersed with a rasping hiss. Largely terrestrial, its nest consists of moss and lichens mixed with mud, which it builds on cliffs and crags as well as under the eaves of hill station houses. Whistling thrushes are found throughout the Himalayas.

Two days later, Fletcher got off the train in Siliguri. The taxi driver, a young Nepali, who had agreed to take him to Kalimpong, set off at a breakneck pace. His car was a vintage Dodge sedan, built for American highways rather than the Indian roads. It smelt of petrol fumes and mildewed upholstery. The first few miles, after leaving the railway station, they passed through crowded markets as the speeding taxi swerved around pedestrians, animals, and other vehicles. After they reached the outskirts of Siliguri, Fletcher could see the mountains ahead, though the tops of the ridges were covered in clouds.

As they raced along the narrow, two-lane road, through sprawling tea estates, Fletcher asked the driver to slow down. The young man grinned but ignored him. Soon enough, they entered the Teesta River valley, overtaking slower vehicles on blind curves. Fletcher could imagine the taxi veering out of the path of oncoming traffic and crashing through the parapet wall before tumbling several hundred feet down into the white-water rapids below. Until now, he had used only English but, out of desperation, he put a hand on the driver's shoulder and spoke to him in Hindi, telling him that if he didn't drive safely, he would report him to the police. More than the threat, the shock of hearing Hindi coming from a foreigner's mouth seemed to calm the driver down, though by the time they reached the Teesta Bridge and the turn-off for Kalimpong, he had picked up the pace once again.

Within a couple of miles, however, they came to an abrupt halt. Near a small settlement of five or six huts, an angry mob of about a hundred men were blocking the road. Several of them were carrying red banners emblazoned with the hammer and sickle. Others were brandishing kukris, with broad steel blades, and looked as if they were eager to chop off someone's head. A couple of ringleaders were shouting slogans, which the rest of the men echoed in a strident chorus, raising their fists. Fletcher couldn't understand what they were saying but he knew it was a political demonstration and the men were Nepalis.

The driver recognized one of the protesters and yelled out a greeting. His friend came across with an unsheathed kukri, eyeing Fletcher as if he might be a suitable candidate for decapitation. He then chatted with the driver, laughing and joking despite the agitation. After the man went back to join his comrades, the driver explained to Fletcher that it was a protest by a labour union against working conditions on one of the nearby tea estates.

Eight or ten vehicles had been stopped on their way up the hill and a long line of traffic coming down. The demonstrators wouldn't let anyone pass. At that moment, a couple of police jeeps came around the corner from above, appearing out of the mist and stopping a short distance away. A dozen constables tumbled out, carrying bamboo staves that the kukris would have easily severed in a single blow. An officer, with a pistol on his hip stepped down and surveyed the demonstration with an arrogant swagger. Fletcher was sure there was going to be trouble as all of the protesters turned to face the police, but then, with a dismissive gesture of his right hand the officer waved the constables back into the jeeps and they turned around, retreating back up the hill.

The road remained blocked for another hour until it began to rain and the demonstrators started to drift away. It was now half-past two and they were probably hungry. The leaders were amongst the first to leave and soon there was nobody in sight, though Fletcher couldn't imagine where all of them had vanished. His driver started the engine and headed on up the hill.

After the humid heat of the plains, the temperature was much cooler as they entered the clouds. On either side of the road the forests were a lush, tropical green. Fletcher could see wild bananas and bamboo growing amidst the dense tangle of foliage. Though the mist reduced visibility, the driver didn't take his foot off the accelerator, trying to make up for lost time. More than once, they screeched around a hairpin bend and narrowly missed a car or truck coming down the hill, its headlights glowing in the fog.

As the road grew narrower, the taxi driver had no choice but to slow down until they eventually came to the Himalayan Hotel. Sullivan had described it as one of the better places to stay in Kalimpong, with a lot of history. Built in the 1920s, the estate had once belonged to David Macdonald, the British Trade Agent for Tibet. His descendants still owned the property.

Though Fletcher didn't have a reservation, a room was available. He intended to stay for a week. His room was on the upper floor and there was a window box full of geraniums, which added bright pink petals to the gloom. As soon as he was alone, he heard a rustling sound that seemed to come from the rafters. At first he thought it might be rats, until he realized that a whistling thrush was foraging in the rain gutter outside his window. With a bright yellow beak and feathers of midnight blue, the bird stared in at him through the windowpane, as if it had spotted an intruder.

◆

'We call it chamong pho and believe it is the first bird to sing every morning. The whistling thrush wakes up all other species before dawn, like an alarm clock. According to Lepcha folklore it also performs auspicious rituals by cleaning sacred lakes in the mountains, removing twigs and leaves floating on the surface.'

Thupten Lepcha was a thin but vigorous man in his forties, dressed in the khaki uniform of the West Bengal Forest Service. His face was clean-shaven and his hooded eyes betrayed a mischievous sense of humour. When Fletcher had called him, Thupten picked up the phone on the first ring and invited him across to his office that morning. The forest department divisional headquarters, a short walk from the hotel, was housed in an old bungalow with a corrugated metal roof, surrounded by gardens full of hydrangeas and gladioli. After Thupten had asked his clerk to bring them tea, Fletcher noticed a whistling thrush outside the window, searching for grubs and insects.

Though he was a DFO, the Divisional Forest Officer, responsible for Kalimpong and the region east of the Teesta, Thupten didn't seem to care much for protocol or hierarchies. Unlike the forest officers Fletcher had dealt with in Bharatpur, he wasn't overawed by his own authority and spoke with easy informality. He made it clear that his first love was birds, the smaller the better. Thupten had done a study of wren-babblers, of which he had identified and described two new subspecies.

'Why wren-babblers?' Fletcher asked.

'Because they're the hardest to see,' Thupten replied. 'You can hear them calling, right in front of your nose, but they're almost invisible in the underbrush.'

'I'm mostly interested in Phasianadae,' Fletcher explained.

'Poultry!' said Thupten, with a dismissive laugh.

'Not just jungle fowl,' Fletcher protested.

'Of course, we have five kinds of pheasant here,' Thupten said. 'Kalij, monal, tragopan, peacock pheasant, and blood pheasant higher up in the hills.'

Meanwhile, as their tea arrived, the whistling thrush hopped onto a wrought iron bench and flared its tail feathers, like a Japanese fan, then flew away beyond a rose trellis at the edge of the yard.

'Is there much poaching in your forests?' Fletcher asked.

'Some,' said Thupten. 'Mostly with snares and traps, when it comes to birds. They save their cartridges for larger game—barking deer and boar.'

'I'd love to go out birding with you some time,' said Fletcher. 'And any advice you have about conducting my survey would be a huge help.'

'Of course!' Thupten gestured with both hands. 'I'm here to help you. Anyone who is interested in birds is a friend of mine. The only problem, this time of year, is the rain and leeches. You'll have to put up with that. Day after tomorrow I'm going on a tour of the Neora Valley, along the border with Bhutan. You are welcome to join me.'

After finishing his tea, Fletcher rose and took his leave. Thupten walked him out to the gate. Though it was raining lightly, the clouds suddenly drifted apart and the sun shone through. The DFO looked up and laughed. 'This means good luck!' he said. 'We call it metok-chharp, blossom rain.'

Taking advantage of the break in the weather, Fletcher decided to explore the town. Earlier, before leaving his hotel, he had made sure that his suitcase was locked. After turning the key in the door, he'd wedged a toothpick into the gap at the top, to signal if anyone entered the room while he was away. Stopping at a store near the hotel, he had bought himself an umbrella as well as a small padlock.

Kalimpong was spread out on the crest of a broad ridge between two forested hilltops. Somewhere to the west lay Kanchenjunga, hidden behind layers of clouds. A few ponies and hand-pulled rickshaws transported tourists along R. C. Mintri Road, the main thoroughfare, also known as 10th Mile. Most of the shops were run by Marwaris and other Indians, though there were a few Tibetan handicraft stalls. As a boy, Fletcher had gone on holiday to Simla with his family and there were elements of Kalimpong that reminded him of that town, particularly the Scottish Church on the crest of the ridge, its bell tower rising above the cluttered mosaic of corrugated metal roofs.

The hill station had a decrepit, waterlogged look, as if another monsoon might wash away some of the taller buildings. By the time he had walked halfway along Mintri Road, it began to rain again, a sudden downpour that made him duck into the nearest shop, which turned out to be a bookstore. Leaving his dripping umbrella at the door, he browsed the shelves. P. G. Wodehouse and W. Somerset Maugham seemed to be popular authors, as well as James Hadley Chase and Agatha Christie. Instead of a novel, however, he picked up a guidebook to Kalimpong, with a bright cover picture of Kanchenjunga and a sketch map at the back. Flipping it open, he read the introduction:

Recently, both Prime Ministers Nehru and Chou En-lai referred to Kalimpong as a 'nest of spies,' which may be an unfair assessment though there is some truth to the fact that this quaint hill station has a rich legacy of intrigue and skulduggery. It has also been called the Gateway to Tibet, serving as a centre for trade, from one side of the Himalayas to the other. Often, shipments of salt, tea, and wool that were carried across high passes like Nathu La, were a means of smuggling contraband and the men who undertook these arduous journeys bartered their lives for valuable secrets as well as dry goods.

During the period of the Great Game, when the British empire was conspiring to outwit the Russians on the Roof of the World, Darjeeling and Kalimpong became the staging grounds for daring expeditions into Tibet. British explorers were forbidden to enter Lhasa's domain, but 'native' agents like Sarat Chandra Das, better known as 'the Babu,' disguised themselves as pilgrims or merchants and crossed over the forbidden frontier. One of the great spy-explorers was Kinthup, a Lepcha surveyor who risked his life to unravel the riddle of the Tsang Po Gorges and the source of the Brahmaputra.

Today, the stakes may not be as high and the romance of duelling empires has waned, but Kalimpong still exudes an air of mystery with its curious assortment of unlikely residents. Along with Russian émigrés and a Greek prince, Burmese royalty have sought refuge here after King Theebaw was deposed, as have a pair of Afghan princesses, the exiled granddaughters of Mohamud Ayub Khan, who defeated the British at the battle of Maiwand. Even the son of Sir Arthur Conan Doyle, the creator of Sherlock Holmes, found his way here, attracted in part, by stories of cloak and dagger....

The rain was hammering on the sheet metal roof. Only one other customer was in the shop. She was wearing a sleeveless kho, a wraparound dress similar to a Tibetan chuba. From her features, Fletcher guessed she might be Sikkimese. Catching his eye briefly, the woman smiled at him, as she surveyed a shelf of books about religion and spirituality. Fletcher guessed she was in her mid-twenties. Her straight dark hair fell below her shoulders. The kho was a rust colour with embroidered medallions of gold and her blouse was a pale cream silk. Eventually, the woman chose a couple of books and went across to the counter to pay. Hearing the rain begin to subside to a steady patter, he followed her down the aisle. After she had finished, he handed the guidebook to the storeowner, along with a hundred rupee note. While waiting for his change, Fletcher glanced over his shoulder and saw the woman pick up his new umbrella, open it, and set off in the rain.

By the time he had finished purchasing his book and hurried to the door, he could see that she was at least a fifty yards down the road, still carrying his umbrella. For a moment, Fletcher had no idea what to do, then he stuffed the guidebook into the pocket of his windbreaker and zipped it up. Running out into the rain, he dashed after the woman.

'Excuse me!' he cried several times, as he caught up with her.

Finally, the woman turned and looked at him with an amused expression.

'I'm afraid that's my umbrella you took,' he said, the rain dripping from his hair and his clothes already wet.

Her face revealed that she knew exactly what she'd done, giving him a careless smile and a helpless shrug. She spoke English fluently.

'Oh, is it yours?' she asked. 'I didn't realize. Do you want it back?'

Fletcher could see that she was playing with him for the woman made no move to return the umbrella. Unlike him, she was relatively dry except for the hem of her kho, where water had splashed up from the road.

'Don't you have one of your own?' he asked.

'Unfortunately, no. I left it at home,' she replied. 'Maybe if you can walk with me to my house, then you can have your umbrella back. I don't live so far from here, just down the road.'

Fletcher was about to lose his temper but something in the woman's manner kept him from erupting in irritation. Smiling at him again, she raised the umbrella a little higher, so there was just enough room for his head and one shoulder beneath the ribbed dome of black fabric. Turning together, the two of them walked on in the rain, sharing the umbrella. A short ways on ahead, the woman gestured for them to turn off Mintri Road, along a side lane that cut down the hill. She tried to make small talk, though Fletcher was in no mood for conversation.

'Are you British?'

'American.'

'Have you been here long?' she asked with innocent eyes. 'I haven't seen you around.'

'I got here yesterday,' he replied.

'And you're a tourist?'

'No.'

'Then what do you do?' she asked, after a pause.

He was about to say it was none of her business, then answered, 'I'm an ornithologist.'

The woman stopped and gave him an enquiring look. 'What is that?'

'I study birds,' he said, urging her to keep moving.

Within a few minutes they arrived at a gate, with the nameplate:

MONTROSE
Dr B. K. Mukherjee.

The house had a gabled roof with a fretted edge along the rain gutters and deep verandas cluttered with flowerpots.

'This is my father's house,' she said, opening the gate and leading him up a flight of steps to the veranda. Finally, she handed Fletcher his umbrella with an earnest, 'Thank you.'

As he turned to escape, she said, 'Wait! I don't know your name.'

He gave her an impatient look. 'Allan Swift.'

'Mr Swift,' she said. 'Forgive me. I'm Kesang.'

She held out her hand. He hesitated then reached out to shake it, both of their hands damp from the rain.

'Maybe you would like to come for a party on Saturday night,' she said. 'Just a few friends. We have a lot of fun. Eight o'clock?'

'I don't think I'm free,' he said, retreating down the steps.

'Please try,' Kesang called after him.

When he got back to the hotel, he could see that nobody had broken into his room, though he had a strange feeling, after his encounter with the woman, that he was being watched. After changing and hanging his wet clothes up to dry, he unpacked his suitcase, putting the tape recorder and his other equipment in the cupboard, which he secured with the padlock he'd bought. The only thing he didn't take out was the Beretta, leaving it in its secret compartment in the empty suitcase, which he slid under his bed. By this time, it was already 6 p.m. and the mist outside was a shroud of shadows.

◆

The next morning he went to the Foreigners Registration Office (FRO), at the Police Station in Kalimpong. Fletcher had been through this process in Bharatpur last year and he knew it would be an unpleasant experience. Carrying his passport and other documents he presented himself shortly after 10 a.m. A lone constable was sitting in a room lined with metal shelves and cabinets stacked with dusty files. When Fletcher explained that he had come to register, the policeman pointed to one of the chairs along the wall and told him that the officer in charge would arrive in ten minutes. Three other people were waiting, all of them Tibetans, who looked as if they had just walked here from Lhasa.

The hands of a pendulum clock on the wall had stopped at two minutes past twelve and the officer didn't arrive for another hour. Around eleven, he strolled in with a casual air of exaggerated authority and indifference. The constable stood up and saluted. Without looking at Fletcher or the others the FRO sat down at his desk. His bulging waist, stubby arms, and mouth full of betel nut, made it difficult to imagine a more perfect caricature, thought Fletcher. He knew better than to get up before he was acknowledged. The Tibetans too remained in their seats.

Finally, the officer glanced over at Fletcher and beckoned. Taking his seat across the desk, he handed over his passport, which was carefully inspected, as if it might be a forgery.

Leaning to one side and haemorrhaging a gout of red paan juice into a spittoon next to his chair, the police officer wiped his lips with the back of his hand.

'American?' he asked.

Fletcher nodded and began to explain the purpose of his research but the officer cut him short.

'CIA?'

Reacting with a shocked look of denial, Fletcher shook his head. 'No.'

'Why are you doing research in Kalimpong?' the officer demanded.

Once again, he began his explanation, only to be interrupted.

'Who issued this visa?'

'The Indian Embassy in Washington D.C.,' said Fletcher, handing over the letters from the Smithsonian and the Bombay Natural History Society.

'When did you arrive in India?'

Leaning across the table and pointing to the entry stamp in his passport, he replied, 'Four days ago, on June 4.'

'You arrived in Delhi. Why didn't you register there?' The officer, whose nametag identified him as J. D. Bhattacharya, was clearly looking for an excuse to turn Fletcher away.

'But on my visa it says that I have a week to register at the place where I intend to conduct my research.' He kept his voice calm.

'You will have to go back to Delhi,' the policeman said.

'No, I can't,' said Fletcher, softly but firmly.

The policeman tossed his passport across the table along with his other papers. 'You cannot remain in Kalimpong.'

'Why not?' Fletcher asked.

'Because you are not registered,' came the curt reply.

'But that's why I'm here,' he insisted.

The officer's mouth had filled with saliva. He leaned back in his chair, tilting his head so that the betel juice wouldn't spill from his lips as he spoke.

'We have no forms available,' he said.

Turning aside, he divulged another stream of red spittle.

'But my visa is valid for a year. Everything is in order,' Fletcher insisted.

The officer shook his head. 'No. Impossible.'

Out of the corner of his eye, Fletcher saw the constable, who was seated in the corner, raise a hand discretely. With a subtle but unmistakable gesture of his thumb and forefinger he hinted that a bribe was expected.

Self-consciously and knowing that the Tibetans were watching, Fletcher reached into his trouser pocket and took out his wallet. Without looking at the officer, he removed five 100-rupee notes and tucked them into his passport before pushing it back across the man's desk. There was a momentary pause, as if the policeman was going to demand more, but then he opened a drawer of his desk and produced three copies of a printed form.

'Fill this out,' he said, then pointed to an empty desk on the other side of the room. 'Over there.'

Fletcher got up and moved aside as the Tibetans were called forward. He began the tedious process of filling out the form in triplicate, as the officer harangued the refugees, accusing them of being Chinese spies.

12

Rufous-throated Wren-babbler

Spelaeornis caudatus

On first glimpse, this appears to be a small, nondescript brown bird but when closely observed it has subtle and distinctive plumage. Its throat is the colour of saffron and its eyes are masked by pale grey patches that extend from its beak to its ears. The rest of its feathers are delicately patterned like a houndstooth tweed. It lives within the dense underbrush of moist forests in Eastern India, Nepal, Sikkim, and Bhutan. As with most wren-babblers, it is usually located by its call, a soft but piercing Chi chee, Chi chee, Chi chee.

Thupten had sent word for Fletcher to be ready to leave at 4 a.m. They had agreed he would bring the parabolic microphone and tape recorder with him to try recording birdcalls. It didn't matter if the microphone got wet but the tape recorder needed to be kept dry and he carried it in a waterproof kit bag. Rain was still falling as he made his way downstairs. Though the main door of the hotel was locked, he let himself out through a back entrance and found shelter under the eaves of the veranda, until he saw the headlights of a jeep at the gate.

'Lovely morning, isn't it?' said Thupten, as Fletcher stowed his gear in the backseat, next to a sullen-looking forest guard, who seemed to be thinking of other adjectives for the day ahead.

A steady drizzle sifted through the headlights as they followed the main route out of town and then turned off on a narrower road that wound its way down into a deep valley, invisible in the darkness. The canvas roof on the jeep sagged overhead and there were a few leaks at the seams but mostly it kept them dry.

'How long a drive is it?' Fletcher asked.

'An hour and a half to Lava, where we enter the Neora Valley,' said Thupten. 'We should get there just before sunrise.'

'Any chance of seeing a tragopan today?' Fletcher enquired.

'Allan! Allan!' Thupten scolded, 'don't ask these questions. You know the first rule of birdwatching: Nothing is certain! We might see a whole flock of *Tragopan satyra* or we might see none. That is the wonderful thing about avifauna. Unlike human beings, they are totally unpredictable.'

Fletcher considered asking Thupten about the girl, Kesang, who had stolen his umbrella, but he thought better of it, deciding to wait until he knew a little more about Kalimpong and its residents. He was also going to mention the bribe he'd been forced to pay at the FRO but felt there was no point raising the issue. In any case, Thupten, barely gave him a chance to speak, launching into a lengthy recitation of the natural history of this region.

'We Lepchas believe that our people have always lived here in these mountains. Everyone else, the Bhotias, the Nepalis, the British, and the Bengalis, they all migrated from somewhere else but our people have been here forever. Our myths and traditions go back to a time before there were countries or kings. We are the children of Kanchenjunga. Our ancestors were born out of her snow.'

Thupten drove as if he knew every corner of the road, though he was not reckless like the taxi driver who had brought Fletcher up the hill. As he spoke, his hands caressed the steering wheel and eased the gearshift from second into third and back again with a practised rhythm that seemed to keep pace with his stories. As they reached the foot of the valley, the rain eased up and Fletcher could see a narrow Bailey bridge across a swollen stream. From there, they began to climb again. The mist closed in around them and the headlights barely penetrated the fog.

'Every bird in these mountains has a Lepcha name,' Thupten continued. 'We have a whole taxonomy, as complex as Linnaeus but much older....'

Fletcher listened in fascination as Thupten rattled off a list of common, Latin, and Lepcha names, each of which identified the birds in different ways, according to their colour, size, distribution, or behaviour.

'Our people were the first biologists,' Thupten insisted. 'They observed everything with a critical eye and classified different species.

Though we believe in spirits and demons, we have no organized religion, just stories and a close connection to nature. It was only when the Bhotias came across the mountains from Tibet that we started to believe in Buddhism. Our people were hunters in the past, using bows and arrows, but we have always been conservationists at heart....'

Fletcher knew there would be plenty of opportunities to steer the conversation in other directions but at this hour of the day he was content to listen to folklore rather than politics. Eventually, as they descended the other side of the ridge, the sky began to reveal the first hint of dawn. When they arrived at the forest checkpoint at Lava, the guards were awake, expecting the DFO. Thupten spoke to them, asking questions with a quiet but respectful note of authority. Fletcher couldn't help comparing his manner to the FRO's arrogant enquiries and commands.

A rough, dirt track wound its way up into the Neora Valley, climbing for a couple of miles before levelling off where the hills opened out. By now the shapes of trees were visible, though it was still dark. After another fifteen minutes, they came to a clearing where Thupten stopped the jeep and switched off the engine. The silence was startling after the constant rumble and squeak of the drive. It took a moment before Fletcher could hear birdcalls but as soon as he stepped out of the jeep, his ears picked up a medley of songs. Thupten had fallen silent and listened attentively to the various calls, from fluting cries to distant trilling, as if the forest were a music box opening its lid at dawn.

In a whisper, Thupten identified the various calls: a red-vented bulbul, a golden-throated barbet, emerald doves. A hoarse cackle sounded nearby. 'That's a peacock pheasant. There are plenty here but they hardly ever show themselves.'

Moments later, Thupten raised a hand.

'What is it?'

'*Spelaeornis caudatus.* Come quickly, and bring your microphone.'

Hauling his equipment out of the backseat of the jeep, Fletcher hoisted the bag containing the recorder onto his shoulder. He had already plugged in the parabolic microphone and held it ready in one hand.

Thupten set off for the edge of the clearing, where a stream flowed out of the woods. They waded through ferns and followed a winding trail into the forest. Though the rain had stopped, the trees were still dripping and the foliage was wet. Stopping every few steps, Thupten listened until he heard the call again. To Fletcher it sounded like any one of a dozen warbles and whistles that rang out on all sides.

'There it is,' said Thupten, grabbing Fletcher's arm in excitement. 'Hear it?'

Reaching into the waterproof bag, he put on a pair of headphones before aiming the microphone in the direction of the sound. The bird called again, a crisp sequence of notes that sounded like somebody worrying a rusty latch.

Turning on the tape recorder, he captured a dozen calls.

'*Twitchy, twitchy, twitchy,*' said Thupten, imitating the bird and grinning with delight. 'Today I'm going to show you a rufous-throated wren-babbler.'

Fletcher had to open the waterproof bag completely to rewind the tape and play the call back but when he did, the recording was sharp and clear. The bird now responded to its own song, '*Chi chee, Chi chee, Chi chee.*'

The light was still poor and the overlapping shadows made it difficult to see. Thupten gestured for Fletcher to play the recording again and after two or three tries, they saw a flittering movement nearby. Out of the moist ferns and shrubbery, the wren-babbler appeared, perched on a branch six feet away. It was no bigger than Fletcher's thumb and he could see the russet patch on its throat as he played back the recording once more. Thinking the song was coming from its mate or an intruder, the tiny bird drew itself up and called again before flying back into hiding.

Retreating out of the forest and back to the jeep, Fletcher checked his legs for leeches. More than a dozen were attached to his boots and gaiters. Picking them off and flicking them away, he wondered how many had penetrated his socks.

For the next couple of hours, Thupten drove along the forest track, stopping from time to time, to show Fletcher a new bird. At one point they came upon a red-headed trogon perched on the lowest branch of an oak. At another clearing they trekked up a trail to a hillock nearby where a flock of giant hornbills were feeding on a ficus tree. By the time the clouds had begun to close in again they reached the upper end of the valley, which was covered in bamboo thickets, as well as a deciduous canopy of maple, oak, and birch.

'About a month ago, I saw *Tragopan satyra* on that slope over there. Bring your microphone and we'll see what we can find.'

Leaving the jeep, they waded into the jungle again until they came to a disused path that threaded its way through the bamboo and emerged into a grove of rhododendron trees. Stopping several times to listen, Thupten led the way. The forest guard, who hadn't spoken so far, followed glumly at the rear. They had gone about two hundred yards, when Fletcher heard a voice behind him.

'Sir,' the guard said in a loud whisper. 'Sak nam.'

Thupten immediately turned and looked up into the trees. Fletcher too scanned the jungle canopy for any sign of movement. The guard pointed to their left at a tall birch overhead. As the mist filtered through the branches they saw a moving shape, though it wasn't a bird.

Reaching for the binoculars around his neck, Fletcher quickly located the red panda on a moss-covered branch. Its ruddy fur was damp and the long striped tail hung down like a plush tassel. As the animal began to retreat along the branch, sensing that it was being watched, Fletcher saw its inquisitive features and pinched black and white nose. Within a few seconds, the red panda quickly turned and scurried down the branch and out of sight.

'We are very lucky,' Thupten whispered. 'I see red pandas only once or twice a year. They are extremely shy.'

Before driving back to Kalimpong, Fletcher removed his boots and found eight leeches feeding on his feet and ankles. They were gorged with blood and he was able to pluck them off his skin like overripe berries. Pulling on his wet socks to staunch the bleeding, he tied up his boots again. He couldn't help noticing that Thupten and the forest guard were both wearing rubber chappals, which allowed them to see the leeches before they latched on.

'We have a story about a vicious demon that used to live in these mountains.' Thupten explained. 'He was finally killed and chopped up into tiny pieces and thrown into the forest. Lepchas believe leeches are the fragments of that demon.'

As they headed back along the twisting road, the rugged landscape that had been hidden by darkness, was now revealed through gaps in the clouds, steep green ridges covered in sub-tropical forest.

'How far are we from the border with Tibet?' Fletcher asked.

'Almost thirty miles as the crow flies. Between us and Tibet, Bhutan is on one side and Sikkim on the other,' said Thupten.

'Are you worried that the Chinese might try to cross over?' Fletcher asked.

'Of course, it is a threat,' said Thupten. 'People are anxious. We hear reports on the radio and read articles in the newspapers about the Chinese causing trouble on the border. The army and the police are supposed to be keeping an eye on infiltrators, but most of the border areas are under the forest department. So, we have also been instructed to keep watch on anything suspicious.'

Fletcher glanced across at Thupten, who had his eyes on the road.

'Have you caught anyone?' Fletcher asked.

Thupten laughed. 'Last month one of our rangers was on patrol near Pedong and he found three poachers skinning a serow they'd shot. They had no papers and refused to answer questions. One of them was wearing a shirt with a label that said, "Made in China", so the ranger thought they might be Chinese spies who had strayed across the border. We reported it to the army and they immediately took them into custody. In the end, of course, it turned out they were Nepalis and the army released them, after confiscating their muzzleloader.'

'It must be difficult when most people don't have identity papers,' said Fletcher. 'But if the Chinese actually invade, it will be easy enough to recognize them.'

'Yes, of course,' said Thupten, 'but among the refugees from Tibet, there are a number of Chinese spies. Several of them have been caught in Kalimpong.'

'Really?' said Fletcher.

'Just last week two lamas were arrested. They claimed to have come from the Pemayangste monastery in western Sikkim. When they rented a room below the main bazaar, people got suspicious because lamas are known to be stingy and never pay rent. When the police went to investigate, they found they had a lot of foreign currency, US dollars and British pounds, worth almost 300,000 rupees. At first they claimed these were donations collected for the repair of a temple, but after the Intelligence Bureau questioned them, they admitted that they had crossed over from the Chumbi Valley. The Chinese sent them to gather information on Indian military installations, especially the Air Force Station in Bagdogra.'

'Were they Tibetans or Chinese?'

'Tibetans, but working for the Chinese,' said Thupten. 'Not everyone in Tibet is against the communists.'

'But they weren't really lamas,' said Fletcher, 'were they?'

'Probably not. Maybe it was a disguise. But even some of the monks are collaborating with the Chinese,' said Thupten.

'There are plenty of communists in India, aren't there?' said Fletcher.

'Yes, the party organizers are active with the labour unions on the tea estates,' said Thupten. 'In fact, a few months ago, the police caught a union leader in Darjeeling who was in touch with the Chinese. He had a wireless transmitter and was sending messages to Lhasa and Yatung, claiming that if the PLA invaded, the tea pickers would rise up to support them because they are exploited and oppressed.'

'Is that true?'

'Certainly, they are oppressed and exploited, that's for sure, but nobody is going to welcome the Chinese, except for a few extremists,' Thupten replied.

'What about Bhutan?' said Fletcher. 'Do you think the Chinese will try to take over there?'

Thupten looked across at him, as if wondering why Fletcher was asking so many questions.

'No,' he said. 'I don't think they will invade Bhutan. There is no purpose really because it is mostly jungle. You saw how hard it was for us to walk half a mile into the forest. If they try to enter Bhutan, the Chinese will never find their way out!'

Fletcher fell silent, as they came to the Bailey bridge at the bottom of the hill before the last climb to Kalimpong.

'So, where do you think I should do my research?' he asked after a long pause. 'In the Neora Valley?'

'Yes, this would be a good place. You've seen how much birdlife there is and I'm sure you'll find plenty of pheasants and partridges.

But I would suggest that first you choose an area at a higher elevation, somewhere in Sikkim, so that you can compare the different altitudinal zones. The Neora Valley is between 500 to 9,000 feet above sea level. If you go beyond Gangtok, towards Lachen, there are higher forests and meadows from 7,000 up to 15,000 feet. This time of year, it is much easier to visit that area because the snow has melted at those altitudes. Then in October you can come back down to Neora, after the monsoon begins to ease off. I can put you in touch with a cousin of mine who is in the Sikkim Forest Department. He will help you conduct your research.'

'That would be terrific,' said Fletcher.

'Do you know when you're going to Gangtok?' Thupten asked.

'Soon, I hope,' Fletcher replied. 'Though I haven't made any plans just yet.'

◆

That evening, after an early dinner, Fletcher picked up a copy of the local paper the *Himalayan Observer* from the lounge downstairs. On the front page was an article about plans to construct a hydroelectric dam on the Teesta with the headline: 'Harnessing the Power of Nature.' The rest of the articles were mostly about politics, including a recent strike by tea pickers on several estates near Darjeeling. On the editorial page he saw an unsigned column with a bold headline:

SCANDALOUS SIKKIM

All is not well in Shangri-La! The Namgyal dynasty continues to dominate and suppress the majority of Sikkim's citizens with a flagrant disdain for democratic ideals. While the Chogyal retreats into myopic isolation, the Maharaj Kumar holds the reins of power with a firm, unyielding grip, refusing to take counsel from even his most loyal advisers. The anguished voices of the poor and needy are ignored while the wealthy line their pockets with filthy lucre. In the immortal words of Shakespeare, 'Uneasy lies the head that wears the crown!' or as Brutus put it: 'Th' abuse of greatness is when it disjoins remorse from power.'

Corruption is the name of the game and all of the largesse that New Delhi has heaped at Sikkim's door has been consumed by the palace elite, as well as their jolly jesters. While pious platitudes are offered and false statements issued in the name of rural uplift and development, it is only the betterment of the Namgyals and their sycophants that is being achieved. Even the swift and sacred waters of the Teesta cannot wash away the dirty stains on palace laundry.

As if that were not enough, the Maharaj Kumar continues his dalliance with an American socialite half his age. Her antecedents are questionable and there are rumours that she reports directly to Washington, selling Sikkim's secrets down the drain. Her Bowery accent clashes harshly with the peaceful quietude of Gangtok while all about her the people cry out for justice and freedom from the yoke of Namgyal oppression.

13

Rose-ringed Parakeet

Psittacula krameri

Also known as the ring-necked parakeet, this bird is native to South Asia,
the Middle East, and Africa but has proliferated throughout the world,
with feral populations in places as far away as South America and Australia.
Adult birds measure approximately fifteen inches, including a long tail.
A vivid green colour with shades of blue, males have a distinctive collar
around their neck. Females have a faint ring or none at all.
The beak on both sexes is bright red. Often kept as a pet, they
can be taught to 'speak'.

The next morning, the manager of the hotel handed him an envelope when he came down for breakfast. It had been delivered a few minutes earlier and when he opened it, he saw a brief note, neatly written on a blank sheet of paper.

Dear Mr Swift,

I'm sorry I stole your umbrella. But please don't forget the party this evening. 8 p.m. at Montrose. Very informal.
    Looking forward to seeing you again.

Kesang

Though he had resisted the idea of accepting the invitation, Fletcher knew that the more he engaged with people in Kalimpong, the more likely he was to gather the kind of intelligence that Sullivan wanted. Besides, Kesang had aroused his curiosity.

The rain had stopped by six in the evening, though he carried his umbrella with him when he set off at quarter to eight. Lamp posts along the road cast enough light for him to see without using the torch in his pocket. He had shaved and put on a collared shirt with a fresh pair of khakis, the only respectable clothes he had. The leech bites on his ankles itched but he had disinfected them and put on Band-Aids. As he passed under a lamp post, he saw dozens of moths circling the light, as well as a few beetles that buzzed overhead.

Turning off the main road, he followed the narrow side street down the hill. Approaching Kesang's house he could hear music and recognized 'Silver Dagger' from an album by Joan Baez. It was a song they'd listened to at The Farm. The singer's plaintive voice, accompanied by guitar, carried through the humid night, with a haunting melody that took him back to America.

Opening the gate to Montrose, he climbed the steps to the veranda and put his umbrella in a stand next to the door, then rang the bell. Another cut from the album was playing now and he could hear excited voices talking over the music. Moments later, Kesang appeared in the doorway.

'You're here!' she said, her voice full of pleasure as she pushed open the screen door. 'I wasn't sure if you would come. Maybe you were mad at me.'

'I was,' said Fletcher. 'But I got over it.'

Kesang leaned forward and kissed his cheek, then took his hand and led him inside. She was dressed in a red turtleneck and slacks, a transformation from the kho she'd been wearing when he saw her last. The party seemed to be on the other side of the house. They entered a drawing room, with pictures and Tibetan thangkas crowding the walls. Through a doorway, Fletcher saw a couple of servants preparing something in the kitchen.

'I'll introduce you to everybody but first I want you to meet my father before he falls asleep,' said Kesang.

Passing through a hallway, they came to a study lined with bookshelves and decorated with brass and copper statues of Buddhist deities, as well as Tibetan masks and other artworks. Seated in an easy chair, a drink on the table beside him, was an elderly man with a parakeet on his knee. The minute they entered, the bird cried out, 'Oh, bloody hell!'

Kesang laughed, still holding Fletcher's hand. 'Don't mind Hari. He has no manners, just like me.'

Fletcher could see that the old man was drunk, slowly lifting his eyes to look at them with an inebriated gaze.

'Daddy, I want you to meet Allan Swift. He studies birds,' said Kesang, speaking slowly, as if to an invalid. Then she turned to Fletcher. 'This is my father, Dr Biswajit Mukherjee.'

The drunk man reached out and grasped Fletcher's hand with surprising strength. 'Allan. With an A or an E?' he asked, his words intelligible but slurred.

'Two A's and two L's,' he answered.

'I had a tutor at Cambridge named Allan Burbage. He spelt his name the same way,' Mukherjee said.

The bird shrieked, 'Believe you me!'

Fletcher recognized that it was a rose-ringed parakeet. He'd had one as a pet when he was a boy, though he hadn't been able to get it to speak.

'Oh, shut up, Hari!' the old man said, reaching into his glass, which was half-filled with gin and ice cubes. Submerged in the drink was a green chilli, which he fished out with his fingers and gave to the bird. Taking it in one claw, the parakeet bit the chilli in half and began to chew on one end.

'He loves them,' said Kesang. 'That's how he got his name, Hari Mirch. It means green chilli in Hindi.'

'Where's your drink?' Mukherjee demanded.

'Daddy, I'll get him one in a moment,' Kesang said. 'Allan just arrived.'

'Good,' said Mukherjee, his chin dropping to his chest. 'Come and see me in the morning, when I'm sober.'

Kesang smiled, guiding Fletcher out of the study and down a set of stairs to a spacious, glassed-in porch, where the music was coming from a record player in a wooden cabinet with built-in speakers. A dozen guests were lounging on sofas and chairs. The lights were dim and the air was thick with cigarette smoke. One of the women was laughing loudly. Through the window, Fletcher could see the lights of Kalimpong spread out across the ridge.

'Hey, everybody,' Kesang called out. 'This is Allan. He's an American. I stole his umbrella!'

As the group turned to look in his direction, Fletcher nodded self-consciously. One of the men nearby reached out a hand.

'Partha Chakraborthy,' he said. 'Let me get you a drink. Scotch?'

'Thanks,' said Fletcher.

Another man on a leather sofa, slid over to make room, as Fletcher completed a circuit of the room, shaking hands.

'I'm afraid I won't be able to remember all your names,' he apologized.

'Don't worry. We've already forgotten yours,' said Partha, handing him a glass with a generous slug of whisky.

Kesang sat next to him, her hand resting on his arm, as if she wasn't going to let him out of her sight. Meanwhile, Fletcher was still processing the parakeet and the drunk man in the study, trying to figure out how an elderly Bengali could be Kesang's father. But there were plenty of other mysteries for him to solve.

To begin with, Eddie Lim—one of the few names he had registered. He was a slender Chinese man with his hair slicked back from his forehead in a pompadour. Eddie got up and changed the record, putting on an Elvis LP. The first song was 'Fever' and he began to dance with one of the women, their bodies writhing slowly to the seductive rhythm and lyrics.

Kesang sang along with Elvis, whispering in Fletcher's ear: '*You give me fever when you kiss me/ Fever when you hold me tight/ Fever in the morning/ Fever all through the night....*'

He took a swallow of whisky that burnt his throat.

'So, this is how you spend your Saturday nights in Kalimpong?' he said.

Kesang smiled. 'Mostly,' she said. 'Do you want to dance?'

'No, thanks,' said Fletcher. 'I'm a terrible dancer....'

'So am I,' said Kesang, putting her head on his shoulder.

He picked up bits of conversation from around the room. One of the girls in the group was getting married and the others were joking about sabotaging the wedding. Everyone at the party was about Fletcher's age and there was a youthful, reckless tone to their voices. The man seated beside him told a long story about getting drunk at the Royal

Turf Club in Calcutta and being thrown out on the street. As soon as he finished, one of the women insisted Eddie change the music.

'C'mon, I'm tired of Elvis!'

'What would you prefer?' Eddie said with a note of disapproval. 'Pat Boone?'

'Cliff Richard,' two of the girls shouted in unison.

Eddie made a face and reluctantly changed the record. Moments later 'How Long is Forever' came on, the crooner's voice smooth as vinyl. As the song continued playing, Kesang got up and whispered.

'Excuse me, I have to go put Daddy to bed. He must have passed out by now. I'll be back in a little while,' she said. 'Don't run away.'

Fletcher noticed Eddie going across to the bar. Finishing what was left of his drink, he headed across to join him. Eddie was fixing himself a gin and lime cordial. Seeing Fletcher, he grinned and nodded.

'Are you enjoying yourself?' he asked.

'Sure,' said Fletcher finding the bottle of Scotch and helping himself.

'Be careful,' said Eddie. 'That's made in Sikkim. They only opened the distillery a year ago. It's pretty raw.'

Ignoring the warning, Fletcher poured himself a small drink.

'Where are you from in America?' Eddie asked.

'Colorado,' said Fletcher.

'The wild west!' said Eddie. 'Are you a cowboy?'

'No. Nothing like that,' Fletcher answered. 'Do you live in Kalimpong?'

'I was born here,' Eddie replied.

'Oh yeah?' Fletcher said. 'Is your family from this area?'

'No,' said Eddie. 'We're Chinese, but not the red ones. My parents came to India after the Nanjing Massacre, when the Japanese destroyed our home in 1937. They arrived by ship in India as refugees, first in Calcutta, then they came up to Kalimpong and opened a restaurant, the Nanking.'

'Is the restaurant still here?'

'Of course,' said Eddie. 'You must come by sometime.'

'I will,' Fletcher promised. 'Can I ask you another question?'

'Why not?' said Eddie.

'What's Kesang's story? I only met her day before yesterday.'

'Aahh!' Eddie wagged his finger. 'Everybody wants to know Kesang's story.'

'I don't mean to gossip,' said Fletcher, 'Just trying to get some context here.'

Eddie took out a packet of cigarettes, offering him one, which he refused. Once he'd got it lit, Eddie looked at the ceiling with an enigmatic smile.

'She introduced me to her father,' Fletcher said.

'Old man Mukherjee,' said Eddie, exhaling a stream of smoke through a gap in his teeth. 'He's her adoptive father.'

'I guessed as much,' said Fletcher.

'Dr Mukherjee was a mountaineer as well as a professor of English Literature at Presidency College,' Eddie explained. 'A very distinguished man, though he's now an alcoholic.'

'Yes, I noticed,' said Fletcher. 'But is Kesang from Kalimpong?'

'Not originally,' said Eddie, glancing over his shoulder. 'I don't think she'd care…but you mustn't let on that I told you.'

He paused then took a sip of his drink. Fletcher also raised his glass to his lips and tasted the harsh flavour of the whisky.

'Her name is Kesang Sherpa. She was born in the Khumbu Valley below Everest but her mother died when she was a few months old. Her father, Dawa Norbu, went on several early expeditions to Everest, with the British in the 1930s. After his wife died, he brought the child to Darjeeling and she was raised by one of his cousins in the Sherpa Basti. By that time, Norbu had met Professor Mukherjee and they went climbing together, mostly around Kanchenjunga, pioneering several new routes on lower peaks. This was during the war, when nobody else was climbing. In 1942, they were climbing near Kanchenjunga and Norbu was killed in an avalanche, buried under tonnes of snow. Mukherjee survived and made his way off the mountain alone. When he got back to Darjeeling, he decided that he would adopt Kesang, who was three years old.'

'Was Mukherjee married?' Fletcher asked.

'No, he's been a confirmed bachelor all his life,' Eddie replied. 'In any case, he hired an English governess to look after Kesang until she could go to school and then he put her in Loreto Convent in Calcutta.

Mukherjee comes from a wealthy family and they have a large home off Park Street. His father bought this house way back in the twenties....'

Fletcher interrupted. 'Did he continue climbing?'

'No. After the accident, he never climbed again,' said Eddie, 'I've heard that's when he started drinking. Eventually, he quit his job at Presidency College and moved up here full time.'

'Kesang seems to be devoted to him,' said Fletcher.

'Totally,' said Eddie. 'He spoilt her silly when she was a young girl. Even today, he lets her do whatever she wants. She's a free spirit, but when it comes to Daddy she's very protective.'

At that point, Kesang and a maid entered the room, carrying two trays of steamed momos, which they put on the coffee table, along with a bowl of hot sauce. Eddie and Fletcher moved across to join the others and there was a feeding frenzy for ten minutes until the trays were empty. By now it was eleven o'clock and the party quickly began to break up. Eddie was the first to excuse himself and he was followed by several others.

When Fletcher told Kesang that he was ready to leave, she gave him a wounded look. 'So early?' she said. 'Please stay, Allan. We haven't even had a chance to talk. Get yourself another drink.'

The whisky made him acquiescent, though he still wasn't sure if Kesang was just flirting with him or actually found him attractive. Fletcher himself was intrigued and watched with a growing sense of arousal as she said goodbye to her guests. Eddie had called her a 'free spirit,' which seemed accurate, though there was a certain maturity about her that none of the others possessed, a quiet confidence in her eyes.

Soon enough, the two of them were alone and she dropped onto the sofa beside him. The music had stopped.

'So, how do you like my friends?' she asked.

'I enjoyed meeting them,' he said.

'No, you didn't,' she teased him. 'I can tell. You're only interested in me.'

He laughed then put his glass on the table.

'You're not having a drink?' he asked.

She shook her head. 'No. Daddy drinks enough for both of us.'

There was a hint of sadness in her voice, but her eyes remained full of amusement and desire, studying Fletcher with an intense gaze. Moments later, she leaned towards him and took his face in both her hands. Kesang's lips were already moist before they kissed and she pressed herself against him with an eager urgency that he couldn't resist.

14

Satyr Tragopan

Tragopan satyra

*Also known as the crimson-horned pheasant, this is one of the most exotic Himalayan birds. Though rarely seen, it is widely distributed throughout the mountains of Nepal, Sikkim, Bhutan, and India, as far west as Garhwal. The western tragopan (*Tragopan melanocephalus*) is found from Kullu through Kashmir. A bright crimson throat and breast gives way to a heavily decorated body and wings, with numerous black and white spots that look like eyes. During the breeding season, male tragopan grow blue 'horns' and wattles that enhance their courtship displays. Females are a dowdy brown, flecked black and tan.*

Kesang was still asleep when Fletcher left her bed and crept downstairs. Daylight was just filtering through the windowpanes as he descended a wooden staircase that creaked underfoot. He thought about removing his shoes but the house seemed deserted and none of the lights were on. Passing through the kitchen, where the sink was piled with glasses and plates from last night's party, he pushed open the door onto the veranda. It wasn't raining but scrolls of mist obscured the mountains and the town.

Just as he was about to retrieve his umbrella and head back to the hotel, a voice startled him. 'Good morning.'

Turning, he saw Dr Mukherjee seated on the veranda, with a tea tray on the table in front of him. He was surrounded by potted fuchsia and other plants.

'Morning,' Fletcher replied.

'You're off early. Come have a cup of tea,' the old man said.

'Thanks, I should get going,' he replied.

'Nonsense,' said Mukherjee. 'Nobody ever has anything urgent to do at this hour of the day. Get a cup and saucer from the kitchen and join me.'

Fletcher did as he was told. When he sat down, the old man removed the tea cosy and poured out the amber liquid. Dr Mukherjee looked as if he was in his seventies, a gaunt man with thinning hair and a grey goatee.

'I hope you don't take milk or sugar, because there isn't any,' he said, handing over the cup. 'What's your name?'

'Allan Swift,' Fletcher said.

'Allan with an 'E' or an 'A'?' Mukherjee demanded.

'Two L's and two A's,' he answered. 'We met last night.'

'That's probably true, but I've forgotten,' said Mukherjee. 'It's one of the prerogatives of being an alcoholic.'

He was sober at this hour and questioned Fletcher about where he came from and what he did. Though it was obvious that he had spent the night with Kesang, the old man didn't seem to care. Learning that he was an ornithologist Dr Mukherjee asked why he'd chosen that field.

'Well, I guess birds have always interested me....' he started to say.

'No, but there must have been something specific that triggered your passion. Nobody devotes a lifetime to studying a particular subject just because of a vague sense of curiosity. For instance, I became a scholar of literature because of one stanza of a poem by Yeats.' He then recited:

The trees are in their autumn beauty,
The woodland paths are dry,
Under the October twilight the water
Mirrors a still sky;
Upon the brimming water among the stones
Are nine-and-fifty swans.

'"The Wild Swans at Coole",' said Fletcher, recognizing the lines.

'Exactly,' said Dr Mukherjee. 'The simple music of those words propelled me into a lifelong pursuit of poetry. There are better lines, perhaps, but I found my inspiration in them.'

'I studied that poem in college, during my freshman year,' said Fletcher.

'But you see, though it was memorable, it didn't make a literary scholar of you. Instead Allan Swift chose to study birds,' he said. 'What was your inspiration? And don't tell me it was swans!'

'No. In fact, it was a satyr tragopan,' said Fletcher. 'I've never been lucky enough to observe one in the wild but when I was a boy, I saw a pair in a zoo. The male's plumage was so spectacular that I couldn't believe a living creature could be so beautiful. Later, I looked up pictures of it in bird books and the crimson colour of its feathers and the brilliant blue on its face fascinated me. When I think back on it, that bird is one of the main reasons I chose to become an ornithologist.'

'Ha! You see, I told you!' Dr Mukherjee exclaimed. 'There's always a catalyst for scholarly passions like ours. Maybe you'll get lucky soon. We have tragopans here in some of the higher forests, though, like you, I've never seen one.'

Fletcher was surprised at himself for telling the story, as if it were some kind of confession that the professor had extracted from him. He could see the old man's hands shaking as he lifted the teacup to his lips.

'Where's your parakeet?' Fletcher asked.

'Still asleep. The lazy bugger doesn't wake up until nine.'

'I had a rose-ringed parakeet for a while when I was a boy,' said Fletcher.

'Where? In Colorado?' said Mukherjee, sharply.

Realizing that he had let down his guard, Fletcher quickly recovered. 'Yes,' he said, after an awkward pause. 'I bought it at a pet shop but it died before I could teach it to speak.'

The old man gave him a dubious look. 'It must have died from the cold.'

Fletcher nodded and changed the subject. 'I understand you're a mountaineer.'

'Who told you that?' said Mukherjee. 'Kesang?'

Again, Fletcher balked, avoiding the question. 'Did you ever try to climb Kanchenjunga?' he asked.

'No, it's a sacred mountain,' said Mukherjee. 'There were some early attempts but after the thirties, the maharajah of Sikkim and his monks forbade anyone to climb it, until Charles Evans and his team went up in '55. Joe Brown and George Band claimed they stopped six feet short of the summit in deference to the gods. Who knows?

Nothing's sacred any more.'

A few minutes later, Kesang appeared at the door in a yellow dressing gown.

'I was wondering who was talking down here,' she said, stepping out onto the veranda and giving her father a kiss on the forehead, while eyeing Fletcher with amusement.

'You can get us some fresh tea, please,' the old man said, leaning forward as if to lift the tray. Kesang took it and disappeared back into the kitchen.

'Which estate is this from?' Fletcher asked.

'Samabeong...north-east of here,' said Mukherjee. 'This is their second flush. Sometimes I wonder whether I'm more addicted to tea or alcohol. Can't do without either. You Americans always drink coffee when you wake up, don't you?'

'I prefer tea,' said Fletcher.

Mukherjee nodded and fell silent until Kesang reappeared with a fresh tray.

'Thank you, darling,' he said in a whisper, as Kesang poured them each a cup.

A few moments later, there was the sound of the gate opening and they all looked up to see a figure ascending through the mist as he climbed the garden steps. Kesang gave a shriek of delight and ran forward, throwing her arms around the man, who embraced her warmly. As she let go, Fletcher recognized who it was.

Captain Afridi wasn't in uniform and his face was bearded and sunburnt but there was no mistaking his chiselled features and the searching look in his eyes.

'Imtiaz, my boy! When did you get back?' Mukherjee shouted, obviously pleased to see him.

'Last night,' said Afridi. 'I knew that if I was going to have a chance to speak with you I needed to come early.'

He nodded in Fletcher's direction and it was impossible to know if he was surprised to find him here.

'Of course,' Mukherjee carried on. 'You know my schedule. Tea until ten. Gin thereafter!'

'This is Allan,' said Kesang, her hand still resting on Afridi's shoulder.

'Yes,' the Captain replied. 'We've met before.'

'Really?' said Kesang, surprised.

'In Kashmir,' Afridi said, extending his hand.

'Good to see you again,' said Fletcher, sensing a wariness in the Captain's manner and wondering whether it had to do with the fact that he was here with Kesang or that he was using a different name.

'Still birdwatching?' Afridi asked.

He nodded.

'Sit down. Sit down,' said Mukherjee. 'I want to hear about your expedition.'

Kesang went to bring another cup for Afridi, as he took the chair next to the old man. Though he knew this wasn't a coincidence, Fletcher wondered what was going on. Afridi explained that he had been up on the lower slopes of Kanchenjunga, doing a recce near the Zemu Gap, starting from the south-west.

'We climbed a couple of unnamed peaks and then we crossed over the Zemu Gap and came down to Green Lake,' said Afridi.

'He's being modest,' said Mukherjee, turning to Fletcher with excitement. 'This would be the first traverse of the Zemu Gap. It's a treacherous route. Even Tilman turned back because of the risks.'

'We were lucky, the weather and snow conditions were good,' said Afridi. 'But the glacier was tough going, heavily crevassed.'

'How long were you up there?' Fletcher asked.

'Four weeks,' Afridi replied, without looking at him.

'Five,' said Kesang, as she poured his tea. 'You left here on 20 April.'

Fletcher could sense a tension between them and wondered if he was the cause. Meanwhile, Dr Mukherjee wanted a detailed account of Afridi's climbs.

'I explored this area with Dawa Norbu in the forties,' he said. 'We didn't attempt the traverse but I'm sure we followed several of the same routes. Did you go up towards Pandim?'

'We climbed it,' Afridi replied. The peeling skin on his face was evidence of the harsh conditions he had endured. 'But we got caught in a storm coming down and had to bivouac until it passed. I got mild frostbite.' He held up his right hand and they could see the discoloured tips of his fingers.

Mukherjee continued to pepper him with questions, recalling some of the obstacles he'd faced twenty years ago. 'There are two gendarmes on the lower part of the summit ridge.'

'Yes,' Afridi confirmed. 'We saw them but avoided that section by traversing to the couloir and following that line to the summit.'

Kesang glanced across at Fletcher and rolled her eyes as they listened to the two men discuss the topography of the mountains, as if it were familiar terrain, every cornice and arête marked in their memories.

'Allan, are you a mountaineer?' Kesang asked.

Fletcher shook his head. 'No. I did a course in rock climbing in Colorado, the summer after I finished high school, but I never took it up seriously.'

Eventually, Mukherjee seemed satisfied with the report. Turning to Fletcher again, he said, 'I'll tell you something. If anyone is capable of climbing Kanchenjunga again, it is this man.'

Afridi waved aside the finger pointed at him.

'I doubt it,' he said. 'But there is something magical about that mountain.'

'Kanchenjunga means "the five treasures of the great snow"', Mukherjee explained. 'The mountain has five summits and the people of this region believe that each of them contains a precious element or mineral, like gold or silver.'

'Have you heard of "terma"?' Afridi asked.

Fletcher shook his head.

'It's a concept in Tibetan Buddhism that suggests the Himalayas contain valuable treasure, which has been buried in hidden places that are difficult to reach,' said Afridi. 'Tibetans believe that ancient saints and sages, like Milarepa, left behind these treasures for others to discover. Sometimes it is gold and jewels, other times it is sacred texts that reveal the truth, and just as often it is something intangible that brings about spiritual enlightenment. Each of these has equal, auspicious value and to search for terma is a noble quest.'

Kesang added, 'That sounds like an excuse to go mountaineering.'

'Indeed,' said Mukherjee. 'The Himalayas are full of treasures we'll never find, but even the most valuable discoveries are immaterial.'

Kesang added, 'Daddy has plenty of terma buried away in this house.'

When Fletcher looked puzzled, Afridi explained, 'Professor Mukherjee's private collection of Himalayan art is one of the finest, outside of major museums. Have you had a chance to see it?'

'Not now,' the old man protested. 'Later sometime, you can show it to him. Right now we should all have a drink. Kesang!'

'Daddy, it's not even eight o'clock.'

'So what? Imtiaz has come back safely and traversed the Zemu Gap. That calls for a celebration!' the old man insisted.

'I'm afraid it's too early for me,' said Afridi. 'I'll come back in the evening and have a drink with you then.'

Fletcher took the opportunity to get to his feet. 'You'll have to excuse me too,' he said. 'I need to get back to my hotel but it's been a pleasure talking to you.'

Dr Mukherjee shook his head reluctantly. 'I hope to see you again. Drop by any time,' he said.

'Where are you staying?' Afridi asked.

'At the Himalayan Hotel,' Fletcher replied, looking out into the clouds that surrounded them. Beyond the edge of the veranda there was nothing but mist.

'Do you have any plans for lunch?' Afridi enquired.

Fletcher hesitated. 'No,' he said.

'Let's meet,' he suggested. 'I want to hear more about your research. The Nanking restaurant at one? It's not far from your hotel.'

'Okay, I'll be there,' said Fletcher, turning towards Kesang. 'Thanks for the tea,' he said, and shook her hand, knowing that Afridi was watching.

With a wave, he set off into the mist, descending the stairs cautiously. But just as he reached the gate, Fletcher heard Kesang calling. 'Allan wait!'

Looking back, he saw that the house had disappeared and there was an opaque void, as if everything had been erased. But then, a shape emerged from the mist, like an apparition draped in a yellow dressing gown.

'You forgot your umbrella,' Kesang cried, holding it like a sword and pretending to fence with him.

As she came close and put a hand behind his neck, she whispered, 'Don't mind Imtiaz, he gets jealous very easily.'

With that, she kissed him gently on the lips, as the saturated air wrapped itself around them in a damp embrace.

15

Crested Serpent Eagle
Spilornis cheela

A mid-sized forest eagle that feeds on snakes as well as other reptiles and small mammals. It is a dark brown colour with speckled feathers on its breast and a flared crest at the nape of its neck that fans out like the brim of a hat when the bird is agitated. Soaring overhead, adults are easy to recognize from the black and white bands on the underside of their wings and tail. It occasionally gives a shrill whistling cry but it is generally a silent hunter that sits and waits on a tree branch before pouncing on its prey.

A section of R. C. Mintri Road, between the hotel and the Nanking restaurant, was being resurfaced and the asphalt had been dug up, a muddy, uneven stretch of about a hundred yards. Working at the side of the road was a gang of day labourers, all of them Tibetans. Men and women were working together, breaking rocks that would later be spread out as the base layer of the road. Playing in the mud near their parents were several young children below the age of five. The road workers were dressed in tattered clothes, their faces exhausted and despondent.

The pounding of hammers was like a solemn drumbeat of misery. To avoid the mud, Fletcher had to walk around and behind the labourers. The children looked up at him with curious eyes, their snotty, grubby features breaking into timid smiles. He wondered how desperate things must have been under Chinese occupation, to force them to escape across the Himalayas, only to be reduced to breaking stones at the side of the road in Kalimpong.

As he passed by, one of the women called out to him, speaking in

Tibetan, which he didn't understand. She waved for him to stop and shouted something. Fletcher turned and waited for her to catch up. The woman's hair was braided and wrapped about her head and she wore a tattered chuba with an apron that was patched and stained with mud. Her feet were bare and her hands were rough and scarred from the work, a rag bandaging one finger. Approaching him, she reached into the folds of her frayed blouse, searching for something. He shook his head instinctively, refusing whatever she might demand of him.

When her hand emerged from the torn folds of fabric, she was holding a small brass figurine, about five inches long. It was tarnished and caked with grime. As the woman gestured for him to take the idol, Fletcher waved both hands and shook his head. 'No, thank you,' he said, though he knew the woman wouldn't understand. He guessed that she was about twenty but looked much older, her face weathered and raw. A toddler clung to the hem of her chuba, the child wearing only an amulet around his neck.

Unable to make the woman understand that he didn't want the brass statuette, Fletcher finally took it from her and examined the figurine. It was obviously a religious deity—half-human and half-eagle. In its beak was a serpent and its wings were spread like a feathered cape behind its shoulders. The weight of the statue surprised him and he wondered how old it might be, as the woman raised the five fingers of her bandaged hand.

Again, Fletcher shook his head and tried to return it, but she was adamant, pointing to the child by her side, then, gesturing with her fingers to indicate that they were hungry and needed food. As he held out the image, the woman pleaded in her own language, refusing to take back the statuette. Eventually, she put up four fingers, indicating the price had dropped.

By this time, all of the Tibetan labourers were watching, as well as a few passers-by, who had stopped to see what was going on. Feeling conspicuous and awkward, Fletcher finally dug his wallet out of the hind pocket of his jeans. The woman was still holding up four fingers but he took out 500 rupees and gave it to her. She quickly tucked it inside her blouse as he walked away, slipping the statue into his jacket pocket as if it were some form of contraband.

◆

The Nanking was a small place, located upstairs above a line of shops selling woollen clothes and shawls, as well as a pharmacy with a red cross on the door. Climbing the dark staircase, Fletcher felt as though he was ascending into an attic but when he entered the restaurant, he was surprised by how bright it was, with light coming through a line of windows overlooking the street. There were about a dozen tables, half of which were empty. Afridi wasn't in sight but Eddie Lim stood next to the cashier's counter, which was decorated with a Chinese screen. On the walls were framed prints of calligraphy and paintings of pagodas and storks.

'Ah, the Colorado cowboy,' Eddie exclaimed. 'Welcome!'

'Thanks, I'm here to meet someone,' Fletcher replied.

'Yes, he's on his way,' Eddie said.

Fletcher shot him a glance. 'You know him?'

'Everyone in Kalimpong knows everyone else,' Eddie said. 'Captain Afridi comes here often, mostly with Kesang.'

'Will she be with him?'

'Not today,' said Eddie, gesturing towards a table by the window. 'Afridi asked me to reserve a table for two.'

Before he could sit down, the restaurant door opened and Afridi arrived. He greeted Eddie with a firm handshake.

'Imtiaz! You've grown a beard!' Eddie said. 'It suits you.'

'Beer?' Afridi suggested, as they sat down.

'No, thanks. Just a fresh lime soda. Sweet,' said Fletcher.

'I'll have the same,' Afridi ordered, 'but with salt and sugar.'

As soon as Eddie had gone to get their drinks, Fletcher leaned forward, his hands folded in front of him.

'How did you know I was coming to Kalimpong?' he asked.

Afridi shook his head. 'I didn't. How could I? I was up in the mountains. You left India at the end of March. When did you get back?'

'A while ago,' Fletcher said, vaguely.

Neither of them was in the mood for small talk and they spoke quietly but with an edge to their words.

'There aren't any ducks or geese up here,' said Afridi. 'So, what are you looking for?'

'Pheasants, mostly,' said Fletcher.

'You seem to prefer game birds,' Afridi observed. 'Are you planning on shooting them?'

'No,' said Fletcher. 'I'm not collecting specimens this time.'

Afridi paused and stared out the window at a rickshaw passing by on the street below, before he spoke again.

'When we met in Kashmir, you told me you weren't with the CIA,' he said.

'I'm not,' Fletcher replied.

'Am I supposed to believe that?' Afridi shot back.

'As much as I'm supposed to believe it was a coincidence that you showed up at Dr Mukherjee's house this morning,' said Fletcher.

'You thought you could hide by changing your name?' Afridi responded. 'Is it Allan Swift or Guy Fletcher?'

'Doesn't matter, does it?'

'Not really,' said Afridi. 'What matters is that your handlers sent you here because they knew I would find you.'

One of the waiters brought their glasses and set them down on the table, pointing out which was sweet and which had sugar and salt. They fell silent until the waiter walked away.

'Why would it matter if I met you?' Fletcher asked.

'Because they think I know something they don't.'

'Maybe you do,' Fletcher said. 'Such as, who shot that man in Delhi?'

'I told you it was the Americans who killed the Cuban diplomat....'

'Yes, and they switched the body with the man I found. That's what you claim. But who killed Emil Zorman?' Fletcher demanded.

Afridi studied him for a moment.

'You really don't know?' he asked.

'No.' Fletcher responded.

'In all likelihood, the Chinese,' said Afridi.

'Why would the Chinese murder an American art dealer?'

'Because he was here in Kalimpong,' said Afridi, 'asking too many questions.'

'When?' Fletcher couldn't hide his surprise.

'Didn't your employers tell you any of this?' said Afridi. 'Emil Zorman was trying to buy a tranche of Tibetan artefacts, worth over a million dollars. They had been smuggled out of Tibet and the Chinese weren't happy about it.'

'Who sold it to him?'

'That's the problem,' said Afridi. 'Nobody did—because the artefacts disappeared. The Chinese were convinced that Zorman had them and when he couldn't reveal where they were, they shot him.'

'What kind of artefacts?' Fletcher asked.

'Mostly statues and idols from the sixteenth and seventeenth century, taken from a monastery in eastern Tibet,' said Afridi.

'This sort of thing?' asked Fletcher, reaching into his pocket and putting the brass figurine he'd just bought on the table.

Afridi reached across and picked it up, 'Where did you get this?'

'From a Tibetan woman at the side of the road. She didn't give me much choice,' said Fletcher.

'How much did you pay for it?' Afridi asked, handing it back.

'Five hundred rupees.'

'It's worth about seventy-five. This is a cheap reproduction made to look like an antique, a copy of a Garuda image, the sacred raptor and vehicle of Vishnu. He is considered the enemy of serpents. Very convincing but it's been recently manufactured, most likely in a sweatshop in Kathmandu.'

'Are you sure?' Fletcher turned the image over in his hands.

'You can see where the marks from the mould have been smoothed out using an electric grinder,' said Afridi, 'It was mass produced.'

Fletcher was seated facing the door of the restaurant, which opened suddenly, admitting a middle-aged European woman with hennaed hair drawn back tightly in a bun, wearing oversized sunglasses. She was dressed in a dark green kho with an embroidered shawl draped across her shoulders. Her face was white as chalk and her eyebrows painted on. Her lipstick was stoplight red. She had a cigarette holder in one hand that she waved about like a conductor's baton.

'Eddie!' she gasped. 'When are you going to get an elevator for this place?'

Lim immediately took her hand and kissed it with exaggerated formality, apologizing for the staircase.

'Are they here?' she asked in a strident voice.

Eddie pointed to a table in the corner, occupied by three young men. As she made her way across, the woman recognized Afridi and stopped.

'Captain sahib!' she said in an imperious tone. 'When did you get back? I hardly recognize you with your beard.'

Afridi rose from his chair.

'I was out of town,' he said.

'Yes, we've been missing you,' the woman scolded, waving her cigarette holder at him accusingly. 'Not enough good looking bachelors around!'

Directing her attention towards Fletcher she studied him through the tinted lenses of her glasses. 'And who is this?' she demanded.

Afridi introduced him. 'May I present, the Kazini Saheba. This is Allan Swift. An American ornithologist.'

The woman's red lips tightened in a scowl. She did not offer her hand while her manner exuded disapproval.

'How *do* you do?' she said brusquely and moved on to her table, where the three young men stood waiting.

Fletcher gave Afridi an enquiring look.

'Elisa Maria Langford-Rae.' Afridi explained under his breath. 'She calls herself the Kazini because she's the wife of Kazi Lhendup Dorjee, a Sikkimese landowner and politician from Chakung. He's just formed the Sikkim National Congress. A political opponent of the maharajah.'

'Is she English?' Fletcher asked.

'Scottish, as best I can tell,' said Afridi, 'Though she claims to be Belgian.'

The Kazini's arrival helped ease the tension between them and both men relaxed after they'd ordered their meal. Eddie had recommended the chicken with bamboo shoots and mushrooms, and they got a prawn chow mein as well.

'Are there many Chinese in Kalimpong?' Fletcher asked.

'A few,' said Afridi. 'There's a Chinese trade mission here but they don't seem to do very much any more. Of course, Eddie's family is different. They're Indian citizens now and don't have anything to do with the communist regime.'

'The men you say killed Zorman, were they with the Chinese Embassy in Delhi?' Fletcher asked, wondering how much Afridi was willing to tell him.

'More than likely,' came the reply. 'Probably intelligence agents, though it's hard to know. They don't advertise their presence.'

Without making eye contact, Fletcher studied the man across the table, trying to gauge his motives. He decided not to mention the jeep station wagon that almost ran him down in Delhi.

As if reading his mind, Afridi asked, 'Why did you leave for the US so suddenly in March?'

'My mother wasn't well. I went back to see her,' he replied.

'I hope she's recovered.'

'Yes, she's fine. Just a minor scare. The doctors found a tumour but it was benign,' Fletcher lied.

'So, now, what's your plan?' said Afridi. 'Are you conducting your research in Kalimpong or Sikkim?'

'Both,' said Fletcher. 'I have a contact in the forest department, the DFO.'

'Thupten Lepcha,' said Afridi. 'Yes, he's a good man. Very knowledgeable when it comes to birds and wildlife.'

'And you're very knowledgeable when it comes to the people I've met,' said Fletcher.

'It's a small town,' said Afridi. 'When do you plan to go to Sikkim?'

'Soon, I hope. Thupten has recommended I spend the next couple of months at higher altitudes and then move back down after the monsoon tapers off.'

'I'm driving up to Gangtok, day after tomorrow. You're welcome to ride with me,' Afridi offered.

'Are you posted in Sikkim?' said Fletcher, cautiously.

'Temporarily.'

'Will you go back to Kashmir?'

'Who knows? I may rejoin my regiment in several months,' said Afridi.

'Which regiment is that?' Fletcher asked, surprised that the Captain was as forthcoming as he was.

'13th Kumaon.' Afridi's eyes were fixed on him, as if daring Fletcher to ask another question.

'The artefacts you mentioned,' Fletcher said. 'Do you think the Chinese have found them?'

'No,' said Afridi. 'They're still looking.'

'And you believe these antiquities are somewhere in Sikkim?'

'This morning, when we were speaking at Dr Mukherjee's place, I mentioned the concept of "terma",' said Afridi.

'Yes, I remember.' Fletcher nodded. 'Buried treasure.'

'After the Dalai Lama escaped into exile, many others followed, including the Karmapa, head of the Karma Kagyu school, also known as the black hat sect. He and some of his followers settled in Sikkim at the Rumtek monastery, near Gangtok. The politics is complicated but the Maharajah allowed him to stay,' Afridi explained. 'One of the oldest and richest monasteries of the black hat sect is the Yangchen Gompa in Kham, in eastern Tibet. In 1958, the Chinese attacked Yangchen and there was an uprising by the monks. The Rinpoche was killed along with most of his lamas. Just before this happened, the antiquities from the monastery were removed and hidden for safekeeping. Later, they were smuggled out of Tibet by a group of Khampa resistance fighters. But somehow they vanished and nobody knows where the artefacts and ritual objects have gone.'

'And that's the same tranche of antiquities Emil Zorman wanted to buy?' Fletcher asked.

Afridi nodded as their food arrived. They served themselves and ate in silence for a minute or two, until the waiter brought a pot of jasmine tea.

'The food's pretty good,' said Fletcher.

'Yes, it's better than most Chinese restaurants in India,' said Afridi. 'Eddie's mother used to do the cooking. She's trained a couple of Nepali boys who do a good job, though it's not quite the same as it used to be.'

After another mouthful of chow mein, Fletcher shifted the conversation back to the lost artworks.

'Has anyone asked the Karmapa what happened to the treasure?'

'Yes,' said Afridi, 'He gave a very Buddhist answer, saying that material objects and wealth are illusory.'

'Meaning, he doesn't want to talk about it,' said Fletcher.

Afridi shrugged, picking up a mushroom with his chopsticks.

'I'm still having trouble connecting the dots,' Fletcher complained. 'If the antiquities disappeared, how could Zorman have known about them?'

Afridi shook his head in mock bewilderment.

'Either you're a very good actor or your employers don't trust you,' he said.

Fletcher put his chopsticks down and poured some jasmine tea into his cup. Taking a sip, he stared back at Afridi with a look of ignorance.

'I don't know the answer,' said Fletcher.

'All right,' Afridi said. 'You can confirm this with your handlers but the Khampas are Chushi Gangdruk guerrilla fighters that the CIA supports. The plan was that Emil Zorman would purchase the antiques on behalf of his clients and the money would go to fund their armed struggle against the Chinese. Back in March, Zorman came here to Kalimpong, pretending to be a tourist but in fact he was sent to negotiate the purchase, only to discover there was nothing to buy.'

'So, when he returned to Delhi,' Fletcher said, 'the Chinese got a hold of him and shot him in the head, after unsuccessfully torturing him to try and get him to reveal where the treasure was hidden.'

'Precisely,' Afridi confirmed. 'And when you found his body the CIA got worried that if the story got out, their whole operation would be exposed. So, they assassinated a Cuban diplomat, who had recently betrayed them, and then paid off the Delhi Police, so they could switch the bodies. Zorman's corpse was flown back to New York in an embassy aircraft.'

Seeing the disbelief in Fletcher's eyes, Afridi added, 'I don't know why you look so surprised, it's called "killing two birds with one stone".'

Fletcher's expression, however, had more to do with the fact that he couldn't understand why Sullivan hadn't told him the truth. Though he wasn't altogether sure that Afridi's story added up, he had to wonder why an Indian intelligence officer would reveal so much, unless he had something more to gain by taking him into his confidence.

'Okay, let's for a minute assume that what you're telling me is correct,' said Fletcher. 'That still leaves us with the question: where is the treasure?'

'Of course,' said Afridi. 'That's why they've sent you here, to look for pheasants but also to discover where the Khampas hid their loot!'

Fletcher knew he was being drawn into a trap and he resisted admitting outright that he was working for the CIA, even if Afridi had blown his cover.

'Do you think that's what they did?' he asked. 'Hide it somewhere?'

'It's the only plausible explanation,' Afridi said. 'Either they had second thoughts about selling the tranche to Zorman or maybe someone offered them more money. It's also possible that the antiquities are still in Tibet. Of course, all of this is speculation....'

Fletcher nodded and pushed his plate aside, leaning forward.

'Okay. Let me speculate for a moment,' he said, trying not to sound too convinced. 'Maybe you've just spent the last four weeks searching for terma in the mountains near Kanchenjunga. I'm guessing your mountaineering expedition was really just a treasure hunt.'

Meeting Fletcher's gaze with a look of confirmation, Afridi nodded and said, 'Perhaps we can work together.'

16

Sultan Tit

Melanochlora sultanea

*Almost the size of a small bulbul, this is the largest tit in the world,
crowned with a bright yellow crest that looks like the sarpesh on a sultan's
turban. The underbelly is the same shade of yellow, while the rest of
the bird is a dark greenish black. It is often found in the company of other
species and distributed from eastern Nepal to Southeast Asia,
ranging as far as Malaysia. The call is a persistent medley of
notes like static on a radio.*

Writing a message to Merlin took a couple of hours because it had to be coded, which was slow work, though Fletcher kept his words to a minimum, as if it were a telegram. The main point of the communication was to let his case officer know that his cover was blown and he was in direct contact with Afridi. As he composed the message, Fletcher could almost smell Sullivan's pipe smoke and wondered if it was true that this was all part of a plan. He felt as if he was flying blind but knew that the only thing he could do was rely on the tradecraft he'd been taught at The Farm and see if he could salvage the operation.

The code he had been given was simple, substituting the letters of the alphabet for each letter in the first line of Kipling's poem 'If—.'

A B C D E F G H I J K L M N O P Q R S T U V W X Y Z 0

I F Y O U C A N K E E P Y O U R H E A D W H E N A L L

1 2 3 4 5 6 7 8 9

A B O U T Y O U A

Though some of the letters were the same, it was easy enough to unscramble the message. Any codebreaker worth his salt could have deciphered it in a day or two but they weren't operating at the highest level of confidentiality. He had been told to use the code only once and switch to another line of poetry for any subsequent messages. It turned out that Sullivan was a Kipling fan and each of the lines was drawn from a different poem. After explaining all this, Sullivan had recited the first stanza of 'If—,' as if it were an exhortation:

> If you can keep your head when all about you
> Are losing theirs and blaming it on you,
> If you can trust yourself when all men doubt you,
> But make allowance for their doubting too;
> If you can wait and not be tired by waiting,
> Or being lied about, don't deal in lies,
> Or being hated, don't give way to hating,
> And yet don't look too good, nor talk too wise....

The code had been given to him a week ago during their meeting at the safe house in Delhi. He was told that a CIA asset in Kalimpong, codenamed Agatha, would pick up and pass on any messages deposited at a dead drop. The procedures were simple and straightforward. Once the message was translated, he burnt whatever notes he'd used. After that, he was supposed to visit an orchid house at the edge of town, where the motor road started to wind its way down into the Teesta Valley.

It was raining heavily as he made his way downhill, his umbrella offering little protection. The mist seeped in from all sides and his shoes and trousers were soaked up to the knees. Fortunately, the orchid house was relatively dry inside despite the humidity, which clouded the panes of glass. The flowers were spectacular, a gaudy array of different species, most of them in bloom. An elderly gardener was working in the main greenhouse, absorbed in preparing pots with moss and soil. Fletcher took his time, admiring the profusion of orchids and wondering how many of them were collected from the forests near Kalimpong.

When he reached the far end of the glass house, he found what he was looking for. One of the wrought iron columns supporting the main structure had rusted out at a point three feet off the ground, exposing a hollow space inside about the diameter of his index finger. Rolling the message up, he was able to slip it into the hole, where it was securely hidden from sight. Fletcher lingered in the orchid house a while longer, as the rain streamed down the panes of glass. With all of the bright coloured orchids, it was a bit like being inside an aquarium full of tropical fish.

In order to signal that the message was ready for collection he had been told to leave a mark on the wall of a public urinal along Rishi Road. The rain had begun to ease as he headed back in the direction of his hotel. By the time he reached the site the rain had stopped completely. Sullivan's instructions had been precise. The urinal was located next to a sign advertising Kashmir Snow cold cream, with a picture of a woman holding a jasmine blossom in one hand. The men's urinal was marked Gents, with an image of a man twirling his moustache.

There could have been no greater contrast between the colourful beauty of the orchid house and the foetid interior of the urinal, which stank of disinfectant and human piss. Leaving his umbrella outside and holding his breath, Fletcher stepped inside, as if to relieve himself. Fortunately, nobody was likely to follow and witness the quick scribble he made on the wall above, writing the Greek letter omega—Ω—with a piece of blue chalk that he'd been given for this purpose. Waiting long enough to make his errand seem plausible, Fletcher hurried out and exhaled before drawing fresh air into his lungs.

In the trees above the road, he thought he saw a yellow orchid growing on a branch but when it moved, he realized it was a sultan tit. He wished he'd brought his binoculars for it was a species he'd never seen before, though he recognized it immediately from an illustration in Salim Ali's bird book. With its dark wings and back, the tit looked as if it were wearing a dinner jacket over a yellow shirt, with a matching cowlick on its head. The bird ducked into the wet shadows of the tree and Fletcher could see that it was part of a hunting party, a mixed flock of nuthatches, green-backed tits, and warblers.

◆

Fletcher debated whether to drop by Kesang's house. He didn't have a telephone number for her and he wasn't sure if he would find her at home. Nevertheless, at four o'clock he set off again from the hotel and arrived at Montrose twenty minutes later. When he rang the doorbell, he heard a voice inside: 'Bloody Hell! Go away!' Taken aback for a moment, he realized it must be the parakeet. A few seconds later one of the servants opened the door, a young Nepali woman he'd seen the night of the party. When he asked if Kesang was in she nodded and led him to the glassed-in porch. As he passed the door of Dr Mukherjee's study, the parakeet called out, 'Stupid Bugger!' The professor was asleep in his chair, an empty glass on the table beside him.

Kesang was seated in the sunroom with another woman, both of them dressed in khos. She seemed pleased to see him and got up quickly, though she didn't kiss Fletcher or give him a hug, on account of her visitor.

'Allan! I'm so glad you came. This is my friend Pema Choden. Allan Swift.' There was a formality to Kesang's words and gestures that was different from two nights ago, as if she was minding her manners.

Without getting up, Pema put out her hand, and he noticed a diamond wedding ring on her finger and a turquoise necklace around her throat.

'I hope I'm not interrupting,' Fletcher said, shaking her hand. 'I didn't know when it might be convenient....'

'Please join us,' said Pema. Her voice was muted and her accent cultured. She had a gracious, privileged style about her. 'We've just been gossiping, that's all.'

Kesang spoke to the maid, asking her to bring a fresh pot of tea.

'Is there much to gossip about in Kalimpong?' Fletcher asked.

'Too much!' said Pema, laughing. 'There's a scandal almost every day.'

'I can't imagine,' said Fletcher, catching Kesang's eye.

'Pema and I studied at Loreto together, in Cal,' she said. 'She was two years ahead of me.'

'You've just arrived in Kalimpong?' Pema enquired.

'Six days ago,' he replied. 'And I'm off to Gangtok tomorrow. Actually, I came to say goodbye.'

Kesang made a face. 'Why so soon?'

'Captain Afridi offered me a ride.'

Pema looked across at Kesang and Fletcher could see them exchanging a glance that suggested Afridi might have been the subject of their gossip.

'Beware of the Indian Army,' Pema said, with a note of sarcasm in her voice. 'They're always up to no good, especially Afridi. He's the worst of the lot!'

'Why do you say that?' Fletcher asked.

'For one thing, he knows he's good looking, which makes me distrust him,' said Pema. 'But beyond that, he's an ardent patriot who will do anything for his country even at the cost of his friends.'

'She's joking,' said Kesang, quickly, before Fletcher could respond.

'No, I'm not,' said Pema. 'He's a dangerous man. Like all the other military officers, Afridi has only one goal. He wants to make Sikkim part of India.'

'How is he going to do that?' said Fletcher.

'Just wait and see,' said Pema. 'They'll topple the Chogyal and take over as soon as they find the right excuse.'

'Aren't they worried the Chinese might invade first?' Fletcher asked.

'It's possible,' said Pema, her eyes suspicious of the question.

'Maybe the Americans will invade,' said Kesang, laughing. 'Once Hope Cooke becomes queen. Everyone says she works for the CIA.'

'I don't believe it,' said Pema. 'She's too naïve. A sweet little girl. But she doesn't have a clue what's going on. Americans are so gullible.'

'Allan's an American,' said Kesang.

'Yes. I guessed from his accent,' said Pema.

The tea arrived and there was a pause in the conversation as Kesang poured them each a cup.

'Will you have a biscuit?' she said, offering him a plate.

'They call them cookies in America, don't they, Allan?' Pema corrected her and Fletcher could see a hint of irritation on Kesang's face.

He took one and sat back in his chair just as the parakeet swooped into the room and perched on a lampshade nearby.

'Hari, get lost!' said Kesang. 'He heard me say biscuit.'

'Biscuit!' the bird demanded.

Breaking one in half, she gave it to him and he took it in his beak before flying back into the other room.

'You need to teach your bird some manners,' said Pema.

'Daddy spoils him,' Kesang replied with a frown.

'Do you think the Crown Prince is making a mistake marrying an American?' Fletcher asked, looking directly at Pema.

She shook her head. 'Frankly, I don't care whom he marries. The important thing is that he needs to guard himself and his country against the Indians. Pandit Nehru says all kinds of reassuring things about Sikkim's independence, but the minute they get a chance, they'll make their move. The Indians already hold most of the power in Gangtok, just as the British did before them.'

'Let's not talk politics, please,' said Kesang. 'It's boring.'

'All right,' said Pema. 'Let's talk about Captain Afridi's beard instead.'

'He's shaved it off,' Kesang replied. 'I saw him this morning.'

'Does he come to Kalimpong very often?' Fletcher asked.

'Often enough,' said Pema. 'Though he spends most of his time up in the mountains, conquering one peak or another.'

'When we were having lunch yesterday, Afridi introduced me to the Kazini,' Fletcher mentioned.

'That's another one to stay away from!' Pema warned him. 'She's the main source of gossip in this town.'

'Who is she, really?' Fletcher asked.

'I've heard she's Belgian,' said Kesang.

'Then why doesn't she speak a word of French?' said Pema. 'I think she's Anglo-Indian, or the daughter of some British Tommy who stayed on in India after '47. She styles herself as some sort of Himalayan diva. Her husband, the Kazi, is a fraud as well. The only money he has, came from his first wife, who died. The Kazini controls him like a puppet while she sits here in Kalimpong writing poison pen letters about the Maharaj Kumar and his American fiancée.'

'Now we're talking politics again,' said Kesang.

'The Kazini hates Americans,' Pema continued, looking straight at Fletcher. 'Several months ago, there was an art dealer from New York who came here for a couple of weeks. Suspicious fellow. The Kazini took a dislike to him immediately. She claimed he was going to steal thangkas from the monasteries in Sikkim.'

'Do you remember his name?' Fletcher asked.

Pema shook her head.

'Emil something, an east European name,' said Kesang. 'He came to see Daddy's collection and offered him a lot of money. He said he represented the Metropolitan Museum in New York.'

'I thought he was a bit of a scavenger,' said Pema, 'though he played bridge quite well. Do you play, Allan?'

Fletcher shook his head. 'I'm no good at cards.'

'That's a shame,' said Pema. 'We're always looking for a fourth.'

'Did the art dealer buy anything while he was here?' Fletcher asked.

'Daddy refused to sell his collection,' said Kesang with a wistful smile. 'He says that someday he wants to donate it to a monastery or some Tibetan charity because most of the artefacts he owns were bought from refugees and he doesn't want to profit on their account.'

'Did this man, Zorman, go up to Gangtok?' Fletcher asked.

'There was some problem about an inner line permit, but eventually he did go up for a few days,' Pema replied. 'Why? You seem very interested in him.'

'Just curious,' said Fletcher. 'There are so many unusual characters in this town, either living here or passing through.'

'You haven't met half of them yet,' said Kesang. 'When you come back, we'll have another party.'

Pema set down her teacup in its saucer with a gesture of finality and got to her feet. 'I must be going,' she said. 'There's a dinner at Bhutan House this evening. The Queen Mother's birthday. Are you coming, Bitchoo?'

Kesang shook her head.

'That's what we called her in school,' said Pema. 'Bitchoo. It means scorpion or stinging nettle, take your pick.'

Fletcher said goodbye and let Kesang accompany Pema to the door. As they passed by Dr Mukherjee's study, the parakeet squawked, 'Believe you me!'

While waiting for Kesang to return, Fletcher noticed a glass display case in one corner of the room, which contained a collection of statuettes, similar in size to the one he'd bought, though he was sure these were genuine antiques, their brassy features staring out at him with the passive omniscience of Buddhist deities. When Kesang came back, she embraced Fletcher and kissed him on the mouth.

'I'm sorry about Pema,' she said. 'She's bitter about a lot of things. After her first husband died, she married a rich Marwari from Calcutta and it hasn't worked out. That's why she's so anti-Indian.'

'I don't mind. It's interesting to hear someone with strong opinions.'

Kesang put her arms around him again.

'Don't go to Gangtok,' she said.

'I have to,' he replied.

'I'm sure Imtiaz offered to give you a ride because he doesn't want to leave you here alone with me,' she said.

'Is he in love with you?' said Fletcher.

'I don't know,' said Kesang. 'That's what he says.'

'And what about you? Are you in love with him?'

She shook her head. 'I don't know.'

Fletcher laughed. 'Did they really call you Bitchoo in school?'

Nodding, she buried her face in his shoulder. After a minute or two he realized that she was crying, gently, her tears seeping through the cotton fabric of his shirt.

17

Green-tailed Sunbird

Aethopyga nipalensis

The green tail on this bird is its least noticeable feature. The male is like a gaudy ornament, with an iridescent blue head and scarlet collar, olive green wings, and a yellow breast tinged with red like a ripe apricot. Its tail is blue above and green beneath. All these colours are concentrated in a tiny body no bigger than a wine cork. It inhabits the jungles of the lower Himalayas and its range extends to Southeast Asia. With a thin, curved bill, it feeds on nectar and insects.

A jeep arrived at the Himalayan Hotel just after 7 a.m. and the driver, a young soldier in uniform, helped Fletcher load his luggage into the back. He explained that they would pick up the 'Captain Sahib' from an army officers' mess. Ten minutes later, the jeep pulled up at an unmarked gate, where Afridi was waiting with a small kitbag in hand. He was dressed in a green camouflage field uniform with a black beret and a pistol in a holster on his hip, as if ready for battle.

'You're travelling light,' said Fletcher, as the driver stowed the kitbag with his suitcase and duffel behind the backseat.

'Actually, I hadn't intended to stay in Kalimpong this long. My original plan was to head back to Gangtok day before yesterday,' Afridi said, as they both climbed into the back. Now that he was clean-shaven, his face looked leaner, as if he'd lost weight since they'd met in Kashmir. Fletcher knew that Afridi had spent the night with Kesang. Yesterday, through her tears, she had admitted that she was expecting him, confessing her confusion and unhappiness, being caught between them. In response, Fletcher had lied, reassuring her that he felt no jealousy.

As they drove down the hill, both men avoided speaking about the matters they'd discussed two days before. Instead, Fletcher asked Afridi about his mountaineering expeditions and the Captain spoke about climbing Trishul and Kamet in Garhwal, as well as several lesser peaks in Kashmir.

'Do you think you'll ever try to climb Everest?' Fletcher asked.

'I would like to, but I don't enjoy being part of large expeditions,' Afridi answered. 'It's better to climb a mountain alpine style, with minimal support. I've heard there are plans to send an Indian expedition to Everest next year, but I'm sure it will be a full-on military campaign, in which case I'll probably not join.'

'What about Kanchenjunga?'

'I was very tempted this time,' Afridi admitted. 'Paljor Sherpa and I went above the Zemu Gap, along the northeast ridge, where we set up our high camp. The weather was perfect and the snow conditions were ideal. We could have made it to the top but, of course, it would have created a political firestorm if anyone found out. The Chogyal is still upset about the British expedition in '55.'

After three-quarters of an hour they reached the border with Sikkim at Rangpo. It was still early and no other vehicles had stopped at the checkpost. Fletcher presented his passport and inner line permit, which the Indian and Sikkimese officials studied with scepticism until Afridi intervened and explained that they were travelling together. After that, the passport was quickly stamped and they let him through. One of the officials warned them that a landslide had blocked the route, fifteen miles farther on. It would take several hours to clear.

The narrow road followed the winding course of the river, climbing at points and then descending as it traced the steep contours. Driving at a cautious speed, the young soldier blew his horn at every corner, though there was no traffic. Most of the route was through heavy jungle and they saw a pair of giant hornbills flying from one side of the river to the other. It was warmer in the valley and the clouds lay several hundred feet above them. After leaving the checkpost, they both fell silent and Fletcher guessed that, like him, Afridi had Kesang on his mind.

After they passed a gorge with a waterfall, the ridge opened up into a series of rocky outcroppings, with dense forest extending several hundred feet down to the river below. Suddenly, without warning, the windscreen shattered. Fletcher heard a loud cracking sound as the glass broke into hundreds of tiny fragments. The driver cried out and swerved in panic, as a second bullet followed the first and struck him in the chest. Before either Fletcher or Afridi could react, the jeep crashed through the parapet wall and plunged down the steep slope. For the next few moments, everything was turned upside down as the vehicle rolled over twice before hitting a tree, and then, tipping sideways, ploughed through thickets of bamboo, finally coming to rest against a mossy boulder surrounded by ferns.

Afridi had been thrown out of the jeep when they collided with the tree but Fletcher had ridden all the way down, slamming his shoulder against the back of the front seat as he was tossed from side to side. He was conscious but dazed. Slowly, he pushed aside the canvas flap at the back and crawled out into a moist bed of ferns. After the crashing sounds of the jeep hurtling down the hill, there was complete silence except for the rushing current of the river below. Disoriented and bleeding from a cut on his forehead, Fletcher looked around for Afridi. The jeep rested on its side, with two tires in the air, and he could smell diesel fuel leaking out. Getting unsteadily to his feet, Fletcher made his way around to the other side of the vehicle, where the canvas roof had been ripped away. The driver was wedged between the steering wheel and the seat, both of which had been twisted and mangled by the impact. Fletcher checked for a pulse but knew the young soldier was dead. Blood was still oozing from the bullet wound in his chest.

Not finding Afridi inside the wreckage, Fletcher was about to call out his name, but stopped himself. Whoever had opened fire on them was likely to come down to make sure they were dead. The angle of the slope was about seventy-five degrees and the jeep had torn a path through the jungle as it fell. Pulling himself up the slope by grabbing onto whatever shrubs and roots came to hand, Fletcher gradually ascended. When he reached the tree that had broken their fall, he could see the edge of the road and the shattered parapet wall, about two hundred feet above him. There was still no sign of Afridi. After casting about for a minute, he spotted a patch of camouflage green amidst the tattered foliage. Scrambling across, he found Afridi face down. He was unconscious but breathing. Easing the injured man onto his back, Fletcher couldn't see any serious injuries though Afridi's face and hands were badly scratched. A moment later, the Captain opened his eyes and looked at Fletcher with a vacant expression, his pupils dilated, staring at the sky.

'You're okay,' Fletcher whispered. 'Can you hear me?'

Afridi's lips moved but no sound came out. His body was limp and Fletcher wondered if he'd broken his back. He knew that moving him could be fatal but if they stayed where they were, their assailants would be able to see them from the road above and could easily pick them off.

When he lifted Afridi by his shoulders, the Captain moved one arm and groaned, which was an encouraging sign. Dragging his body over level ground would have been difficult enough but on the densely forested slope, which was littered with rocks hidden beneath the undergrowth, it was nearly impossible. In the end, Fletcher hoisted Afridi onto his back as he stumbled downhill at an angle through jungle until he came to a fallen tree, covered with ferns and fungi. Next to it was a large rock on which the moss had spread a thick pile of green. Laying Afridi behind the rock, Fletcher took his revolver out of its holster and checked to see if it was loaded. The Captain had a Smith & Wesson .38; all six chambers were full.

Though they were safely hidden from sight, at least for the time being, he could hear voices above them now and a couple of loose rocks tumbled down. Whoever had fired at the jeep was descending the hill to finish them off. Until now, Fletcher hadn't had time to wonder who the attackers might be. Because of the landslide, there was no traffic from Gangtok and it would be another hour before vehicles from Siliguri reached this stretch of the road. No settlements or army camps were located nearby. Just before the crash, they had passed a milestone that showed they were still twenty-three miles from Gangtok.

Afridi was slowly regaining consciousness, moving his legs and moaning softly. Fletcher leaned across and put a finger to his mouth to warn him to be quiet, though the injured man was still in shock and didn't comprehend the danger they were in. Keeping as low to the ground as he could, using the tree trunk as cover, Fletcher waited with the revolver cocked and the safety off.

Moments later, he saw a movement to his left, about ten yards up the hill. The flash of colour startled him and for a few seconds he thought it might be one of their attackers creeping through the jungle, but almost immediately he realized it was a sunbird. The bright plumage was dazzling, even in the shadows, and he wasn't sure which species it was, though he guessed it could be either Mrs Gould's sunbird or a green-tailed sunbird. Earlier, knowing that he was likely to find both species in the eastern Himalaya, he had studied his bird books in anticipation and could now clearly see that it was *Aethopyga nipalensis*.

Though momentarily distracted by the bird, out of the corner of his eye, he saw a human figure moving through the foliage about forty feet away. The man was slightly built, dressed in a grey t-shirt and khaki shorts. It was impossible to see his face but it was easy to make out the military carbine in his hands.

Fletcher held his fire, hoping that Afridi wouldn't make a sound, as a second armed figure passed in front of them, following the path of the jeep downhill. Neither of the men said a word to each other and they looked like shadows passing behind a tangled screen of trees and vines. He knew it would take another few minutes before they reached the wreckage, after which they would return to track them down. Until now, Fletcher had been operating on adrenaline but as he lay on the cushion of ferns, he could feel his shoulder throbbing with pain. One of his fingers was broken too. Holding the heavy revolver was difficult and he rested it on the fallen tree trunk for support.

The sunbird had disappeared and the forest was still. On Afridi's boot Fletcher noticed a leech inching its way up the toe and onto the laces. He knew that there were plenty of others, ready to suck their blood, even as the human killers stalked them through the jungle.

Their survival depended on remaining hidden. Fletcher realized that he could probably kill one of the men with the revolver but the minute he fired, it would give away his location, and the second man would certainly find them. Unlike their field training at The Farm, this was no simulation in which the enemy was firing blanks. Shooting at targets, he had often wondered if he would be able to kill a man. It was easy enough to pull a trigger while aiming at one of the black and white human silhouettes in a firing range, but here he knew that every shadow could be alive. At the same time, he felt no hesitation, having seen the fatal wound in the driver's chest. He knew that he needed to be ruthless and decisive if he had to use the weapon in his hand to defend himself and Afridi.

The Captain moved again, this time trying to sit up. Fletcher put out a hand to restrain him, holding his arm and pulling him down. When he glanced across, their eyes met and this time he could see that Afridi was finally coming around. A look of concern and confusion passed over the injured man's face, as he began to comprehend what was going on. He lowered his head and kept one eye on Fletcher.

No sounds came from their assailants, and he guessed they were barefoot. Fletcher could picture the armed men moving stealthily back up the hill. Through a maze of twisted limbs and leaves, Fletcher caught sight of one of the men ascending the slope that he himself had climbed. The marks he'd left in the mud would be clearly visible. Minutes later, the man reached the spot where Afridi had been lying. Though Fletcher couldn't see him now, he could hear a rustle of bamboo stems and imagined bloodstains on the leaves that betrayed their presence nearby.

If Afridi hadn't been injured, Fletcher might have been able to slip away into the forest but it was too late for that now. Any sound he made would betray their hiding place. Blood was still seeping from the cut on his forehead and he had to wipe it away as it flowed into his right eye. The revolver was pointed in the direction of the killer and Fletcher's finger was on the trigger, though he could see nothing.

Moments later, off in the distance, he heard the sound of a horn. It was coming from somewhere upriver, in the direction of Gangtok. A few seconds later, he heard it again. The landslide must have been cleared and traffic was now moving downhill. He had no idea how long it would take the vehicles to reach them or whether they would stop.

The shooters must have heard it too and Fletcher saw the leaves part, as one of the men took cover. His companion soon joined him and they conversed in whispers. Crouched behind the buttressed roots of a tall silk cotton tree, they were no more than twenty feet away, though the foliage made it impossible to get a clear shot. If they came towards him, he might be able to shoot them both, though it would take him at least three seconds to get off the second shot, long enough for one of the men to drop and fire his carbine. Fletcher released his breath slowly and tried to steady his hand, despite the pain in his broken finger.

Suddenly, the two men rose to their feet and before he could take a shot, they ducked out of sight and moved uphill, away from him. A branch snapped as they hurried off, disappearing into the jungle like predators abandoning their prey. Fletcher looked at Afridi and shook his head. They could both hear the horn again, as the vehicle took another turn coming down the valley.

Five minutes later, the roar of engines and a loud blast from a horn, sounded on the road above, followed by the squeal of brakes. Fletcher heard doors opening and excited voices from above. They must have seen the shattered glass, skid marks, and the broken parapet wall. Uncocking the pistol and putting the safety back on, Fletcher reached across and replaced the revolver in Afridi's holster.

'They've gone,' he said, as the Captain struggled to raise himself onto one elbow. His eyes were clearer now and focused.

'What happened?' he asked, his voice a hoarse whisper.

'Somebody shot our driver and we went off the side of the hill,' said Fletcher, hearing shouts from above. 'How badly are you injured?'

'Everything hurts,' the Captain replied, 'but I'll be all right.'

Getting to his feet was harder than Fletcher expected and he stumbled as he made his way forward. Soon afterwards he passed the buttressed roots of the tree where the two assassins had been crouching less than ten minutes ago. After that, he pushed aside a branch that had been broken by the jeep as it crashed through the jungle. A chorus of voices greeted him, as he lurched into view. Three men were already on their way down, scrambling over the ferns and rocks on the precipitous slope, coming to their rescue.

◆

It took almost an hour for the men to carry Afridi back up onto the road. Fletcher had needed help as well. He could tell from the expressions on the faces around him that he looked in bad shape. The cut on his head had bled down one side of his face and soaked his shirt. His jeans were torn and he could see that his finger had swollen to twice its size. Ten or twelve vehicles had stopped, including a bus, so there was a crowd of fifty onlookers or more. Someone offered Fletcher water. He drank a little and spat out the rest. Two Indian army vehicles, a jeep and a truck, were in the convoy. As soon as they saw Afridi, the soldiers took charge, laying him on the backseat of their jeep. Meanwhile, some of the others had gone down to the wreckage, to retrieve the driver's body. When they finally carried him up to the road, they stretched the limp corpse on the ground. Until then, the excited jabber of voices had been full of laughter and relief that Afridi and Fletcher had survived, but now, with the dead man in front of them, everyone fell silent. Fletcher had been sitting with his back against the parapet. He stood up slowly and went across to see the driver. His face was masked in blood and his arms and legs contorted in death. Though Fletcher could see the bullet wound in the dead man's chest, nobody else had noticed, there was so much blood on his shirt.

The rescuers had also carried up the suitcase and other bags. Fletcher's luggage was battered but intact. Most of the crowd argued insistently that they should return to Kalimpong or go on down to the military hospital in Bagdogra, at the foot of the hill. But Afridi was now fully conscious and alert. He insisted that the army transport turn around and take them on up to Gangtok.

18

Common Green Magpie

Cissa chinensis

*Distributed throughout the Himalayan foothills, as far west as Garhwal,
this close relative of jays and crows, is more common in the subtropical
forests of the eastern Himalayas. Predominantly green, of varying shades,
it has a distinctive black mask that extends over its eyes from its red beak
to the nape of its neck. Its wings are a rusty hue, edged with black and
white bands, and the tip of the tail is also white. When this bird dies
its feathers turn from green to blue, which has been noted with
specimens collected by ornithologists.*

The Medical Inspection room at the army camp on the edge of
Gangtok was a prefabricated shed that looked a bit like the Orchid
House in Kalimpong. Afridi was carried in first, as soon as they arrived.
The doctor on duty, Major Mathur, examined him and performed
whatever triage was required. He had suffered a concussion and one of
his ribs was cracked but other than that, he had only cuts and scrapes,
as well as a number of leech bites. Fletcher learnt all this when his turn
came, for the doctor was a talkative man. He explained that most of
the emergencies he dealt with were road accidents. The highway up to
Gangtok was treacherous, especially if someone was driving too fast. The
cut above Fletcher's right eye required three stitches and the doctor set to
work before the local anaesthetic had fully taken effect, so that it felt as if
he was being stung repeatedly on the forehead by a wasp. More painful
than that was his little finger. They had no X-ray facility in the MI room,
but Major Mathur reset the bone between his first and second knuckle
and taped it up with a splint. Fletcher's right shoulder was badly bruised

though nothing seemed to be broken. He had lost a good deal of blood but the doctor didn't feel he needed a transfusion.

'By tomorrow, you'll be ready for battle again,' the doctor joked.

Fletcher thanked him, though he didn't appreciate the sentiment. Afridi and he were shifted to an officer's ward in an adjacent building. The doctor insisted that he wanted both patients to remain under observation for twenty-four hours. An army nurse had cut away Fletcher's bloodstained clothes and dressed him in a blue medical gown. By the time he lay down, his whole body ached.

'Major Mathur doesn't have the gentlest touch, does he?' Afridi muttered, from his bed.

'How are you feeling?' Fletcher asked.

'It could be worse,' came the reply. 'At least my head has cleared— though I'm still seeing double.'

The two of them were lying on their backs, staring up at the ceiling. With some difficulty and pain, Fletcher turned his neck and saw Afridi's bandaged head resting on a pillow five feet away.

'Have you told anyone that we were attacked?' Fletcher asked.

'I wanted to speak to you first,' Afridi answered. 'The CO, Brigadier Narayan, is on his way. I'll report to him. He's been up at Nathu La and should be here any minute now. Please tell me what happened. I have no memory at all except for waking up in the jungle behind that fallen tree.'

Fletcher explained everything he could recall, describing the gunshots that shattered the windshield and killed the driver, as well as the two men who had pursued them down the hill.

'I don't think they expected the jeep to go off the road,' Fletcher said. 'In that sense, we were lucky. The accident saved our lives.'

'Where were the men when they first fired at the jeep?' Afridi asked.

'I didn't see them, but I got a sense they were on the ridge above us,' said Fletcher. 'It took them a while to get down to the crash site.'

'What language were they speaking?' Afridi questioned him.

'I couldn't tell. They didn't say much,' Fletcher replied.

'Where did they go?'

'They just disappeared, melting away into the forest.'

Afridi was silent for a minute and then spoke. 'They obviously knew we were coming. Who did you tell, that I was giving you a ride?'

'Thupten Lepcha,' Fletcher said, pausing to think, 'and the hotel manager.'

'Nobody else?'

Fletcher hesitated.

'I did tell Kesang,' he said, 'and her friend Pema Choden.'

Afridi did not respond for ten or fifteen seconds.

'When did you see her?' he asked.

'Yesterday afternoon. I went across to say goodbye,' Fletcher explained, realizing that Kesang must not have told Afridi that he had been to Montrose.

'What was Pema doing there?' Afridi's voice had changed with a note of suspicion in his words.

'They were having tea together. She said they were gossiping.'

'About whom?' Afridi asked.

Before Fletcher could answer, they were interrupted by the sound of voices outside and boots on the MI room floor. Seconds later, Brigadier Narayan entered and stood at the foot of Afridi's bed. He was a tall, balding man with a fleshy face and a pencil-thin moustache. His glasses made him look more like a bureaucrat than a soldier. Afridi raised his right hand in a painful salute.

'Captain, are you badly hurt?' the Brigadier asked.

'Just a bit banged up, sir,' he replied.

The CO looked across at Fletcher.

'And who is this?'

'Allan Swift,' Afridi said. 'I was giving him a ride.'

A look of disapproval crossed the Brigadier's face, as he acknowledged Fletcher with a brusque nod of his head before switching to Hindi.

'What were you doing with a foreigner in your vehicle?' he demanded.

Fletcher expected Afridi to warn the Brigadier that he understood what was being said but the Captain replied in Hindi, explaining vaguely that they had met each other in Kalimpong at a party.

'And what happened to your driver?' the CO enquired. 'Major Mathur says he has a bullet in his chest.'

Afridi recounted how the accident had occurred, explaining that their assailants had killed the driver during the ambush before the jeep rolled down the hill. Without giving too many details he repeated Fletcher's account, including their rescue when the convoy of vehicles arrived after crossing the landslide. Listening to Afridi retell the story, Fletcher felt a strange sense of detachment, as if the violence had happened to someone else.

The Brigadier stayed for half an hour and continued to quiz Afridi in Hindi, trying to determine who the attackers might have been. From the questions he asked, the CO seemed to think they must have been insurgents opposed to India's military presence in Sikkim. Afridi sounded sceptical, though he didn't offer an alternative explanation.

At the end of his visit, the CO finally turned to Fletcher and spoke in English. 'You are welcome here,' he said, in a stern, reprimanding voice, 'though foreigners are forbidden from entering our camp. But this was an emergency. I hope you will be discharged soon.'

After he left, Fletcher glanced over at Afridi, whose eyes were closed.

'I'm surprised you didn't tell him that I speak Hindi,' Fletcher said.

Afridi winced as he took a breath.

'It's better you keep your cover intact,' he said. 'If anyone finds out who you really are, they'll lock you up.'

Later, they had other visitors, including the Crown Prince. He was a soft-spoken man with a mild stammer. Dressed in a plain brown kho, he had a round, handsome face and tousled hair. Accompanying him were a couple of palace officials but the visit was far less formal than the Brigadier's interrogation. The Prince presented each of them with white khata scarves, as a mark of welcome and respect. He seemed genuinely concerned about their injuries and had a sympathetic look in his eyes. The Maharaj Kumar asked Fletcher where he came from and nodded when he learnt about his project, saying that he had been told that someone was coming to research birds in Sikkim.

'If there is anything we can do, please don't hesitate to ask,' he said.

He spoke awhile longer with Afridi and it was obvious that they were on familiar terms, certainly close acquaintances, if not friends.

'Once you're on your feet again, Captain,' the Maharaj Kumar said, 'You must come over to the palace for a drink. You too, Mr Swift.'

After he had left, Afridi explained that the Maharaj Kumar held the honorary rank of a lieutenant colonel in the Indian Army.

'Does Sikkim have an army of its own?' Fletcher asked.

'Not really,' said Afridi. 'There's the Sikkim Guard, a palace militia. Our treaty provides for the country's defence, as well as its foreign relations.'

The last visitor was the Political Officer, who dropped by late in the afternoon, when most of the painkillers had worn off. He was an Indian Civil Service officer with a starchy British accent, wearing a suit and tie. Fletcher found him pompous and Afridi seemed to share that opinion, though he answered the PO's questions politely. By the time the PO left, it was growing dark outside the single window in the ward. Fletcher could see what looked like some sort of fruit tree outside and a distant ridgeline with conifers. In the gathering twilight, he saw a scruffy-looking bird, about the size of a small crow, land on the tree. From his bed, it was difficult to make out what it was, though Afridi had a better view.

'Green magpie,' the Captain said, without being asked.

◆

Major Mathur discharged Fletcher at noon the next day but decided to keep Afridi in bed for another twenty-four hours. Despite the dull ache in his forehead, the throbbing pain in his finger, and a sore shoulder, Fletcher felt much better. He was able to get a change of clothes from his duffel and an army vehicle dropped him and his luggage at the Blue Poppy Guesthouse, which was next to the only petrol pump in town. Thupten had recommended it as one of the few places to stay in Gangtok. The owner spoke very little English but they were able to come to an agreement that he would rent a room for a week. The accommodation was cramped but comfortable, with an outside entrance. A couple of simple restaurants were located near the guesthouse, where he could get his meals.

Unpacking his suitcase, Fletcher tried to assess the damage. He was relieved to find that almost everything was intact, though something inside the night vision scope had shattered. Listening to the bits of glass rattling about, he could tell it was beyond repair. The parabolic microphone was dented but seemed to work, as did the tape recorder.

His camera and field glasses were undamaged though several of the syringes and glass vials that he used for collecting blood samples had been reduced to fragments. All things considered, he was surprised that nothing else had broken. Unzipping the lining of the suitcase and opening the cover of the hidden compartment, he took out the Beretta and inserted a loaded magazine. Making sure the safety was on, he slipped the handgun into his jacket pocket.

Half an hour later, he stepped outside to get something to eat. At one of the restaurants nearby he ordered a bowl of thukpa noodles with chicken. The hot sauce he added made his mouth burn and his ears ring. Unlike Kalimpong, which was situated along the top of a high ridge, Gangtok lay at a lower elevation, on a protruding spur overlooking a broad valley with higher mountains on all sides. Though it had rained in the morning, the sky was mostly clear and he could see prayer flags waving all around him. A line of shops stretched along the main road, beyond which lay the two-storey palace with its double peaked roof. Off to the right, on another hillock, stood the Residency, a colonial-style structure where the PO lived. Fletcher recognized the buildings from photographs in the dossier he'd been given in Delhi, though everything looked somewhat different now that he was here. In many ways, he preferred Gangtok to Kalimpong—it seemed less cluttered and rundown.

Taking advantage of the clear weather, Fletcher headed out to explore the town, wandering as far as the palace gate and down a winding road that passed through a neighbourhood of clustered huts. A number of birds were about, including a pair of green magpies that he noticed in a tree above the road. By six in the evening, the sun had started disappearing behind the clouded ranges to the west. The snow-clad peaks were hidden, though he could tell that the higher country began farther up the valley to the north, where the ridgelines converged.

Returning to the Blue Poppy, Fletcher saw a car parked out front, across from the petrol pump, a grey Fiat 1100. As he headed towards his room, he noticed that the door was ajar; he was sure he had locked it when he had gone out. Immediately, his right hand went into his jacket pocket and found the Beretta. With the splint on his little finger, holding the pistol was awkward at first. He was able to grasp it firmly enough once his index finger wrapped itself around the trigger.

Moving forward quietly, Fletcher positioned himself outside the door and listened. Someone was in the room for he could hear a faint rustle of fabric. Keeping the pistol concealed in his pocket but ready to fire, he pulled the door towards him and stepped inside. Every nerve in his body was primed to react and he was already pressing the trigger, when he saw who it was.

Kesang was standing with her back to him, holding aside the curtain on the window, looking out. She turned and smiled, as he slipped the safety catch back on.

'Hey,' he said, trying not to sound alarmed. 'I thought someone had broken into my room!'

'I did,' she said, coming across and putting her fingers to the wound on his forehead, then kissing him gently.

'How did you get in?' he asked, as soon as he could move his lips.

'The hasp on your door is broken,' she said. 'All I had to do was slide the bolt in the other direction.'

'So much for security,' he said.

'Nobody locks their doors in Gangtok,' said Kesang.

'So, how'd you get here?' he asked.

'I drove,' she said. 'Daddy never uses his car but it still works. When I heard about the accident, I had to come. Are you okay?'

'Just a few stitches up here and my finger is broken.' Pulling his hand out of the pocket, he showed her the splint. She took his hand gently in hers as if she was holding an injured bird.

Kesang was casually dressed in a white blouse and jeans. Her eyes blinked once as she stared at Fletcher then held him in her gaze.

'Did you see Afridi?' he asked.

She nodded.

'He got hurt a little worse than me but he'll be all right.'

'You're both lucky to be alive,' she said. 'I saw the place where the jeep went over. An army recovery team was winching the wreckage up the hill.'

'What did Afridi tell you?' Fletcher asked.

She took a deep breath. 'He said you saved his life.'

'Yeah?' said Fletcher. 'Are you sure?'

'He wouldn't have told me if he hadn't meant it,' Kesang replied, putting out her hand and touching his right arm. Fletcher couldn't help but wince.

'What's wrong?' she asked.

'I bruised this shoulder, that's all,' he said.

'Imtiaz told me there were two armed men who tried to kill you,' she said. 'Why?'

'I have no idea,' he said.

'Is that why you're carrying a pistol?'

'You noticed?'

She slipped her hand into his jacket pocket. Fletcher was about to stop her but then he let Kesang take the Beretta out and examine it. Something about the way she held it made him realize that she knew how to fire a gun.

Setting the weapon aside on the dressing table, she reached over and bolted the door from inside, then pulled him against her and began unbuttoning his shirt. Fletcher kissed her forehead and smelt the fragrance of her hair. Kesang gently examined the bruises on his body as well as the scrapes and cuts on his arms and legs. At the same time, her hands caressed him with sensuous intimacy. The splint on his finger made it difficult for him to reciprocate but he responded with the other hand, stroking her face and throat as she kissed him passionately. Buttons, clasps, and zippers were loosened as they shed their clothes. Submitting to her guiding touch, Fletcher let himself be lowered onto the bed, ignoring the ache in his shoulder as Kesang's agile fingers aroused every impulse of desire.

The pain of his injuries was nothing compared to the pleasure of feeling her smooth skin against his and the soft friction of her thighs as she straddled his hips. Taking him deep inside herself, Kesang closed her eyes and threw her head back as he arched his body against hers. It was as if the two of them were possessed by a single, animated spirit that made them writhe together in an ardent trance. Moving in unison to the rhythmic pulse in their veins, their hearts pumped faster and faster, until, finally, they both cried out as one.

When their breathing eased and their limbs relaxed, Fletcher felt a last shudder of pleasure as he closed his eyes.

'Did I hurt you?' she asked.

'No,' he said. 'Not at all.'

They were silent for several minutes.

'Imtiaz told me you work for the CIA,' she said.

He laughed.

'Don't believe everything he says,' Fletcher answered, brushing her hair away from her face.

Kesang rolled aside and lay down beside him, careful to rest her head on his uninjured shoulder.

'He said your name isn't Allan Swift,' she whispered. 'Is that true?'

'The truth...' he answered, 'is that you and I hardly know each other. We met less than a week ago. I'm sure you have as many secrets as I do.'

'What do you mean?' she demanded.

'When we first met, it wasn't a coincidence, was it?' he said. 'You walked off with my umbrella on purpose.'

'Of course I did,' she said, laughing.

'Then why should I trust you?' he asked. 'If everything's a game....'

'Is that what you think it is?' said Kesang, rolling her eyes. 'Do you think I've made love to you because I'm trying to lure you into some kind of trap?'

'Honestly, I'm not sure what's going on between us,' he said. 'There are things I still don't understand.'

'Such as?' Kesang said, lifting herself onto one elbow and looking him directly in the eye.

'What's your relationship with Afridi?' he said. 'It's almost as if you were playing the two of us off each other.'

She smiled with a mischievous expression, as if he'd taken the bait.

'But you told me you weren't jealous,' she said.

'So, I lied,' he admitted.

'What else have you lied about?' Kesang asked. 'Why can't you just tell me the truth?'

'Because it's not that simple,' he said.

'Because you don't trust me,' she complained, looking hurt, though he could see it was an act. He wondered if Afridi had actually told her that he worked for the CIA or if that was just a ploy on her part.

'I wouldn't lie to you about anything important,' he said.

'What's more important than the fact that I'm here in bed with you?' said Kesang, 'Neither of us has any clothes on. We have nothing to hide.'

Fletcher studied her with a wary look.

'Then don't ask me questions I can't answer,' he said. 'That way I won't need to lie to you.'

After a while, they began to make love again but this time more slowly, with patient persistence and conspiratorial gestures, allowing their bodies to interrogate one another in the absence of words, searching for concealed secrets and exploring covert desires. In the darkness they seemed to exchange identities as if it were a fluid game of hide-and-seek. Forbidden questions formed on their lips and slipped off their tongues, answered by intriguing sensations, like knotted riddles waiting to be solved. Even as they sought to unmask each other, neither of them felt any urgency to arrive at the truth....

They had all night.

19

Rufous-necked Hornbill

Aceros nipalensis

Though smaller than the great hornbill (Buceros bicornis),
this is one of the largest birds in the Himalayas. The male has a rufous
head and neck, with a distinctive blue eye patch and a red wattle at its
throat. Instead of the giant hornbill's double casque, the rufous-necked
hornbill's upper mandible has four to six grooves on either side that look
like black stripes. Most of the body and wings are black, with a broad
white band on the tip of its tail.

The day after Afridi was discharged from the MI room, he and Fletcher met for a cup of tea at a small canteen near the Blue Poppy Guesthouse. The Captain's head was still bandaged but his beret covered most of his injury. In a small town like Gangtok the accident was big news. Recognizing who they were, the owner of the canteen insisted on serving them chang instead of tea. Two bamboo flasks were filled with fermented millet over which the proprietor poured warm water. Sipped through a reed straw, the infusion had a sour, refreshing flavour.

'How do you like it?' Afridi asked.

'Not bad,' said Fletcher, 'though it doesn't taste much like beer.'

'The alcohol content is low but you can get drunk on it if you try hard enough,' Afridi explained.

'I think I'll hold back,' said Fletcher. 'The last thing I need right now is a hangover.'

'Well, I should warn you then—we've been invited to the palace tomorrow evening for drinks and dinner. They pour generous pegs of whisky in Sikkim,' said Afridi.

'Is it a special occasion?' Fletcher asked.

'No,' said Afridi. 'The Maharaj Kumar sent word that he wants to celebrate our recovery. He's always looking for an excuse for a party.'

'Will it be a formal event?'

'Not at all,' said Afridi. 'Very casual. The palace isn't particularly grand and the social circle in Gangtok is even smaller than in Kalimpong.'

'And have you had any progress finding our attackers?' Fletcher asked.

'No, but there is some interesting news. The ambush was carefully planned and there must have been more than just two of them. The landslide was caused by dynamite detonated a few hours before we got there. I had a suspicion and sent a team to find evidence of the blasts.' Afridi paused as the owner of the canteen refilled the bamboo flasks with more water. 'The other piece of news is that we were able to recover a bullet from the driver's body. There was also a slug embedded in the radiator of the jeep. Both of them came from an M1 carbine. An empty brass casing was found just above the road. China still manufactures the M1, copied from American weapons dating back to World War II.'

'Would anyone other than the Chinese have had an M1?'

'It's possible, but unlikely,' Afridi replied. 'Most of the weapons here are antique muzzle loaders and old three-naught-threes.'

'Do people know that we were ambushed?' Fletcher asked.

'We've kept it quiet,' Afridi replied. 'Of course, the CO and the Political Officer are aware, as is Major Mathur and the Crown Prince but beyond that, it's strictly confidential. I'm sure that eventually the word will get out. It's impossible to keep a secret in Gangtok. I hope you haven't told anyone.'

Fletcher shook his head. 'Has the driver been cremated?' he asked.

'His body was sent back to his home in Bihar. Except under extreme circumstances, the Indian Army usually ships a soldier's remains to his family, so they can conduct the final rites,' Afridi said.

'What was his name?' Fletcher asked.

'Sepoy Gambhir Yadav,' said Afridi. 'From Kishanganj.'

Fletcher took another sip of chang and fell silent for few moments.

'So the Chinese must have agents operating in Sikkim on their behalf,' he said. 'Do you think they were after you or me, or both of us?'

'I doubt if you were the target,' Afridi said. 'They must have been trying to kill me. I'm sure it's connected to the antiquities from Kham. The Chinese are searching for the relics and they don't want us to find them first.'

'For that matter, I'm sure the Tibetans don't want you to find the terma either,' said Fletcher.

'Nor do the Americans,' Afridi added with a knowing look. 'When do you want to head up to Lachen?'

'Maybe after I get these stitches out,' said Fletcher.

Afridi nodded then looked him in the eye. 'Did Kesang visit you?'

'Yes, she did,' said Fletcher, without blinking. 'I was surprised to see her.'

'Did she spend the night?' Afridi asked.

'No,' Fletcher lied, then added, 'But even if she had I wouldn't tell you. Has she gone back to Kalimpong?'

Afridi nodded and looked away. 'Be careful. She's not as innocent as she makes out.'

'Oh yeah?' Fletcher responded. 'What do you mean by that?'

'Well, for one thing, she's a member of the Communist Party,' said Afridi with a tense smile.

Fletcher shrugged. 'That's perfectly legal in India, isn't it?'

'Yes, of course, they contest elections and hold political rallies,' Afridi conceded. 'Dr Mukherjee has been a member since the 1940s, though he doesn't get involved any more. Kesang is also a trustee for an organization called the Tibetan Rehabilitation and Welfare Society, TRWS. Pema Choden is a founding member. Its patron is Princess Coocoola, the Maharaj Kumar's sister. They do charity work with refugees and they're also promoting the idea that Sikkim should become a new homeland for Tibetans in exile.'

'That sounds like a plan,' Fletcher said.

Afridi continued. 'Though a few of the refugees have settled here, along with the Karmapa and his monks, most Tibetans have moved on to other places like Mussoorie, Delhi, or Dharamshala. The government of India prefers to keep them away from sensitive border regions. Historically, the royal family and the aristocracy in Sikkim have always had strong ties with Lhasa. Coocoola and Pema were both married to wealthy, influential Tibetans. Before the Chinese takeover, however,

people from Lhasa always treated the Sikkimese like poor cousins, so
there's an undercurrent of resentment, now that those same people from
Tibet have been displaced.'

Afridi stopped for a moment and looked at Fletcher intently.

'I'm oversimplifying,' he said, 'because the politics is byzantine,
even by Himalayan standards. Essentially the problem in Sikkim is
that the Buddhist Bhutias and Lepchas, who consider themselves the
original inhabitants of this country, have become a minority in their
own homeland because of an influx of Hindu migrants from Nepal.
The electoral system is heavily weighted in favour of the Bhutias and
Lepchas. The Durbar, or royal assembly, is controlled by the Chogyal
and the Kazis, who are the large landowners and nobility. Nevertheless,
the Nepali population is beginning to grow restive and more vocal,
demanding majority rule. One faction of the National Party, which
represents Bhutias and Lepchas, advocates granting Sikkimese citizenship
to a large number of Tibetans in order to counterbalance the Nepalis. It's
ethnic politics in a raw and undiluted form. Sikkim has about 100,000
eligible voters and just under 70,000 are of Nepalese origin. Bhutias and
Lepchas make up only 30,000 and the rest are smaller ethnic groups.
Adding another 50,000 names to the rolls isn't an insurmountable task.
Demands like that, however, are political dynamite and the government
of India will never agree to the plan.'

'Kesang's family came from Nepal originally, didn't they?' Fletcher
asked.

'Yes, but the Sherpas are Buddhists and their ties are closer to Tibet
and the Bhutia community,' Afridi explained. 'When she studied at
Loreto Convent in Calcutta, Kesang became close to Pema and several
other women from Sikkim. Though she's not an aristocrat by birth, her
adoption by Dr Mukherjee gives her a privileged position in a small
town like Kalimpong. She has humble roots but wealth and influence,
which is a useful combination when it comes to politics.'

'I still don't get it,' Fletcher said. 'If Kesang is a communist, why
is she allied with the palace?'

'It's more a matter of identity than ideology,' said Afridi. 'Most
Buddhists in Sikkim are opposed to the Sikkim National Congress,
which is pro-India and pro-Nepali. Ironically, the SNC is headed by

Kazi Lhendup Dorjee from Chakung, who happens to be married to Elisa Maria Langford-Rae, better known as the Kazini.'

'The woman I met with you the other day at the Nanking restaurant,' said Fletcher, trying to fit the pieces together.

'Yes, and she's the one who keeps stirring up trouble, writing unsigned articles in the press and circulating rumours against the Crown Prince. More than that, though, she has begun to cultivate a clique of young Nepali activists. The Kazini herself is close to one or two Congress Party leaders in India, whom she has known since she lived in Delhi in the fifties.'

'I think I read one of her pieces in the *Himalayan Observer*,' said Fletcher. 'Does she live in Kalimpong or Gangtok now?'

'Mostly Kalimpong, because she refuses to give up her British passport and become a Sikkimese citizen. The government of India won't issue her a residential permit because this is a border area, across the inner line. Of course, she comes and goes on a regular basis, along with the Kazi. He's the owner of this petrol pump, by the way, and the building next to your guesthouse.'

'I suppose everybody has to make a living,' Fletcher said, glancing across at the pump where a motorcycle had stopped to fill up on fuel.

'The situation in Sikkim is gradually becoming volatile,' Afridi continued. 'Things may not explode immediately but there are members of the National Party who are suggesting that any Nepali who has lived here for less than five years should be expelled. Meanwhile, there are demands for expanding the Sikkim Guard, which has mostly a ceremonial role though the Crown Prince has hinted that he would like them to be more of a royal militia. The Political Officer and the Indian Army aren't likely to allow that to happen.'

◆

The next evening, Fletcher set out for the palace on foot. Afridi had told him the invitation was for 7.30 p.m. and it was already dark. Gangtok had no streetlights, except near the main bazaar, but the paved road was broad enough so that he had no trouble seeing his way. As he approached the main gate, a white Ambassador car, flying the Indian flag, passed by. The driver sounded his horn impatiently to let them through. By the time Fletcher got to the palace, it had started to rain.

A dignified gentleman in a black suit with shiny lapels and a narrow tie, held in place with a steel clip, met him at the door. He looked as if he might be a butler, or at least styled himself as one, with a long face and sober eyes.

'Good evening, sir,' he said, 'I'm Mr Manuel, please follow me.'

'Has Captain Afridi arrived?' he asked.

'Not yet, sir.'

They passed through a couple of gloomy rooms that looked as if they were used only for formal occasions, full of heavy Victorian furniture. A wooden staircase led to the private quarters upstairs. When they entered the drawing room, it was brightly lit, with low cushioned divans and Tibetan carpets on the floor. A cluster of four people was standing to one side. Fletcher recognized the Political Officer, who had visited them on the day of the accident.

'Ah! The walking wounded!' he said, catching sight of Fletcher. As the others turned to look at him, the PO continued, 'How are you, dear boy?'

Fletcher didn't bother to reply as he recognized Hope Cooke from photographs he'd seen. She was dressed in a neon blue kho, her eyes heavily made up. Another young woman was with her, as well as an older American man. The PO introduced them with a wave of his hand. 'Mr Simpson and his daughter, Rose.'

'I'm so sorry you had such a horrible experience on your way up to Gangtok,' said Hope, in a throaty whisper, as if she'd lost her voice. 'We were all so terribly upset. Maharaj Kumar was just saying that the road has to be widened.'

'Where are you from in America?' Rose's father asked.

'Colorado,' said Fletcher. 'But I went to Wesleyan, in Connecticut. In fact, I've even visited Sarah Lawrence.'

'What a coincidence!' Rose said. 'We just graduated from there!'

'I know. Did you ever meet someone named Sage Carlyle?' he asked.

The two women shook their heads.

'I guess she would have been a few years ahead of you,' he said.

'An old girlfriend?' Hope asked, tilting her head to one side in a coquettish gesture. There was a strange combination of naivete and sophistication to her manner, like a schoolgirl performing the part of an older woman in a play.

'Not really,' said Fletcher with a shrug. 'Nothing like that.'

'Old flames never die!' said Rose's father in a jocular tone.

The PO interjected, 'Mrs Kennedy studied at Sarah Lawrence, didn't she?'

'No, Vassar, then Grenoble,' said Hope, lowering her voice to a husky murmur. 'But her sister, Lee Radziwill is a Sarah Lawrence grad.'

Fletcher suddenly remembered where he'd heard the hushed voice before. Moments later, a striking woman entered through a pair of embroidered drapes that covered a doorway on the opposite side of the room. She was in her late thirties and beautiful in an elegant, unapproachable sort of way. Her dark hair had been carefully pinned up and she wore a multi-coloured pangden apron over her kho. Her skin was flawless and her eyes shone like sapphires. The only jewellery she wore was a coral necklace with matching earrings, a bright salmon colour.

She exchanged kisses with Hope, though their lips didn't touch each other's cheeks.

'May I present, Princess Coocoola,' said the PO, adding an extra syllable to her name. 'This is Mr Allan Swift.'

'Ahh!' Coocoola gasped, raising one hand to her mouth dramatically. 'You're the one who had the dreadful accident. I hope you're not in pain.'

The stitches and bruise on his forehead had turned from dark purple to a livid yellow that made it look even worse than before.

'Nice to meet you,' Fletcher said.

'Where is the Maharaj Kumar?' said the PO, abruptly, looking around with a haughty air of having been snubbed by his host.

'He's playing mah-jong upstairs with his chums,' said Coocoola. 'Please come, Your Excellency. Let's interrupt them. They've been at it all afternoon.'

As the two of them left the room, Hope turned to Fletcher again, 'You're an expert on birds, aren't you?' she said in her first lady whisper.

'I guess,' he admitted, 'I'm planning to do part of my fieldwork here in Sikkim.'

'Of course,' said Hope. 'Maharaj Kumar is a bird lover. In fact, he commissioned a book on the birds of Sikkim that just came out.'

'I have a copy,' said Fletcher.

'We saw an unusual species today,' Rose interjected. 'Maybe you know what it is. Almost as big as a turkey but longer, with black wings and body. The head was a chestnut colour and it had bright blue patches around its eyes. Its beak was huge and curved with black lines that looked like Apache war paint.'

'Probably a rufous-necked hornbill,' said Fletcher.

Mr Manuel coughed politely at the door as a group of five Indian Army officers entered the room, Afridi amongst them. All of the men were in uniform. The other officer Fletcher recognized was Major Mathur from the MI room. Hope made a welcoming gesture, throwing up both hands and greeted them effusively.

'Now, the party can begin!' Rose cried and her father winked at Fletcher.

'Are you staying in Sikkim for a while?' Fletcher asked.

'Just for a month or so,' Mr Simpson said. 'I'm here as a chaperone. The Crown Prince invited us along with Hope. He didn't think it would be proper if she came alone, even though they're engaged.'

Major Mathur interrupted with a cheerful, 'So, how is my patient?'

When Fletcher reached out his right hand the doctor examined the splint. 'The swelling is going down,' he said. 'What about the cut on your head?' He probed it roughly with his fingers, and Fletcher flinched. 'Still painful, is it?'

'Yes,' said Fletcher.

'Come by next week on Tuesday and I'll take the stitches out,' he said.

Afridi had joined them now and, with the officers off duty, the mood was light-hearted. Someone mentioned that the CO had been called away to Calcutta, which meant they could all relax. Meanwhile, Mr Manuel had rallied the palace staff to open up the bar and everyone quickly got themselves drinks. The Crown Prince appeared soon afterwards and greeted his guests with quiet sincerity. He seemed to know each of the army officers by name.

Princess Coocoola and the PO reappeared, along with several Sikkimese courtiers who shook hands with everyone, while Rose and Hope set up the record player and shuffled through a stack of albums. As more guests arrived, Fletcher could hear the sound of the storm outside, a rumble of thunder and rain spattering against the windows and drumming on the roof. There was a stilted, uneasy feeling to the gathering until the alcohol began to take effect. Someone had put a large whisky soda in the Maharaj Kumar's hand and he raised it in a toast.

'To Captain Afridi and Mr Swift...your good health and rapid recovery,' he said, suppressing his stammer. 'Cheers!'

Hope touched her glass to Fletcher's and whispered. 'I hate it when they drink too much. Hopefully the dancing will distract them.'

Rose had put on Chubby Checker and one of the young officers gave an enthusiastic catcall and began to twist with her. The PO watched with disapproval, though Princess Coocoola tried to get him to dance. When he refused, she caught hold of Major Mathur and the party gathered momentum after that. Outside the palace there was thunder and lightning, with wind battering the windows. Suddenly, the power went off and the music ground to a halt. There were groans of disappointment and after a few seconds, several cigarette lighters and matches flared in the darkness. But just as Mr Manuel was lighting candles, the lights came back on again and everyone blinked at each other.

Fletcher could see that Afridi had taken a seat in one corner, nursing his broken rib. Using his injuries as an excuse not to dance, Fletcher watched from the sidelines, a glass of beer in hand. A few more women appeared from somewhere within the palace but things were too lively and chaotic now for anyone to be introduced. From behind the curtain covering the doorway, Fletcher noticed two young boys peering out at the adults. He guessed they must be the Crown Prince's sons, from his first marriage.

Eventually, the PO came across to where Fletcher was leaning against the wall. He took out a silver cigar case and offered him one.

'No thanks, I don't smoke,' said Fletcher.

Lighting up, the PO puffed on his cigar and then studied Fletcher with a cold-blooded gaze, as if his eyes were searching for answers to unspoken questions.

'By the way,' he said, at last, 'On Captain Afridi's recommendation, I've approved your permit to visit the Lachen Valley and Yumthang. We don't usually allow foreigners into that region, even guests of the palace. It's a border area and a highly sensitive zone.'

'Thank you,' said Fletcher.

'I'll warn you, however,' the PO continued. 'If there's any nonsense, any trouble of any kind, you'll be on your way back to America before you know it.'

'Of course,' said Fletcher. 'I'll be doing my research, that's all.'

The PO's expression made it clear that he didn't believe him. A loud crash of thunder exploded outside and the lights flickered but didn't go out.

'And if you're free day after tomorrow,' the PO added. 'I'm having a little dinner party at The Residency. You're most welcome to join us,' he said, with a note of cultivated disdain that even his colonial predecessors couldn't have matched. 'Unfortunately, the social scene in Gangtok is somewhat limited and you'll meet the same people all over again. It's such a bore. We're always grateful when someone new arrives to break the monotony.'

'Sure,' said Fletcher, 'Thanks.'

Pointing dismissively at the dancers with his cigar, the PO added a postscript: 'You know that all of this is a farce, a charade.'

'In what sense?' Fletcher asked, surprised by the old man's candour.

'The Crown Prince believes that he rules Sikkim and blunders on with grandiose plans for economic development and self-sufficiency. But he doesn't realize that the age of monarchies is finished. We are in the twentieth century now,' the PO said. 'This palace. The Durbar. The Chogyal. They are nothing but medieval anachronisms. I can assure you, Mr Swift, that India is very much in control of Sikkim and we will make sure that whatever happens here, it serves our purposes and not some delusional fantasy of Shangri-La.'

20

Rusty-cheeked Scimitar Babbler

Pomatorhinus erythrogenys

An elusive bird that is heard more often than seen. It is the size of a small thrush and has a generally dusty colouration that varies from olive brown above to umber below, with a white throat and breast. The beak, which it uses to forage in the dead leaves for insects and worms, is relatively thick and curved like a scimitar, from which it derives its name. Often found in groups of five or six birds, it pairs off during the mating season. The male and female perform a 'duet', their combined calls sounding like a single bird.

The next morning, Fletcher had just finished eating breakfast at a restaurant next door to his guesthouse, when a Sunbeam Alpine sports car pulled up, with the roof down. Seated behind the wheel was the Crown Prince, who beckoned with a friendly wave. Fletcher was surprised by this sudden show of familiarity. The night before at the palace, the Maharaj Kumar had been cordial but reserved.

'Good morning...Allan,' said the Prince. 'I'm sorry to disturb you.'

'No, of course not, no problem,' said Fletcher.

'Are you busy?'

'Not at all, I just had a late breakfast and was wondering what to do next,' Fletcher answered.

'Hope was telling me and the children this morning that you have a device for recording birdcalls,' said the Prince.

'Yes, a parabolic microphone,' Fletcher confirmed. He had explained how it worked to Hope and Rose the night before.

'It would be wonderful if you could come over and give us a

demonstration,' said the Prince. 'The palace gardens are full of songbirds.'

'Right now?' said Fletcher.

'If it's not inconvenient,' the Maharaj Kumar replied.

'Sure, it will take me just a minute. I'll be right out,' Fletcher said, heading across to his room. The Prince's informality had flustered him but he quickly gathered up his equipment. Once he was settled in the passenger seat of the Sunbeam, they sped off to the palace.

'Nice car,' said Fletcher.

'Though not the best for the monsoon,' said the Maharaj Kumar with a laugh. 'Usually, I have to keep the top up because of the rain.'

When they reached the palace, Fletcher was introduced to the Prince's two sons, Tenzing and Wongchuk, who were ten and eight years old, as well as his daughter Yangchen, who was five. Hope, Rose, and their father were there as well, along with an elderly Englishman, Colonel Basil Norton, whom Fletcher had met briefly the night before. He was wearing a terai hat with a bush shirt over khaki shorts and matching knee socks. Together they walked across to a small gazebo in the garden. Overgrown hedgerows surrounded the flowerbeds, which were full of dahlias and gladioli, as well as monsoon weeds. Setting up the Grundig tape recorder and connecting the microphone, Fletcher explained how it worked.

'What this does is focus individual sounds. Depending on where I point it, the microphone picks up and amplifies a specific birdcall that gets recorded on the tape. After that, I can replay it and lure the bird to come closer,' he said, as Tenzing and Wongchuk watched with serious, studious eyes.

After a few moments, they heard a sharp chirping call from a hedge on the other side of a flowerbed. Fletcher held up one hand to signal silence. Putting on his headphones, he directed the microphone towards the call and pressed a button on the tape recorder. The sound was crisp and clear in the headphones—*Que Pee!... Que Pee!... Que Pee!* Between each call was an interval of five or six seconds and Fletcher waited until he had recorded six of the bird's shrill cries.

The Crown Prince was holding his daughter's hand and held up a finger to his lips, signalling for her to be quiet. After rewinding the tape, Fletcher took off the headphones and pressed the Play button. The whole process was much easier here than it had been with Thupten in the Neora Valley.

On the second call, there was a rustling movement in the hedge and moments later a brown bird emerged, darting about aggressively. Its dark eyes, ringed with white, looked indignant. Flying up onto a hydrangea bush, the bird cocked its head so its crescent-shaped beak was clearly visible. When the recording had finished, Fletcher rewound it and played back the call once more. This time there was a response from the other side of the hedge, a muted *churr* of a female. The babbler on the rosebush gave a loud *Que Pee!* and flew off to reassure his mate.

Everyone in the group applauded, as Fletcher took out his copy of *The Birds of Sikkim*, and flipped through the pages until he came to a coloured plate on which he showed them a couple of different scimitar babblers.

The Prince's sons smiled and nodded. Just then another bird called, from the trees along the edge of the garden. There were four distinct notes, *Cu coo Cu coo!*

'I recognize that call,' said Colonel Norton. 'The Indian Cuckoo.'

Fletcher repeated the recording process but by the time he finished, the bird had flown away. After they listened to the call played back, Fletcher explained how Salim Ali reported that tea planters interpret the cuckoo's cry as *O-range Pe-koe!*

The Colonel added, 'Others say it means *One more bot-tle!*'

After the performance, they all retreated to the veranda for coffee and the children ducked out of sight indoors.

'Thank you so much,' said the Crown Prince. 'I'm sure this is something my children won't forget. I hope you make a collection of birdcalls from Sikkim, and please send me a copy.'

Fletcher nodded. 'I'll do that.'

'It's good you're not shooting and collecting specimens, like most ornithologists,' the Prince continued. 'As Buddhists we believe that all life is sacred and killing is taboo, even in the name of science.'

Before the coffee arrived, one of the palace attendants came out and leaned down to speak in the Prince's ear.

'If you'll excuse me, please,' he said, getting to his feet. 'His Majesty, my father, has asked to see me upstairs.'

After the Maharaj Kumar left, two servants brought around cups of coffee on a tray, along with plates of cake and biscuits. Turning to the Englishman who was seated beside him, Fletcher asked. 'How long have you been in India?'

'Half a century,' said Colonel Norton.

'Do you live in Gangtok?'

'No, Kalimpong mostly,' he said. 'I'm retired, of course, but I help recruit young men for the Gurkha regiments of the British Army.'

'From around here?'

'Not so much in Sikkim but in the hill districts of West Bengal. A number of Magars and Gurungs have settled near Darjeeling and Kalimpong, also Rais and Limbus. Those are the ethnic groups we select from. Of course, our main recruitment centres are in Pokhara and Kathmandu, but I keep an eye out for promising prospects in these parts.'

'Were you an officer in a Gurkha regiment?' he asked.

'The Fourth Gurkha Rifles, which used to be known as the Prince of Wales's own Fourth Gurkhas. I had the honour of commanding the regiment before I retired.' Colonel Norton was eyeing the bruise above Fletcher's eye. 'Don't mind me asking, but how is that knock on your head?'

'Much better, thanks.'

'Bloody shame. Did the driver lose control?' Norton asked. 'So many of them drive too fast, but accidents usually occur when they're going downhill.'

'It all happened so quickly, I really can't remember much,' said Fletcher.

'Of course,' said the Colonel. 'I drove up the day after it happened and saw the spot. Odd place for a vehicle to go over....'

He left the thought unfinished, plucking at the ends of his furled moustache.

'What brings you to Gangtok?' Fletcher asked.

'The Maharaj Kumar has asked me to advise him on the reorganization of the Sikkim Guards. It's a bit of a mess right now, not much training or discipline. He wants to make them more of a fighting force,' said the Colonel.

'Who would they fight against?' Fletcher asked.

'Good question,' said Norton, with a shrug. 'Perhaps you should ask your friend, Captain Afridi.'

'Do you know him?' Fletcher asked.

'Not exactly,' said the Colonel. 'I've met him several times in Kalimpong. He's always been a bit standoffish. I suppose it's because he's with Military Intelligence. One of their rising stars!'

'Really?' Fletcher responded.

'Though he's still a junior officer, even the generals listen to him. Very few people know the Indian Himalayas as well as him. Afridi is a rare bird. There aren't many Muslims in India's intelligence services.'

'How do you know all this?' Fletcher asked in surprise.

'Gossip,' said the Colonel with a wave of his hand.

◆

They met again the next evening at the Residency, which was also known as the Burra Kothi, or big house. It stood on a hill overlooking the palace and its architecture was more like the government buildings in Kalimpong. Thunder and lightning threatened from the higher mountains but there was no rain.

'Hello, again,' said the Colonel, raising his glass. He had changed into a tweed jacket with a regimental tie. Instead of shorts he wore grey flannels that bagged at the knees. Fletcher guessed he was in his late seventies, but active for his age. Across the room, the Political Officer was holding forth on the merits of Nehru's latest Five-year Plan, surrounded by a group of guests who didn't seem to care at all about 'infrastructure development' and 'industrial capacities'.

The Colonel leaned towards Fletcher and lowered his voice. 'Poor bugger,' he said. 'This is not a plum posting for the ICS. Being the PO in Sikkim is like overseeing a small municipality. Bit of a backwater. He'd rather be prowling the halls of power in New Delhi but, from what I've heard, he botched a posting in Kashmir and they've sent him here for six months until he retires.'

Fletcher and the Colonel chatted for a while longer, mostly about the political situation in Sikkim. Norton claimed that the palace was trying to build up sympathies within the international community but the Indian government would block any attempts at gaining membership to the UN. Just as he was saying this, the Crown Prince and his fiancée arrived. Though most of the guests turned to greet them, the PO kept expounding his theories on 'domestic expenditure and gross national product,' until he pivoted dramatically and hailed the Maharaj Kumar with exaggerated enthusiasm.

'Do you think the Crown Prince is marrying Hope Cooke because he believes it will make the United States sympathetic to his situation?' Fletcher asked.

The Colonel raised an eyebrow with an amused expression and scoffed, 'That's very cynical of you, Mr Swift!'

'Well, I don't really know what's going on....' Fletcher backtracked.

'No, I think they're very much in love,' said Colonel Norton. 'But, of course, in any royal marriage there are considerations that must be taken into account, which have nothing to do with romance. A lot of people are opposed, the Indians primarily, but also his sisters, Coocoola in particular. The Maharaj Kumar's first wife was Tibetan and the Princess feels that if he wants to remarry it would be better to find a match from amongst their own people. There's a lot of superstition in the court. Some believe the Namgyal dynasty is cursed. The air crash that killed the Maharaj Kumar's brother. The Chogyal's ill health. And the death of the Crown Prince's first wife. It's all on account of evil omens, if you believe in that sort of thing.'

By now there were about thirty guests in the room, which was filled with a general hum of conversation. Unlike at the palace party, there was no music or dancing, and Fletcher noticed that the drinks were much weaker. When he mentioned this to the Colonel, the old man nodded.

'The PO is a chotta peg sort of man, stingy with his drinks and penny-pinching when it comes to yielding power,' said the Colonel before his face suddenly contorted in a look of alarm. 'Good God! Look who's arrived!'

Fletcher heard a woman's voice even before he turned around, a sharp, nasal accent that conveyed as much officious disdain as the PO's polished vowels and varnished consonants.

'Her Exalted Eminence the Kazini Saheba of Chakung,' said Colonel Norton under his breath, with a note of exasperation.

After making her entrance, the Kazini approached the PO, who greeted her indulgently, though they were too far away for Fletcher to hear what was said. The Kazi was several inches shorter than his wife, a wizened old man in a brocade green and gold kho and a matching hat on his head. The Kazini was also wearing a silk kho but a deep ochre colour with a yellow blouse. Draped over her shoulders was a fur stole that looked like a fox skin. She had on a necklace of amber beads and her face was powdered snow white.

As he watched her move about the room, Fletcher was aware of the political ripples she caused in the gathering, as some of the guests moved towards her, while others retreated. She greeted the Maharaj Kumar and Hope Cooke with an overly dramatic gesture of affection, throwing out both arms as if she was going to embrace the two of them together but then retracting her limbs before making contact.

'What a darling couple you make!' Fletcher heard her cry out. 'Perfect for the cover of *Life* magazine.'

Hope's response was inaudible but the Maharaj Kumar made a remark that perhaps their photograph might appear in the *Himalayan Observer* instead.

Colonel Norton muttered, 'Intolerable woman! The minute he turns around, she'll stab him in the back.'

A few minutes later, however, the Kazini spotted them. Brushing aside the other guests, she made a beeline for Fletcher.

'Poor Mr Swift!' she cried, as if they'd known each other for years. 'Your first trip to Gangtok and it was almost your last!'

She handed her ivory cigarette holder to her husband, who was following in her wake. As Fletcher shook her limp hand, the Kazi took out a packet of cigarettes and fitted one into the holder.

'Where is your fellow survivor?' she asked.

'Captain Afridi hasn't arrived yet,' said Colonel Norton.

There was a pause as the Kazini took the holder then let the Kazi light her cigarette. She then waved it about like a wand, as if casting a noxious spell.

'Oh, Colonel Norton. Fancy meeting you here! We don't see enough of each other in Kalimpong, do we?' Her voice changed when she spoke to him, going up a register and the accent becoming even more affected than before.

'Good evening, ma'am,' the Colonel said curtly.

'Still chasing Gurkha boys, trying to sharpen their khukris?' she asked, then turned to Fletcher who was studying her fur stole. 'Be careful, young man, Colonel Norton has a glad eye that would make Oscar Wilde blush.'

The Colonel seemed immune to her comments and didn't respond. Meanwhile, the Kazini kept her green eyes fixed on Fletcher. Her large-rimmed glasses and her painted eyebrows gave her a look of alarm.

'Excuse me...' said Fletcher, cautiously. 'Your fur stole.... Is that what I think it is?'

'And what do you *think it is*?' she snapped. The smouldering tip of her cigarette was only a few inches from his face, while the fingers on her left hand brushed the striped tail that dangled over her bosom.

'A red panda?' Fletcher asked.

'I prefer to call it a firefox,' she huffed.

'Isn't it an endangered species?' said Fletcher.

'All of us are,' she said, turning away brusquely, as if taking offence.

'Good riddance,' muttered the Colonel.

The rest of the evening went by slowly and painfully, as the Kazini held forth while the PO humoured her and most of the guests tried to keep out of her way. As soon as the buffet dinner was served and they finished eating, everyone rushed to depart. Fletcher was surprised that Afridi hadn't shown up. He was prepared to walk back to his guesthouse, but Colonel Norton offered him a ride in his jeep. Dropping him off, he pointed to the building next to the petrol pump, immediately behind where Fletcher was staying.

'Beware!' said Colonel Norton. 'The Kazi and Kazini have a flat next door.'

Minutes later, after Fletcher was safely inside his room, he heard them arrive. Through a gap in the curtains, he saw the Kazini march into the building with two young men at her heels. The Kazi followed, his shoulders stooped. Lights came on inside the ground floor of the building and Fletcher could see figures moving about, as chairs were drawn up. The Kazini's profile appeared in a window, about thirty yards away.

Fletcher quickly set up the Grundig on the dressing table and turned off the lights, then opened his window. After replacing the tape he had used that morning with a fresh reel, he threaded it through the guides on the machine. Attaching the parabolic microphone, he put on his headphones and pressed Record. Seconds later, he could hear the grating sound of the Kazini's voice as she lectured the two young men in a combination of English and broken Hindi.

21

Blue-winged Laughingthrush

Trochalopteron squamatum

Laughingthrushes are one of the most common families of birds in the Himalayas, with more than fifteen species found in different regions. The blue-winged laughingthrush, as its name suggests, has a thin azure band on its outer wing. The rest of this bird is a mottled bronze or brown with a black eyebrow and tail. Not as gregarious as other laughingthrushes, it is usually found in small parties. Call is a high-pitched whistle.

The trail from Gangtok to Lachen and Yumthang dropped down into the Teesta Valley, heading north. There was no motor road and this route was used mostly by shepherds and yak herders who migrated up to the high pastures in summer. With the help of Thupten's cousin in the Sikkim Forest Department, Fletcher had been able to hire three mules to carry his gear and supplies. It was about a forty-mile trek to Chungthang, after which he would need to hire yaks to take him further on up. Altogether, he planned to spend a month exploring the upper reaches of the valleys and he had purchased rice and flour, as well as lentils and other basic foodstuffs. Afridi had warned him that there would be little more than a forest rest house at Lachen and beyond that, nothing at all. One of his purchases was a canvas tent with bamboo poles, which made up most of the load for one mule.

Though he had been tempted to spend another week in Gangtok before setting out, Fletcher was glad to get moving and leave civilization behind. As he and the muleteer set off at dawn with the line of pack animals, it felt as if he was heading into uncharted terrain. Soon enough they were out of earshot of the town. Though it wasn't raining, the mist enclosed them and he could see only ten to fifteen feet ahead. The path was about four feet wide and slippery, with slick rocks and clay. He kept a lookout for birds and, after hearing the ascending notes of a fluting whistle, he spotted a laughingthrush on a branch above him. In Gangtok he'd identified several other species, including the white-throated, spotted, striated, and grey-sided, but this one was different and with his binoculars, he was able to see the blue streak on its wing, though the light was poor.

The first three days of trekking passed through lower valleys, where it was warm and humid. It rained much of the time and they covered about twelve miles a day, spending the first night in a village and the next two in shepherd's huts, which were crude shelters full of dung and mud. The muleteer, Lakhpa, was a resourceful man and he made the huts as habitable as possible, getting a fire burning and cooking their evening meal. Though he spoke no English or Hindi, Lakhpa was able to communicate through gestures and Fletcher was happy enough to be away from conversation, after all of the socializing in Kalimpong and Gangtok.

His finger was still in a splint but the cut on his forehead had healed. By the time they reached Chungthang at the end of the fourth day, his body was used to the rhythm of the journey and he looked forward to climbing higher into the mountains. With Lakhpa's help, he found a yak herder who was willing to take him on to Lachen. Though the herdsman, Lobsang, was a rougher character than Lakhpa, he was pleasant enough and knew the route well. The yaks were ponderous, stubborn creatures with sharp horns but, most of the time, they were docile and followed Lobsang's commands. One night was spent in a stone shelter, over which they rigged a tarpaulin for a roof. The rain blew in from the sides and Fletcher didn't get much sleep but in the morning he woke up to clear skies for the first time. Climbing towards Lachen, they left most of the leeches behind, though there was a moment of panic when a green pit viper uncoiled itself from a branch overhead and dropped onto Fletcher's rucksack. Fortunately, he was able to shrug it off quickly and the snake escaped into the weeds at the side of the path.

Lachen was situated in a high valley at an altitude of 9,000 feet, amidst a thick forest of giant oaks, hemlocks and firs. It was a lonely place and they arrived late in the afternoon on the sixth day out of Gangtok. A cluster of wooden huts bordered the path, with a few children peering out from between gaps in the rough-hewn boards. The forest rest house lay on a knoll above, a compact building with two bare rooms and an outhouse where the forest guards lived. They had received word that Fletcher was coming and had swept the floors and cleared most of the spider webs from the rafters. Lobsang joined the guards in their quarters, while the yaks grazed on the front lawn. In the evening they brought Fletcher a heaped plate of rice and dal, his standard meal. As daylight faded, the clouds lifted and he could see snow peaks at the head of the valley.

Lighting a candle, he wrote up his notes for the day, which included a brief summary of the trek and descriptions of the birds he'd seen along the way. Unlike the months he'd spent in Bharatpur, observing ducks and geese on the water, here in the mountains, the landscape and ecology was constantly changing as he passed through several different altitudinal zones in the course of a single day. The variety of species was much greater than it had been on the plains, from a common merganser—the only duck he'd seen along the Teesta—to the bright sunbirds and red-billed leiothrix higher up. There were many birds he could not identify on first sight and he poured over his field guides by candlelight.

Fletcher's plan was to stay a couple of days in Lachen and make this his base, from where he could trek up into the higher valleys. The border lay along the ridgeline of high mountains to the north, no more than ten or twelve miles away. As Afridi had explained, pastoralists from Tibet often brought their herds over the high passes at this time of year and there was no one to check their coming and going. Other than the two forest guards, the government of Sikkim had no officials posted here. The Indian Army sent occasional patrols but mostly the region was wild and untouched by any political or military presence.

As he fell asleep, his first night at Lachen, Fletcher felt he had reached a point where he could rely only on his instincts. All of Sullivan's instructions and Afridi's advice was useless now. He had no maps, no dossiers, no means of communication and certainly no contacts. In the cold darkness of the empty room he felt he was staring into a void, even after he shut his eyes.

◆

Before departing from Gangtok, Fletcher had met with Afridi several times at the White Hall Club, a colonial building, near the Sikkim Guard's barracks, which had been outfitted with a bar and a badminton court. They had discussed Fletcher's plans in detail. At one point, he had asked why Afridi himself hadn't explored this region and the Captain explained that his presence would immediately signal that the Indian military was scouting for something. He was too well known in Sikkim and the Chinese would find out soon enough about his activities near the border. Fletcher's cover as an ornithologist gave him the freedom to wander about with his binoculars and camera, ostensibly searching for birds but at the same time, keeping a lookout for suspicious activity.

As always, their conversations were governed by a level of caution on both sides, as each man withheld facts and revealed only necessary details. Though he would not give Fletcher a survey map of the area, Afridi had shared a good deal of information on the terrain above Yumthang, including the location of two high passes into Tibet that were seldom used but navigable at this time of year. For his part, Fletcher had reported on some of the conversations he'd had in Gangtok but didn't tell Afridi that he had recorded the Kazini on the night of the PO's party.

By now, it was mid-July and the snow had retreated well above the tree line. Though he was impatient to explore the areas along the border, Fletcher continued to play the role of a researcher doing his fieldwork. He was now at an altitude where *Phasianidae* were more plentiful. So far, he had seen plenty of kalij pheasant, as well as common hill partridges but in the forests near Lachen, he discovered the monal or impeyan pheasant, a flamboyant bird with iridescent blue, violet, green, and russet plumage. The monals crowed loudly at dawn just above the forest rest house and, when he went in search of them, exploded from the bushes with shrill cries of alarm before sailing down the hill on fixed wings.

Lobsang was happy to transport his tent and equipment to higher camps, where Fletcher spent three or four days exploring one valley after the other. It was wild country and lonely work but he enjoyed it.

The only company he had were the occasional shepherds grazing their flocks on the high summer pastures. Three weeks went by quickly, as he trekked through the rhododendron forests of Yumthang. The clusters of trumpet-shaped flowers were different shades of pink and lavender, while a smaller yellow rhododendron grew close to the ground. At several places he set up his mist nets and caught finches and accentors that he held in his hands, examining their feathers, making notes and comparing the birds to their descriptions in the field guides. It was always with a sense of pleasure that he released the captives and watched them fly away. He had removed the splint from his finger by now and it was gradually regaining its flexibility.

Wild sheep, known as bharal, roamed the upper slopes of the valleys. Some of them were so tame they came sniffing at the flaps of his tent. Marmots burrowed amongst the rocks and called out their shrill alarms as he walked by. One day, Fletcher climbed a rib of moraine overlooking a small glacier and found what looked like a disused path. At places the trail vanished and then reappeared as he followed it up to the crest of the ridge. After three hours of strenuous trekking, he stood on a snow-covered pass that looked into the Chumbi Valley. Far below him he could see a motor road with Chinese trucks driving back and forth, trailing plumes of dust. Snow peaks stood on either side and he made a point of deliberately stepping across into Tibet, wondering if anyone would find the footprints he left in the snow.

One day, in another remote valley, he was scanning the slopes for snow partridges, which had been calling, when he saw a blurred movement amongst the rocks. A herd of bharal was grazing nearby and he thought it was one of the wild ewes at first. But focussing his binoculars, he caught sight of a snow leopard stalking the sheep. For half an hour, he watched the hunt, as the predator moved from rock to rock, creeping within range. Finally, the big cat, with its ghostly pelage, raced from cover and chased the sheep down a steep cliff, bounding after them as they scattered across the vertical terrain. Just when Fletcher thought they had escaped, one of the bharal doubled back and the leopard lunged, catching it by the throat.

The kill was only a couple hundred yards away and Fletcher watched as the leopard fed for an hour or so. Eventually it dragged the carcass under the shelter of a rock before disappearing up the slope. Curious to take a look at the remains, he climbed to the spot and found the dead bharal. Its hind leg had been eaten to the bone. Unsheathing his knife, he cut a foreleg away at the shoulder and carried the meat back with him. That evening, and for several days afterwards, his tedious diet of lentils and rice was supplemented by wild mutton.

All this time, Fletcher kept a lookout for any sign of human beings but beyond the stray shepherds and a few yak herders, the area seemed desolate and deserted. At a number of places, he came upon cairns, some of them stacked with mani stones on which Tibetan verses had been carved. The piles of rock seemed to have been there forever, longer than the mountains themselves. In one of the valleys he discovered ruins of stone huts but these too looked as if they had been abandoned centuries ago. Scouring the mountains for any signs of life, he found a few caves, though none of them were inhabited. One night, he got stranded by a hailstorm, with thunder and lightning. Taking shelter in the lee of a giant boulder that looked as if it was about to break loose and hurtle down the hill, he spent the night awake, huddled in his anorak, both arms hugging his knees.

The cold was brutal and he imagined this must be what Afridi experienced while climbing high mountains, the solitude and darkness so complete that it felt as if the world had come to an end. At times like this, disturbing thoughts circled in his mind. He wondered if Afridi was using him as a decoy to lure the Khampas out of hiding. Fletcher speculated too about Jack Sullivan's motives and whether the whole operation wasn't meant to accomplish something else altogether, a ploy to recruit Afridi perhaps, or to undercut India's political machinations in Sikkim. He felt like a pawn that had escaped from the predictable grid of squares on a chessboard.

Sitting by a campfire in the evenings, with juniper smoke in his eyes, he thought mostly of Kesang, imagining her at home in Kalimpong, listening to music or laughing with her friends, sitting with Dr Mukherjee and feeding green chillies to the parakeet. He also imagined her in bed with Afridi, making love to him with the same unrestrained passion that he remembered from their last evening together. He felt a knot of jealousy tightening somewhere below his ribs. He thought of Sage too, remembering their weekend in bed several years ago and the tumult of emotions that she had aroused. Alone in the mountains, he wondered if he would ever experience those sensations again.

The only way that he kept track of the days and weeks that passed were the entries in his journal, which he updated every evening. On 12 August 1962, Fletcher made a note:

Three days trek from Lachen, I entered a broad valley leading up to Pauhunri peak, which straddles the border. The mountain rises above Khangchung Tso, a large lake that fills the upper end of the valley, fed by a glacier that we crossed. It is as desolate and empty a place as I have seen anywhere in Sikkim. Lobsang had difficulty getting his yaks over the pass from Yumthang. It didn't look as if anyone had taken this route in recent years. We had to cut our way through the bamboo and rhododendrons until we reached the tree line.

Yesterday, I was lucky to come upon a flock of blood pheasant in a grove of birches at about 12,000 feet. At first I saw a female, which is a dull moss-colored bird and I wasn't sure what it was but then two males appeared in front of me in full regalia. Their silver and grey feathers were streaked with red and green and their faces tinged a bright scarlet.

The valley that extends southeast from Khangchung Tso is bounded on all sides by serrated ridges that rise above 20,000 feet. Pauhunri is the highest peak in this range, 23,000 plus, a huge, untidy mass of snow and ice. There is one high pass at the top of a lateral valley, about a day's trek from the lake. Known as Kallis Col, it is named after Alexander Kallis, a Scottish mountaineer who was the first to climb Pauhunri in 1911. Lobsang will leave me in the valley below the Col for a week and retreat to lower altitudes, where grazing is better along the lakeshore, returning on the seventh day.

What he didn't write in his journal was that Afridi had told him that the pass and valley were often used by Tibetan guerrilla fighters. Kallis Col was one of the most difficult but direct routes into Tibet, avoiding most of the Chumbi Valley. Fletcher had decided that if he had no luck in the next few days, he would return to Gangtok empty-handed. His supplies were almost depleted.

After trudging up the open, windswept valley for several hours, they came to a swift stream flowing down from a notch in the cliffs. The water was the chalky blue colour of glacial melt and Fletcher decided to follow it up to its source. Beyond the narrow aperture in the cliffs, they entered a canyon and climbed over a rock fall that the yaks had difficulty negotiating. Eventually the animals waded into the icy stream and made their way up the channel, while Lobsang threw stones in their direction to keep them moving. Within an hour the valley opened out into an expansive cirque, where the glacier must have extended centuries ago. The ice had retreated at least two miles upstream leaving a giant amphitheatre of loose debris amidst which were patches of green though the landscape was mostly dull brown and grey. Above the glacier, at the far end of the cirque, Fletcher could see a dip in the ridge and a broad saddle covered in snow—Kallis Col.

Lobsang seemed to disapprove of the place and gestured for Fletcher to turn back, waving his arms in the direction of the glacier and shaking his head. Nevertheless, it seemed safe enough. They found a strip of grass and wildflowers next to the stream, sheltered by boulders. The surrounding cliffs were at least three quarters of a mile away on either side, so there was no danger of falling rocks or avalanches. As Lobsang helped set up the tent, before heading off in the early afternoon, there seemed to be no one else around. Clouds obscured the highest peaks and a drizzle of rain fell until dusk, when the light changed abruptly and Fletcher could see a few scarred pinnacles catching the sunset and turning gold.

On their way up, they had collected juniper branches and a gunnysack of dried yak dung, so he had enough fuel for several nights in camp, though he would have to use it sparingly. Lighting a fire, he made some tea and thought about whether to cook a meal or not. He wasn't hungry and wondered whether the altitude had robbed him of his appetite. Today he would rest and tomorrow he planned to explore farther up near the glacier. Lobsang had given him a bag of tsampa, roasted barley flour, that he could make into a paste, mixed with his tea.

As he sat and drank the hot, sweet brew, Fletcher was convinced that his search would end in failure. His mission, as Sullivan had explained, was simply to explore and observe the areas near the border to gauge a growing Chinese presence. Most of that information he had gathered in Gangtok, particularly through his conversations with Afridi. But Fletcher felt that he also needed to locate the tranche of antiquities, which the CIA hoped to buy. The fact that Sullivan had lied and never mentioned that part of the conspiracy made him even more determined to uncover the truth. If nothing else, it would help him gain Afridi's trust. By cultivating his relationship with a military intelligence officer, he would be able to deliver the kind of intel that Sullivan sought. Though he recognized that Afridi would never agree to work for the CIA, there was always the possibility of sharing information.

A herd of wild sheep was grazing at the foot of the cliffs to the north and Fletcher could see them begin to climb the rocks as shadows lengthened. Leaping from ledge to ledge, the animals sought shelter in the perpendicular expanse of stone that rose a thousand feet or more into the clouds. He watched them through his binoculars, their movements choreographed by instincts of survival.

Lifting the aluminium cup to his lips and finishing the dregs of his tea, Fletcher suddenly heard a sharp report, like a hammer striking a rock. He knew immediately that it was a gunshot, a single round fired from a high-powered rifle. The sound reverberated from one side of the valley to the other like a clap of thunder. At the same moment, he saw one of the wild rams lose its footing and stagger backwards off the rock face, tumbling lifeless to the ground.

22

Hodgson's Grandala

Grandala coelicolor

The male of this species is a bright, indigo blue. The female has more subdued plumage, mostly brown with a touch of blue on the rump. About the size of a small thrush, it lives at extremely high altitudes, from 14,000 to 17,000 feet. Grandalas are usually found in small flocks though they sometimes congregate in much larger numbers. According to one report, cited by Salim Ali, approximately 1,000 birds were seen above Lachen, Sikkim, flying together in a swarm.

The following morning, Fletcher was preparing a pot of cracked wheat porridge boiled with powdered milk and sugar for breakfast, when he noticed two men approaching. They looked as if they might have stepped out of another age, several centuries ago. Both of them were wearing rough-spun woollen coats of a dull brown hue. These were worn with one loose sleeve, exposing their right arms and shoulders. Under this, they had on vests and tunics, all of which were gathered at the waist with braided ropes of yak hair. The coats reached to their knees, beneath which they had on woollen trousers, as coarse as burlap, and felt boots with hard leather soles. Their long tresses were braided and coiled about their heads. Both men were unshaven though their facial hair was sparse—a few strands of chin-whiskers and thin, unruly moustaches that drooped over cracked lips. Their features were chapped and weathered like rawhide.

Fletcher assumed they must be the hunters who had shot the bharal last evening. Raising a hand in greeting, he received no response, as the two men strode up to him with expressions of arrogant aggression. The only things about them that seemed part of the twentieth century were the .303 rifles slung across their shoulders. They were taller and more strongly built than most of the shepherds and yak herders he'd met so far.

Without saying a word, one of the men stepped around the burning hearth and threw open the tent-flap. Fletcher knew better than to try and stop him but he was glad that the Beretta was in the pocket of his anorak. The second man also went across to the tent and began rummaging through the bags of supplies. After three weeks in the field, not much was left but they picked up a depleted sack of rice and helped themselves to a couple tins of butter, as well as a bottle of sugar.

'What are you doing?' Fletcher said, speaking English though he doubted the men would understand.

One of them gave him a surly look and gestured with two fingers raised to his mouth, demanding cigarettes.

'No, I don't have any.' Fletcher shook his head.

The other man took the rifle off his shoulder and casually pointed it at him. Fletcher tried not to react, holding perfectly still. After a minute or more the weapon was lowered and the man slung it back over his other shoulder as he picked up an almost empty bag of flour, along with the rice. Turning abruptly, the two men set off in the direction from which they'd come.

There was nothing subtle or furtive about the robbery and the thieves walked away casually, without looking back, as if they feared no reprisal. After finishing his breakfast, before it went cold, Fletcher examined what was left of his supplies. A handful of lentils remained and the cloth pouch full of tsampa that Lobsang had given him. Other than that, there were some tea leaves and a few ounces of salt. Fletcher realized that the porridge he had just eaten would probably be his last full meal until he returned to Lachen, if he got back alive. The encounter with the Khampas made him wonder if he should pack up and head out of the valley, but there was no way that he could carry his gear and Lobsang would only return in another six days.

Meanwhile, a flock of grandalas seemed to have adopted him. They had arrived outside his tent before he got up this morning and surprised him with their bright blue feathers, the minute he stepped outside. He had tried to photograph the restless birds but they wouldn't hold still, moving about constantly though never flying away. Even while the two Khampas were busy looting his supplies, the grandalas had flitted about, perching on the guy ropes of the tent for a brief moment, before opening their wings and settling on a rock nearby.

Fletcher knew that he was in danger and there was no reason why these men wouldn't return later and cut his throat. He had no idea if they were guerrilla fighters or just ordinary bandits. Without food, there was no point in remaining there. The safest option was to wait until dark and then make an escape, taking whatever he could and abandoning the rest.

Before leaving, however, Fletcher was determined to see if he could get a look at the men's camp and take some photographs. Having watched the two Khampas walk back up the valley and disappear into the rocks to the west of the glacier, he had a good sense of where they were camped. If he climbed onto a shelf of moraine on the opposite side of the glacier, he guessed it would give him a clear view of the upper end of the cirque.

Packing his camera and whatever valuables he had into his rucksack, he draped the binoculars around his neck. The pistol remained in his pocket. In case he was being observed, Fletcher crossed the shallow current of melt water, leaping from rock to rock, then set off downstream for a ways, until he came to a gulley heading the other direction, back up into the higher moraine. Keeping his head down, he moved cautiously. The gulley soon narrowed into a trench, about ten feet deep and twelve feet across. At places he had to scramble over loose scree or detour around boulders but after about an hour of walking, he felt that he must be near the snout of the glacier. By now the moraine rose up in a series of eroded ridges radiating down from the eastern wall of the circular valley.

Marmots shrieked at him from their burrows and a bearded vulture soared overhead but, other than that, there were no signs of life. The rocks were decorated with lichens but hardly any grass or plants that he could see, a wasteland of packed earth and talus. Above him, to the north, he could just make out the snow-covered Kellas Col that led into Tibet. On either side were imposing walls of rock and snowfields that stretched towards the clouds.

Scaling a 45-degree slope of shale and ice he reached a level patch of ground overlooking the glacier. Fletcher crawled across the frozen surface to a heap of rocks that provided some cover. At over 16,000 feet the air was thin and the exertion made him gasp for breath. Once he had settled into position, he discovered that he had climbed higher than planned, though it gave him a perfect vantage point from which to see the upper reaches of the valley. The pass was about 200 yards above him and a quarter mile to his right. A few rocks protruded from the snow but it was mostly a smooth white surface, like a ski slope. The glacier was covered with rocks and dirt. At places, where crevasses had opened up, he could see evidence of the frozen core. Along the far edge was the jagged outline of a bergschrund where the ice had separated from the rocks. The slopes of the higher ridges were caked with fresh snow.

As he traced the line of descent from Kellas Col, Fletcher could see where the route funnelled down into a boulder field that levelled out onto a sparse meadow. Through his binoculars, he caught sight of two tents of black woollen fabric pitched over rough stonewalls. Three yaks were grazing a short distance away. Removing his camera from the pack, he attached an 80-300 mm zoom lens. The light was still good, though the sky was overcast, and he was able to take photographs that showed the location of the camp, across the glacier, about three quarters of a mile away. With his binoculars, he could just make out several figures moving around and estimated that there must be four to five men in the camp.

It was now well past noon and a breeze had picked up. He could see spindrift blowing across the col. Fletcher waited for a few more minutes, though he could feel the cold seeping through his layered clothes. Then, just as he was about to leave, two figures appeared on the crest of the pass. Silhouetted against the white snow, they were as black as the line of yaks that followed them. Through the binoculars, he could see that the pack animals were heavily laden, sinking into the snow up to their flanks. Within five minutes the entire party came into view. Most of the men were on foot, though he could make out the silhouette of a rider on one of the yaks. Fletcher counted eleven pack animals and fifteen men, all of whom were armed. Steadying his camera on the rocks, he took a couple more photographs as they slowly worked their way down the slope. Moments later, he heard shouts from the camp and answering cries from the group above, as they caught sight of each other.

The caravan of yaks was making slow progress as the men from the camp headed up to meet them, climbing through the boulder field to the snowline. It was like watching a procession of ants. Even from a distance, Fletcher could feel his eyes burning from the glare off the snow. After the first few shouts, there was silence.

Half an hour later, when the caravan had descended two thirds of the way down, almost level with the shelf on which Fletcher lay, he spotted more figures coming over the pass. These too were armed men but Fletcher could see, through his binoculars, that they were wearing bulky white uniforms. Though he couldn't be sure, they looked like PLA soldiers as they trooped down the slope, following the trail that the yaks had ploughed through the deep snow.

As if to confirm his suspicions, he heard a warning cry from the group below. Six of the armed escort separated from the yak train and took up defensive positions facing the soldiers coming down from above. He could only assume that the Chinese troops had crossed the border in pursuit. There were twenty-five of them, altogether. Fletcher got his camera ready.

The first shots were fired by the men below, as the line of yaks continued to blunder down the snowfield. Fletcher estimated that the distance between the two groups was four hundred yards. The soldiers had now fanned out, returning fire sporadically. The sharp reports of their rifles echoed across the glacier and between the cliffs on either side.

With a bird's eye view, Fletcher could see the skirmish play out. Three Chinese soldiers broke away and headed towards the glacier, trying to outflank the caravan. The rest advanced straight downhill in a disciplined formation, one group descending while the others provided covering fire. The Khampas were less organized, each of them picking his own ground. As his binoculars followed the action, Fletcher saw one of the Chinese soldiers fall forward and lie still. Two of the Khampas had been hit as well and one fighter was retreating, dragging his leg. A shot rang out and he collapsed in the snow. The wind had picked up, muffling the shouted commands and warning cries. Meanwhile, the line of yaks was now fifty yards from the boulder field.

Though he was safely hidden on the ledge where he lay, Fletcher could feel the tension of the conflict. It reminded him of when he was a boy, playing with toy soldiers on the rumpled sheets of his bed, a tableau of tiny figures arranged against a bleached field of white. The deep snow made the combatants move slowly as they floundered about, trying to find cover. Scanning the slope with his binoculars he saw streaks of blood staining the snow red. The crackle of gunfire continued as the Chinese troops held a clear advantage, positioned above the Khampa fighters.

Three more PLA soldiers had detached themselves and crossed over onto the glacier. Hidden by a ridge of moraine, they made their way down the rugged surface, avoiding crevasses. Fletcher could see that like the other detachment they were working themselves into position to attack the Khampas from behind. Meanwhile, the yak train had reached the camp and six more men had turned back, heading up to reinforce their compatriots.

Fletcher also noticed that two of the Khampas had set up a mortar just above the snow line. Seconds later he heard a dull thump as the shell was dropped into the tube and shot up through the air towards the Chinese. Its errant trajectory was marked by a feathery trail of smoke as the mortar round missed the PLA troops by several hundred yards, exploding on the slope above their position. At first, it seemed a futile, ineffectual response to the volleys of gunfire, until Fletcher noticed the snowfield begin to shift and heard a deep rumble.

Thousands of tons of deeply packed snow on the face of the mountain began to move, trigged by the mortar shell's detonation. An enormous slab of the frozen surface, almost 200 yards wide, sloughed off and slid downhill. At first it seemed as gentle as a white cloud blown by the wind but then, as a deep, booming roar silenced the gunfire, the terrifying force of the avalanche was unleashed.

Fletcher watched in horror and amazement as the soldiers and guerrilla fighters began to run for their lives. Instinctively, he took several photographs as the white wave descended, throwing up a mist of ice crystals. For most of the soldiers there was no escape as they struggled to run uphill towards the pass. Seconds later they disappeared beneath the avalanche. Several of the Khampas, too, were overwhelmed. The momentum was relentless, burying everything in its path, and Fletcher wondered if it would destroy the camp as well. Four Khampa fighters were sprinting through the boulder field as the avalanche sent blocks of ice tumbling after them, as well as a cloud of debris. The Chinese troops on the glacier were not spared. The cascading wall of snow engulfed them too before they could retreat.

Suddenly realizing his own vulnerability, Fletcher could see a dense cloud of frozen particles billowing up towards him. As he scrambled to his feet a powerful gust of air hit him and knocked him back to the ground. For several minutes, he struggled to breathe as the blast left a vacuum in its wake.

Though the avalanche had finally stopped, it took ten minutes for the air to clear. Fletcher was covered in powdery crystals that clung to his hair and beard, as well as his clothes. Brushing off the camera and binoculars he hoped there was no damage. On the other side of the valley, where the huge slab of snow had broken free of the slope, a broad delta of frozen debris extended halfway across the glacier. Two of the PLA soldiers had escaped and he spotted them climbing up to the pass. None of the others had survived.

The camp on the meadow was dusted with snow, as if a fresh flurry had just fallen. After wiping the eyepieces and lenses on his binoculars, Fletcher could see the yaks huddled together, their fur frosted white. He could count at least six or seven survivors. The avalanche had inundated most of the boulder field, within thirty yards of the tents, both of which had been uprooted by the blast. He guessed that the two men who had fired the mortar were now entombed beneath the icy shroud they had unfurled.

Having witnessed the devastation, Fletcher felt a hollow void in his chest. Taking a couple more photographs to record the aftermath, he turned away and headed back down towards camp, numbed by the cold but more by the unrelenting force of the avalanche. In his mind, he kept seeing the white tidal wave spilling down on the crouched figures until, each time, his thoughts went blank.

When he finally reached the stream, it was beginning to grow dark, though beams of sunlight illuminated the upper rim of the cirque through gaps in the clouds. As he was about to step across the stones protruding from the chalky current, Fletcher glanced up and saw the train of yaks a long way off, coming down the valley towards him.

Cautiously, he retreated to the shelter of a large rock nearby. It was about his height and at least ten feet wide, large enough to hide behind. The Khampas were leaving the valley before the Chinese could return. As he waited, he wondered if the yaks were carrying the antiquities Afridi had described.

Soon enough, the caravan came in view again. The men walked on either side, exhausted and distraught. Their rifles hung loosely from their shoulders and they looked like a procession of mourners, having lost more than half their number. Fletcher watched as they passed by his tent. The bundled loads the yaks carried looked heavy, though it was impossible to know what they contained. Two of the party were lamas, wearing ochre robes under woollen coats. Neither of them was armed. As he aimed the zoom lens at the ragged party, some of their faces came into focus. He recognized one of the men who had visited him that morning, though this time none of them stopped, moving on into the canyon below.

Two riders were mounted on one of the yaks. Through the viewfinder on his camera, Fletcher could make out a young woman, swaying with the animal's slow gait. Her shoulders were wrapped in a maroon blanket. Seated in front of her was a boy, no more than three or four years old. The woman had tucked the corners of the blanket around him to shield the child from the wind. He wore a fur hat that covered his ears, but his eyes and face were clearly visible, fixed in an impassive but attentive gaze as he surveyed the mountains on all sides.

The shutter release on the camera clicked three times, capturing their image in the fading light.

23

Tibetan Snowcock

Tetraogallus tibetanus

About the size of a well-fed chicken, this bird resembles an overgrown partridge in shape and behaviour. Generally grey and buff, it has a distinct collar of white and black across its breast, below which the belly is striated. Its beak is a bright colour. Found in flocks of four to five, it runs on the ground when alarmed or climbs atop a rock before gliding away on outspread wings. The call is a repeated chuk...chuk...chuk as well as a piercing whistle. When alarmed it emits a loud cackle. Found at altitudes above 13,000 feet.

After spending a restless night, disturbed by repeated visions of the avalanche and haunting images of the departing survivors with their train of yaks, Fletcher rose at dawn and packed whatever he could carry into his rucksack. He then wrapped the remains of his gear in the tent and cached it in a sheltered niche between two large rocks. Now that he was heading back to Gangtok, all he needed was the tea, salt, and tsampa that remained, as well as a box of matches and small cooking pot. His down mummy bag, camera, and binoculars made up the rest of the load. The tape recorder and parabolic microphone had been left behind at the forest rest house in Lachen, along with some of his clothes.

The sun had risen by the time he made his way out of the canyon. After scrambling over the fallen rocks, he felt warmer though the temperature was still below freezing. Entering the main valley, he headed back towards the lake, Khangchung Tso, and the glacier at the source of the Teesta River. Keeping a lookout for the Khampas and their yaks, he spotted them camped near the lakeshore. Instead of circling around

Khangchung Tso, he decided to cross the glacier, just as he and Lobsang had done on their way up. The river of ice creaked and groaned beneath him. At one point, his foot broke through a crevasse but he was able to avoid falling and eventually made it across.

Fletcher had no idea where Lobsang might be grazing his yaks. He had already decided that if he didn't find him, he would continue on his own. The first day, he covered two stages of the route and, just before nightfall, found a ring of stones built by shepherds as a windbreak. On a rise to the east were a few stunted junipers, about a quarter mile away. Though Fletcher was exhausted, he set off to gather firewood.

Approaching the junipers, he heard a chuckling cry and realized a covey of snowcocks was nearby. Having eaten nothing since the night before, he knew that he should put something in his stomach, though the altitude dampened his appetite. The snowcocks were on the other side of the rise. From their calls, he estimated they were about fifty yards away. Lowering himself to the ground, he crawled up the last few feet of the slope and positioned himself behind one of the twisted junipers, taking the Beretta out of his pocket. The muted calls meant the birds had not sensed any danger. He had seen a number of snowcock before, though most flocks had flown away before he had got within a hundred yards.

The wind tugged at the hood of his anorak while he waited and he could feel a chill in his limbs as the sun disappeared beyond the mountains to the west. The lower end of the lake was visible, turning from a bright blue green to the colour of lead. A few moments later, the first snowcock came into view, about thirty feet to his left. It strutted forward and glanced around, then pecked at something on the ground. Another bird appeared, the feathers on its breast a streaky white. This one moved closer until Fletcher could see the salmon pink beak and its eye gleaming like a topaz. His hand, which held the pistol, rested on the ground. Exhaling slowly, he squeezed the trigger.

The Beretta jumped in his grip, as if it had suddenly come to life, and the gunshot sounded much louder than it actually was in the surrounding silence of the high valley. Three snowcocks took to the air with frightened cries of alarm, fixing their wings and sailing off down the slope. The fourth was fluttering where it lay, as if pinned down by an invisible hand. Running forward, Fletcher picked it up and snapped the bird's neck. After collecting an armload of juniper twigs and dry branches, Fletcher retreated to his camp, carrying the bird by its feet.

The snowcock's raw flesh gave off a pungent, unpleasant odour as Fletcher gutted it and plucked the feathers. Once the fire was lit, he tilted two rocks together over the hearth to hold the bird in position, rotating the carcass with his hands until the skin was charred. Parts of the legs were underdone but the breast meat was edible. Sprinkled with salt it tasted like badly barbecued chicken.

◆

The higher altitudes were easier to navigate and traverse but as soon as Fletcher crossed over onto the southern slopes of the ridges south of Khangchung Tso and descended below the treeline, he found himself in an almost impenetrable jungle of rhododendrons and bamboo. Caught in a downpour, he lost his way at the upper end of the Yumthang Valley. Fletcher knew that it would be another two days of walking, at least, before he reached Lachen but as he floundered about searching for a path, it seemed he might be lost forever. Now that he was below 12,000 feet, the clouds and mist closed in around him and he had trouble getting his bearings, even with his compass and altimeter.

On the second night, he had been able to start a fire, though most of the wood was wet. He made some tea and mixed it with tsampa, the starchy gruel quelling his hunger. Fletcher's mummy bag had got wet in the rain and the goose down no longer provided much insulation, though the farther he descended the warmer it got. On the third night, he found himself in a deep valley, with a rushing stream below and rocky crags above, hemmed in on all sides by pleated folds of greenery.

He chose a small clearing for his camp, such as it was, and left his rucksack at the foot of a moss-draped oak to climb the slope and try to find dry wood for a fire. Though there was nothing left to eat, the warmth would be comforting and might help his clothes dry. Rhododendron wood burnt badly, with a lot of smoke, and though the lowest branches of the oaks and firs were too high for him to reach, he did manage to find a stand of yews about a hundred yards above the clearing. Just as he was about to start breaking dead branches, he heard the wailing cry of a child.

The sound had an eerie resonance, as if an infant had been abandoned in the forest and was calling out for its mother. After the cries were repeated several times, Fletcher guessed what it was and took the Beretta out of his pocket. Lying down in the damp cushion of needles beneath the yews, he waited, as the wailing continued, drawing closer.

A female tragopan appeared first, her brown feathers flecked with white spots. She crossed about twenty feet above Fletcher. He could have easily shot the hen but he knew a male was following her. Moments later, the cock appeared, stepping through an opaque curtain of mist and displaying his crimson breast feathers, beaded with white speckles like pearls. Though Fletcher had seen photographs of *Tragopan satyra* and he had examined a couple of skins in the collection at Cornell, observing this bird in the wild, less than fifteen feet away, made him hold his breath, afraid to make a sound. The pistol was nestled in his hand and all he needed to do was move the barrel a few inches to the left. The tragopan raised its beak and let out another piercing cry. As the bird descended and turned broadside, he could clearly see the black face and tufted feathers that looked like horns, as well as its bright blue chin. The rest of the pheasant was like a Fabergé egg, so ornately decorated that it looked as if it belonged in an art gallery rather than a Himalayan forest. After more than a minute, Fletcher exhaled and flipped the safety back on. Though he knew the bird would be good eating, he could not bring himself to fire the pistol. Seconds later, the tragopan ducked into a stand of bamboo and disappeared from sight, after one last cry.

The dry branches from the yews burnt well and Fletcher stretched out in his sleeping bag by the fire, exhausted and hungry, but strangely satisfied as only a birdwatcher can be, when the dead language of a Latin name finally comes to life.

Hours later, before first light, it began to drizzle. He tried to revive the fire but the few embers that remained were buried within the sodden ashes and the wet kindling refused to ignite. Stuffing the damp sleeping bag and the rest of his gear into the rucksack, he began the slow trudge downhill as a murky dawn seeped through the clouds. Within an hour, he came upon a trail that angled across the slope and he could see the prints of goats and sheep in the wet clay.

The shepherds, who were camped on a broad meadow, welcomed him cautiously, as if he were an apparition from the forest. They gave him salted tea laced with goat butter, along with a bowl of tsampa, which he devoured. The overpowering stench of goats and the mire of mud and dung that surrounded their hut was a squalid contrast to the high, arid valleys he'd left behind. Another six hours of walking brought him to the rest house at Lachen, where the guards greeted him with surprise.

The next day, as he departed, Fletcher left money for Lobsang, who was sure to return here after discovering that he had decamped. A muleteer from Lachen was happy to accompany him to Gangtok. Travelling downhill with a much lighter load they covered the distance in three and a half days. Even the rain let up for this stretch of the journey though there were still plenty of leeches. Along the way, they stopped at a hot spring where Fletcher soaked and bathed before changing into fresh clothes. By the time they marched past the Chogyal's palace and arrived at the Blue Poppy, he looked a little less haggard and not completely unwashed.

◆

It was now 18 August. He had been away for four and a half weeks. Gangtok seemed deserted. Almost everyone had left. Hope Cooke and her chaperones had gone back to New York, accompanied by the Crown Prince, who had travelled with them as far as London. Princess Coocoola was away on an extended shopping spree in Hong Kong. Colonel Norton, the Kazini and Kazi, were all in Kalimpong. And the PO was in Delhi for consultations with the government. Only Afridi remained and he listed the departures for Fletcher when they met that evening at the White Hall Club.

'So, what other news is there?' Fletcher asked.

'Marilyn Monroe died,' said Afridi, 'a little over a week ago. I heard about it on the BBC.'

'How did it happen?'

'An overdose of sleeping pills. Looks like suicide.'

Fletcher paused, then said, 'I never thought of you as a Hollywood fan.'

'I'm not,' Afridi replied. 'I just thought you might want to know.'

Once they'd got their drinks, Fletcher filled Afridi in on what had happened at Kellas Col, the Chinese troops pursuing the caravan of yaks, the gunfight, and the avalanche. Though he did not mention the photographs he'd taken, he described in detail how the pack animals were heavily loaded, as well as the woman and child he'd seen riding on one of the yaks.

'Do you know where they were headed?' Afridi asked.

'I have no idea, but I think they must be on their way here. Where else would they go?' said Fletcher.

'There is a longer route than the one you took, a permanent track used by shepherds that follows the river,' said Afridi, 'about a twelve day journey.'

'Do you think they're carrying the relics?' Fletcher asked.

'They could be,' said Afridi. 'If the Chinese were willing to pursue them across the border, they must have been transporting something valuable.'

'Maybe the Chinese will send more troops to catch them.'

'Probably not. It's one thing to intrude a short distance into Sikkim but it's another matter to cross over and set up camp for several days. I'll ask the CO to authorize a patrol to locate the caravan but also to scout the valleys around Khangchung Tso and Pauhunri. We'll find out soon enough what's going on.'

'The Khampas weren't particularly friendly,' said Fletcher.

'I'd be surprised if they were,' Afridi responded. 'They have plenty of reasons to distrust everyone. Were there any lamas with them?'

'Two that I could see,' said Fletcher.

'And the mother and child riding on the yak, what did they look like?'

'The boy was about four or five. I assumed the woman was his mother but I can't be sure,' Fletcher replied.

'What were they wearing?'

'They had a blanket wrapped around them and their heads were covered with fur hats. That was all I could see,' said Fletcher.

Afridi fell silent for a while, his eyes clouded with thought.

After a long pause, Fletcher asked, 'What about the men that attacked us? Any progress there?'

'No.' Afridi shook his head. 'All of our leads have dried up. They've disappeared.'

'And nobody's tried to kill you while I was away?' Fletcher asked.

'Not that I know of,' said Afridi, with a smile. 'I was in Delhi for a couple of weeks and only got back a few days ago. Aside from the gunfight on the border, how was your birdwatching?'

'Plenty of interesting species,' said Fletcher. 'I finally saw a tragopan, six days ago, as I was coming down the Yumthang Valley.'

'Lucky man!' Afridi exclaimed with a distracted nod. 'I keep hoping I'll see one sooner or later.'

'It's a spectacular bird,' said Fletcher, 'but the call spooked me.'

'That's what I've heard. There's a folk tale that says it's the spirit of a stillborn child crying out for its mother,' said Afridi.

Fletcher shuddered. 'I can believe it.'

'Another rum?' Afridi asked, raising a hand to catch the bearer's attention.

'I'll go slow,' said Fletcher. 'This is the first alcohol I've had in four weeks.'

'Have a small one,' said Afridi, 'and we'll get something to eat. You must be hungry.'

'It's nice not to be living on dal and rice, or tsampa,' said Fletcher.

'Yes, I know what that's like,' Afridi agreed. 'So, what are your plans now?'

'I'm not sure, I was thinking of staying here for a few days until the caravan shows up, then heading back down to Kalimpong,' said Fletcher.

'I saw Kesang on my way back from Delhi,' Afridi said, his gaze wandering to one corner of the room. 'She asked about you.'

'Oh yeah? What did you say?' Fletcher responded.

'I told her you were herding yaks.'

'How is she?'

'Good,' said Afridi, 'Though Dr Mukherjee hasn't been well. He caught pneumonia and she's had her hands full looking after him.'

This time there was less tension between them as they spoke of Kesang though Fletcher could sense that Afridi was on guard.

'I'm sorry to hear that,' he said. 'By the way, how much does she know?'

'About what?'

Fletcher caught his eye. 'About my reasons for yak herding?' he said. 'The last time I saw her, Kesang said you told her that I'm a CIA agent.'

'Are you?' Afridi asked, with a mischievous smile.

Ignoring the question Fletcher said, 'I thought we were working together?'

'We are,' Afridi agreed. 'But that doesn't necessarily mean we're on the same side.'

24

Indian Lesser Racket-tailed Drongo

Dicrurus remifer tectirostris

*A dark purple bird that appears black, it is usually found in pairs and frequents Himalayan forests up to 4,500 feet above sea level. Two thin feathers, like strands of black wire, form the tail, at the ends of which are plumes that look like delicate paddles. Unlike the greater racket-tailed drongo (*Dicrurus paradiseus*) it does not have a crest. Sexes alike. Feeds on insects.*

Standing in the courtyard of Rumtek monastery, Fletcher and Afridi watched a group of lamas waiting at the gate. Several of them were beating drums in a solemn tempo and two of the monks carried long brass and copper horns that they blew with a resonant blast. Coming up the main trail to the monastery, which twisted its way along the brow of the ridge, was a procession of yaks with their armed escort. The mother and child were in front, flanked by the two lamas accompanying them.

Afridi's informants had already extracted the story of their journey and he had shared the information with Fletcher. The boy was a tulku, a reincarnation of the Rinpoche from Yangchen Gompa, who had been killed four years ago by the Chinese when they destroyed his monastery. A search for his successor had been conducted in secret. The child was discovered and identified in a remote settlement in Amdo province. He was kept hidden for almost a year until an opportunity arose to bring him across the border. The Chinese had tried to stop the young Rinpoche from escaping over the high pass into Sikkim but the Khampa fighters had protected him, though they had lost half their number. The young tulku was four years old and had never visited Yangchen though he recognized some of the personal effects of his predecessor, the murdered Rinpoche. During her pregnancy his mother had a dream of Yangchen Gompa, as it used to be, before the Chinese destroyed the monastery. Afridi had also explained, with some disappointment, that the yaks were not carrying relics or antiquities but a library of sacred texts that came from another monastery in Amdo. These were of great spiritual value but only dated back to the nineteenth century.

'So, there is no treasure,' Fletcher said, in resignation.

'Well, the boy, the incarnate Rinpoche, is the precious one,' said Afridi. 'He's the gem or jewel that has been smuggled out of Tibet.'

'I guess it's hard to assign a dollar value to that,' Fletcher said.

'Perhaps we put too much faith in material wealth,' was Afridi's response.

'Do you believe in reincarnation?' Fletcher asked.

Afridi shook his head. 'I believe that we pay for our sins in this life.'

'And good deeds?'

'I'm a soldier, not a philosopher,' Afridi replied. 'Don't ask me about spiritual rewards.'

By now the party of refugees had arrived at the gate and the monks offered them white scarves while chanting prayers. Fletcher could see that the boy was dressed in maroon and yellow robes. His head was shaved and he looked around him with curiosity, eyeing a stupa with its gold finial and painted symbols on its plinth. The lamas attending him helped the boy off the yak and presented the welcoming party with scarves in return. As Fletcher watched, he found it a simple, moving ceremony, the white fabric like scraps of mist torn from the clouds that drifted over the surrounding hills.

'When the sixteenth Karmapa came to Sikkim in 1959, he chose this monastery as his base. It was in ruins at that time, abandoned long ago, but Rumtek had once been occupied by the Karma Kagyu sect, so he decided to rebuild and restore it as his seat of spiritual authority,' Afridi explained.

The boy and his two lamas were ushered through the gate and Fletcher could see the child glance anxiously over his shoulder at his mother, who stood apart from the others, letting her son go on ahead. Crossing the courtyard to the accompaniment of drums and horns, the incarnate Rinpoche climbed the steps to the main hall of worship, which had an ornate facade with coloured flags, bunting, and a peaked yellow roof. The restoration of the monastery was still underway and a team of artists were crouched atop scaffolding, painting murals on the walls. Bowing at the entrance to the sanctuary, the boy obediently followed whispered instructions from the lamas who guided him into the presence of the Karmapa.

Fletcher and Afridi followed the group inside and watched from the back of the temple. A large gilded idol of the Maitreya Buddha, seated in meditation, dominated the shrine. The pillars and walls were heavily decorated with images of deities—green and white goddesses in calm but seductive repose, guardian figures with swords drawn, dozens of different bodhisattvas in teaching postures. On an ornate throne at the centre of the temple was a cheerful looking man in his forties, dressed in ceremonial robes and a large black cap.

'They believe that the Karmapa's crown was woven from the glossy black hair of celestial nymphs, known as dakinis,' whispered Afridi.

The four-year-old tulku was hesitant to go forward on his own. After the bleak and barren wastelands he had travelled across, the temple must have seemed like a gaudy hallucination. Butter lamps with flickering flames provided most of the illumination though there was some light from a line of windows overhead. Realizing that the boy was afraid, the Karmapa spoke to him softly and beckoned. Then, with a benevolent smile, he stepped down from his throne and greeted the boy, who presented him with a scarf. Despite the formality of the setting there was a tenderness to the Karmapa's gestures, as he reached out and patted the boy's cheek.

◆

The taxi Fletcher hired to take him to Kalimpong was owned and driven by a young man named Gopal Rai, of Nepali origin but born in Sikkim. His Ambassador car was only two years old and he kept it in good condition. A small dashboard shrine to the goddess Kalimata was decorated with a fresh floral offering of marigolds. As they drove down the hill, Rai recounted all of the injustices his family had suffered at the hands of the Namgyal dynasty and their courtiers. He claimed that

Nepalis were treated as second-class citizens by the Bhotias, who were corrupt and arrogant.

'The Maharaj Kumar goes off on foreign trips that cost thousands of rupees while people here can hardly put food in their stomachs,' he complained.

'But isn't India providing aid to Sikkim?' Fletcher asked.

'All of that money goes into the pockets of the Chogyal and the Kazis. There is nothing left for us,' said Rai, with a cynical wave of his hand.

'Then how did you buy this taxi?'

'I took a loan from the State Bank of India,' he said. 'It is hypothecated.'

'What does that mean?'

'If I don't pay my monthly instalments, they can take it back,' said Rai.

'You must be doing good business, though. There aren't many taxis in Gangtok,' Fletcher said.

'When there are passengers like you, it is good,' the driver replied, 'But for the last three days I had no work. Whatever I earn goes to buy off the police. I have to pay bribes in Sikkim as well as in West Bengal. All of them are thieves. By the end of the month, I hardly save enough to pay the bank. Hopefully, there will be more tourists coming. Now that the Maharaj Kumar is marrying an American girl, people from all over the world are hearing about Sikkim. Last week there was a couple from Texas who came here to see this "Himalayan Paradise" they'd read about in *Time* magazine. I told them it is a paradise for some, but not for most of us.'

As Rai continued with his litany of complaints, they passed the place where the jeep had gone over the side of the hill. Fletcher could see that the parapet wall hadn't yet been repaired. He was tempted to stop but also impatient to reach Kalimpong and see Kesang. Though he had thought of telephoning her from Gangtok, the line was down because of recent storms.

When they arrived at the Himalayan Hotel, the manager recognized him and gave him the same room, which still smelt of mildew but with an added fragrance of stale cigarette smoke from the last guest who had stayed there. Opening the windows, Fletcher looked around for the whistling thrush. A light rain was falling and the trees at the edges of the garden were laden with ferns and moss. It was about three o'clock in the afternoon, though the overcast sky made it seem much later.

The umbrella he'd purchased two months ago had been destroyed on his trek, blown inside out by strong winds. He borrowed one from the hotel and set off to see Kesang but also to leave a signal, requesting a live drop with Agatha. Once again, he entered the same public urinal on Rishi Road and, this time, wrote the Greek letter sigma, Σ, in blue chalk on the wall. The stench hadn't changed in two months, though someone had sprinkled powdered bleach on the road outside, as disinfectant. After leaving the signal, he couldn't be sure when or how Agatha would contact him. Jack Sullivan had said that he should only request a live drop under extreme and urgent circumstances. Though Fletcher wasn't facing a life-or-death situation, he was tired of operating in the dark and wanted answers.

When he arrived at Montrose, the rain had stopped and he noticed a racket-tailed drongo perched at the top of a tall maple that stood behind the house. Silhouetted against the sky the bird was completely black. When it took off and circled above him, he could see the two long strands of its tail, streaming behind the drongo like ribbons.

Most of the lights in the house were off but when he rang the bell, Hari, the parakeet, cried out from inside, 'Bugger off!' It took a while for someone to answer the door but eventually the maid unlocked it from inside and peered out at him with a worried look. When he asked if Kesang was in, she shook her head. Speaking a mixture of Hindi and Nepali, the maid explained that Kesang had taken Dr Mukherjee to Calcutta because he was very sick. They had left two days ago and she didn't know when they would return.

The early twilight was depressing as Fletcher retraced his steps to the hotel. The drongo had disappeared and the dark monsoon clouds hid the sky. Though he passed a number of people on the road, he felt more alone than he had ever been, even high up in the mountains. Coming towards him was a hand-pulled rickshaw hauled by two men who were struggling up the incline. Fletcher stepped to one side just as he heard a familiar voice call out.

'Roko! Roko! Stop!' The Kazini cried, leaning forward under the canopy of the rickshaw so that Fletcher could see her pale features. 'Mr Swift! I heard you were in town!'

Startled, he replied, 'But I only got here a couple of hours ago.'

'Don't worry, I have my sources!' she said as her red lips parted in some semblance of a smile.

The rickshaw pullers were breathing heavily, sweat and rain streaming down their faces.

'I hear you're staying at the Himalayan Hotel,' said the Kazini. 'It's not far from Chakung House. Please come and have a drink and dinner with us this evening. Sevenish.'

Fletcher was about to refuse but it suddenly occurred to him that this might be the live drop he had requested and the Kazini could be Agatha. If so, she'd been quick to respond.

'Thank you. Are you sure?' he said.

'Of course, I'm sure. We'll see you soon,' the Kazini exclaimed, then shouted at the rickshaw pullers, 'Chalo! Chalo!'

The two men strained to get the awkward vehicle moving again, their bare feet slipping on the wet asphalt as the rickshaw rolled slowly uphill.

◆

The manager at the hotel directed him to Chakung House and he found his way without much trouble. The building was a ramshackle bungalow, the veranda overgrown with honeysuckle and wisteria vines. There was no bell but he rapped on a window and a young boy opened the door and greeted him with folded hands, then guided him into the Kazini's salon. It was a large room, with a bay window overlooking a shadowy garden. A roll top desk stood against one wall with an old-fashioned typewriter positioned at its centre, as if ready to receive the Kazini's latest opinion piece for the *Himalayan Observer*. The walls were draped with several large thangkas, alongside a number of photographs of the Kazi meeting dignitaries like Pandit Nehru and the king of Nepal. Furnished in an eclectic mixture of European chairs and Oriental divans, the salon resembled a depleted gallery of antiques in which all of the good pieces had been taken and what remained were cheap reproductions and bric-a-brac.

Five minutes after he arrived, the Kazini swept into the room. A half-smoked cigarette smouldered in the long ivory holder she held in one hand. Her pale green kho looked as if it had been hastily wrapped, like a dressing gown.

'Ah, Mr Swift, how punctual of you! Right on time,' she cried, holding out her hand as if she expected him to kiss her topaz ring. 'What do Americans say? Time is money. Here in the east, everyone arrives late.'

'Sorry. I didn't know how long it would take me to walk over,' said Fletcher.

'Please don't apologize. I'm so glad I ran in to you today,' she said. 'Where were you coming from?'

There didn't seem to be much point in avoiding the truth so Fletcher replied, 'I went to see Dr Mukherjee and Kesang, but they've gone to Calcutta.'

'Yes, poor sod. I'm afraid he's not long for this world,' she said. 'Kesang had been trying to get him to a hospital for more than a week but he refused. It was only after he got much worse that she was able to take him to Cal.'

'I heard it was pneumonia,' said Fletcher.

'Yes, and other complications. His liver and kidneys are in a bad way on account of his drinking,' she said. 'Of course, Mukherjee and I haven't been on speaking terms for several years. But still, you feel sorry for the man....'

'You had a disagreement?' Fletcher asked.

'He had the audacity to lecture me on Buddhist culture and said that I should show more respect for Sikkim's heritage,' she declaimed. 'I told him I'd shown enough respect by marrying my husband and then I called him an "old fart", which he took personally. After that we avoided each other, though I've always had a soft spot for Kesang. Are you in love with her?'

'No,' said Fletcher, a little too quickly, and the Kazini raised her eyebrows.

'Actually, I'm glad you're here before the others arrive. Just a few friends, a couple of journalists, and an agent from IB. Of course, he'll deny it, just as you will deny working for the CIA. Anyway, there was something I wanted to ask you in private.' She had seated herself in an upholstered chair and waved for Fletcher to sit beside her on a low divan.

Taking a puff from her cigarette, she let her bosom heave and then exhaled a jet of smoke from her crimson lips.

'I need you to get me an appointment with the US ambassador, Professor Galbraith. Week after next I plan to be in Delhi and I need to discuss a very sensitive matter with him,' she said in a conspiratorial voice.

'Sorry,' said Fletcher. 'I don't know the ambassador and I have no connections with the Embassy. I'm just a visiting ornithologist....'

'Nonsense,' said the Kazini. 'I know who you are and I'm sure you can get onto your walkie-talkie and give Galbraith a buzz. Tell him that the Kazini Saheba has an urgent message that affects Indo–American relations.'

'I really can't,' said Fletcher, trying to sound apologetic.

'No, you must not refuse me, young man,' she insisted, leaning forward. 'It is of the utmost importance. You see, I intend to warn him about that chit of a girl, Hope Cooke. They must do something to break off her engagement with the Crown Prince. It will be a diplomatic disaster.'

'Why?' Fletcher asked.

'Because India will take it as an affront, a direct breach of protocol,' she said.

'How do you know that?'

'The 1950 treaty gives India complete control over Sikkim's foreign affairs,' the Kazini said, in an assertive voice.

Fletcher had to laugh. 'But I'm sure that doesn't include the Maharaj Kumar's personal affairs with a foreigner,' he said.

'Don't make light of it!' the Kazini scolded him. 'The Red Chinese will use the marriage as an excuse to invade Sikkim. They won't tolerate an American queen in Gangtok! Now, promise me that you will pass on my request for an appointment with your ambassador.'

'You have to believe me, I have no influence at the Embassy,' Fletcher protested. 'But I do know someone who might be able to help.'

'Who is this?' she demanded in a haughty voice.

'A friend who has contacts at the Embassy,' he said, trying to get her off his back. 'I'll speak to him. Of course, I can't promise....'

She looked at him suspiciously.

'But you must! I won't take "no" for an answer,' she said, reaching over and picking up a brass bell that she rang loudly. 'Now, let's get you a drink.'

Seconds later the young boy appeared.

'Kancha!' she ordered. 'Drinks lao!'

Any suspicions Fletcher might have had that the Kazini was Agatha, had already been dispelled, though he still wasn't sure what she was after.

The boy came in carrying a tray loaded with bottles and glasses. As he set it down on a side table, there was a loud knock at the front door. Kancha ran to answer it. Moments later, three men entered and greeted the Kazini politely.

'This is Tariq Chaudhury of *The Statesman,* Ranjan Bose of *The Telegraph,* and Deepak Malhotra of the Intelligence Bureau. Allan Swift. CIA,' she announced. 'We have no secrets here!'

They all shook hands and there was a brief moment of awkwardness as Malhotra corrected her. 'I'm actually with the Tourism Development Council.'

Fletcher smiled, then added, 'And I'm researching birds.'

'Rubbish,' said the Kazini. 'Nobody believes either of you. Ranjan why don't you pour drinks while Tariq gives us the latest headlines from Delhi?'

The others were obviously used to the Kazini's theatrics. They were soon comfortably settled with drinks in their hands and cigarettes lighted until the smoke in the room was almost as thick as the mist outside. Tariq's summary of the news from Delhi included a remark about a delegation from the Ministry of External Affairs going to Peking for consultations.

'They must be careful,' the Kazini cautioned. 'The Chinese aren't known to be inscrutable for nothing! One minute they'll be saying that India is their closest ally and the next they'll create a border incident and demand another hundred square miles or two.'

The others chimed in as the informal soiree continued under the Kazini's command. Though she nursed a single brandy soda, she encouraged the others to drink up. Soon enough the Kazini was berating the Crown Prince for his duplicity.

'You can be sure he's meeting with the Chinese ambassador in London just as his sister Coocoola is off cultivating her contacts in Hong Kong. They don't realize that they're playing with dynamite,' the Kazini insisted.

'May I quote you on that?' Tariq asked.

'Certainly not!' the Kazini replied, 'I'm in enough hot water with the palace, as it is, though you can attribute it to an unnamed but reliable source.'

Fletcher listened in on the conversation without saying much. At one point the Kazi appeared and greeted them hurriedly then left soon afterwards.

'My husband has a meeting with some of his supporters tonight,' the Kazini whispered. 'They have to wait until dark because the Chogyal's spies are everywhere.'

At quarter past ten, the evening finally ended, immediately after dinner. By this time the two journalists were drunk and their hostess had run out of conspiracies to unravel. As the four men staggered out of Chakung House together, the Kazini called out: 'Remember your promise, Allan! I'm counting on you.'

25

Red Junglefowl

Gallus gallus murghi

The wild progenitor of domesticated chickens, which human beings first
raised for eggs and meat approximately 8,000 years ago. Though somewhat
smaller than its captive cousins, the rooster has a bright red comb and
orange hackles. The rest of its feathers are different shades of red, black, and
a dark, metallic green. It crows at dawn with a high-pitched shriek.
*A related species, the grey junglefowl (*Gallus sonneratii*),*
is found in South India.

Fletcher dropped by the Forest Department office to see Thupten
Lepcha the next morning. He briefed him on his fieldwork in
Lachen and Yumthang, omitting his encounters with the Khampa
fighters. After all of the debate and discussion in the Kazini's salon
the night before, it was a relief to have a conversation with a fellow
birder that focused only on the identifying traits, distribution, and
behaviour of feathered creatures, rather than political intrigue. Thupten
was particularly interested to learn that Fletcher had spotted a red-eared
bay woodpecker (*Blythipicus pyrrhotis*) above 9,000 feet, much higher
than where it was usually found. As he described the satyr tragopan he'd
seen, he could tell that Thupten understood his excitement in a way that
others could never appreciate. Together, they made plans for the second
part of his survey, here at lower elevations.

Leaving the DFO's office at quarter to twelve, Fletcher set off for his
hotel in the rain, though this time the weather didn't dampen his spirits.
A short while later, as he was passing a tea shop on Mintri Road, a
young man called out to him, 'Hello mister...my friend, change dollars?'

Shaking his head, Fletcher moved on but he was aware that the tout was following him and tried to wave him aside.

'Pound Sterling?' the man persisted. 'Deutsche Marks?'

'Nothing,' said Fletcher, impatiently. 'Go away.'

Leaning towards him, until their umbrellas touched, the stranger said, 'Tomorrow morning. Six o'clock. Be ready.'

◆

He had assumed that Agatha was a woman, though Fletcher knew from his training at The Farm that codenames weren't supposed to provide any clues to a person's identity or gender. The same young man who had accosted him the day before arrived on a motorcycle and picked him up from the gate of the hotel at six. They drove about eight miles southeast of Kalimpong to an unpaved sidetrack, which had a sign for Upper Invergarry Tea Estate. The motorcycle strained on the incline as it passed through a dense forest laden with vines and creepers. A few minutes later, they emerged into the manicured expanse of the tea garden that spread like a plush green cloak over the rolling hillsides. At the end of the road stood a large bungalow, beyond which were other buildings, including a factory for processing tea.

As the bike pulled up at the gate two cocker spaniels came barking across the lawn and he saw a familiar figure step out into the garden. Colonel Basil Norton was dressed in a khaki shirt, shorts with knee socks, and his broad-brimmed terai hat. He whistled for the dogs and they raced back to their master, as Fletcher got down and walked up to the bungalow.

'Agatha,' said the Colonel, introducing himself, 'But you can call me Basil, since we've already met.'

'I wasn't expecting it to be you,' said Fletcher.

'Please,' said the Colonel gesturing towards the veranda. 'Join me for breakfast.'

'Is this your house?' Fletcher asked.

'No,' said the Colonel. 'A good friend manages this estate. He's away in Assam at the moment but he lets me stay over whenever I want. I have a small cottage in Kalimpong but this is more discreet, no prying eyes.'

A fleece of mist lay over the tea bushes but there had been no rain since the night before. As they reached the veranda, Fletcher heard a shrill cry from the edge of the forest.

'You recognize that, don't you?' said Norton, taking off his hat and hanging it from a hook on the wall.

'Red junglefowl,' said Fletcher.

'Yes, indeed,' the Colonel confirmed. 'One of the boys who works here found a nest a couple days ago and he brought us four eggs. We'll have them for breakfast.'

'What do they taste like?' Fletcher asked.

'Very similar to a chicken's egg, though they have a little more flavour and the yolk is a brighter colour,' Norton explained.

The spaniels sniffed at Fletcher's ankles, as he scratched behind their long ears. 'What are their names?' he asked.

'Somerset and Maugham,' said the Colonel. 'The male is Somerset and Mom is the bitch.'

One of the servants had brought a tea tray and placed it on a glass-topped rattan table. The Colonel offered Fletcher a seat and then settled into a chair, his pink knees jutting out of his shorts like swollen knuckles.

'This is a beautiful spot,' said Fletcher looking out across the surrounding gardens as the sun broke through the clouds.

'Yes, it is, though the tea is mediocre at best,' said the Colonel pouring him a cup. 'Upper Invergarry was badly managed for a number of years until my friend took it over in '53, but by then the damage was done.'

The two dogs lay at his feet and looked up expectantly.

'Are you a fan of W. Somerset Maugham?' Fletcher asked.

'I enjoy his work, mostly the lighter novels like *Cakes and Ale* or *Up at the Villa*. *The Razor's Edge* is heavy going in parts—too much philosophizing. What I enjoy most are his Ashenden stories, about the British secret agent in World War I. Have you read them?'

Fletcher shook his head and both of them fell silent for a minute as they watched a white-collared black bird hunting for worms on the lawn. Eventually, Fletcher turned to Colonel Norton.

'Thank you for responding to my signal so quickly,' he said.

'My pleasure,' Norton replied. 'I apologize for the urinal. It's not the most pleasant place to leave your mark but it happens to be located along the route I take for my morning walk every day. And at my age, it's important to keep an eye out for public conveniences.'

'I need to see Merlin as soon as possible,' said Fletcher, leaning forward. 'I'd like to talk to him face to face.'

'I'll let him know,' said Norton. 'Is there a problem?'

'Yes,' said Fletcher, 'or at least I think so. I have a couple of things I need to give Merlin but I also have some questions.'

Norton's eyes narrowed as he studied him from beneath his untrimmed eyebrows, which were a shade darker than his moustache.

'How was your trip to North Sikkim?' he asked.

'Interesting,' Fletcher replied, not sure how much he should share with Agatha. 'Some areas were very remote and desolate. Have you been up there?'

'Only to the base camp of Kangchenjunga but no further,' he said. 'I accompanied the British Expedition in 1955. Helped organize their porters.'

A full English breakfast arrived on two trays that were placed in front of them, the plates loaded with bacon, sausage, fried tomatoes, and baked beans, along with toast and two boiled eggs each, in matching ceramic cups.

'This looks serious,' said Fletcher.

'Planters eat well,' said Norton, 'and our host has an excellent cook. By the way, the eggs are soft boiled. I hope you don't mind. It's the only way to cook them. Everyone eats omelettes these days, which is sacrilege as far as I'm concerned.'

Fletcher watched as the old man picked up a table knife and topped his two eggs with a practised flick of the wrist. His own attempt was less successful but eventually, he got them cut open. Peeling away bits of the shell with his fingers he sprinkled salt and pepper over the viscous white flesh inside, which reminded him of the oysters he'd eaten with Sullivan, back in April. Following the Colonel's lead, he broke the yolk with one corner of his toast and then spooned it into his mouth.

'How do you like it?' asked the Colonel.

'Very good,' said Fletcher. 'You're right, it has a slightly stronger flavour than ordinary eggs, sort of yeasty.'

The Colonel nodded, chewing his toast. Fletcher waited a few seconds before he asked, 'What's your assessment of the situation on the border? Do you think the Chinese will invade?'

'That's a difficult question,' said Norton. 'The simple answer is "yes", but the complicated part is "where". They've been making a lot of provocative statements and engaging in aggressive manoeuvres at different points along the McMahon Line but it's hard to know what their strategy will be.'

'Wouldn't Nathu La be the obvious place for them to cross over?' Fletcher asked, before taking a mouthful of bacon and beans.

'It is, and that's what most people expect, which is why I'm not sure, because an invasion like that requires an element of surprise,' the Colonel explained. 'I have a feeling they will choose another pass, maybe two or three that aren't guarded, where they can slip several small detachments across without being challenged.'

'Won't they need supply lines?'

'Eventually, but the PLA troops are very good at living off the land. Each soldier can be self-sufficient for as long as a week. That would give them enough time to regroup and attack the Indian positions from the rear. At the same time, they'll launch a simultaneous assault from the north. The Indian soldiers will be trapped in between,' said Colonel Norton.

'But surely India must be anticipating something like that,' said Fletcher.

'I would hope so but there's a sense of complacency in the Indian Army these days that worries me. Nehru has ignored seniority and appointed generals to positions of command who are politically adept but have little experience in the field. Most of the old guard, who fought in World War II, have been retired.'

'Like you,' said Fletcher. 'Do you ever wish that India was still part of the British empire?'

'Absolutely not,' said Norton with a stern look of disapproval. 'I'm not one of those "koi hais", who have a lot of nostalgia for the Raj. We left when our time was up. It wasn't easy but it was the right thing to do.'

'You've stayed on, though,' said Fletcher.

Norton turned his gaze to the hill above, where a group of women were picking tea on the slope, carrying bamboo baskets as the mist swirled around them.

'Personally, I had no desire to go back to a bedsit in Muswell Hill,' said Norton. 'I've never felt entitled to India, as many of my countrymen did, though I will admit that this country owns me.'

They ate in silence for a while. Norton buttered a piece of toast, then broke it in half and fed it to his dogs.

'If the Chinese take Sikkim, do you think they'll stop there?' Fletcher asked.

'Probably not,' Norton replied. 'I think they'll wring the chicken's neck, if you know what I mean.'

Fletcher nodded as Norton continued: 'Once the Chinese reach Gangtok there's nothing to stop them from moving on to Siliguri. Darjeeling and Kalimpong can be dealt with later. If they control Nathu La, they can move a whole division across in a matter of days. The Indian Army will fight back but it's only twelve miles from Siliguri to the border with East Pakistan. And if they cut off that corridor, then they've essentially amputated Assam and NEFA. All you have to do is look at a map and it's obvious. Of course, Pakistan would welcome the Chinese at their border and maybe even give them assistance. After that, the Northeast will be cut off and vulnerable, no roads, no rail links.'

'What about the Indian Air Force?' said Fletcher.

'They won't make it easy for the Chinese but one of the strengths of the PLA is that they have the largest army on earth. They'll just keep marching more men across the mountains and they're willing to take heavy casualties.'

'What will the rest of the world do?' said Fletcher.

'Not much, I suppose. The UN will pass a resolution condemning Chinese aggression. I'm sure that you Americans will offer plenty of aid and assistance. Britain will do the same. But once a chicken's neck has been wrung, it's very hard to bring it back to life.'

'Have you told all this to Merlin?' Fletcher asked.

'He knows already,' Norton replied.

'Why do you think he sent me here?' said Fletcher.

Shaking his head, the Colonel pushed his plate aside. 'I really can't say.'

'When you came up to Gangtok last month, you were checking on me, weren't you?' Fletcher said.

Norton nodded. 'Merlin wanted to know if you were all right, after the jeep went down the khud.'

'What about Afridi? You told me that he's with military intelligence,' said Fletcher. 'Am I supposed to recruit him?'

'I doubt if that's possible,' said Norton.

'But Merlin must have known that I'd meet Afridi and my cover would be blown,' said Fletcher.

'You'll have to ask him that yourself,' said the Colonel, glancing at his watch. 'Now, if you'll excuse me, I've booked a trunk call for half past eight. Let me see if I can get through.'

The spaniels got up as soon as their master rose from his seat and followed him inside. A short while later, two servants cleared away the breakfast trays and Fletcher was left on his own, staring into the mist, which had crept closer until everything beyond the veranda had been erased.

It was almost half an hour before Colonel Norton returned.

'My apologies, the connection was dreadful and we could hardly hear each other. Though it's a secure line, one hates to be shouting while trying to be discreet,' said Norton.

'What did Merlin say?'

'He'll meet you in Calcutta, day after tomorrow. You should be able to get a train from Siliguri, without much trouble. Stay at the Grand Hotel in Chowringhee. Merlin will contact you.' The Colonel spoke softly but firmly as if he were giving a command.

'Have you known him for a long time?' Fletcher asked.

'Who?' said Norton.

'Merlin.'

'Long enough,' the Colonel replied. 'We worked together during the war.'

26

House Crow

Corvus splendens

Somewhat smaller than the jungle crow (Corvus culminatis), it is distinguished by a grey neck and less prominent beak. Crows are amongst the most intelligent birds on earth and have learnt to live in close proximity to human beings. An omnivorous species, they often scavenge through household garbage. Commonly found in urban areas, large flocks congregate near rubbish heaps and slaughterhouses. The call is a raucous cawing though crows also 'sing' to each other in muted tones of varying pitch.

The Darjeeling Mail pulled into Sealdah Station an hour late at 7 a.m. Though the only ticket he'd been able to buy was a third-class unreserved, Fletcher had been assigned a first-class berth after bribing the conductor. For the last hour of the journey the train had rumbled through the outskirts of Calcutta, passing slums and factories along the route. With the monsoon still underway there was a lot of standing water, much of it a scummy grey. A few groves of trees and stands of bamboo provided a bright green contrast to the sullen visage of urban squalor and decay. An anaemic, yellow sun rose through the clouds.

Just before reaching the station, the train stopped at a siding and Fletcher noticed a flock of crows feeding on a pile of garbage next to the tracks. They were handsome birds with glossy black feathers and bright, alert eyes. As he watched, one of them picked up a crust of bread in its beak and leapt onto the steel railway track, strutting about. Immediately, another crow attempted to snatch the bread away and the two of them tussled to claim the prize, twisting their heads back and forth, trying to wrench the bread free. Finally, the crust broke in two and each of the crows went off with its share.

The platform where Fletcher got down was swarming with passengers. Though he could have easily carried his own luggage, he hired a railway porter, wearing a red shirt with a brass badge on his arm, to help him navigate through the crowd. His suitcase, balanced on the porter's head, bobbed its way up a staircase and across a walkway, then down another set of stairs to the exit. Once they were outside, he got a taxi to the Grand Hotel. This was his first visit to Calcutta and it was already overwhelming. The density of population and the sultry fug in the air made him want to turn around and head back up to the hills.

Before leaving Kalimpong, he had been able to find out from Eddie Lim that Dr Mukherjee had been admitted to the Medical College Hospital, which was not far from the hotel. After checking into his room and showering, Fletcher had a quick breakfast and headed out to find Kesang.

Trams, buses, cars, and rickshaws competed with bicycles and pedestrians for right of way; there seemed to be no order or pattern to the traffic. A harried policeman stood on a platform at the centre of a busy crossing, waving his arms frantically, as if signalling to be rescued from the flood of humanity and mechanized transport that flowed around him.

The hospital was enormous, its main entrance designed like the facade of a Greek temple with Corinthian columns and a sloping roof, a remnant of colonial grandeur. Trying to find Dr Mukherjee's room, Fletcher felt as if he was trapped in a Kafka novel but after half an hour of wandering through the crowded halls, he finally found someone who could direct him to the private wards. More than a dozen patients were named Mukherjee but eventually he found the right room and knocked softly.

Kesang opened the door and stared at him for a moment, as if she didn't recognize who he was. But then, with a startled gasp, she embraced Fletcher and held him tightly. Over her shoulder, he could see Dr Mukherjee in the hospital bed with an oxygen mask on his face and an intravenous drip in his arm. His eyes were shut and his face looked sunken. No one else was in the room. After the crowds he had passed through that morning, it felt as if he had crossed a threshold between the chaos and clutter of life and the stillness and solitude of death.

'How did you find us?' Kesang asked, finally letting him go and wiping tears from her eyes.

'It wasn't easy. This place is more chaotic than the railway station,' he said, then looked across at the bed. 'How is he?'.

Kesang shook her head and he could see her lower lip trembling with emotion, unable to speak. As he approached the bed, he could trace the frail outline of Dr Mukherjee's body under the white sheet, which rose and fell with his breathing. He looked like a child with an old man's face. His left hand, which lay outside the sheet, was a bundle of dried twigs.

'He hasn't regained consciousness since we left home five days ago,' Kesang whispered, 'The doctors are surprised that he's survived this long.'

'I heard it was pneumonia,' Fletcher said.

She nodded. 'He was always stubborn about taking medicines and wouldn't let me call a doctor in Kalimpong,' she said, reaching out to touch the old man's forehead. Then all at once, despite her grief, she began to laugh.

'What is it?' Fletcher said.

'Daddy used to boast that whenever he climbed a mountain he never once used oxygen,' she said. 'Now he's here at sea level breathing from a bottle.'

'Is there anyone else to help you here?' Fletcher asked.

'His family has been by to see him. He has a younger sister and several nephews and nieces. But they were never close to him and they've always disapproved of me,' she said.

'Where are you staying?'

'Here, mostly,' she said, pointing to a small day bed in the corner. 'I can also go to Pema's flat, which is nearby. She's in Kalimpong but gave me the key and there is a servant who does some cooking.'

Fletcher could see that Kesang looked exhausted, worn down by the strain of waiting by her father's sickbed. Just then, there was a knock at the door and a nurse entered. She looked at Fletcher with surprise but said nothing, going across to the bed to change the glucose drip.

The room had only one chair so they sat together on the day bed, once the nurse had gone. After her initial tears, Kesang pulled herself together and seemed less distraught. She asked Fletcher where he was staying. When he mentioned the Grand Hotel, she smiled.

'Luxury, for a change!' she said. 'How long are you staying?'

'I don't know,' said Fletcher. 'I'm meeting someone.'

'Who?' she asked.

'Someone from the Smithsonian,' he lied. 'I'm supposed to report on my research.'

From the look in her eyes, he could tell that Kesang didn't believe him.

'But I'll stay as long as you need me,' he reassured her.

'Thank you,' she said, looking across at Dr Mukherjee's bed, 'though there's not much anyone can do.'

'It's strange,' said Fletcher. 'I met him only once, that morning before Afridi showed up, but I still remember our conversation.'

'Daddy told me that he approved of you,' said Kesang, lowering her voice as if the sick man could hear her. 'He didn't like most of my friends but he thought you were a "decent chap"—that's what he called you.'

Fletcher made a face. 'At least I'm not indecent,' he said.

Kesang smiled. 'Have you seen Imtiaz recently?' she asked.

'We met in Gangtok,' said Fletcher. 'I think he's still up there. He told me that your father was sick but I don't think he understood how serious it was, or that you had brought him here to Calcutta.'

'Would you mind sending him a telegram from me?' said Kesang.

'Of course,' said Fletcher.

She reached over and picked up her handbag, from which she took out a small notebook. Kesang carefully wrote down the address and a short message, then tore out the page and handed it to him:

KUNCHOK BHUTIA LAL BAZAAR GANGTOK SIKKIM
DADDY SERIOUSLY ILL STOP IN CAL STOP PLEASE COME
SOON STOP K

Seeing the puzzled look on Fletcher's face, as he read the address, she put a hand on his arm and said, 'Don't worry, it will reach him. Otherwise, I have to send it to the Army Field Post Office and it will take forever.'

◆

He returned to the Grand Hotel after spending a couple of hours with Kesang, promising to come back as soon as possible. The concierge agreed to send the telegram for Fletcher, who gave him a hundred rupees and told him to keep the change. There was no message from Merlin and he ordered room service for lunch, a club sandwich and a Coke. While he waited for it to arrive, he watched a flock of crows circling the rooftops outside his window.

Nothing happened for the rest of the day or that night and he stayed in his room. The next morning, at half past ten, his phone rang but when he picked it up there was silence. Changing into a fresh shirt and shouldering his backpack, he went down to the lobby, where a wedding party had gathered. The Bengali groom was wearing a conical white hat that looked as if it was made out of Styrofoam. Scanning the room, he caught sight of a man holding a blue umbrella in his right hand. Fletcher followed him out the door and onto the street. The man walked for about a hundred yards and then entered a music store with guitars in the window, as well as a harmonium and a sitar. Fletcher went inside and glanced around at all of the instruments, as well as a display of records. As he stood there, the man he'd been following picked up one of the albums, Trini Lopez's *America/If I had a Hammer*. After a couple of minutes, he put the record down and brushed past Fletcher, handing him a scrap of paper.

He wondered if such an elaborate ruse was really necessary as he browsed the albums for a few more minutes and then went out and hailed a taxi. The yellow and black Ambassador was stuffy and smelt of stale incense smoke. He rolled the window down after giving the driver the address on the piece of paper: 23 Bijoy Basu Rd, Apt 301. The drive took fifteen minutes, though he could have walked there in ten. The building, which must have been a grand mansion at one time, was in disrepair and from the outside it looked ready to collapse. An ancient lift, like a large birdcage, took him up to the third floor, which was as high as it went.

Merlin answered the door, a few seconds after Fletcher rang the bell. Though they shook hands, he noticed that his handler didn't seem pleased to see him. An air conditioner was humming in the background but even the cool air in the flat was a few degrees warmer than the cold reception he got.

'What's up?' Sullivan said, with an impatient frown.

'We need to talk,' Fletcher replied.

'Okay, I'm listening,' said Sullivan, leading him across to a couch with two matching chairs, where they sat down across from each other. 'I hope you have a good reason for making me fly all the way here from Delhi.'

'I'd like to know what's going on,' said Fletcher. 'This whole operation, Staghorn.... I feel like I'm in a movie but nobody's given me the script.'

'What do you need to know?' said Sullivan, taking out his pipe and stuffing it with tobacco.

'Well, let's start with Emil Zorman,' Fletcher said. 'Why did you lie to me? He wasn't a Cuban diplomat. He was an American expert on Asian art. I read his obituary in the *Tribune*. He didn't die of a coronary. He was tortured and then shot in the head.'

Sullivan was silent for a moment, as he fired up his pipe, the match burning almost to his fingertips before he dropped it in an ashtray.

'So what?' he said. 'I withheld some of the facts.'

'Yeah, but I keep finding out things from Afridi that you could have told me beforehand,' said Fletcher. 'Why was there any need for a cover up?'

'Well, the fact that Afridi is talking to you justifies the whole operation,' said Sullivan. 'Of course, he's not telling you everything....'

'No, I realize that,' said Fletcher impatiently. 'But my cover was blown within twenty-four hours of reaching Kalimpong. Everybody knows I'm with the CIA, from the foreigners registration officer to the Political Officer in Gangtok!'

'They *think* you're with the pickle factory but they don't know for sure...' said Sullivan. 'There's a big difference.'

'Afridi knows,' said Fletcher.

'Okay. But he's your source,' Sullivan replied. 'You've done a good job of cultivating that relationship. You've gained his trust.'

'But he's not telling me anything that you don't know already,' said Fletcher.

Sullivan exhaled and shook his head. 'We'll get to that in a minute, but let me begin by answering your first question. Emil Zorman worked for us as a contractor. He was an influential guy in New York, very well connected. In fact, he knew the first lady and was a friend of Lee Radziwill who had bought several expensive pieces of art from his gallery. So, when you found his body the day before Jackie Kennedy's visit to Delhi, it could have become a public relations disaster. Because he was working for us, we had to clean up the mess.'

'What about the Cuban?' said Fletcher.

'Collateral damage,' said Sullivan, 'but he had it coming.'

'Afridi told me that he was selling secrets.'

'That's about right,' Sullivan confirmed.

'He also told me about the Tibetan antiquities that Zorman was hoping to buy and the scheme to fund Tibetan guerrillas from the proceeds....' said Fletcher.

'You see,' said Sullivan, smiling for the first time. 'Afridi is a useful source.'

'But you knew all of that already,' said Fletcher.

'Of course,' said Sullivan. 'But we weren't sure how much the Indians knew, or the Chinese....'

'Well, I guess it doesn't matter any more,' said Fletcher, 'because the tranche of relics doesn't exist. The Chushi Gangdruk fighters smuggled their treasure out of Tibet but it wasn't a hoard of twelfth-century statues, it was a four-year-old boy, "the precious one", an incarnation of the Rinpoche of Yangchen Gompa.'

'You're sure about that?' said Sullivan, with a look of suspicion.

'I saw them bring him across Kellas Col,' said Fletcher. 'And twelve days later, Afridi and I were at Rumtek monastery when he arrived.'

He then told Sullivan about the gun battle and the avalanche, as well as the library of sacred books that the yaks were carrying. At Rumtek, Afridi had questioned the Khampas through an interpreter and they claimed to know nothing about the treasure, insisting that the Chinese had destroyed all of the relics and thangkas at Yangchen. Sullivan quizzed him closely, as if he felt there was something missing in the story that left him unconvinced.

Finally, taking the roll of film from his pocket, Fletcher handed it over.

'What's this?' Sullivan asked.

'Evidence,' said Fletcher. 'I didn't have it developed because I didn't want some photo studio in Kalimpong making copies.'

Sullivan set the film canister down on the coffee table, as if it were a chess piece. Nodding with satisfaction, he asked, 'Good. What else have you got?'

Fletcher opened his backpack and took out the spool from the tape recorder.

'You know who the Kazini is, don't you?' he asked.

'Yeah,' said Sullivan. 'Elisa Maria Langford-Rae. I knew her in Delhi before she married Kazi Lhendup Dorjee. A character.'

'Well, I recorded a conversation between her and an Intelligence Bureau agent. Some of it's garbled but they're talking about overthrowing the Chogyal in Sikkim and sabotaging the Crown Prince's marriage to Hope Cooke. Some of it is crazy stuff because the Kazini is a lunatic, but a lot of what they say is dead serious. Indian intelligence is doing everything it can to undermine the palace,' said Fletcher. 'The Kazi was part of the discussion too. IB is promising that they'll make him Prime Minister if he cooperates with them.'

'Does Afridi know about this?' Sullivan asked, taking the tape and turning it over in his hands.

'No,' said Fletcher.

'Swell!' Sullivan set his pipe aside. 'You see, this is why I didn't think you needed a script.'

'It would have been helpful if you'd told me some of this stuff before sending me into the field,' Fletcher complained.

'As I explained before, ignorance is your best defence,' said Sullivan. 'Besides, you're a rookie, a greenhorn. I can't tell you everything.'

'So, you weren't really interested in what the Chinese were doing on the border?' said Fletcher. 'You were using me to get to Afridi.'

'We're interested in anything you might uncover,' said Sullivan, 'but, yes, Afridi was the main target and the antiquities from Tibet, of course. We guessed he was aware of what was going on but the whole thing was a moving target. Now, you're telling me there isn't any treasure, just some kid in ochre robes.'

'Did you know about Afridi before I met him in Kashmir?' asked Fletcher.

'Not really,' said Sullivan, 'but after he spoke with you about Zorman, we checked him out. He's obviously one of their golden boys. They give him a lot of autonomy for military intelligence.'

Now that the tension had eased between them, Fletcher had a chance to look around the room. It was a comfortable, modern flat, despite the building, which looked as if it hadn't been maintained for years.

'What is this place?' he asked.

'It belongs to the US Consulate. No one is staying here at the moment, but it's usually assigned to one of the USIS people, Cultural Affairs,' said Sullivan. 'Do you want some coffee? A drink?'

'No, thanks,' said Fletcher, getting up to examine a framed picture on the wall. It was a reproduction of a Mughal miniature.

'I hate coming to Calcutta,' said Sullivan.

'Yeah, it's a pretty awful place….' said Fletcher.

'No, that's not what I mean,' Sullivan interrupted him. 'I love this city. During the war I used to come here for R&R. It was full of life, even with the Japanese on our doorstep. A party every night. Even after independence in forty-seven, it had its own special character—the nightclubs, the crooners, a cosmopolitan mix of eccentric personalities. A lot of castaways washed ashore here, Jews and Czechs, Russians and Brits. Compared to Delhi, it was the most entertaining place on earth.'

'Then why do you say you hate coming here?' Fletcher asked.

'Because I can't go out and enjoy myself, the way I used to do,' said Sullivan, his face etched with regret. 'I can't walk into Firpo's and sit down at the long bar and order a brandy soda. I can't play tennis at the Tollygunge Club or take a walk in the park around the Victoria Memorial.'

'Why not?'

'Because people recognize me here,' he said. 'I had too many friends. I can't be anonymous. They know who I am. It's one of the liabilities of this job. Some of my happiest times were spent in Calcutta but now I have to sneak in and sneak out of the city like a thief in the night.'

'To me it just seems like a crowded, crazy, polluted place,' said Fletcher. 'I prefer Gangtok or Kalimpong over this.'

Sullivan looked at him with a sympathetic smile. 'Well, I've got some news for you,' he said. 'You're not going back.'

'How come?'

'I'm pulling you from the field.' He glanced at his watch. 'A car is going to pick us up in half an hour. We'll stop by your hotel and collect your luggage, then go to the airport. The Convair will take us to Delhi tonight.'

'Why? What's the rush?' said Fletcher, trying not to sound alarmed.

'Your work is done. Congratulations! Good job,' said Sullivan. 'Now that you've discovered that the antiquities aren't in Sikkim, there isn't anything else that needs to be done.'

'But I've got my research to finish,' said Fletcher.

Sullivan gave him a sceptical glance. 'You can go back to your ducks and geese in Bharatpur,' he said. 'Tomorrow is September twentieth. They'll be migrating from Tibet in less than a month. We need to find out if any of them are radioactive.'

'No way. I've got to go back to Kalimpong,' said Fletcher. 'I can't just disappear without any reason.'

'Why not?'

'Because I've left stuff there,' he said.

'Or is it because of the girl?' said Sullivan. 'Kesang Sherpa.'

Fletcher was still standing next to the miniature painting with his back to the wall, no longer trying to hide his dismay.

'That's part of it,' he said. 'Sure.'

'But she's here in Calcutta,' said Sullivan. 'You saw her this morning.'

'Her father is dying. I told her I'd stay here for a few days if she needs my help,' said Fletcher, realizing there was no point in lying.

'Sit down,' said Sullivan, waving him back to the sofa. 'I've got to tell you something important.'

Fletcher obeyed though he was determined not to let Sullivan persuade him to leave. The older man's eyes studied him with a weary expression.

'What is it?' Fletcher demanded.

'She's a Chinese spy,' said Sullivan. 'We've been watching her for a while and we have confirmation. She has a contact in Kalimpong through whom she communicates with a man named Bo Lin Gu at the Chinese Embassy in Delhi. They recruited her four or five years ago, through the Communist Party.'

'I don't believe it,' said Fletcher.

'She's played you like a banjo,' said Sullivan. 'Don't kid yourself. You've been compromised.'

'Why would Kesang be working for the Chinese?' Fletcher asked. 'It doesn't make sense.'

'Maybe for the money,' said Sullivan. 'Or politics. She is a card-carrying communist after all. So is her father.'

'But that's not....' Fletcher began.

'Listen, your life is in danger,' said Sullivan. 'You're lucky to have survived the ambush on the jeep and that crash. She obviously tipped them off and they were waiting for you and Afridi. We also have hard evidence that she's the one who informed the Chinese about Zorman. After he visited Kalimpong, she sent a message to Bo Lin Gu, and told him that Zorman was trying to buy Tibetan antiques. As soon as he got back to Delhi, they picked him up from his hotel and interrogated him. When he didn't provide them with the information they wanted, they shot him. Kesang is directly responsible for Zorman's death.'

27

Brown-headed Gull

Chroicocephalus brunnicephalus

*Common throughout Southern Asia, this coastal seabird frequents
inland lakes and waterways. In late spring it migrates to the Tibetan
Plateau, where it lays its eggs on the shores of high-altitude wetlands.
The chocolate-coloured head is a feature of breeding adults and is not
seen on juveniles and non-breeding birds. In flight, it is pale grey and
white with black primaries marked by distinct white windows.
Emits a loud croaking call.*

As Fletcher entered the Grand Hotel, he could see that the wedding reception was still underway in the ballroom, which was packed with guests. The celebrations spilt out into the lobby. A man's voice could be heard singing a nostalgic Bengali love song accompanied by a Hawaiian slide guitar and drums, while children ran about recklessly through the reception area. Fletcher asked for his key and took the lift up to the fourth floor. Sullivan was waiting in a car parked on the street outside, a Ford station wagon with tinted windows.

Stepping into his room, he felt a bewildering sense of indecision and confused emotions. Though Fletcher didn't want to accept what he had been told, it all made sense. From their first encounter until now, he had imagined that Kesang was working for India's Intelligence Bureau in collaboration with Afridi, but never guessed that she might be a Chinese agent. He had been blind to her motives, seduced by her carefree manner and reckless charms. At the same time, part of him still wanted to deny the truth and see Kesang again, so that he could ask her himself. Reluctantly, he collected his toothbrush and razor from the bathroom and began to pack his clothes.

Just as he was about to shut his suitcase, the phone rang. Fletcher hesitated, then picked it up. The connection was poor, with a lot of static, but he recognized Kesang's voice.

'Allan? Is that you?' she said. 'Allan? '

'Yes,' he replied. 'Kesang? Hello!'

'Daddy's died…. Can you come?' he heard her say. After that, the line went dead. Fletcher stood there for a minute holding the receiver, as if it were a useless toy that no longer worked. Putting it down in the cradle, he reached over and picked up his backpack, feeling the reassuring shape of the Beretta through the canvas fabric. Leaving his suitcase, he went out into the hall and locked the door.

Riding the lift downstairs, he tried to collect his thoughts and wondered what he would say to Sullivan. His mind felt as if it were racing in two opposite directions while running in place. The music was still blaring in the lobby but he could barely hear it as he walked out of the hotel and opened the car door.

'Where's your suitcase?' Sullivan demanded.

'I'm not going,' Fletcher said.

'What? Come on, Guy, knock it off,' said Sullivan.

The driver was listening, though he sat facing straight ahead like a stone statue. Fletcher knew he had to keep it brief.

'Dr Mukherjee has died,' he said. 'I need to stay.'

'You're crazy,' said Sullivan. 'It's not safe. I told you.'

'Yeah, I know, but I need to make sure for myself,' he replied.

The older man's face was lined with disapproval, a look that seemed to reject any argument he might have made, though there was a long silence between them.

'Our plane is already on the ground,' Sullivan said, his voice as flat as a hacksaw blade. 'We're getting late. Just go and bring your suitcase now.'

'No,' said Fletcher. 'I'll get to Delhi whenever I can.'

He knew that Sullivan wasn't used to being contradicted, particularly when he'd issued a clear command. At this moment, all of the good humour and avuncular charm had drained away and Fletcher could see only anger in his case officer's eyes, a hardened, unforgiving stare.

'If you don't come with me now, we're done,' Sullivan growled. 'You're on your own!'

Fletcher wished he had time to argue and persuade him, but he had no choice. He saw the driver's eyes in the rear-view mirror, knowing that for the moment there was nothing more he could do.

'I'll take my chances,' he said and got out of the car.

His hands were shaking and his breathing was uneven as he let the door close behind him and walked away, heading in the direction of the hospital. Thirty seconds later, when he looked back, the Ford was gone.

◆

Vagrants. A small flock of seagulls drifted on the swollen brown waters of the Hooghly, paddling about ten feet from shore. At this time of year, they were supposed to be a thousand miles farther north, on Tibetan lakes, but these gulls had decided to stay behind, ignoring their breeding instincts for an easier life on the riverbank in Calcutta.

Five pyres were burning at Nimtala Ghat as the sun descended over the arched silhouette of Howrah Bridge, a steel skeleton of criss-crossing girders and beams. The other pyres had burnt down to embers and the mourners had left. Dr Mukherjee's cremation had been conducted by the family priest, who had chanted Sanskrit prayers and poured ghee and sprinkled sandalwood shavings on the pyre. Two of his nephews attended, observing the final rites with mute indifference. No other women from the family were there, except for Kesang who had insisted on accompanying the body to Nimtala Ghat and now stood beside Fletcher watching the flames, as if in a trance. The heat was intense and they stepped back as the men who managed the crematorium tended the pyres with long poles to make sure that the bodies were consumed. A smell of burnt flesh filled the air and Fletcher felt sweat trickling down his face. Despite the grim surroundings, there was a reassuring sense of finality in the flames.

He remembered his own father's death and the sterile atmosphere of the funeral parlour, the polished wooden coffin, the embalmed corpse, and the neatly dug grave. The cremation on the ghats by the river seemed much more real, raw, and conclusive. Kesang and he had hardly spoken since he had met her at the hospital, where the body was being

transferred to a battered ambulance that served as a hearse. The silence
between them allowed him to set aside his doubts and hold his questions
at bay, at least until the pyre had burnt out.

A garland of marigolds floated on the water, detached from one
of the biers. Fletcher could see the gulls swim towards it, their beaks
tugging at the flowers and then turning away in search of fish or charred
scraps from the pyres. While watching the birds squabbling, he caught
sight of a familiar figure.

Fletcher nudged Kesang's arm. She looked up through the smoke
as Afridi came and put his arm around her. Kesang placed her head on
his shoulder while the two men acknowledged each other with a nod.
No one said anything as they watched the fire burn down while the sun
disappeared behind Howrah Bridge and the gulls flew off downriver.
Finally, the priest gestured that it was time to go and the two nephews
folded their hands and departed without saying a word. Kesang didn't
seem ready to leave but then turned and walked away.

'Where do you need to go?' Afridi asked, once they were on the
street outside, surrounded by the traffic and congestion.

'I'll go to Pema's flat,' she said. '18 Wood Street. Behind St Xavier's.'

Fletcher hailed a cab and got in the front seat, while Kesang and
Afridi sat in the back. None of them spoke on the drive and when
they arrived at the address, Kesang studied the two men with a wistful
smile, then shook her head.

'Thank you both for coming,' she said. 'But if you don't mind, I
think I'd like to be alone this evening.'

'Of course,' said Afridi. 'Are you sure you'll be all right?'

'Yes,' she said. 'I'll be fine. Thank you.'

With that, she opened the door and got out, waving to them before
she disappeared through the entrance to the apartment building. It
was already dark and the streetlights had just come on. The two men
looked at each other.

'Shall we get a drink somewhere?' Fletcher suggested.

'Where are you staying?' Afridi asked.

'The Grand,' said Fletcher.

'Then we'll go to Firpo's. It's just down the street from your hotel.'

Fletcher's clothes still smelt of smoke and perspiration kept trickling down his face but when they entered the restaurant it was cooler than the street and almost empty, too early for other patrons. The bar was off the main dining room. As they went inside, Fletcher could see the long counter of polished wood, extending the length of the room. It looked as if it might have been cut from a single teak tree that once towered over a forest somewhere in Burma. The overhead lights gave off a warm amber glow that glinted off shelves of glasses and bottles. The waiters wore turbans with white and yellow tunics. Firpo's was an old fashioned yet timeless place and Fletcher could imagine Sullivan drinking here during the war.

They ordered beer and when it arrived, Fletcher drained most of his glass in a single swallow. He hadn't realized how thirsty he was.

'So, you got the telegram?' he asked.

'Yes, I left Gangtok straight away,' said Afridi. 'I'm sorry I got here too late.'

'It wouldn't have made any difference. He wasn't conscious,' said Fletcher.

'When did you arrive?'

'Yesterday morning.'

'And you came here just to see Kesang?' Afridi asked.

Fletcher nodded.

'She's a strong woman,' said Afridi. 'Naturally, she's upset, but she'll be all right in a couple of days.'

'It's not something you get over that quickly,' Fletcher responded.

'Of course not,' said Afridi. 'Dr Mukherjee was a good man, and a fine mountaineer. Watching the flames today, I couldn't help thinking how Kesang lost her real father to ice so many years ago and now the man who adopted her has been consumed by fire. In the end, we all go back to the basic elements, don't we?'

'I suppose,' said Fletcher. 'My father went into the earth.'

'As did mine,' said Afridi, 'though I'm not sure any one method of disposal is better than the other. In Tibet, they have sky burials and feed you to vultures, like the Zoroastrians.'

'Speaking of vultures,' said Fletcher. 'I got confirmation that Emil Zorman was shot by the Chinese.'

'No surprise,' Afridi replied, gesturing for the barman to bring two more beers, adding, 'One gets dehydrated in this weather, despite the humidity.'

The two of them watched the barman taking bottles out of the refrigerator and arranging them on a tray, with fresh glasses and a bowl of masala peanuts. After these had been placed in front of them, Fletcher broke the silence.

'I have to ask you something,' he said, 'about Kesang.'

Afridi looked him in the eye. 'Yes, what is it?'

'I was warned that she's a Chinese spy,' said Fletcher. 'Is that true?'

'Who warned you?' Afridi asked, tilting his glass as he poured the beer.

'It doesn't matter,' Fletcher answered.

'Of course it does,' said Afridi. 'If you want me to answer your question, I need to know who's making the accusation.'

'Okay, forget it,' said Fletcher, pouring his beer, 'Never mind. I'm sorry I asked.'

Afridi laughed softly. 'The fact that you won't tell me, gives it away.'

'What do you mean?' Fletcher shook his head.

'It must be your friends from the Embassy, the duck hunters,' Afridi suggested. 'Are they the ones that also told you the Chinese killed Zorman?'

Fletcher took a long pull at his beer. 'So?'

'I would have thought we'd stop playing these games by now,' said Afridi.

'That's why I'm asking you about Kesang,' said Fletcher. 'I don't believe it.'

'You mean you're hoping that I'll tell you she isn't a Chinese spy,' said Afridi. 'What makes you think I would know?'

'Come on,' Fletcher said, 'You're the one who warned me that she's not as innocent as she seems.' Taking a spoonful of peanuts and transferring them to his cupped palm, he then put them in his mouth, one by one.

Afridi seemed to be studying the assortment of bottles behind the bar.

'All right,' he said, at last. 'It's not as simple as you think. I can't give you details but, yes, she is working for the Chinese and has been for several years.'

Fletcher nodded.

'What your friends don't know,' said Afridi, 'is that she also works for me.'

'A double agent?' said Fletcher.

'That's what they call it in the movies,' Afridi replied. 'Though I'm never quite sure what that means. Kesang's loyalties aren't divided. She is my asset and has been from the start.'

'But she passes on information to the Chinese?' said Fletcher.

'Yes. I provide her with enough to make it seem plausible but nothing that seriously affects our security,' said Afridi.

'Who is her Chinese contact?'

'As I said, I can't get into details,' Afridi demurred. 'I've already revealed more than I should.'

'Did she tell the Chinese that Zorman worked for the CIA?' Fletcher asked.

Afridi was now studying the cardboard coaster with Firpo's crest and a damp circle where his beer glass had stood.

'Yes,' he said at last. 'But I was responsible for that. She just passed on the information I gave her.'

'How did you recruit Kesang?' Fletcher asked.

Afridi shook his head. 'That's not something I can reveal.'

'You seduced her?' said Fletcher.

'Of course not,' Afridi answered. 'I may have fallen in love with her, but only after we started working together.'

'Love?' Fletcher smiled. 'That's very unprofessional of you.'

'I told you it was complicated,' Afridi admitted. 'I keep trying to get her to quit and break off her contacts, but she refuses.'

'Is she in danger?'

'All the time,' said Afridi, 'and not just from the Chinese. I've kept her identity hidden from the Intelligence Bureau and my own superiors. She reports only to me.'

'Then why would you tell me?' Fletcher said.

'Because you asked,' said Afridi.

'No, but...'

'I want you to protect her,' he said. 'From your duck hunting friends or anyone else who might want to harm Kesang. Strange as it may seem, you're one of the few people I can trust.'

'Why's that?'

'Because I know you're in love with her too,' said Afridi, raising his hand to catch the barman's eye. 'I'm going to switch to Scotch. Will you join me?'

'Sure,' said Fletcher. 'Why not?'

'Two large Vat 69s,' Afridi told the barman. 'Ice. No water.'

'Don't you think Kesang can take care of herself?' Fletcher asked.

'Most of the time, yes,' said Afridi. 'But I don't like the idea of leaving her alone. You see, I'm going back to rejoin my regiment.'

'In Kashmir?'

'Ladakh,' Afridi said.

'When do you leave?'

'Soon,' said Afridi. 'Day after tomorrow, I'm flying to Delhi. I won't be going back to Kalimpong or Sikkim any time soon.'

They finished their drinks and Fletcher paid up. Afridi seemed more pensive than usual and appeared to be weighing the risk of having told Fletcher the truth about Kesang. As they were leaving Firpo's, he gestured to a set of framed photographs on the wall. Men in uniform were leaning against the long bar, drinks in one hand, cigarettes in the other.

'You might be interested in these,' Afridi said. 'They're from the war. Those are American pilots that flew over the hump. Firpo's was one of their favourite watering holes.'

28

Ibisbill

Ibidorhyncha struthersii

*Though very similar to other waders, such as stints and plovers, the ibisbill
is unique enough to merit its own genus. About the size of a small hen,
it has a broad black band across its breast and a black face with a long,
curved red beak. The belly is white and its wings and neck are grey,
providing perfect camouflage amongst the round rocks that line the banks
of Himalayan riverbeds, where it forages, probing under stones
for worms and other invertebrates.*

Dr Mukherjee had wanted his ashes immersed at the confluence
of the Rangit and Teesta Rivers. Kesang instructed the taxi
driver to stop there on the way up from Siliguri to Kalimpong. The
Teesta was swollen and a muddy brown colour from monsoon run-off
and snowmelt but the Rangit was almost clear, a smaller stream that
spilt into the larger river with a ruffled current. Walking down to the
confluence, Kesang carried a clay pot that contained her father's remains,
its mouth sealed with folded layers of red cloth tied with a cord. Fletcher
followed a few feet behind. The white sand tapered to a point where the
two rivers met and there were scattered boulders and polished stones at
the water's edge.

Kicking off her sandals, Kesang waded into the confluence up to
her knees, unknotted the cord and then unwound the cloth covering.
Watching her, Fletcher thought how much more peaceful it was here
than at the burning ghat in Calcutta. The mountains rose up on every
side, covered with dense green forests, while the roar of the two rivers
drowned out all other sounds. Tipping the urn, Kesang let the ashes

and fragments of bone fall into the flowing water. Once the clay pot was empty, she let it float away until it capsized in the current and disappeared.

At that moment, Fletcher saw two ibisbills flying upriver towards them, no more than three feet above the water, their wings beating in tandem. He hadn't seen this species before but the curved bills and long, extended necks were unmistakable as the pair flew past them and then landed in the rocks further on, where they vanished immediately from view.

'Most of this water comes from the Kanchenjunga,' said Kesang, as she waded out onto the sand and held Fletcher's hand for a moment. 'The Rangit flows off the southern slopes and the Teesta comes down from the north. There's a Lepcha story that says they are two lovers who meet here at the confluence and are joined together forever.'

Letting go of his hand, she made her way up the riverbank to where the taxi was parked. Though Kesang had asked Fletcher to accompany her back to Kalimpong, three days after her father's cremation, he was careful to give her the space and time to mourn. Afridi had seen her to say goodbye before he left Calcutta for Delhi. The past few days had seemed surreal and Fletcher kept replaying the conversation with Sullivan in his mind, remembering his last words, 'We're done. You're on your own!' Though he wondered what would happen next, at the same time, there was a part of him that didn't care.

They drove across the Teesta Bridge and turned off uphill to Kalimpong. Soon they were in the clouds again and the cool, clammy air was strangely comforting. When they reached Montrose, Fletcher let Kesang go ahead, as he paid off the taxi and then carried their bags up the steps and onto the veranda. As soon as he got to the door he heard the parakeet squawk, 'Bloody hell!'

Kesang had insisted that he stay with her instead of going back to the Himalayan Hotel. There was a spare bedroom on the ground floor, at the rear of the house, and the maid, Sunita, showed him the way. Montrose felt deserted and most of the lights were off. He drew aside the curtains on the window, which looked out onto a steep hillside and a retaining wall covered in ferns and moss. With the mist, it was impossible to guess what time it was, though his watch read 5 p.m.

After opening his suitcase and taking out the Beretta, he checked to make sure it was loaded, then tucked the pistol beneath his pillow. Lying down on the bed, Fletcher closed his eyes and tried to forget whatever he'd been told, though his thoughts kept returning to Afridi's words. Their emotions were tangled together just as their motives and missions were entwined. He knew he wasn't *done*, despite what Sullivan had said, and he certainly wasn't *on his own*. More than anything, Fletcher felt a strong desire to shield Kesang from danger. At the same time, he also knew that he would use her, just as Afridi had been using her until now. She was his lover but also an 'asset', and in the strange, distorted vocabulary of their secretive existence, it wasn't so much that they trusted each other but that they had simply set aside their distrust.

Half an hour later, Sunita brought him a cup of tea and a plate of biscuits.

'Didi has gone to bed,' said the maid. 'She told me to tell you that she will see you tomorrow, when she gets up. But I can make some food, if you'd like.'

'No, thank you,' he said. 'I don't need anything more right now.'

◆

The next morning, Kesang was up early and they had breakfast together. She was subdued but calm and spoke about her father's idiosyncrasies.

'He wasn't the easiest person to live with,' she said. 'But at least he didn't get angry or abusive when he was drunk. For a while I tried to make him stop but he couldn't give up alcohol. He called it "liquid poetry" and loved to recite Yeats after a couple of drinks, though if he had two or three more his memory dissolved.'

She told Fletcher how he had inherited a fortune from his grandfather, who had been a major landowner in Birbhum District, though Dr Mukherjee hated spending any of his wealth on himself.

'He was always generous, giving people loans that he never collected,' she said. 'But Daddy refused to buy himself a new shirt, even though all of his collars were frayed. I think it was part of his stubborn Marxist ideology.'

'You're a Marxist too, aren't you?' Fletcher said, smiling.

Kesang shrugged. 'I used to be, but not any more. Daddy never pushed me to join the party but he would talk to me about it sometimes. The idea of class struggle and capitalist exploitation made a lot of sense, when he spoke about it. He was always more in favour of Lenin than Mao, and very critical of Stalin.'

Soon after 10 a.m., people started arriving to offer condolences. Pema Choden was the first to show up and she stayed with Kesang most of the day, while a steady stream of visitors came and went. In the living room, where she received them, was a framed photograph of Dr Mukherjee, from his younger days, and Kesang had put a vase of flowers beside it. Fletcher remained in the background. Just before noon he went across to the Forest Department Office, hoping to see Thupten but he was told that the DFO was away in Darjeeling and wouldn't return until tomorrow. When he got back to Montrose, Eddie Lim was there to pay his respects. A little while later, Colonel Norton showed up, wearing a tweed coat and tie. He placed a comforting hand on Kesang's cheek, as if she were a child, and spoke softly with her for a while. As he was leaving, he shook hands with Fletcher though neither of them said anything to each other.

Around six in the evening, the last of the visitors departed and Pema finally went home as well. Kesang looked exhausted and Fletcher expected her to excuse herself and go to her room, but she sat down beside him and leaned her head on his shoulder, as he put an arm around her.

'Your father obviously had a lot of admirers,' said Fletcher. 'There must have been more than a hundred people who came by today.'

'I suppose they feel a need to show sympathy and honour his memory,' Kesang said. 'But there are also those who come out of a sense of morbid curiosity, or for other motives.'

'What do you mean?' Fletcher asked.

'I'm sure that a lot of people wonder what's going to happen to me and they think that Daddy's family will throw me out of this house, now that he's gone,' she said. 'Whenever there's property to be inherited, it always leads to disputes and it's no secret that Daddy's sister and her sons never liked me.'

'Do you have a good lawyer?' Fletcher asked.

'Yes, I'll be fine,' she said. 'Daddy wrote a will and made sure that everything he owned would come to me. Ten years ago, he put this house in my name and added my signature to all of his bank accounts and investments.'

'Do you think they'll challenge the will?' he asked.

'I suppose they might, but it's registered in court. Anyway, I don't want to think about it right now,' she said, closing her eyes and leaning against him.

They were quiet for a while as the setting sun shone through the mist outside, turning everything saffron and gold.

'Imtiaz said he spoke to you,' Kesang murmured, her eyes still shut. 'He told you that I have a Chinese contact.'

'Yes,' said Fletcher.

'What else did he say?' she asked.

'He was worried about your safety and asked me to protect you,' said Fletcher.

She began to laugh, softly. 'Why do men always think that women are so vulnerable and helpless?'

'I don't think you're helpless,' said Fletcher, 'but your life could be at risk. They must know that I'm staying here.'

'Of course. They know all about you,' she said.

'Who is your Chinese contact?' Fletcher asked.

'It's better that I don't tell you,' Kesang replied. 'He was here today. He came to offer condolences but also gave me instructions.'

Fletcher looked at her with surprise.

'What did he ask you to do?'

'They want me to find out from you where the CIA has hidden the relics that were smuggled out of Tibet,' she explained.

'There aren't any relics,' said Fletcher.

'I know,' said Kesang. 'But they still think the Khampas brought them across the mountains and hid them somewhere in Sikkim.'

'Afridi must have told you about the boy, the Rinpoche....' Fletcher began before Kesang interrupted him.

'They don't believe that story,' she insisted. 'They are convinced the treasure exists and that the CIA is still planning to sell it and use the money to support Chushi Gangdruk insurgents. Today, when my contact spoke to me, he said I must get the information from you...to prove that I'm not working for the Americans.'

'That's impossible,' said Fletcher.

'Damn fool!' the parakeet cried, startling them both. He had been sitting silently in his cage until now.

Kesang laughed. 'Hari misses Daddy. There's no one to swear back at him.'

Fletcher studied the parakeet for a moment and wondered if the bird was capable of understanding that Dr Mukherjee had died.

'You can tell your contact that I know where the relics are,' he whispered after several minutes of silence.

Kesang looked up at him puzzled.

'Tell them that there was an avalanche on 12 August, caused by a gunfight between the Khampas and PLA soldiers below Kellas Col, on the border of Sikkim and Tibet,' Fletcher explained. 'A number of men were killed and the yaks that were carrying the antiquities were buried under the snow. The Rinpoche escaped but the relics from his monastery are gone. They can confirm this with the Chinese officers commanding that unit. There were only two survivors on their side.'

'Is it true?' said Kesang.

'Most of it,' said Fletcher. 'At least enough to convince them for a while.'

'You saw it happen?' she said.

He nodded. The parakeet gave another cry but this time there were no words, just a demanding screech. Kesang got up and went to the kitchen. Several minutes later, she came back with a green chilli that she fed to the bird through the bars of its cage. Fletcher could see the worried look on her face.

'There's something more,' she said, sitting down beside him again. 'They want to know when you're planning to go out in the field again and where you'll be doing your research.'

Her right hand brushed against Fletcher's and she interlaced her fingers between his. Kesang closed her eyes again and he kissed her forehead gently.

'You can tell them I'm planning to go up to the Neora Valley next week on Tuesday. There's a forest hut, at a place called Tenga Camp, about eight miles beyond Lava. I'll be staying there on my own.'

29

Sikkim Bay-owl

Phodilus badius saturatus

*Extremely rare. According to Salim Ali, there has been only one recorded
sighting in the Teesta Valley (20 November 1915 by G. E. Shaw).
Presumed to be a subspecies of the Oriental bay-owl, it is closely related
to barn owls. About the size of a pigeon and a chestnut brown colour,
it has large, pale eye discs surrounded by a white ruff trimmed with
darker feathers. Bay-owls are found in other parts of
Asia and are entirely nocturnal.*

Thupten had offered to send one of his forest guards to accompany
Fletcher but he had declined, saying that he was happier working
on his own. A jeep-taxi dropped him off at Tenga Camp in the early
afternoon. The hut was deserted and it didn't look as if anyone had
stayed there for years. He had a key to the padlock on the front door.
Inside, the single room was full of cobwebs and one of the windows
was broken, through which a number of creatures had entered, leaving
their dung on the floor. There was also a leak in the roof and one wall
was covered with slime. Rather than stay indoors, Fletcher decided that
he would sleep on the veranda, which was open on three sides but deep
enough to shelter him from the rain.

The location was dramatic, at a point where the valley narrowed
into a gorge, with cliffs on one side of a swift mountain stream that
flowed two hundred feet below the hut. On one of the overhanging
rock faces, eight hundred yards above, he could see a cluster of large
beehives hanging from the underside of a cliff. Thupten had warned
him about these.

'Rock bees are more dangerous than most predators we have in our forests,' Thupten had said. '*Apis dorsata laboriosa* is the Himalayan giant honey bee. They usually mind their own business but if disturbed they will viciously attack anything that comes in their way. A swarm can kill a horse or a man. The hives above the hut have been there for years and you should avoid that area.'

'Does anyone collect the honey?' Fletcher had asked.

'There are a few Nepalis who know how to harvest the hives,' Thupten had explained. 'The honey is poisonous but valuable as medicine. The bees gather the nectar from toxic flowers like rhododendrons. Even a small drop on your tongue makes your mouth go numb. It can cause hallucinations.'

The jungle had been cleared in front of the hut, right up to the edge where a cliff fell away into the gorge. At the back, however, the branches of trees touched the rusty metal roof while monsoon shrubs and weeds had grown close to the walls. Directly in front of the building was a dead birch with skeletal limbs and a trunk around two feet in diameter. As he studied the location and surrounding terrain, Fletcher considered his options.

Unpacking the mist nets, he strung up two of them behind the forest hut. Each of the nets was thirty feet long and eight feet high, made of nylon mesh. Securing the upper corners to the branches of trees and tying the lower edges to sturdy shrubs, he created an invisible barrier on either side. Though it wasn't raining, the clouds were slowly descending and the beehives were now hidden from view. His equipment and sleeping bag lay at the centre of the veranda. As it began to grow dark, he broke off several dead branches from the birch and lit a fire outside. Opening a tin of sardines, he ate them with a couple of cold parathas, wrapping the oily fish inside the flat, leathery pieces of bread.

Plenty of sounds came from the forest, mostly birdcalls but also the repeated alarm cries of a barking deer on a ridge above. The only motorable route into the Neora Valley was the unpaved jeep track he had taken, though there were other paths and game trails through the forest. The cliffs directly below the hut were too steep to climb without ropes and he felt sure that if anyone approached, they would come from the rear. As it grew dark, Fletcher lit a candle. Dripping wax on the concrete floor, he stuck the candle in the centre of the veranda so that it cast a pool of light near the door of the hut. He also stuffed his sleeping bag with some of his supplies so that it looked as if he had gone to bed. Taking the Beretta out of his rucksack, along with a small torch, Fletcher positioned himself with his back to the dead tree, hidden within its mossy shadows, beyond the dim circle of firelight.

Soon after he finished his meal, Fletcher was watching sparks rise with the smoke when a bird flew past him on his left. It was completely silent and all he saw was the blur of its wings as it swooped away from the light and disappeared into darkness. He knew immediately that it was some kind of owl. Its flight reminded him of barn owls he'd seen in America, though the bird was much smaller.

Several months ago, at The Farm, one of the instructors had spoken about the need to rely on first impressions, 'because sometimes that's all you have,' he'd said. 'An agent in the field has to depend on a lot of guesswork, sorting through scraps of information to try and piece together some shadow of the truth.' This idea had appealed to Fletcher because it was similar to birdwatching, in which there was always an element of ambiguity. He had mentioned this to the instructor, explaining how even a professional ornithologist depends on something called 'jizz' to help identify species that aren't clearly seen or heard. 'Jizz' or 'giss' stood for 'General Impression of Size and Shape', which allowed an experienced birdwatcher to speculate about what kind of bird he had seen. The same ability to interpret incomplete and fragmented information was a prerequisite for intelligence work, when only a few stray facts were available.

Every spy is a hunter-gatherer, Fletcher thought as he sat facing the fire and the hut. For all of his planning and careful calculations, he knew that he must rely on primal instincts. While the flames burnt down, he waited for the owl to return, as well as for the arrival of his unknown assailants.

◆

After passing on the information to her Chinese contact, Kesang had tried to persuade Fletcher to cancel his visit to Tenga Camp, but he had assured her that the element of surprise was on his side and he would be careful. Nevertheless, she seemed conflicted and uncertain. He wondered how much of it was because of her father's death or if there was something more that she hadn't told him. Two nights ago, they had made love again but he could tell their relationship had changed. The spontaneous passions, which had brought them together, were now restrained by doubts and uncertainties, as well as mistrust.

Earlier that day, Kesang had been going through Dr Mukherjee's study, sorting some of his papers and belongings. From his cupboard she had taken out an old ice axe with a wooden shaft, showing it Fletcher.

'I think I'll give this to Imtiaz,' she'd said. 'I know he'll appreciate it.'

She had also showed Fletcher her father's collection of Tibetan artefacts, some of which were on display in the main rooms of the house, including more than two dozen thangka scroll paintings. In the old man's bedroom were several trunks filled with ritual objects, one of which was a ceremonial horn made from a human shinbone, encased in ornate silver. There was also the upper half of a man's skull that had been fashioned into a chalice. Many of the images were grotesque and frightening, reflecting the mythology of Tantric Buddhism, a mysterious and macabre realm of demons and deities. Picking through the stash of antiques, Fletcher examined a copper oil lamp shaped like a lotus.

'Many of the refugees that came through Kalimpong in 1959 and afterwards were carrying objects they had salvaged from shrines and temples. They were desperate for money and Daddy would pay them whatever they asked,' said Kesang, picking up a brass dorjee, or thunderbolt. 'He used to tell me that if anyone asked him to return what they'd sold, he would happily give it back for free. He wasn't a serious collector. After a while I don't think he even knew what he possessed.'

'What are you going to do with all of this stuff?' Fletcher said.

'I don't know. The American art dealer told us it was valuable,' she said. 'Maybe I'll open an antique shop.'

'You know that he was killed, don't you?' said Fletcher. When Kesang gave him a questioning glance, he added, 'the art dealer, Emil Zorman.'

'No,' she said.

'Afridi didn't tell you?' he asked.

Kesang looked confused and he could see that she had no idea what he was talking about.

'Who killed him?' Kesang asked.

'The Chinese,' said Fletcher. 'They thought he knew where the terma was hidden.'

'Why would they care so much?' she said, impatiently.

'You should ask your contact,' Fletcher suggested.

'He wouldn't know,' she said. 'He's just a postman delivering messages back and forth.'

'Do you know who receives your messages?' Fletcher asked.

'I don't know his real name. He only signs his communications as Comrade Jiu, which means the number nine,' she said.

'Do you know where he is? Delhi? Peking?' said Fletcher.

'Delhi, I think, or maybe Calcutta,' said Kesang. 'He once asked me to find out if the Maharaj Kumar of Sikkim trusted Nehru. He wanted to know if the Prince would let his country become a part of India.'

'What did you say?'

'Imtiaz gave me a copy of a letter from the Maharaj Kumar to Nehru, insisting that his country must remain independent but asking Delhi for financial help so that Sikkim could develop its economy and become self-sufficient,' Kesang explained.

'And was the letter real or a forgery?'

'It was a carbon copy typed on the Crown Prince's stationery,' she said. 'Comrade Jiu seemed pleased to get it.'

'Why can't you tell me who your contact is?' Fletcher asked. 'The postman?'

'Because I want to protect him. Even Imtiaz doesn't know who he is,' she explained.

Fletcher didn't push Kesang any further but he decided to use the dead drop once again, hoping that Agatha would pass on a message to Merlin. This time, the code was taken from the first line of 'Recessional,' another poem by Kipling that Sullivan had chosen. Fletcher wrote out the verse, 'God of our fathers, known of old/ Lord of our far-flung battle-line,' as well as the corresponding letters of the alphabet. As before, he kept the message simple and brief, reporting that Kesang worked for Afridi and not the Chinese, though she was operating as a double agent. Fletcher also informed Merlin that he was going to the Neora Valley for a few days and if anything happened to him, Kesang should not be held responsible.

◆

Sitting in the dark, watching the birch branches smouldering as the fire died out, Fletcher wondered if Sullivan would believe him when he deciphered the message or if he would still think that his rookie agent had been outplayed in a treacherous contest, a novice who had waded in over his head. The Beretta felt almost weightless in his hand and he wished he was armed with something more substantial. By now, most of the night sounds had fallen silent, except for a few insects humming in his ears and the furtive rustle of a mouse or some other small creature moving about in the grass.

The candle had melted down to less than half its original height, though the guttering flame continued to illuminate the veranda with a flickering aura. Layers of mist had enveloped the hut and the burning wick seemed farther away than before. Fletcher remained wide awake but his eyes struggled to penetrate the shadows. Suddenly, he heard an abrupt yelp, several hundred yards behind him, the alarm call of a barking deer. The cry was repeated three times and Fletcher could tell that the deer had been startled by something in the dark.

Listening attentively, he waited for at least ten minutes before he heard wet leaves brushing against each other, though he could not locate the sound. It might have been the breeze, which ruffled the mist and teased the candle flame. But again, there was a discernible noise, so soft that it could have been the last whisper of the fire, though he knew it was something more. Perhaps the owl had returned, its feathers as silent as smoke. There was no sign of any movement. The darkness was complete beyond the glimmering puddle of light on the veranda.

He could now hear the distinct footsteps of someone approaching, cautiously and slowly, but with a determined tread. Rather than coming from behind the hut, as he had expected, the direction of the sound seemed to be somewhere off to his right, where the jeep track came up the valley and entered the gorge. Fletcher had set up the nets hoping they would signal the arrival of his attackers, but now they served no purpose and all he could do was try to trace the faint sounds.

For more than a minute there was silence and he wondered if his ears had deceived him until he saw a figure slip out of the shadows and onto the veranda. The man was dressed in shorts and a singlet, with a chequered cotton scarf draped over his shoulders, the kind that labourers used to wipe away their sweat. He had an M1 in his hands. Seconds later, a second killer emerged from the darkness into the halo of candlelight. This man had a carbine too. Without hesitation, he lifted it to his shoulder and fired at the sleeping bag.

The gunshot sounded brittle, like a dry branch snapping in two. The first man stepped forward and kicked the mummy bag with his bare foot. Saying something to his companion, he leaned down. Suddenly, realizing that they had walked into a trap, the two men turned to face the darkness.

Fletcher had his pistol raised, as he called out in Hindi for them to drop their weapons. Instead, both men immediately fired in the direction of his voice, missing him by several yards. The first bullet from the Beretta caught one of the shooters in the chest and he fell back against the door of the hut, almost knocking down the candle. Struggling to raise his carbine, the man fired once more, just as Fletcher's second bullet hit him in the face. The other shooter tried to escape, darting out of the light and into the shadows behind the hut. Fletcher got up and ran forward, his left hand reaching for the torch. As he turned it on, he could see the man tangled in the net, yanking it free from the branch overhead but unable to escape into the jungle beyond. The torch beam held him in its unrelenting gaze. Once more, Fletcher shouted in Hindi, telling his attacker to surrender, but the assassin twisted around and fired his carbine wildly in the direction of the light. The Beretta barked twice, a sharp, decisive sound.

Fletcher could see from the wavering beam of the torch that his hand was shaking and he took several deep breaths. Crossing quickly to the veranda, he checked on the dead man, kicking the carbine aside as a precaution. Fletcher's fingers searched for the carotid artery in the killer's neck but there was no pulse. He could see where his second bullet had entered just below the man's right eye.

After replacing the magazine in his Beretta, he went across to the mist net, which was wrapped around the second shooter like a spider's web. Pulling the nylon mesh aside, he rolled the body over and saw that one of his bullets had entered the man's gut, near his navel, while the other had gone straight to his heart. He could almost hear his instructor at the firing range on The Farm, congratulating him for hitting the bull's eye, though Fletcher felt no sense of elation or satisfaction.

He had killed two men who had tried to kill him. That simple equation justified whatever he'd done, though he felt a strange sense of anger and remorse at having been forced to take human lives. He had warned them, but they had no intention of surrendering. Though he wasn't sure if these were the same men who had ambushed the jeep, it seemed likely.

Fletcher knew that he had to get rid of the bodies, but first he retrieved his camera from the rucksack. Attaching a flash, he took pictures of the dead men's faces in case they needed to be identified. Both of them looked as if they might be Chinese, but he wasn't sure. They could have been from any one of a dozen tribal communities that lived in these mountains, their ancestry as opaque as the mist. Staring down at the lifeless, anonymous features he realized that he would probably never know who they were, nameless foot soldiers in a revolution that promised freedom but delivered death. Shaking off these thoughts, Fletcher calculated the odds of someone searching for the bodies in the gorge.

Neither of the men was carrying anything in his pockets, except for extra ammunition. Dragging the first shooter off the veranda, Fletcher hauled his limp corpse across the wet grass to the far edge of the clearing. Shining his torch into the gorge, he could see that there was a straight drop of two hundred feet, at the bottom of which lay a thicket of bamboo. The dead man tumbled as he fell, striking the rocks several times before plunging headfirst into the dense foliage below. The second victim followed the first and after disposing of both, along with their carbines, Fletcher scanned the bamboo thicket with his torch. It was as if the green abyss had swallowed them whole.

There was a streak of blood on the veranda but Fletcher was able to wipe most of it up with a handful of wadded leaves that he tossed over the edge. More than an hour had passed since the shots had been fired and the night was silent again. As he added another branch to the fire and stoked the flames, he heard a rustling sound from the far side of the hut.

Shining his torch in that direction, he saw that a bird was entangled in the mist net, fluttering its wings in a futile attempt to escape. He could tell it was an owl with broad eye discs and russet brown feathers. Picking up his camera again, Fletcher took three pictures. Blinded by the flash, the owl didn't react when he reached out and caught it by the wings, gently pulling it free of the net. Examining the bird closely, he knew that his guess had been right. It was an Oriental bay-owl, probably the subspecies *Phodilus badius saturatus.* Looking into its wide eyes for a moment longer, he let the bird go and watched it vanish into the night.

◆

Rain fell for a couple of hours before dawn and when there was finally enough light, Fletcher cleared up any remaining evidence of the shooting, collecting the spent shell casings and washing the bloodstains off the veranda. He took down the mist nets and rolled them up carefully. Nobody was likely to visit the hut for several weeks but he knew that he should take precautions, no matter how unpleasant it might be. Searching for a path leading into the gorge he finally found a ravine half a mile below the hut where he was able to descend to the stream. Heading up the narrow valley he reached the foot of the cliff. The bodies were lying where they'd fallen though they had stiffened overnight. It was difficult to pry them loose from the bamboo but eventually he was able to drag them across to an eroded trench, parallel to the stream.

Though everything was wet from last night's rain, there was plenty of driftwood along the stream bed. Using the papery leaves and dead stems of bamboo, he was able to get a fire burning. Smoke mingled with the mist and the flames were a translucent orange in the green shadows of the gorge. He kept adding wood and let it burn for most of the day. The two carbines were also added to the blaze, after Fletcher unloaded them and tossed the bullets into the stream. By late afternoon only ashes remained, a few charred bones and the blackened barrels of the guns, which looked like burnt sticks. Collecting stones from the stream bed, Fletcher buried the remains of the fire until there was nothing but a heap of rocks like the debris from a flash flood. He knew that the jungle would cover it completely within weeks, long before anyone else set foot in the gorge.

30

Verditer Flycatcher

Muscicapa thalassina

One of several Old World flycatchers found throughout the Himalayan range, this sky blue bird, about the size of a sparrow, is often seen perched on the tops of trees or on electric lines from where it hunts for insects in the air. It has a black eye stripe and an indistinct black mark on the forehead. Nests on the ground beneath rocky overhangs. The female is also blue but not as bright as the male, tending towards grey. It has a faint trilling call, like the ringing of a tiny silver bell.

Kanchenjunga was visible for the first time since Fletcher had come to Kalimpong. The monsoon clouds finally parted, revealing the enormous white massif rising above a green panorama of intervening ranges. A couple of days had passed since Fletcher had returned from the Neora Valley. He and Kesang were on their way to lunch at the Nanking, when he spotted the mountain. Used to seeing the layers of monsoon mist and cumulus formations, he mistook it for a cloud at first. The huge cluster of white summits rose up in the distance like a thunderstorm gathering on the horizon.

'Is that what I think it is?' Fletcher asked, stopping in his tracks.

'Yes,' said Kesang. 'I've seen Kanchenjunga for as long as I can remember, ever since I was a little girl. But it always takes me by surprise.'

'It's a beautiful mountain, though I don't think I'd ever want to climb it,' said Fletcher. 'Looks too cold and steep.'

Kesang nodded. 'I don't know what it is that drives someone to try and conquer a mountain. It's much better to look at them from a distance, like this, rather than risking your life and freezing to death.

Daddy tried to explain it to me, many times, but I couldn't understand.'

'Afridi obviously feels an urge to get to the top,' said Fletcher.

'I think it's a very selfish thing to do,' said Kesang.

He looked at her, surprised.

'How come?'

'People risk their lives trying to reach the summit and when they die it's supposed to be heroic, some kind of noble sacrifice, but really it's just a stupid way to lose your life, isn't it?'

'I suppose,' said Fletcher.

'My real father, Dawa Norbu, was killed up there,' she said, pointing toward the massif. 'On one of outlying peaks called Jannu, which is also known as Kumbakarna, the sleeping giant. He climbed with Daddy because he was paid to do it. That's the only reason Sherpas climb mountains, because it's a job. For Daddy it was an obsession, a challenge that made him feel alive and successful and brave but for my real father it was how he earned a living. That's the difference, I suppose.'

'Do you remember your real father?' Fletcher asked.

'No. I was only three years old when he died,' she said.

'Do you have any photographs of him?' he asked.

'Yes, there are several with Daddy, standing on a summit somewhere, or at base camp before they started to climb. They're posing for the camera and smiling, with their arms across each other's shoulders,' she said. 'I always wondered, if my father hadn't died on the mountain, what would have become of me?'

The two of them stared at Kanchenjunga for a few minutes more and then moved on in silence until they came to the staircase leading up to the Nanking. Eddie Lim greeted them enthusiastically and kissed Kesang on both cheeks.

'I'm glad to see you out and about,' he said.

Music was playing softly in the background, an instrumental number by The Shadows. Eddie led them to a table in the corner, next to one of the windows overlooking the street. A few other customers were in the restaurant. Kesang waved to one of them as they sat down.

After Eddie left and they were alone, she said, 'There were times when I used to blame Daddy for my father's death, usually when I was angry with him because of something else.'

'I suppose it's only natural...' Fletcher started to say.

'And if you'd been killed by those two men,' she said. 'I would have blamed myself for putting you in danger.'

'It wouldn't have been your fault,' said Fletcher, with a smile. 'It's not the same thing, really.'

He had told Kesang most of what had happened at Tenga Camp, explaining how he had set the trap and shot the two attackers then thrown their bodies over the cliff and burned them. The recent memory still made Fletcher catch his breath, not so much out of fear but because he had pulled the trigger without hesitation, becoming a predator like the two men he'd killed.

'What do you think will happen now?' Kesang asked.

'It's hard to know,' he replied. 'Honestly, I don't think anyone's going to care much about those men. The real problem is that they failed to kill me.'

'Do you think they'll try again?'

'It's possible,' said Fletcher, as the waiter arrived to take their order. Kesang knew the menu by heart and he let her decide what they would eat.

'I think you should go away from here, maybe back to America,' said Kesang, after the waiter had gone. 'It's not safe for you to stay in Kalimpong. Things are getting worse. Everybody is getting paranoid about the Chinese.'

'I don't want to leave just yet,' said Fletcher. 'Unless you want me to go.'

'Of course, I don't,' said Kesang. 'But for your safety....'

'What about yours?' he said, reaching across the table to touch her hand.

'Don't worry. I can take care of myself,' she said.

Though he could still see the sadness in her eyes, Kesang seemed more at ease, away from the house. Outside the window, and across the street, were several strands of electric wires. Perched on one of these was a verditer flycatcher.

'What kind of bird is that?' Kesang asked.

'*Muscicapa thalassina*,' said Fletcher. 'A verditer flycatcher.'

She looked at him and laughed. 'How do you know all that?'

'I'm an ornithologist, remember?'

'Of course,' she said. 'I almost forgot. But why would anyone give a little blue bird a complicated name like that?'

'Verditer means a chalky blue,' said Fletcher. '*Musca* is a fly in Latin and *capere* is to catch. Taxonomists put it together as *Muscicapa*. And *thalassina* is the colour of the sea.'

Kesang rolled her eyes. 'All I asked for was the bird's name, not a lecture on natural history!'

Soon after their meal arrived, they could hear the sound of rowdy voices coming up the stairs and a group of four young men entered the restaurant, speaking loudly in Bengali. As they swaggered into the room, Fletcher could tell they had been drinking from the way they moved and the dull aggression in their eyes.

Kesang made a face. 'Tourists!' she said, under her breath.

Eddie had come out from the kitchen and spoke to the men, who demanded a table near the windows. One of the waiters appeared and the tourists beckoned to him, asking for beer and ignoring Eddie, who was trying to steer them toward a table at the back. Suddenly, one of the men erupted in anger.

'Chinese bastard!' he shouted in English.

'No. I'm Indian,' Eddie responded in a stern but even tone.

'Look at your face,' the man said, loudly, then spat on the floor.

'Please leave,' said Eddie, quietly but firmly. 'You're disturbing the others.'

'Don't you tell us to leave, Chinky boy,' said one of the others. 'This is our country. Not yours! Go back to China!'

By now, two more waiters had emerged, along with one of the cooks. They tried to herd the tourists out the door but they resisted, yelling more abuse.

Fletcher and Kesang pushed back their chairs and stood up. When the tourists saw them coming, one of them blurted out, 'Foreigner, fuck you!'

'Go on. Get out,' said Fletcher. 'You've been told to leave.'

One of the men responded with an ugly laugh. The others leered at Kesang.

'Oi, Chin Chin Choo. Hello darling, how do you do?' two of them started to sing the lyrics of a popular film song.

Kesang replied in Bengali, her voice full of indignation and rage. Stepping between Eddie and the four men, she pointed her finger in their faces. Fletcher couldn't understand a word of what she said but the four tourists quickly backed down, turning away with surly expressions and moving toward the exit. As they left, one of them muttered something back at her, before they escaped.

Eddie looked shaken though the waiters were all grinning because of Kesang's tirade. The guests at one of the other tables applauded, as she and Fletcher went back to their meal and picked up their chopsticks. Moments later, Eddie came across and thanked them.

'It's getting bad,' he said, shaking his head. 'People just don't understand. With all the trouble on the border, anyone who looks Chinese is seen as the enemy.'

'What did you say to those goons?' Fletcher asked Kesang.

She shook her head. 'Never mind.'

Eddie smiled and put a hand on her shoulder. 'Some things don't translate that easily,' he said. 'Bengali is a poetic language but the obscenities are particularly colourful, especially when they're delivered by a Loreto Convent girl.'

'What would you have done if they hadn't backed off?' Fletcher asked.

'I knew they would,' said Kesang with a shrug. 'They're cowards. Anyone who talks like that about someone else, it's because they're afraid of people who don't look like themselves.'

◆

A Zenith shortwave radio sat on a side table in the living room at Montrose. Kesang explained that it hadn't been switched on in months. Dr Mukherjee would listen to BBC broadcasts from time to time and she occasionally tuned in to Radio Ceylon for the Binaca Hit Parade.

With the escalating situation along the border, Fletcher began listening to the English news on All India Radio every morning and evening, though the reports were vague, referring to 'increased provocation' by China, both in Ladakh and NEFA. A couple of times the newsreaders mentioned Sikkim and Nathu La but there seemed to be no immediate cause for concern. The BBC and Voice of America reported belligerent rhetoric coming out of Peking, accusing Indian troops of intruding into their territory, though it was difficult to tell how serious things actually were. The *Himalayan Observer* published alarmist headlines and an unsigned opinion piece, titled 'Chinese Whispers', in which the author, probably the Kazini, claimed that the communists were brainwashing Sikkimese villagers and shepherds along the border, in order to create a cohort of insurgents who would come to their aid when the PLA poured over the passes. *The Statesman* and the *Times of India* were more restrained, though by the third week of October there was a growing sense of anxiety about Chinese intentions. The government of India's official statements, however, expressed confidence that these were minor disputes that could be easily resolved through negotiation.

Rumours began to circulate in Kalimpong and Kesang got several phone calls from friends, warning her to stock up on supplies because the Marwari merchants were planning to close their shops and run away to the plains. Someone else reported that the main water tanks, which supplied the town with drinking water, had been poisoned by Chinese saboteurs and everyone should collect their own rainwater instead. The Scottish Mission Hospital had supposedly treated several patients for gunshot wounds and injuries from Chinese bombs—it later turned out they were PWD labourers who had been injured while clearing a landslide. Meanwhile, Kesang's contact hadn't been in touch since their last communication. Both Merlin and Agatha had fallen silent too, though Fletcher checked the dead drop at the orchid house and found that his last message had been picked up.

Through Thupten, Fletcher befriended a young civil servant from Bhutan, named Palden Wangchuk, who was related to the royal family and stationed at Bhutan House. He was a liaison officer for the Queen Mother who lived in Kalimpong. They met a couple of times for coffee, on the pretext of getting permission for Fletcher to do research on birds in Bhutan. Palden was talkative and reported that the Bhutanese government was growing worried about the Chinese threat. Their army consisted of only 1,400 volunteers, most of whom were armed with flintlocks and other outdated weapons. He explained that the main route from Bhutan to Sikkim passed through the Chumbi Valley and for the past few weeks the Chinese had been stopping people from going back and forth.

Fletcher wrote up a coded report on his conversations with Wangchuk and left a signal for Agatha to check the dead drop. He deliberately didn't mention the two men he had killed, knowing that Sullivan's suspicions about Kesang would be aroused. A couple of times, he had seen Colonel Norton from a distance, walking his spaniels in the morning, but he knew better than to request another meeting. Staying indoors most of the time, he browsed Dr Mukherjee's library, which consisted almost exclusively of poetry and books on mountaineering.

Four days after the incident with the tourists at the Nanking, Fletcher and Kesang were sitting together in the living room after dinner. Sunita, the maid, had washed the dishes and left for the night. The news on the radio that evening had more of the same. Pouring himself a couple fingers of whisky from Dr Mukherjee's bar, he opened a copy of Maurice Herzog's *Annapurna*.

'I got a letter from Imtiaz today,' Kesang said. 'He asked about you.'

'Does he know that I'm staying here?' Fletcher answered, taking a sip of his drink and feeling the alcohol numbing his lips.

'Why do you care?' she said.

'Just asking,' he said, pretending to read the book. 'What else did he have to report? Is he in Ladakh?'

'He doesn't say…but I think he must be,' she said.

Fletcher nodded and turned the page. Out of the corner of his eye, he could see Kesang rise from her chair and go across to the birdcage where Hari sat on his perch. 'Good night,' she said softly and the bird replied with a shrill 'Good night!' as she covered his cage.

Kesang came across and took the book out of Fletcher's hand. She then kissed him and they began to make love on the sofa. When Fletcher reached over to switch off the reading lamp, Kesang told him to leave it on.

'I want to be able to see you,' she said.

Undressing him, she ran her fingers over the back of his neck which was sunburnt and traced the line of his collar, below which his skin was pale.

'You're so white!' she said, laughing. 'I've never understood why people want to be fair-skinned. There were girls in school with me who used to cover their faces with cold cream every night, trying to lighten their complexions.'

'When I was growing up in Delhi,' Fletcher said, 'some of the kids I played with would tease me, calling me a "gora" because I was white. They also called me a red monkey because of the way I blushed when I got angry or embarrassed. I remember wishing I was brown, so that I could blend in and not be seen as a foreigner all the time.'

Stroking his shoulders and chest, Kesang compared her skin colour to his.

'If I was a bird,' she said. 'What colour would you say I was?'

He thought for a moment. 'Fulvous,' he replied.

'And you?' she asked.

'Pallid.'

As her hands moved lower, Fletcher pulled Kesang towards him. In the amber light from the reading lamp their naked bodies were moulded into one. Fletcher closed his eyes and let his other senses take over, inhaling the musky fragrance of Kesang's skin, hearing the choked intake of her breath, tasting the salt in her saliva, and feeling the warm touch of her tongue as their nerves were braided together. Opening his eyes, Fletcher could see their shadows projected on the wall behind them, a moving silhouette that looked like an outlandish two-headed creature with four arms and four legs, wrestling with itself. When the struggle finally ended, he kissed her shoulder and pointed towards the wall, as their bodies disengaged.

'At least our shadows are the same colour,' he said.

Collecting their clothes from the floor, they switched off the lights and went upstairs to Kesang's room. She put on a nightgown as he pulled on his shorts and a t-shirt. Holding each other in bed, they spoke in whispers, talking about nothing that mattered. Lulled by the sound of each other's voice, they gradually fell asleep.

◆

Sometime later that night, Fletcher woke up with a start, as he heard a familiar cry from downstairs: 'Bloody hell! Bugger off!'

He knew it was Hari, the parakeet, but couldn't figure out why he was calling in the middle of the night. Lying still, Fletcher listened but there was silence. Turning over, he found that Kesang was not in the bed beside him. The room was completely dark though he could see the outline of the window and the shape of a wardrobe nearby. He wondered if Kesang had gone to the bathroom but then heard someone coming up the staircase from the living room. Realizing the parakeet must have sensed an intruder, Fletcher remembered that the Beretta was in his room downstairs. An artery pulsed in his neck as the wooden steps creaked.

For a moment, he thought Kesang might have gone downstairs for some reason but there was something about the footsteps that alerted him to danger, a cautious, stealthy approach. Fletcher was lying on his right side, with the covers pulled up over his left shoulder. He knew that the door was five feet from the foot of the bed. Calculating the distance, he figured that if he waited until the intruder entered the room, he would be able to throw himself out of the bed and reach him in a couple of strides. His muscles tensed in anticipation while his left hand was ready to fling off the covers.

The door opened slowly, admitting a faint glow from a bulb on the veranda. He saw the shape of a man appear and he could see a revolver in his hand. Fletcher began to count the seconds as the figure took a step forward...one...two....

As he tossed the sheet and blanket away from his body and lunged off the bed, there was a gunshot. Before he could reach the figure in the doorway, the man had fallen backwards, grunting with pain as he collapsed on the floor. In the same instant, he saw someone step from behind the wardrobe and knew it was Kesang. She moved towards the doorway and switched on the light.

The sudden glare of electricity was blinding. Kesang held a pistol in her hand as she approached the man lying in the hall outside. He had on a pair of jeans and was wearing sneakers, his legs splayed out and his body twisted at the waist with his face to the floor. The revolver lay inches away from his outstretched hand. Fletcher stepped past Kesang and knelt beside the man, feeling for a pulse.

'Is he alive?' she asked.

'I think so,' said Fletcher, rolling him over.

As he did, the man's eyes stared up at them and he coughed, a trickle of blood spilling from his lips.

'Oh, my God!' Kesang said. 'Babu!'

The victim seemed to recognize his name but when he tried to speak there was only a harsh gurgle, for the bullet had caught him in the throat and Fletcher could see a growing pool of blood on the floor behind his head. Within seconds his eyes rolled back in their sockets and his body went limp.

Kesang lowered the pistol, her eyes still fixed on the dead man's face.

'You know him?' said Fletcher.

She nodded, then whispered, 'My contact, Babu Chettri.'

31

Himalayan Golden-backed Three-toed Woodpecker

Dinopium shorii shorii

Often confused with Tickell's Golden-backed Woodpecker
(Chrysocolaptes guttacristatus). The primary difference is that
the latter has five thin black stripes on its throat while the former has no
hallux, or inner hind toe. Otherwise, both species are virtually identical
with a bright golden back, crimson crown, and black facial markings.
The underbelly is fulvous and scalloped with black lines. The three-toed
woodpecker is found in forests at lower altitudes, seldom above 2,000 feet.

October 22, 1962. Listening to radio broadcasts in the evening, Fletcher learnt that fighting had broken out between Chinese and Indian troops in two separate regions of the Himalayas. The armed conflict had begun three days ago, on 20 October. One theatre of conflict was in NEFA, on the Thagla Ridge, immediately to the east of Bhutan. The other was in Ladakh, along the perimeter of the Aksai Chin and in the Galwan Valley, adjacent to disputed border areas of Pakistan. In both cases the fighting was at high altitudes, between 12–14,000 feet above sea level.

The Indian soldiers in NEFA were heavily outnumbered and outgunned by the PLA forces, estimated as two battalions, equipped with artillery and mortars. According to the limited information available from military sources, an Indian detachment had been routed, with many casualties. The Chinese were advancing on the town of Tawang, which was about twelve miles inside the McMahon Line. There were no motor roads in this area of the mountains and the only access from the Indian side was either by foot or by helicopter.

In Ladakh the situation was also dire, though Indian troops had been able to hold back the Chinese at several points despite heavy shelling. The arid terrain provided little cover and, as winter was approaching, temperatures had dropped below freezing. Much of the Aksai Chin had already been occupied by the Chinese, through earlier incursions. This area consisted of desolate, high-altitude desert and salt plains, with a few lakes like Pangong Tso to the south. In Ladakh, it was easier for the Indian Army to supply their troops because of airfields in Leh and Chushul as well as a seasonal highway from Kashmir.

On account of the remote locations where the fighting was taking place, no journalists were present in either theatre and the only information came from a Ministry of Defence spokesman, who was less than forthcoming about details. All India Radio reported that the fighting was essentially an escalation of earlier skirmishes but the BBC was now referring to it as an all-out war. Prime Minister Nehru had issued a statement asking every Indian to remain vigilant in the face of Chinese aggression, which he referred to as a serious betrayal of Indo–Sino relations.

The United States, Great Britain, and the Soviet Union were calling upon both countries to exercise restraint. The United Nations had also issued a statement condemning the hostilities and encouraging India and China to resolve their dispute through diplomacy rather than warfare. One of the newsreaders on AIR speculated that Pakistan would side with China and use the conflict to advance its claims in parts of Kashmir. If that occurred, India would be hard pressed to defend its borders on two separate fronts in the Western Himalayas, as well as in NEFA.

Soon after Fletcher switched on the news, Kesang joined him in the living room and they listened together in silence. There was no mention of Sikkim or the Chumbi Valley. Nevertheless, it sounded as if the war could easily spread to this part of the mountains.

'Looks like Afridi got to Ladakh at just the wrong moment,' said Fletcher. 'I wonder if his regiment will be part of the fighting.'

Kesang took a deep breath and exhaled.

'I hope not,' she said. 'But knowing him, he'll be in the middle of the action.'

'It doesn't sound good,' Fletcher replied. 'The Chinese seem to have the upper hand right now.'

At that moment, the phone rang in the other room and Kesang got up to answer it. Fletcher could hear her speaking for a few minutes, after which she returned to the living room.

'That was Pema,' she said. 'According to her, the electricity is going to be switched off for the rest of the night and from tomorrow we have to black out all our windows. The army has ordered a curfew from 7 p.m. to 7 a.m.'

'Do you think your contact, Babu Chettri, knew this was happening?' Fletcher asked. 'I don't think it's a coincidence that he showed up last night.'

Kesang nodded. 'The Chinese must have known that the fighting had started on the border and after that it would be difficult to send someone to kill you.'

'Are you sure he was only targeting me?' Fletcher asked.

'Maybe both of us,' said Kesang. 'But it doesn't matter any more.'

◆

Last night, after Kesang shot Babu Chettri, they had wrapped his body in a tarpaulin and carried it out to the garage, where Dr Mukherjee's car was parked. The trunk of the Fiat was barely wide enough to accommodate the dead man, even with his knees folded up to his chin, but with a lot of shoving and twisting, they had been able to fit him inside. By the time they'd cleaned up the blood in the hallway, it was beginning to get light and the two of them set off in the Fiat, with Kesang driving. Unlike the bodies that Fletcher had disposed of in the jungle, Chettri's corpse posed a bigger problem.

Kesang had explained who he was, as she manoeuvred the car down the twisting hill road, its headlights weaving through the mist.

'Babu was a local activist and folk singer,' she said. 'Everybody in Kalimpong knows him. He was an active party worker and organizer. I met him through Daddy...he was amusing and entertaining. In the end, however, the Chinese used him badly. They blackmailed him into doing their dirty work.'

'What did they use against him?' said Fletcher.

'He was homosexual,' said Kesang. 'But only a few of us knew it and if it had been publicized it would have ruined him. Many people here in Kalimpong are small-minded, especially within the communist party. They pretend to be forward thinking but most of them are prejudiced and puritanical.'

'How did he recruit you?' said Fletcher.

'In the beginning we weren't especially close but he would often come to the house and talk with Daddy. Eventually, he asked me if I could help him gather information,' she said. 'I didn't really understand what he meant but he said he wanted me to tell him things about my friends, like Pema and Princess Coocoola, particularly their work with Tibetan refugees. He made it sound harmless but when I refused, he got upset and told me that if I didn't help him, he would be in serious trouble. "Didi," he told me. "They are vicious people and I am trapped." Then he explained how the Maoists were going to expose him. They had photographs and some letters he had written to one of his boyfriends. I felt sorry for him, so I agreed to give him bits of gossip now and then. I knew I shouldn't have done it because soon enough, his Chinese handler, Comrade Jiu, started asking specific questions. Around that time, Imtiaz came to see Daddy. I knew he was with army intelligence so I told him what was happening. He wanted to know what questions the Chinese were asking and he said that I could get out of it but I didn't want to betray Babu. At the same time, I thought I could help turn the tables on the Chinese. By then, I had stopped believing in the communist party and it seemed the right thing to do but I never thought it would come to this.'

After her initial shock at having shot Babu Chettri, Kesang had pulled herself together and kept her emotions under control.

'Did Dr Mukherjee know?' Fletcher asked.

Kesang shook her head. 'He wouldn't have understood and I wanted to leave him out of it because of his drinking. Sometimes he was very indiscreet.'

'But Babu never threatened you, did he?' said Fletcher.

'No. Sometimes the messages he delivered had a menacing tone but Babu himself was a gentle person. I still can't believe he showed up with a gun.'

'They probably gave him no choice,' said Fletcher. 'And where did you get your pistol from?'

'Imtiaz gave it to me for my protection. He taught me how to use it,' she said.

'That's fortunate for me,' said Fletcher. 'If it weren't for you, I'd be the one in the trunk of this car.'

'You were sound asleep. Hari called out twice before you woke up. I knew there was someone in the house,' she said. 'I thought of warning you but I didn't want to make a sound.'

Fletcher remained silent, as the car descended out of the clouds and he could see the river below them. No other vehicles were on the road. It was still less than an hour after dawn and the valley lay in darkness. As they reached the Teesta Bridge, he saw a sign: Photography Prohibited.

A small cluster of shops stood next to the bridge and there was a guard post on the opposite side. Though everything was shuttered and deserted at this hour, it was too risky to try and throw the body off the bridge. Instead, they drove about half a mile upriver to a point where the road was only thirty yards from the water's edge. Kesang nodded as Fletcher pointed to a spot, where she pulled over. With the engine switched off, there was complete silence, except for the roar of the swollen current.

Opening the trunk, they pulled the body out, still wrapped in the tarp. Moving as quickly as they could, the two of them hauled it over the side and down a rocky slope. The Teesta was a murky brown colour with white-water rapids, its current fierce and unrelenting. Chettri's corpse slid out of the canvas tarp and into the stream, face down. The swirling water pulled him away from the riverbank and the last they saw of him was a dark shape, like a piece of driftwood, carried off by the rapids. They let the tarp float away as well, after which Fletcher flung Chettri's revolver into the water.

The overcast sky was brighter now, a smoky light filtering through the clouds. Just as Fletcher hoisted himself back onto the road, he heard a steady rattling sound, like someone hammering away on a typewriter. Realizing what it was, he looked up and saw a woodpecker on the tree next to where the Fiat was parked. Even in the gloomy light, its golden back and bright red crest were visible. The bird was their only witness.

◆

Good evening, my fellow citizens. This government, as promised, has maintained the closest surveillance of the Soviet military build-up on the island of Cuba. Within the past week, unmistakable evidence has established the fact that a series of offensive missile sites is now in preparation on that imprisoned island. The purposes of these bases can be none other than to provide a nuclear strike capability against the Western Hemisphere.

Upon receiving the first preliminary hard information of this nature last Tuesday morning (16 October) at 9 a.m., I directed that our surveillance be stepped up. And having now confirmed and completed our evaluation of the evidence and our decision on a new course of action, this government feels obliged to report this new crisis to you in the fullest detail....

The morning of 23 October in India was the evening of 22 October in the United States. After learning on the BBC that there was a crisis in Cuba, Fletcher tuned into Voice of America, which broadcast President Kennedy's speech.

The president went on to explain the risk of nuclear war posed by the Soviet Union's actions and he detailed the United States's response. In essence, Kennedy warned that the Cuban Missile Crisis represented the greatest threat to the free world since World War II and raised the spectre of global annihilation. He warned that if any missiles were launched from Cuba, the United States would strike back at the Soviet Union with every weapon in its nuclear arsenal. Though he hoped for peace, Kennedy assured Khrushchev and Castro that he was prepared for war. He ended his speech with a righteous exhortation: 'Our goal is not the victory of might, but the vindication of right—not peace at the expense of freedom, but both peace and freedom, here in this hemisphere and, we hope, around the world. God willing, that goal will be achieved.'

'Do you think there's a connection between what the Russians and Chinese are doing?' Kesang asked.

'Probably not, but either one of them could trigger a larger conflict and, sooner or later, they'll join forces.'

'Maybe, but Moscow and Peking don't agree on very much,' said Kesang. 'I wonder how India will react to the situation in Cuba. Pandit Nehru has always spoken about non-alignment but this will be a time for countries to take sides.'

They kept the radio on all morning, switching between the BBC, VOA, and AIR. Fighting continued along the Himalayan border and there was news that Tawang had fallen to the Chinese forces, while Indian troops had pulled back to defend the Sela Pass. No updates had been received from Ladakh.

The day before, Kesang had found a pile of old blankets in one of Dr Mukherjee's cupboards and they had cut these up and tacked them over the window frames to black out the main rooms of the house. Montrose now felt like a cave, even with the lights on, and Hari kept shouting with alarm, 'bugger off! bloody fool!' sensing tension in the air. Sunita reported that there were long lines at the ration shops in town and everyone was afraid they would run out of food. Most of the tourists had already left town, escaping back to Calcutta or wherever they'd come from. The government had imposed restrictions on the sale of petrol, diesel, and kerosene, diverting all of the fuel for the army.

Later in the morning, Pema dropped by to see Kesang. She seemed surprised to discover that Fletcher was still there.

'I've heard that all foreigners must leave border areas, including Kalimpong and Darjeeling. Inner line permits to Sikkim have been cancelled,' she said. 'The Kazini is already on her way to Delhi.'

'Nobody has told me to leave,' said Fletcher, 'but I guess they wouldn't know that I'm staying here instead of at the Himalayan Hotel.'

'Maybe it's just a rumour,' said Pema. 'Everyone's in a panic. Yesterday I got a call from one of my friends in Siliguri. She said she'd heard that the Chinese were only a few miles from Kalimpong.'

The radio kept repeating the same reports while the newspapers arrived later than usual and sodden with rain because of a downpour. While Pema and Kesang sat on the glassed-in porch, Fletcher carefully spread *The Statesman* on the living room floor to dry. He scanned the articles for information, though there was very little that hadn't been reported on the radio. The headlines trumpeted a shrill alarm: CHINESE PUSHING FORWARD INTO NEFA and NEHRU WARNS PAKISTAN NOT TO INTERFERE. Though most of the articles sounded a patriotic note and supported the government and the army, an opinion piece on the editorial page was critical of Krishna Menon, the defence minister, who had diverted resources away from the army and embarked on expensive projects like designing an indigenous aircraft. The writer, a retired brigadier, argued that Menon was pursuing priorities that left India's conventional forces without adequate arms and supplies. Indian infantry stationed in the high mountains weren't even equipped with warm clothing and they had only enough ammunition for two or three days of fighting.

Amid all this, Fletcher wondered what he should do. If foreigners were being told to leave, he would probably have no choice but to go, even if Kesang stayed behind. Now that hostilities had erupted, he felt sure there was no danger the Chinese agents would come after her again. One of the articles in *The Statesman* reported that a number of Chinese diplomats had been expelled from the country. The only thing that worried him was that sooner or later someone would find Babu Chettri's body and they might link his death to Kesang.

Pema stayed only for an hour and said she had to hurry back home because she was expecting friends to arrive from Sikkim. Those who were able to leave Gangtok were trying to get as far away from the border as possible.

After lunch, Kesang told Sunita to go home and come back the next morning. She lived in a settlement on the other side of town called Bong Basti and it was at least an hour's walk away. The rain was still coming down and added to a feeling of being besieged. Finally, after it stopped around 4 p.m. Fletcher was about to make a pot of tea, when he heard the doorbell ring. As always, the parakeet shouted abuse while Kesang went to answer the door. From the kitchen, Fletcher heard her greet the visitor.

'Colonel Norton!' she said. 'What a surprise!'

32

White-capped Redstart

Chaimarrornis leucocephalus

A small, active bird, slightly larger than a sparrow, with a black back and wings, its belly and rump are a rusty red. A chalk white cap is the most visible feature, especially when light is poor and the rest of the bird vanishes into the shadows. Usually found near water, either singly or in pairs. The tail is often flipped up and down or fanned out as it sits on rocks by a stream. The call is extremely high-pitched and almost inaudible, particularly with the sound of flowing water nearby.

Agatha had broken the first rule of tradecraft by showing up at Montrose but he had an excuse to cover his tracks. When Fletcher came out of the kitchen, the two of them shook hands.

'I was just going to make us some tea,' he said.

Norton laughed. 'I didn't know that was something Americans were capable of doing.'

'I'll try not to poison you,' Fletcher said.

'So, the two of you know each other?' Kesang asked.

'We met in Gangtok,' said Norton. 'Socially.'

'Please come, let's sit in the sunroom,' Kesang said.

'Actually, I don't mean to intrude. I just came by to return a book that I borrowed from Dr Mukherjee over a month ago,' Norton explained, holding up a hardcover volume. 'I'm sorry I didn't bring it back earlier.'

'Daddy never loaned his books to anyone except Colonel Norton, because he knew they would always be returned,' Kesang told Fletcher. 'He used to say that he would rather loan someone money before he let them borrow a book.'

'What's the title?' Fletcher asked.

'*The Secret Rose* by William Butler Yeats. A bit too romantic for my tastes, but the professor persuaded me that it was worth reading,' said Norton, as they entered the glassed-in porch where he took a seat on the leather sofa.

Fletcher went back to the kitchen and set up the tea tray. A kettle of water was boiling on the stove and he filled the pot then covered it with a tea cosy. After two weeks at Montrose, he knew the domestic routines. When he returned to the porch, Kesang and Norton were talking about the fighting on the border.

'I'm not sure if you can call it a war just yet, more like tactical strikes,' said the Colonel. 'But it will probably escalate in the next few days.'

'Do you think the Chinese will cross over Nathu La?' Kesang asked.

'It depends on what their intentions are,' said Norton. 'If it's just to challenge the McMahon Line, then I think they'll restrict themselves to NEFA and Ladakh. It's interesting that they decided to strike Tawang. That's the same route that the Dalai Lama used when he escaped from Tibet in '59. I think the Chinese chose that location for symbolic reasons as well as strategic importance.'

'What about Bhutan?' Fletcher asked.

'Probably not just yet,' said Norton, 'though they'll make threatening noises, I'm sure. Right now, their adversary is India and when you pick a fight you don't want to make too many enemies all at once. Of course, they could take over Sikkim and Bhutan within a matter of days but that would stir up an even greater outcry from the UN because they are defenceless countries, whereas India has an army and is at least capable of fighting back.'

'Are you going to stay in Kalimpong?' Fletcher asked. 'We were told that all foreigners must leave.'

'Where would I go?' Norton replied. 'I'm part of the furniture. There have been rumours about foreigners being evacuated but I don't think that will happen, unless there's a direct attack on Sikkim.'

'We heard that the Kazini has left,' said Kesang.

'Good riddance,' said Norton, with a chuckle. 'For all of her bellicose rhetoric, she's the first one to put her tail between her legs and run.'

'Do you think I should stay?' Fletcher asked.

Norton looked up and met his gaze. 'I wouldn't know,' he said. 'But if you have other reasons to leave it's probably a good time to go.'

Kesang didn't seem to suspect anything and Fletcher changed the subject to the news from Cuba. Norton snorted his disapproval of Kennedy's handling of things. 'Too soft,' he said.

Just then, the phone rang and Kesang went to answer it.

As soon as she was out of the room, the Colonel pointed to the book. 'You might be interested in that,' he said to Fletcher. 'Merlin has sent you a message.'

◆

YOU WILL RECEIVE IMPORTANT DOCUMENTS TOMORROW, WEDNESDAY. THESE NEED TO BE HAND CARRIED TO DELHI. USE ALL PRECAUTIONS TO KEEP THE DOCUMENTS FROM BEING DISCOVERED IN YOUR POSSESSION. GO DIRECTLY TO BAGDOGRA AIRPORT ON THURSDAY. A PLANE WILL PICK YOU UP AT 11:00 A.M. THE PILOT WILL BE WAITING IN THE MAIN TERMINAL.

It took Fletcher almost an hour to decode the message, using Kipling's lines, 'Take up the White Man's burden / Send forth the best ye breed'. He wondered if Merlin understood the irony of picking a poem written to celebrate America's conquest of the Philippines, when the US first planted its flag in Asia. In a seminar on colonial history, one of his professors at Wesleyan had called it, 'racist doggerel'.

The message had been tucked inside the book that Norton had returned. Fletcher retrieved the single, folded sheet of paper before Kesang put the book back on the shelf in Dr Mukherjee's study. He didn't mention the message to her and deciphered the words in his room downstairs.

Later that evening, they made an omelette for dinner and listened to the news on the radio. Fighting had intensified in both Ladakh and NEFA and it was clear that the Indian troops were taking a severe beating. Meanwhile, in the western hemisphere, Kennedy had ordered a naval blockade of Cuba, demanding that the Soviets dismantle and remove their missiles. Tensions in Europe were high, particularly in Berlin, where American troops stood toe to toe with Russian soldiers in divided sectors of the city.

Though he was confident that nobody would break into the house again, Fletcher made sure that he had his Beretta under the pillow, when he and Kesang went to bed. Neither of them felt like making love, though she lay with her head on his shoulder as he wrapped an arm around her.

'I keep expecting to hear something from Imtiaz but I suppose there's no way he can communicate from Ladakh,' she said.

'As an intelligence officer, he's probably stationed in Leh, not on the front lines,' Fletcher tried to reassure her.

'He used to tell me that the Chinese were India's most dangerous enemy, much more of a threat than Pakistan,' she said. 'Imtiaz explained that we could defeat the Pakistanis because we had more tanks, artillery, and airplanes, but none of those things would help us if China attacked because there are very few roads in the Himalayas and the tanks and artillery can't reach the border. The air force might be able to bomb and strafe the Chinese but, in the end, mountain warfare has to be fought on the ground.'

'Fortunately, neither India nor China has nuclear weapons, at least not yet,' said Fletcher. 'With the Soviets in Cuba it may not be hand-to-hand combat but an awful lot of innocent people could die. Hopefully, that will deter them.'

After a few minutes silence, Kesang asked, 'Have you made up your mind? Are you going to leave?'

'Yes,' said Fletcher. 'Day after tomorrow.'

'So soon?' she said.

'It's better that way,' he said. 'I hate prolonged goodbyes.'

'Where will you go?'

'I don't know. Maybe back to the States,' he said.

'Will I see you again?' she asked.

'I hope so,' he replied. 'Though I wouldn't count on it.'

Kesang was quiet, as they lay in the dark.

'I won't forget you,' she said, after a while.

'But both of us knew, from the beginning, that this wasn't going to last,' he said as he felt her turn toward him.

'You've never told me that you loved me,' she said.

'Is that what you wanted me to say?' Fletcher asked.

'No,' said Kesang. 'Love is a stupid word.'

'But what about Afridi? He says he loves you,' said Fletcher.

'Because he thinks it's the right thing to say,' she replied. 'He's not cynical like you and me.'

'There's a part of me that could stay in Kalimpong forever,' said Fletcher. 'I'm very content lying here like this…you and me…probably happier than I've ever been before, but I know I have to leave because the world is so fucked up and there's nothing we can do to make it right, is there?'

'You see? You are a cynic,' said Kesang.

'Not really,' he said. 'I just don't think I believe in anything any more.'

'Are you afraid?' she asked.

'Sort of…. Sometimes,' he said. 'You mean, afraid of dying?'

'Or being alive, when everyone else is dead,' she said. 'I always knew that Daddy would die one day but when it happened, I wasn't ready….'

'I don't think you can ever be prepared,' he said.

'But what if Imtiaz dies?' she said.

Fletcher turned his head and kissed her forehead.

'He won't,' he said, trying to sound as if he believed his own words. 'Don't worry, he'll survive, one way or another.'

◆

The next morning, Fletcher walked across to the forest department office to say goodbye to Thupten. They were able to speak for only a few minutes because the DFO was getting ready for an inspection tour to check on forest roads that needed maintenance after the monsoon. The army had sent two engineers to accompany him and make sure that the routes were open and the bridges in good repair. Thupten seemed disappointed to hear that Fletcher was leaving but agreed that there was no point in trying to continue doing research with the conflict going on. Access to all of the forests along the border with Sikkim and Bhutan had been closed to anyone other than authorized officials. Fletcher thanked him for his help and said he hoped to get back to Kalimpong someday.

After that, he met Wangchuk at the same coffee shop as before and listened to his concerns about the fighting spilling across to Bhutan. A number of Indian soldiers, escaping from the Chinese in NEFA, had crossed over into Bhutan and there were fears that the PLA might pursue them or blame the Bhutanese for giving them refuge. The tribal people of that region were closely related to the Monpas of Tawang and Wangchuk said nobody was sure about their loyalties.

As they were sitting at a table outside, Fletcher saw three police jeeps drive by, full of constables with bamboo riot shields and staves.

'Do you know what's going on?' he asked Wangchuk.

'Yes, some people attacked the Nanking restaurant this morning and tried to set it on fire,' said Wangchuk. 'It was part of an anti-Chinese demonstration.'

'But the owners are Indian citizens,' said Fletcher. He finished his coffee and gestured to the waiter for the bill.

'These days anyone who looks Chinese is being targeted. Even I have been called names by Indians, who don't know any better,' said Wangchuk.

Excusing himself, Fletcher walked quickly down Mintri Road towards the Nanking, where he could see a crowd waving banners and shouting slogans. Police were blocking the road and when he approached, one of the constables signalled for him to stay away. Fletcher could see that some of the restaurant's windows had been smashed but the crowd had moved on towards the Chinese Trade Mission. Owners of the shops along the street were standing outside, watching as the demonstrators chanted, 'Mao Tse Tung Murdabad! Death to Mao!' and 'Chini Harami Hai Hai! Chinese bastards, Hai Hai!'

There was nothing Fletcher could do so he turned back in the direction of Montrose. He wondered whether Eddie was inside the restaurant but knew that Kesang would find out. By the time he got back to the house, she already knew.

'Eddie and his family were taken away this morning by the police, on the district magistrate's orders,' she said.

'Where to?' he said.

'We don't know for sure. Someone said they're being sent to an internment camp in Rajasthan. A place called Deoli,' she said, shaking her head in disbelief.

'Rajasthan?'

'It's more than a thousand miles from here, in the desert,' said Kesang. 'Supposedly the internment is for their protection but the government doesn't want any Chinese people near the border. My friend Partha says that even in Calcutta they've rounded up some of the Chinese. He drove up from Siliguri this morning. The police are checking cars at Teesta Bridge for weapons and explosives.'

'Everybody's getting paranoid,' said Fletcher.

Kesang had sent Sunita out to buy groceries and when she came back, the maid said that all she could get was a kilo of rice and half a kilo of sugar. The Marwari, from whose shop they got their supplies, had promised that he would try to keep aside more rice and lentils when he got his next delivery but he had no idea when it would arrive. There were shortages of cooking oil and vegetables too.

'Are you sure you don't want to come away with me?' said Fletcher.

Kesang gave him a discouraged look and shook her head. 'No,' she said. 'I can't leave now. I need to be here.'

A little while later, he went to his room and began to pack his suitcases. He thought of discarding things and taking only what he needed, but realized that it was better to carry everything to Delhi and get rid of it there, even the sleeping bag which was stained and torn. He didn't want to leave anything behind.

Outside the window, he could see some of the ferns on the trees turning brown, now that the rains had ended. Beyond the house, at the edge of the property, was a seasonal stream that flowed down the eastern slope of the hill. In the shadows, he saw a flash of white, as if it were a scrap of paper blowing on the wind. Opening the window, he picked up his binoculars. For a moment there was nothing to see but then he spotted a white crest and brought the bird into focus. During the past three months he had seen plenty of white-capped redstarts and immediately recognized what it was, perched on a moss-covered rock, bobbing up and down.

At that moment, he heard a hesitant knock. Closing the window and latching it shut, he called out, 'Come in.'

Sunita opened the door and told him that someone was here to deliver a package. Surprised, he followed her out to the veranda, where a young man was waiting at the top of the steps. He looked as if he might be Nepali and was casually dressed in a polo shirt and trousers.

'Mister Swift?' he asked.

'Yes,' said Fletcher.

'For you.' He handed him an envelope and immediately turned away, as if he wanted to avoid any questions.

Sunita was watching from the door but quickly went back to the kitchen as Fletcher examined the brown paper envelope. It was sealed and had nothing written on the outside. Though he knew these were the documents Merlin had mentioned, he was surprised they had been delivered without any secrecy or precautions.

Returning to his room, he wondered if he should open the envelope or not, but soon decided it was safer to know what it contained. Slicing it open with the blade of his pocketknife, he took out a sheaf of papers, realizing immediately what they were. He could see two holes, where a clamp had once held the documents together, though they had been removed from their file. At the top of the first page was a rubber stamp that said TOP SECRET in red ink. Below this was the emblem of a shield and the rising sun with the heading 'Eastern Command'. At the bottom of the page was an illegible signature followed by a line: 'Received 21/10/1962'.

Leafing through the papers, Fletcher understood why Merlin had asked him to hand carry the documents and the reason an embassy aircraft was being sent to pick him up tomorrow. The file contained a complete description of the Indian Army's Forces in Sikkim, including the names and rank of the officers and the number of troops under their command. A map was also included giving the exact locations of encampments and other installations such as gun emplacements, ammunition dumps, and bunkers along the ridge near Nathu La.

A carbon copy of typed orders from Army Headquarters in Delhi outlined a detailed strategy in the event of a Chinese attack from the Chumbi Valley. Skimming the pages, Fletcher absorbed enough information to understand that the Indians were prepared to fight back but there was also a contingency plan to retreat downriver, beyond the southern border of Sikkim, to the Teesta Bridge. Included in the file was a memorandum from a Major Darshan Yesudas of the Madras Sappers, reporting that the army engineers had made preparations to destroy the bridge with explosives to stop the Chinese from advancing into West Bengal.

33

Emerald Dove

Chalcophaps indica

A relatively small dove with a metallic green back and wings. The rest of the bird is a pinkish grey with a pale crown, ranging from ash to white. The beak is coral coloured. It feeds on the ground under dense foliage, pecking for seeds and berries amongst dead leaves. Usually found in pairs, it has a swift, agile flight. The call is a soft, two-note cooing sound, repeated at intervals of one or two seconds. Distributed throughout most of Asia.

Standing in the shade at the side of the road, Fletcher noticed a feather lying on the ground by his foot. It was no larger than one of his fingernails—a brilliant, iridescent green with white fluff along the lower quill. Picking it up, he turned it over in his hand, recognizing that it came from an emerald dove. None were in sight but the bamboo thickets on the hillside above would have provided the right kind of habitat for this timid bird.

Fletcher's patience was running out. He had been detained at a police checkpoint on the west side of the Teesta Bridge. Traffic coming up from Siliguri was being stopped and checked but vehicles coming down the hill were allowed to go through without delay. His taxi, however, had been waved over by two constables, who insisted on seeing the driver's licence and car registration. They seemed to be in no rush, wasting time on purpose. The driver, someone Kesang had recommended, was arguing with the police, saying that his papers were in order. Wondering if they were expecting a bribe, Fletcher was about to reach for his wallet, when he saw two men approaching from the other side of the bridge. They weren't in uniform but, from the constables' reaction, it was obvious they were senior police officers. One of them came up to Fletcher and looked him over, as if he were trying to recognize his features. Dropping his cigarette butt on the ground he crushed it beneath the heel of his shoe.

'Where are you going?' he asked, in English.

'Bagdogra airport, then Delhi,' said Fletcher.

'And coming from?'

'Kalimpong.'

'Passport,' demanded the man, who had a thin moustache and wary eyes. Fletcher guessed that he and his companion were with the Intelligence Bureau.

'Swift, Allan,' the man read his name in the passport. 'Open your luggage.'

'What is this for?' Fletcher asked.

'Checking,' said the man. He then spoke to the driver in Bengali, ordering him to open the trunk.

'Why aren't you checking other vehicles?' Fletcher asked. 'Why am I the only one being stopped in this direction?'

The man didn't answer but simply waved a finger. 'Open!'

Fletcher unlocked the suitcase, which contained mostly clothes and a few books and papers. The officer gestured to one of the constables and told him to take everything out. They carefully examined his journals and notes and picked through each article of clothing. Fortunately, though they felt about at the bottom of the suitcase, they did not discover the secret compartment where the Beretta was hidden. It was obvious they were searching for the documents.

After letting Fletcher repack the suitcase as best he could, they pointed to the duffel bag, which he unzipped. Again, the constables emptied everything and the officers focused on the papers and notebooks it contained. They examined the tape player too and the parabolic microphone but when he explained that it was for making recordings of birdcalls, they lost interest. When they didn't find what they were looking for, the officers made him take out the contents of his rucksack— binoculars, camera, and the thermos flask, which they opened and sniffed.

'Drinking water,' said Fletcher as they handed it back to him. He took a swig before closing the lid.

The two officers consulted with each other, mumbling in Bengali.

Then one of them went off to the other side of the bridge, perhaps to make a phone call. Twenty minutes later he appeared again and shouted something. Finally, the other officer reluctantly waved Fletcher through. Altogether, his taxi had been stopped for two-and-a-half hours. It was now 10.30 a.m. and the driver estimated that it would take two more hours to reach Bagdogra.

When they arrived at the airport, armed soldiers in full battle gear guarded the main entrance. It was a military facility with a small terminal for commercial flights. Fletcher expected that he would have to open his bags again but after he explained that a US Embassy aircraft was waiting for him, the armed guards let him through. Nobody stopped him as he hauled his luggage inside the empty terminal. The Indian Airlines flight to Calcutta had already departed and the only other flight was in the evening. A man appeared through a door at the far end of the room and Fletcher recognized the pilot who had flown them from Kashmir to Delhi in March.

'You took your time,' the pilot said, checking his watch. 'We were supposed to be out of here an hour and a half ago.'

'Sorry,' said Fletcher. 'I was stopped by the police on my way down.'

'Everything okay?' asked the pilot, extending his right hand. 'Chuck.'

'Allan.' He put down his bag to shake hands, after which Chuck picked it up and led him out onto the tarmac, where a Cessna was parked. After stowing his bags, Fletcher settled into the seat behind the cockpit, strapping himself in.

'We've got to stop in Patna, on the way to Delhi, to pick up a diplomatic pouch from Kathmandu. Most of the commercial flights have been cancelled,' Chuck explained, 'because of the war. The army is using Indian Airlines planes to fly troops and supplies to Assam and Ladakh.'

After take-off, the pilot shouted over the roar of the engine, 'It's a clear day. If you look out your window, you'll be able to see most of the Himalayas. That's Kanchenjunga over there. Everest will be coming up in a little while.'

Through the oval window, he could see the white shape of the 'five treasures of the snow' looming against the sky. Kanchenjunga had an ethereal beauty that made it seem so far away and yet so close. Fletcher realized that this was the same view that migratory birds observed as they approached the mountains before flying across. Watching the panorama of snow-covered summits glide past, he remembered the gunfight he'd witnessed at Kellas Col and imagined the soldiers who were now battling over an invisible border somewhere along that frozen ridgeline. He thought how insignificant and futile the conflict seemed against the backdrop of a mountain range as old and high as this.

After the stop in Patna, he slept for a while and opened his eyes just as they descended into Delhi. From the air, the city looked green and orderly. He spotted the dome of Humayun's tomb and the golf course with its fairways and sandstone monuments. They were only a few hundred feet above the ground.

The pilot glanced over his shoulder and explained. 'We've got permission to land at the old airport, at Safdarjung instead of Palam.'

Fletcher could see Lodhi Gardens out of the window. Directly below him was Jor Bagh. He spotted his old house and Reggie's home across the street, as the pilot descended over the treetops. After landing, they taxied back down the short runway to the apron in front of the terminal building. A car was waiting to pick him up and take him to the safe house in Sundar Nagar, where Sullivan sat in the living room, wreathed in pipe smoke. The windows were covered in blackout paper, which made it feel like a bunker.

Shrugging off his rucksack, Fletcher extended a hand to shake. He noticed a moment's hesitation on Sullivan's part, as if he still hadn't been forgiven for what had happened in Calcutta.

'Welcome back,' the older man said, the smouldering pipe still clenched in his teeth. 'But if you ever pull a stunt like that again, I'll bench you for good.'

Fletcher gave him a sheepish look and apologized, 'Sorry, coach.'

'How was the flight?' Sullivan asked. 'You got here much later than expected. Any trouble on the way?'

'Only at the beginning. They stopped me at a checkpoint below Kalimpong,' said Fletcher. 'Two Intelligence Bureau officers were looking for the documents. I could tell they were on to me.'

'How'd you get through?' Sullivan asked, his eyes narrowing.

'When the envelope was delivered to the house, I got suspicious. No dead drop. Not even the pretence of tradecraft, just a guy knocking on the door and handing me a sheaf of military secrets and plans. It didn't make sense. Was it Agatha who sent them?'

'No. Someone else,' said Sullivan.

'The IB officers were expecting me this morning. They went through my suitcases, frisked me, even made me take off my shoes and remove the insoles.'

Sullivan was quiet for a minute or two, as he tamped down the tobacco and relit his pipe. 'So, how'd you shake them off? Did you get rid of the papers?'

'No,' said Fletcher, opening his rucksack. 'I brought them with me.'

Taking out the thermos flask, he unscrewed the lid and drank the last bit of water. Then he twisted the outer, metal sleeve and removed the glass cylinder inside. Surrounding this was a space, about half an inch wide all around. He removed the documents, which he'd wrapped in a plastic bag.

'I'm afraid they're a little crumpled,' he said, handing them over to Sullivan. 'And more than likely, they're useless. Whoever your source is, he obviously tipped off the IB. Most of that file is probably out of date, or made up.'

'No shit,' said Sullivan, closing his eyes.

'Was it a military source who sent you these documents?' Fletcher asked.

'Yeah, but he obviously screwed me over.' Sullivan swore under his breath. 'Or somebody got to him and turned things around. If the Intelligence Bureau had found you carrying these papers, you'd be in jail.'

'That file would have had much more value for the Chinese than it has for us,' said Fletcher.

'Sure, but it's good to know the strength of your friends as well as your enemies,' Sullivan replied. 'The problem is that there are key individuals in the IB who are dead set against American interests. They would like nothing better than to expose and embarrass us, even if we are providing military aid.'

'Too bad Afridi has gone to Ladakh,' said Fletcher. 'He told me that he kept Kesang's identity hidden from the Intelligence Bureau. She reports only to him.'

'And you're absolutely sure that she's not working for the Chinese?'

'Positive,' said Fletcher, taking a roll of film out of his camera bag and handing it over.

'More pictures?' Sullivan said. 'By the way, those shots of the avalanche and the PLA running for their lives were spectacular. I had them blown up and sent copies to Langley. The guys in the Far East Division love that kind of stuff. So, what am I going to see when we develop this film?'

'Some pictures of a Sikkim bay-owl and three dead men,' said Fletcher.

'Who are they?'

'Chinese agents. The first two had no IDs. I shot them after they tried to kill me. I'm pretty sure they were the same guys who ambushed our jeep,' said Fletcher.

Sullivan nodded. 'And the third one?'

'He was Kesang's contact, a man named Babu Chettri, her go-between with the Chinese handler,' Fletcher recounted. 'Chettri broke into Kesang's house in the middle of the night. I would be dead if she hadn't shot him.'

'She killed her contact?' said Sullivan.

'Yeah, this was the night of October 21, just before we learned that the fighting had broken out on the border,' Fletcher explained. 'He probably would have killed us both, but I think I was the primary target.'

'And you were in bed with her when this happened?' said Sullivan.

Fletcher shrugged. 'Afridi asked me to look after her.'

'Okay, I'll get these developed,' said Sullivan pocketing the roll of film.

'So, what's the latest news from Cuba?' Fletcher asked.

'It's a stalemate right now,' said Sullivan. 'Khrushchev and Kennedy are playing chicken and we'll see who flinches first. The blockade seems to be working, at least for now, but depending on who you talk to in Washington, it's either going to end in mushroom clouds or somehow the Soviets will back down, as long as they can save face. A military strike by the US is still on the table.'

'And what about the situation over here? Do you have any news on what's happening along the border?' Fletcher asked.

'Not much. There's a lot of static and garbled information so it's hard to read the situation,' said Sullivan, 'but the Indian Army is retreating in NEFA and the Chinese are advancing. It looks as if the Sela Pass is going to fall before long and after that it's a straight shot to Assam. The Indian generals are still trying to bluff their way out of it, but it looks as if they're going to suffer a serious defeat.'

'What's the US going to do about it?'

'We're already airlifting shipments of arms and other military supplies. The ambassador was away in London but he returned the next day to reassure Nehru and his government that we've got their back. I don't think we'll be sending in the Marines but India will get the hardware it needs,' Sullivan explained.

'So, what am I supposed to do now?' Fletcher asked.

'Well, as I told you in Calcutta, you've done your job. Despite your blatant insubordination, it's been a successful operation and the desk jockeys at headquarters asked me to tell you that they're impressed. As I said, they loved the pictures of the Khampas fighting with the PLA, though there's some disappointment that there wasn't any treasure. The Khampas had promised to deliver the relics in exchange for our support.'

'But the CIA has plenty of money,' said Fletcher. 'Why do you need to get into the antiques business?'

'That's a good question,' said Sullivan. 'I've asked it myself....'

'And?' Fletcher enquired after a long silence.

Sullivan blew out his cheeks and started to refill his pipe.

'As far as I can tell, there are two answers,' he said. 'The first one is that the operations in Tibet have been run out of our station here in Delhi but once Galbraith became the ambassador, he wanted the whole thing shut down. Our boys were counting on dipping into the PL480 slush fund—rupees that India owes the US for wheat shipments during the fifties, which is millions of dollars that have to be spent over here. But the ambassador nixed that and after the Bay of Pigs disaster, the Kennedy administration lost its appetite for covert insurgencies. So, the idea was that the Khampas would fund themselves by selling the artefacts. The agency was just acting as middleman, facilitating cash flow and ensuring plausible deniability.'

Lighting a match, he got his pipe going again and exhaled a cloud of blue smoke. 'The second part of the answer is something nobody

wants to talk about. Four years ago, one of the CAT C-130s that flew
into Tibet crashed in the mountains, after delivering its payload. There
were two Americans aboard, the pilot and co-pilot. Both were presumed
dead. The Chinese weren't aware of the accident. We sent a team of
Khampas to explore the crash site and they found the burnt-out shell of
the plane at the head of a valley at about 15,000 feet. They recovered
the remains of the pilots, a few charred bones that's all, and brought
them down to the Yangchen Gompa monastery, where they were kept
along with the relics. When the Chinese destroyed the monastery a year
later, the two fliers' remains were rescued along with the artefacts to be
smuggled out of Tibet.'

'But the problem is that everything has disappeared,' said Fletcher.

'That's right...and we haven't been able to get any confirmation about
what happened or where they might have gone,' Sullivan said, making
a gesture with one hand to show that it had vanished into thin air.

'I guess, with the war on right now there isn't much chance of
tracking it down,' Fletcher added.

'No, we'll just have to give up on that for the time being,' Sullivan
agreed. 'Meanwhile, the other thing we've got to do is get you out of
here. The Intelligence Bureau obviously knows who you are and other
than staying in this safe house until things blow over, the only real
option is for you to leave India.'

'Where am I supposed to go?' Fletcher said with resignation.

Sullivan smiled. 'I was thinking Bangkok.'

'What am I going to do there?'

'Take a week off. Enjoy yourself. You've earned some R&R,' said
Sullivan. 'After that, you can come back.'

Fletcher shook his head, confused.

'Allan Swift departs tomorrow morning at 3 a.m. on TWA, Delhi–
Bangkok direct,' said Sullivan, handing him a folder of air tickets and
his old passport. 'A week later, Guy Fletcher flies back into Delhi on a
Thai Airways flight. You switch passports and reclaim your identity as
a Fulbright scholar doing fieldwork on migratory geese.'

34

Common Kingfisher

Alcedo atthis

A striking little bird that frequents ponds, streams, and tidal marshes throughout South and Southeast Asia, as well as most parts of Europe. It has bright turquoise and blue spangled feathers on the upper parts of its body, a white chin, and a vivid orange breast and underbelly. Often seen perched on a branch overlooking a waterbody, from where it swoops down to pluck minnows just below the surface with its long, streamlined beak.

After Kalimpong and Delhi, Bangkok was chaotic but in a different way than Calcutta. It was a cleaner, more polite city with a languorous air of crowded civility. Sullivan had arranged for one of the CIA staff at the Embassy ('the boys in Bangkok', as he called them) to meet Fletcher's flight and show him around. Terry was about his age, mid-twenties, and came from Tulsa, though he'd gone to college at the University of Virginia. As they drove into the city, traffic gradually congealed into a sluggish current that eventually poured into Sukhumvit. Along the way, Terry pointed out landmarks and spoke about Bangkok as if he'd lived here all his life.

'How long have you been in Thailand?' Fletcher eventually asked.

'Three months,' Terry answered. 'I love this place, though I can't take the spices in the food. That's my only complaint.'

Fletcher was dropped off at a small, discreet hotel, the Siam Pagoda, a few blocks from the Chao Phraya River. A relatively quiet part of town compared to the areas they'd passed through, the streets here were lined with European architecture that gave the neighbourhood a colonial ambience. Terry told him that his hotel stay was being covered by the agency and he could sign for his meals. He also suggested that they get together for dinner, 'with a couple of other guys. I'll pick you up at six.'

After checking into his room, Fletcher went down to the coffee shop to get some lunch. The table he was given overlooked a tropical garden with a small goldfish pond in the middle, surrounded by bamboo, flowering ginger, and other ornamental plants. It was like staring into a painting by Rousseau. Suddenly, he saw a flash of blue as a kingfisher dove into the pond like a turquoise dart, the water splashing up as the bird emerged with a tiny minnow in its beak. Perched on a stem of bamboo, the kingfisher quickly swallowed its prey. Fletcher had seen the same species many times before at Bharatpur but its presence here in downtown Bangkok took him by surprise.

Having entered Thailand on his old passport, he now had his own name and identity back. It felt as if an invisible mask had been peeled off his face. The whole time he'd been in Kalimpong and Sikkim there was an underlying tension, as he maintained the fictitious identity that Sullivan had assigned him. Even with Afridi and Kesang there was never a moment when he could be completely at ease. But now, as he sat alone and ate his lunch—a green papaya salad and red beef curry with sticky rice—he felt utterly anonymous and entirely himself.

Over the next six days, Fletcher spent his evenings with some of the younger CIA officers in Bangkok. Like the JOTs at The Farm, all of the men he met through Terry kept certain parts of themselves screened off, though they talked openly about the operations in which they'd taken part. An earnest yet secretive esprit de corps animated the group, tempered by an ironic sense of humour when it came to the dangerous consequences of their work.

For the first time, Fletcher realized how many American agents there must be in the Far East Division, hundreds of undercover operatives in every country in Asia from the Philippines to Indonesia, Cambodia, and Vietnam. Laos was a hotspot right now and a couple of the men who joined them for drinks at the St Louis Bar on Patpong Street had just returned from Vientiane. They had been conspiring to subvert and subdue the Pathet Lao communists by supporting Vang Pao and his Hmong tribesmen from the highlands. According to them, the Hmong were sworn enemies of the Vietnamese and ready to slaughter the communists.

One of the CIA field officers paid the Hmong a dollar an ear for their victims. At the same time, the young operatives complained about the lowlanders in Laos, being the 'laziest SOBs on earth! Fucking lotus-eaters!' as one of the men said. While Fletcher listened to their stories and the way in which the agents romanticized the Hmong, he couldn't help wondering how long these men had actually been here and whether, like Terry, they had instantly become experts after a few days on the job.

It was a bit like the Peace Corps, but the dark side, a shadowy fraternity working to preserve democracy and freedom, though most of what they did was undermine popular uprisings and replace them with totalitarian regimes and corrupt despots. But that didn't seem to trouble these men. They were in it as much for the game as they were for their convictions and they justified their actions through metaphors of sport, joking about how they'd exposed a political leader in Laos using 'a perfect double play', 'sacked the quarterback' in Muang Kham, or made an 'end run' around the Ho Chi Minh Trail. With locker room banter they tallied up their 'wins' and 'losses'. Fletcher understood that he was part of this game too, though he felt out of place. When they asked him, 'So, what are you up to in Inja?' he shrugged and said, 'Nothing exciting. Just the usual grunt work.'

On his second night in Bangkok, the Embassy received word that Khrushchev had agreed to disassemble and remove Soviet missiles from Cuba. America's policy of containment had prevailed and, for the time being, the threat of nuclear war had been averted. This added to the mood of self-assurance and bravado in their group. After a couple of beers, the others at the table were convinced that stopping the communists in Laos would be a 'slam dunk' as long as they put 'a full court press' on the Viet Cong. Listening to the conversation, Fletcher had a strange premonition that things would end badly in this part of the world.

◆

By the time he returned to India on 4 November, there was a lull in the fighting along the Himalayan frontier, though tensions remained high. Neither India nor China had actually declared war, even if that was what the international press was calling it. Mounting casualties on both sides proved that it was anything but an ordinary border skirmish.

The PLA had pushed the Indian Army back in both theatres and there were reports in the papers that Nehru and Chou En-lai were exchanging letters, attempting to reach some sort of ceasefire agreement.

The boys in Bangkok had helped sort out the entry and exit stamps in Fletcher's passport, so that when he returned to India it looked as if he had travelled from the United States, via Thailand. In any case, his research visa was still valid and the immigration official at Palam Airport didn't take more than a couple of minutes to let him through.

Now that he no longer needed to stay at the safe house, Fletcher checked into the YMCA Tourist Hostel near Connaught Circus. Though several notches below the Siam Pagoda, it was comfortable enough for a short stay. The Fulbright office was nearby, where he reconnected with the administrators and made plans to go to Bharatpur as soon as possible. Delhi was on edge because of the border conflict but almost everything was open during the day and, in any case, the capital shut down early in the evenings.

He called Reggie Bhatia on November 7 and they agreed to get together for lunch at the Golf Club the next day. Taking an autorickshaw, Fletcher arrived at 1 p.m. and found his friend sitting outside on the lawns under a sun umbrella, reading a book.

'Where have you been, Guy Bhai?' Reggie complained. 'You suddenly disappeared and I had no idea where to find you.'

'Sorry. I had to go back to the States,' Fletcher explained vaguely, 'and I got stuck there longer than expected.'

Reggie didn't seem to want to know any more details as he beckoned for one of the bearers to bring them two beers. Fletcher was glad he wouldn't have to lie to his friend. It was strange to be back in Delhi again, as if nothing had happened. Seven months of his life seemed to have been erased.

'What are you reading?' Fletcher asked. 'I don't think I've ever seen a book in your hands.'

Reggie showed him the cover, which had an image of skeletal fingers picking up two cards, a queen of diamonds and an ace of spades, with a switchblade stuck between the bones on the back of the hand.

'*Thunderball*,' he said. 'James Bond. You should read it. Action. Sex. Suspense. I've read everything by Ian Fleming.'

'I'll have to give it a try,' said Fletcher.

'Brilliant stuff!' said Reggie.

Fletcher moved his chair into the shade of the umbrella as he sat down.

'Speaking of international intrigue, what do you think's going to happen with the Chinese?' Fletcher asked.

'It's hard to say,' said Reggie, who always seemed to have inside information. He had studied at St Stephen's College at Delhi University and several of his classmates were aspiring politicians and members of the Youth Congress. 'But you can be sure, when it's all over, heads will roll. Krishna Menon is already being pushed aside and Nehru has taken over the defence portfolio. General Kaul has been disgraced and promptly came down with pneumonia. Meanwhile, America is sending military aid, but it's all happening a little too late.'

'What about Nehru himself?'

'I think he's taken it very hard,' said Reggie. 'He trusted Chou En-lai and was badly betrayed. Politically, it's damaged Nehru, though I think he'll survive. People are rallying behind the government, donating gold jewellery to the National Defence Fund and knitting woollen sweaters and socks for the troops.'

'What about the Soviets?' Fletcher asked as their beers arrived, along with a plate of finger chips.

'They've been distracted by Cuba,' Reggie said, 'and though there's no love lost between the Russians and the Chinese, Moscow is probably reluctant to send too much military hardware that might be used against their fellow communists. Of course, the other wild card is Pakistan and they seem quite ready to exploit the situation. Things could get worse before they get better.'

Temperatures in Delhi had cooled off at last and it was pleasant sitting outdoors in the shade. Mostly they talked about the conflict with China, but Reggie also spoke about his plans to travel to England in December, where one of his clients had asked him to attend a conference. Unfortunately, it was the wrong season for golf, otherwise he would have made a side trip up to Scotland. After they finished their beer, they headed into the dining room for lunch. Reggie excused himself to go to the men's room, while Fletcher waited in the lounge. Just then, he heard a familiar voice call out.

'Oh, Mr Swift, is that you?'

He turned to see the Kazini seated in one corner of the lounge along with an elderly couple. She was waving at him from across the room, her cigarette holder poised in the other hand.

Fletcher froze for a moment but then collected himself and walked across to greet her. She was seated in a large, overstuffed chair and held out her hand with a regal gesture.

'I'm very cross with you,' she said. 'You broke your promise. You were going to get me an appointment with John Kenneth Galbraith.'

'Forgive me. Things have been crazy....' Fletcher said.

'Yes, indeed! When did you leave Kalimpong?' she asked.

'A while ago,' he said.

The couple that was seated with the Kazini watched in amusement.

'May I present Mr and Mrs Mirchandani, dear old friends of mine,' said the Kazini, 'And this is Mr Allan Swift, an American ornithologist, or so he says.'

Glancing over his shoulder, Fletcher saw Reggie emerging from the rest room. He shook hands with the couple and tried to extricate himself.

'How long are you in Delhi?' the Kazini demanded.

'Just until tomorrow,' Fletcher replied, taking a step backwards. 'I'm sorry. Will you please excuse me? I've got a friend waiting.'

Raising an arched eyebrow, she waved her hand to dismiss him.

'Who was that?' Reggie asked, as they headed into the dining room.

'The Kazini,' said Fletcher.

'Who?' His friend gave him a puzzled look.

The head bearer led them to a table at the far side of the room.

'She's married to an aristocrat from Sikkim. I met her at a Fulbright event,' Fletcher said.

Accepting Fletcher's explanation, Reggie began to recount the plot of the book he'd been reading. 'An international crime syndicate, SPECTRE, steals two atomic bombs from NATO and holds the world at ransom. Agent 007 travels to the Bahamas and teams up with Felix Leiter, a CIA operative who also works for the Pinkerton Detective Agency. Bond seduces the villain's mistress, Dominetta, better known as "Domino"....'

'Stop,' said Fletcher, holding up both hands. 'Reggie yaar, don't tell me any more. You'll spoil the ending.'

◆

The next day, November 9, was a Friday and Fletcher went across to the Embassy, ostensibly to register as a Fulbright scholar with the consular section but mainly to see Sullivan. Mark met him and took him downstairs, through a locked door where he punched in a combination before they were admitted to the maze of hallways beneath the Chancery building.

Sullivan's office didn't seem to have changed since his last visit, though Fletcher noticed a duck decoy on top of the filing cabinet. It was carved out of wood and painted to look like a spotbill, with mottled brown feathers. The duck's bill was black with a yellow dot at the end and a red patch above the nostrils.

'Where did you get that?' Fletcher asked, admiring the quality of the workmanship.

'From a Kashmiri merchant, Abdul Hamid. He had a dozen of them made for me in Srinagar, carved out of willow wood. I'm going to try them out at Sultanpur Jheel this weekend. Want to come along?' Sullivan said.

'No, thanks,' said Fletcher, 'I think I'll head down to Bharatpur tomorrow. Most of the birds must already be there.'

'So, how was Bangkok?'

'Nice. Your friends took good care of me,' said Fletcher.

'Yeah. I like Thailand for a change, once in a while,' Sullivan replied.

'There seems to be a lot of activity in that part of the world. Laos in particular. Also, Saigon,' said Fletcher.

Sullivan nodded. 'A bunch of cowboys and yahoos strutting around. But it's not going to amount to anything more than a hill of beans.'

'Any more news from Sikkim?' Fletcher asked.

'All quiet on the eastern front, though the Chinese still have a significant presence in the Chumbi Valley. Ladakh is heating up, if you can say that about a place where the temperatures are sub-zero. The PLA have been shelling an Indian airfield at Chushul. Your friend Afridi must be feeling the heat,' Sullivan said. Unscrewing his pipe, he began cleaning it with a reamer and scraping off the tar on the edge of an ashtray.

'So, what am I supposed to do now?' Fletcher asked as he watched Sullivan probing the burled briar bowl with a pipe cleaner.

'Go back to being an ornithologist,' said Sullivan. 'Work on your research and lie low. Right now, we don't need you for anything. When we do, I'll get in touch.'

'What about the bar-headed geese and checking for radioactivity?' Fletcher asked. 'Do you still want me to collect blood samples?'

Sullivan was silent for a minute or more, as he reassembled his pipe.

'It's a good thing you don't smoke,' he said, glancing up. 'Look at all this crap that goes into my lungs.'

The decoy was watching them with its black beaded eye, as Sullivan seemed to be chewing over the question.

'Nah, I think we'll give up on the geese,' he said, at last. 'It was an interesting experiment but the results were too iffy. Besides, we've got reliable intel that the Chinese are still a few years away from developing a viable nuclear device. The facility at Lop Nur is just getting started.'

'Is there any way to stop them before they get a bomb?' Fletcher asked.

'I wish there was,' said Sullivan, 'but somehow, it seems inevitable. Look at Cuba. That was a near miss. I don't think people realize how close we came to global annihilation.'

35

Red-wattled Lapwing

Vanellus indicus

A common wader found throughout India, its long, yellow legs give it the appearance of walking on stilts. A fleshy wattle extends from the beak to encircle the eyes and resembles a pair of red spectacles. It has a black breast bordered by white lapels and brown wings with black stripes that are only visible in flight. The lapwing's sharp, seemingly accusatory call is often translated into English as: 'Did you do it? Did you do it?'

The BSA thundered along the two-lane highway between Delhi and Mathura, from where the road turned west toward Bharatpur. Altogether, it was a six-hour drive. The motorcycle hadn't been started for eight months, since it was left parked at Sullivan's house. Fletcher had given it to a mechanic in Lodhi Colony for servicing and had the rear shock absorbers replaced. The bike was now running better than it had ever done before. Two canvas saddlebags contained all of his belongings, including the notebooks in which he had recorded the results of his fieldwork last year. He had also brought along the tape recorder and parabolic microphone, which was strapped onto the carrier.

As he drove past fields of sugar cane and other winter crops, Fletcher felt he was turning back the clock, to a year ago. While the sun was warm and bright, there was a suggestion of colder days to come, especially in the early morning, as he'd left Delhi. The mud-walled villages along the sides of the road looked like anthills or humble sandcastles and the flat, open landscape was a stark contrast to the forested mountains where he'd been only a few days ago. Though it was a relief to leave behind the tensions and struggles of the past few months, he couldn't help thinking of Kesang as he drove along, imagining her seated in the glassed-in porch at Montrose, or asleep in her bed. Crossing the state border from Uttar Pradesh into Rajasthan, he remembered that Eddie Lim and the other Indian–Chinese were imprisoned at an internment camp somewhere nearby.

When he reached Bharatpur, the dusty outskirts of the town were familiar and, for a moment, he felt as if he was returning home. He had no idea if his old flat would be available for rent but when he stopped in front of the mechanic's shop, his landlord was welding the chassis of a jeep. They greeted each other warmly and within half an hour, he was reinstalled in his rooms upstairs.

The war in the Himalayas seemed far away but he had brought a transistor radio to keep up with the news. That evening, after eating dinner at one of the dhabas nearby, he tuned into All India Radio. Melville de Mellow was the newsreader, with a voice as sonorous as his name. Fletcher had heard him many times before but this evening the reassuring baritone struck an ominous note as he reported that, after the recent pause in hostilities, fresh fighting had broken out in NEFA and Ladakh. The Chinese had crossed the Sela Pass and were advancing on the district headquarters in Bomdila. From there, it was only a few days' march to Tezpur, on the north bank of the Brahmaputra River in Assam. In Ladakh, the Chinese were also pressing forward and threatening the Rezang La Pass, which would give them access to the Galwan Valley.

The next morning, Fletcher was up before dawn and drove out to the bird sanctuary, which was only three miles from where he stayed. Parking by the locked gate, he ducked under strands of barbed wire and walked out along the bund, listening to the muted sniggering of ducks on the water. Acacia trees on either side were draped with weaverbird nests. A number of species were calling at this hour, from the deep, reedy whoop of a coucal to the stuttering rattle of painted storks.

'*Did you do it?... Did you do it?*' He heard a red-wattled lapwing piping its persistent query. This was one of the birds that Fletcher remembered from his childhood in Delhi and it always sounded as if it were taunting a guilty conscience. A pair of lapwings took off from the water's edge and he recognized the distinctive cadence of their wings, threshing the air.

After walking for half a mile, he spotted another figure farther down the bund, a short, wiry man with a floppy green hat and white beard. At first, he couldn't believe his eyes but lifting the binoculars and focusing on the man, he confirmed who it was. Though Fletcher had never met Salim Ali before, he owned all of his books and admired his work as an ornithologist and conservationist. Often referred to as 'The Birdman of India,' he was a regular visitor to Bharatpur. The winter before, Fletcher had missed meeting him on several occasions but he had seen Salim Ali's name and signature in the guest register at the forest rest house.

Not wanting to intrude on the quiet reverie of another birdwatcher, Fletcher kept his distance as he scanned the algae covered surface of the water near the shore, spying moorhens and grebes, as well as sandpipers and stilts. Eventually, though, he caught up with Salim Ali, who nodded with a friendly squint, then pointed at a palm tree leaning over the lake shore.

'There's a Pallas's fish eagle over there,' he said.

Fletcher trained his binoculars on the line of trees and saw the pale-headed raptor perched on the shaggy fronds of the palm.

'It's a real honour to meet you, sir,' he said, after studying the bird for a minute. 'I'm a big fan of your books. Right now, I'm doing my fieldwork for a PhD at Cornell and I'm here on a Fulbright.'

'Splendid! What's your research topic?' Salim Ali asked.

'Bar-headed geese. I'm studying how they interact with other migratory species. I'm also comparing the physical condition of the birds when they arrive in the fall and then again before they leave in the spring,' Fletcher explained.

'So, you're collecting specimens?' Salim Ali said, removing his glasses and wiping the lenses with a handkerchief. Though he was in his mid-sixties and his beard was completely white, there was a boyish quality to his face.

'A few,' said Fletcher. 'I check their weight, take blood samples, and measure the amount of fat in their bodies.'

'I hope you eat the birds you shoot,' said Salim Ali, with a mischievous look in his eyes.

'Some of them, yes,' said Fletcher.

'Very good,' said the old man. 'I've always believed that you can never understand a bird completely until you know what it tastes like!'

Both of them laughed.

'Are you staying for a while?' Fletcher asked.

'No, unfortunately, I'm leaving in a couple of hours. I've been here a week and just came out this morning for a last look around before I head back to Bombay,' he said, indicating that he was going to turn around here. 'Good luck with your research and I hope we meet again.'

Fletcher watched as the old man waved and headed back towards the gate. There were so many things he would have liked to ask him, especially about the birds he'd seen in Sikkim, but for now he had to keep those questions to himself. Nevertheless, meeting Salim Ali like this, alone on a quiet November morning in Bharatpur, was like sighting a rare bird.

◆

Plenty of work needed to be done to restart his research, and Fletcher was grateful for the distractions this provided. He had a number of letters to write, particularly to his supervisor at Cornell, explaining that he was back in India. After registering with the FRO, which involved several unpleasant hours at the police station, he called on the Divisional Forest Officer, who was new to his post and demanded to see all of his documents and permissions. Unlike Thupten Lepcha, this DFO seemed uninterested in birds and wasn't particularly helpful. There was also a lot of red tape involved in renting a shotgun from a gun shop in Bharatpur. The owner had let Fletcher use an old, single-barrel twelve-gauge the year before. This winter he arranged to get a double-barrelled gun, along with a box of twenty-four cartridges, his permitted quota for the month. Of course, he still had the unlicensed Beretta.

Before settling into the routine of observing and counting birds, he also arranged to hire a small boat from the forest department that allowed him to move about in areas of the sanctuary that weren't accessible on foot. The leaky flatbottomed craft had no motor or oars, just a long bamboo pole, with which he could manoeuvre about at roughly the same pace as the flapshell turtles that eyed him suspiciously from the weedy shallows near the shore.

Fletcher was able to get *The Statesman* and the *Times of India* from a newsagent near the railway station in Bharatpur, but the papers were always a day late. The radio remained his primary source of news and he listened to the broadcasts every evening. Though there had been indications that the Chinese were going to enter Sikkim, nothing new had happened there. However, reports from Assam were disturbing. The PLA appeared to have reached the foot of the hills. Tezpur was being evacuated and government officials had been ordered to destroy files before abandoning their offices. Even currency reserves had been burnt. All of NEFA was now under Chinese control and hundreds of Indian troops were trapped in the region of the Sela Pass. Meanwhile, in Ladakh, the PLA had mounted a full-scale assault on Rezang La and, from what little information was available, the Indian Army had suffered severe casualties. Despite the ongoing 'arms lift' of American military aid, Indian troops were hampered by a lack of weapons and ammunition, as well as warm clothing.

It looked as if the war would stretch on into December, with temperatures dropping steadily in the mountains and the risk of snow blocking the high passes. But then, on November 22, the Chinese took everyone by surprise, declaring a unilateral ceasefire, effective within twenty-four hours, and promising to withdraw from most of Indian territory by the first of December.

Suddenly, it was all over and there was a general sense of disbelief. Chou En-lai announced the ceasefire through the China News Service, Xinhua. Even the Prime Minister of India learnt about it through press reports. Befuddled journalists and commentators weren't quite sure what to make of it. The whole campaign seemed as if it had been nothing but a show of force by the Chinese to assert their claims to the Aksai Chin and other areas along the border that they had occupied well before the fighting started.

Over the next few days and weeks, more details emerged as Fletcher continued to carefully follow the news. Eventually, he learnt that the battle of Rezang La, which took place on November 18, had been particularly fierce. Out of a force of 120 men from the 13 Kumaon regiment, posted at Rezang La, 114 had been killed, including the commanding officer Major Shaitan Singh. Rather than abandon their post, they stood their ground and fought the Chinese to the final bullet. Reading this report in the newspapers, Fletcher was stunned, remembering that 13 Kumaon was Afridi's regiment, which he had rejoined a few months before.

His first instinct was to call Kesang but almost as soon as he thought about it, Fletcher rejected the idea. He knew that the Intelligence Bureau would be tracking any calls to her number in Kalimpong. If he tried to get in touch, they would be able to trace him to Bharatpur without much difficulty. He also considered contacting Sullivan to get some news. Though he had a number at the Embassy to call in an emergency, not knowing what might have happened to Afridi didn't rise to the level of a crisis. He recognized that he needed to be patient.

Disciplining himself, he carried on with the routines of fieldwork even as he scanned the newspapers every day for any word on the casualties at Rezang La. Soon after the ceasefire, there were a few reports of wounded soldiers being airlifted out of Leh. The papers also indicated that the Chinese had taken a number of prisoners, both in NEFA and in Ladakh. Peking had issued assurances that the POWs were being treated humanely, according to the terms of the Geneva Convention, but none of their names had been released by either side.

After his initial impatience, Fletcher was reconciled to waiting for word from Sullivan. He guessed that the CIA station in Delhi probably knew that Afridi's regiment had taken severe casualties at Rezang La and they would discreetly find out through their military sources what had happened to him. At the same time, Fletcher realized there was little he could do, regardless of the situation.

It was soon the middle of December and the days went by with monotonous regularity, though he felt he was making progress with his research, collecting data on the geese and taking notes regarding their behaviour. One flock in particular had grown used to his presence and let him approach to within a few yards. For hours, he watched them feeding and preening along the lakeshore. Using the tape recorder and microphone, he recorded the different sounds they made from subdued bickering noises to loud honks of alarm. A few weeks earlier, soon after he arrived, Fletcher had collected a dozen geese on the far side of the wetlands. Being a scientist, not a sportsman, he had shot them while they were on the ground rather than in the air.

Most of his mornings were spent in the boat, circling from one wetland to another. The sanctuary included a number of different ponds, connected by canals. By now it was cold at dawn and there was a dense mist over the water that often lingered until noon. In some ways it reminded him of the monsoon in Kalimpong, though it wasn't the same. Punting his boat out into the fog, using the bamboo pole, he sometimes felt as if he was floating through a cloud, as if the world had been erased and he was the only survivor.

Just before Christmas, he got a package from Sullivan, delivered by a driver who left it with his landlord downstairs. He opened the parcel expectantly and found that it contained mostly food from the Embassy's commissary, a couple of tinned hams, several bars of chocolate, and boxes of cookies. There was also a bottle of Wild Turkey bourbon. Fletcher hunted through the package for a hidden message but found nothing. That evening he sat on the flat roof above his apartment, listening to the night sounds of the town, and finished a quarter of the bottle. He hadn't had any alcohol since arriving in Bharatpur. The bourbon gave him a good buzz and watching the stars come out he wondered about the future in a philosophical sort of way, reflecting on the dangers of his work but also the kick of adrenalin that he felt when he was working undercover.

Reggie had sent him a postcard inviting him to Delhi for a New Year's party he was throwing at his house. Fletcher thought of driving up for a couple of days but he was getting used to the solitude and felt a comfortable sense of inertia. Sometimes he felt depressed or bored but seldom lonely. Having saved a third of the bottle of Wild Turkey, he got drunk by himself on New Year's Eve and fell asleep before midnight. Though he was glad to see the end of 1962, Fletcher had no illusions about the next year being any better.

36

Black Partridge

Francolinus francolinus

*Despite its name, only the head and breast on this partridge is black, with
a speckled underbelly of white spots, a chestnut throat, and white cheeks.
The wings are patterned different shades of tan and brown and its back
is pied. Distributed throughout North India, it is usually found in open
grasslands and scrub jungle, though it also frequents cultivation.
Its call is easily recognizable, like the horn on a Lambretta scooter:
teet tara ta rara.*

Soon after dawn in early February, as the first rays of sunlight burnt
the mist off the water, Fletcher was bailing out his boat before setting
off for the day. He usually tied up next to a stunted babool tree that
grew along the shoreline, where someone had placed a few bricks in the
mud as stepping stones. Just as he was scooping the last inch of water
from one corner of the boat, using an old Dalda tin, he was suddenly
aware that someone was watching him.

Looking up, he saw a figure standing on the embankment, one arm
in a sling. The second their eyes met, the man raised his right hand in
a gesture of greeting.

'Hey there!' Fletcher called out in surprise. 'Long time no see! I've
been wondering where you were!'

'May I join you?' Afridi asked.

'Of course. Welcome aboard,' said Fletcher.

Afridi made his way down to the water and Fletcher pulled on
the rope to bring the boat next to the shore. They greeted each other
warmly as Afridi stepped on board. Moments later, Fletcher cast off.

Using the bamboo pole, he pushed them free of the mud and they drifted out into the green water. Two moorah stools, made of reeds and straw, provided the only seats in the boat. Afridi tested one of them for stability before making himself comfortable in the prow.

'I've been worried about you,' said Fletcher. 'Was your arm injured fighting the Chinese?'

'Yes,' said Afridi, 'A flesh wound. Nothing too serious.'

'And you were at Rezang La?'

Afridi looked out across the water at a purple heron standing perfectly still amidst a cluster of reeds.

'I was,' he said, 'but the night before the main assault, I took two men with me on patrol, which probably saved my life. We climbed a high ridge, eight miles north of the pass to try and get a look at the PLA forces. Early the next morning, just after dawn, we heard gunfire and realized what was happening. The three of us immediately turned around and came back down but by then the Chinese had overwhelmed the post. Our company was outnumbered more than ten to one and they couldn't call in artillery support because of an intervening ridge. By the time we got there, most of the Chinese had moved on down to a position on the other side of the pass. We exchanged fire with a couple of men that remained behind and I was wounded by a stray bullet, just as it was getting dark. The next morning, we crawled down to the pass, which the PLA had abandoned. It was a terrible sight, trenches littered with bodies. Out of a 120 of our men, only six survived.'

Afridi's voice was still raw with pain, two and a half months after the battle. Fletcher didn't know what to say in response, as he steered the boat across the pond, towards a canal that connected to a larger waterbody beyond. Ahead of them was an island covered with acacia trees on which dozens of painted storks were roosting.

'How did you get out of there?' Fletcher asked at last.

'It took us three days to walk to the nearest Indian Army encampment where a helicopter picked us up and took us to Leh. From there I was airlifted to Delhi and spent a couple of weeks in the military hospital. When I was released, they let me go back to Kalimpong.'

'Kesang must have been glad to see you,' said Fletcher.

'I was able to write to her from the hospital, so she knew I was all right,' said Afridi. 'By then, of course, the war was over.'

'Some journalists are saying it wasn't a war,' said Fletcher.

Afridi shook his head. 'Well, if it wasn't, then I'd hate to see what a real war is like. The Chinese are still holding a number of our men and officers as POWs.'

After they passed through the canal and glided out onto an open expanse of water, dotted with hundreds of ducks and geese, Fletcher drew the pole into the boat and sat down.

'So, you've been in Kalimpong all this time?' he asked.

'Mostly, but I also went up to Gangtok. We were lucky the Chinese left Sikkim alone. I still don't understand why. It would have been a much greater blow to India if they had crossed over Nathu La,' Afridi said.

'The whole thing seems so pointless,' said Fletcher, 'as if the PLA were just flexing their muscles for no reason at all.'

'When did you get here?' Afridi asked.

'In November,' Fletcher told him. He went on to explain how he'd decided to come back to Delhi once the fighting began. Without going into details, he let Afridi know that there had been a risk that he might be arrested by the Intelligence Bureau. Kesang had told Afridi about the two men he'd killed and Babu Chettri, whose body had been found twenty miles downstream from Teesta Bridge. Afridi reported that his death had been blamed on Chinese agents and no one suspected Kesang or Fletcher. It felt strange to be talking about things that had happened in Kalimpong because it seemed so far away and long ago. Fletcher didn't say anything about his trip to Bangkok, though he assumed Afridi knew he'd switched passports.

'Can I ask why you're here?' said Fletcher, eventually, after a pause in their conversation. 'I'm guessing you haven't come to Bharatpur for birdwatching.'

Afridi smiled briefly, then shook his head.

'I need your help,' he said.

'Sure,' said Fletcher. 'What for?'

'On 14 November of this year, while the fighting was still going on, our Prime Minister approved the establishment of a Special Frontier Force of Tibetan fighters. It's also known as "Establishment 22". The whole operation is top secret, run by the Intelligence Bureau with assistance from the CIA. Many of the fighters that have been recruited were part of the Chushi Gangdruk insurgency in Tibet. Originally, the government of India was reluctant to support them because it would have antagonized the Chinese but after hostilities broke out it was seen as an effective strategy to hit back at the PLA.'

'Okay...' said Fletcher, trying to figure out how this involved him.

'I've been helping with recruitment and screening,' said Afridi. 'Over the past two weeks I was in Chakrata interviewing some of the men who have applied for the SFF. One of the Khampas I spoke with is an older man, in his late forties, obviously an experienced fighter. I got him talking about the work he'd done for the CIA and it turned out that he parachuted into Tibet on two occasions and blew up a couple of bridges. Eventually, he told me that he had helped collect the antiquities from Yangchen Monastery just before the Chinese attacked. He described the relics in detail, remembering many of the images and thangkas that were salvaged. Altogether, there were three yak loads that were packed into six large sacks. When I told him that I didn't believe there was any treasure, he laughed at me and said he himself had been part of the team that carried it out of Tibet.'

'Does he know where it is?' said Fletcher.

'I think so, but after starting out being talkative, he suddenly grew cautious,' said Afridi. 'He wouldn't tell me which route or pass they'd used and said he really wasn't sure, though he wanted to speak to some American named Mr Jack, with whom he had worked back in 1957.'

'Weren't there any Americans in Chakrata?' Fletcher asked. 'You could have put him in touch with one of them.'

Afridi was silent for a moment. A fishing eagle circled overhead and the ducks grew restless as the raptor's shadow passed over the water.

'I thought it would be better if I came to see you,' he said.

'So, you want to start this treasure hunt again?' said Fletcher.

'I want to finish it,' said Afridi.

'Okay, let me see what I can find out,' said Fletcher. 'What's the Khampa's name?'

'Temba Lekshi. He's still in Chakrata and I've made sure he stays there,' said Afridi. 'If you can find Mr Jack, then maybe we can get him to talk.'

'I'll do my best,' said Fletcher.

◆

Bharatpur had only three Public Call Booths, one of which was near the railway station. Fletcher had used it a couple of times, the year before, to phone the Fulbright office in Delhi. It was nothing more than the back corner of a ration shop, with a plyboard partition and a single black telephone with a frayed cord. The owner of the ration shop spoke to the operator and booked a trunk call. After that, Fletcher waited until the operator called back and connected him. It took half an hour and he drank a lukewarm bottle of Coke while he waited. The ration shop was full of bags of rice and flour, as well as bins of spices and other basic commodities. It had a refrigerator for cold drinks that wasn't working. Eventually, when the call went through to Sullivan's office, his secretary answered and there was a delay as she went to look for her boss. Fletcher finally recognized Sullivan's gruff voice. They spoke briefly without any pleasantries or small talk.

'Yeah, okay,' Sullivan agreed, after Fletcher said he wanted to meet. 'Why don't we do this? I'm going to be in Sariska on Saturday, staying at the maharajah of Alwar's hunting lodge. It's about two hours away from you. Come over on Saturday morning and we'll have lunch together.'

'Sounds good,' Fletcher said, just before he heard the receiver click on the other end of the line.

It was Thursday. Afridi had already gone back to Delhi and on to Chakrata, a hill station in the foothills between Simla and Mussoorie. Fletcher had never been there though he'd heard the name. On Friday, he pulled together his papers and notes and returned the twelve-gauge to the gun shop, knowing that he might have to leave without warning. He also paid his rent for February and March, explaining to his landlord that he would probably be away for a while.

The road from Bharatpur to Sariska was badly potholed and Fletcher drove slowly. There wasn't much traffic except for bullock carts and a few camels. It took three hours instead of two but he finally found his way to the hunting lodge. An imposing, two-storey structure with turrets, it had wings of guest rooms on either side of a broad staircase leading up to a columned entrance. He could see a dozen embassy vehicles parked out front, as well as several Forest Department jeeps. Leaving his motorcycle in the shade of a palm tree, off to one side, he went up the stairs and entered a cavernous hall full of stuffed tigers and leopards, as well as deer trophies on the walls.

An obsequious gentleman in a pink turban emerged from one of the side rooms and greeted him with a deferential bow.

'Is Mr Jack Sullivan here?' Fletcher asked.

The man nodded and gestured with one hand, leading him through a drawing room and up a staircase to the second floor. At one end of the hall was a teak doorway that looked as if it could admit an elephant. The man in the turban knocked loudly and there was a shout from inside, telling them to come in. Fletcher entered an enormous suite, with twenty-foot ceilings.

His turbaned escort had disappeared, closing the door behind him. Moments later Cocoa appeared, wagging her tail and greeting Fletcher with affection. She was followed soon afterwards by her master, who emerged from the bathroom stark naked, a towel in one hand. He seemed to be in a cheerful mood.

'Guy!' he said, pulling a pair of plaid boxers out of a suitcase and starting to get dressed. 'It's good to see you.'

'What brings you here?' Fletcher asked.

'Bird shooting,' said Sullivan. 'A delegation of US senators is with us for the weekend. They've come here to make sure our arms shipments are being gratefully received, but they wanted to do some hunting on the side. Mostly sandgrouse but also partridges and quail. We just got back from a couple of beats this morning and I thought I'd have a shower before you showed up.'

'Isn't Sariska a wildlife sanctuary?' Fletcher asked.

'Technically, yes,' said Sullivan, 'but they've bent the rules for us. After all, we're not shooting tigers.'

'Cocoa seems to be happy.' Fletcher stroked her head as she sat contentedly at his feet.

'She retrieved her first peacock today.' Sullivan laughed. 'The senior senator from Nebraska mistook it for a partridge, or at least that's his excuse for shooting India's national bird.'

Pulling on his trousers and buttoning his shirt, Sullivan picked up his pipe and they went out onto a balcony that opened off the suite, overlooking the lawns and gardens at the back. After he got his pipe burning, Sullivan pointed to a pair of lounge chairs positioned in the shade.

'So, what have you got for me?' he said.

Fletcher leaned back in the chair and put his hands behind his head. 'Afridi came to see me, day before yesterday.'

'Oh, yeah? What does he want?' Sullivan asked.

'He told me about the Special Frontier Force and how we're helping the Intelligence Bureau recruit and train Tibetan guerrillas,' Fletcher said.

After a long pause, Sullivan mused, 'It's interesting.... Now that we're supplying military aid, after the Chinese attack, suddenly India and the United States are bosom buddies. We're doing all kinds of things together.'

'Afridi was up in Chakrata and met one of the Khampas who used to work for us, a guy named Temba Lekshi....' Fletcher paused to see if there was any reaction but Sullivan maintained a poker face, so he continued. 'He claims to have been one of the Chushi Gangdruk fighters who rescued the antiquities from Yangchen Gompa monastery and brought them across to Sikkim.

'Did he tell Afridi where this stuff is?' said Sullivan.

'No.' Fletcher shook his head.

Sullivan threw up both hands in a gesture of frustration.

'Oh, come on! What is this?' he said. 'First you tell me there's no treasure and it's just some kid, "the precious one". Now you're saying there is a pot of gold at the end of the rainbow after all, but nobody knows where it is. Get it together, Guy! We need solid evidence, not just rumours and wishful thinking....'

'Temba says he's willing to talk,' said Fletcher. 'But the only person he'll speak to is Mr Jack.'

The pipe smoke filtered upward, catching a breeze and swirling out into the sunlight where it disappeared.

'Is that so?' Sullivan said, after another prolonged silence. 'What did you say his name was, again?'

'Temba Lekshi.'

'I have a tough time remembering Tibetan names,' Sullivan mumbled. 'They all sound the same.'

'He says the Americans called him "Ted".' Fletcher explained. 'He's in Chakrata. Afridi has kept him there.'

'Did you tell Afridi about the pilots' remains?' Sullivan asked.

'No, I saved that for later,' said Fletcher.

'Atta boy!' Sullivan responded with approval.

'So, if we find this tranche of relics,' said Fletcher. 'Are you still interested in buying them?'

'It depends where the money goes,' Sullivan answered.

'To support Chushi Gangdruk, of course,' Fletcher said.

'No, we're handing that programme off to the Indians. We can't be in the business of supporting insurgents,' said Sullivan, after sucking on his pipe. 'Maybe if there was some other organization that would give us some cover.... The phrase of the month right now is "plausible deniability".'

The two of them exchanged a glance.

'But even if we cover our tracks, what is the agency going to do with twelfth and thirteenth century bronzes, now that Emil Zorman isn't there to sell them for you?' Fletcher asked. 'Are they going to decorate the halls at Langley?'

'Zorman wasn't the only art dealer in New York. We can always unload them on someone else,' said Sullivan. 'Besides, if we get the remains of those fliers back, that's my first priority.'

'So, you'll talk to Temba?'

Sullivan drew on his pipe with an almost imperceptible nod of his head. At that same moment, they both heard a staccato call from the far edge of the yard. *Teet tara ta rara!*

Cocoa looked up expectantly, cocking her ears.

'*Kaala teetar,'* said Sullivan in Hindi. 'Black partridge. We used to say it was calling out, "Paan-bidi-cigarette", like those vendors on railway platforms, but I've always thought its call sounded more like Morse Code.'

They tried to spot the bird but it was hidden in the underbrush somewhere beyond a bougainvillea hedge that marked the limits of the yard.

'Do you want me to come with you to Chakrata?' Fletcher asked.

'No, it's better if you stay out of this for the time being,' Sullivan said. 'Depending on what I learn, I'll get in touch with you.'

37

Oriental Dollarbird

Eurystomus orientalis cyanocollis

*A stout, stubby bird, about the size of a pigeon, though it often appears bulkier than it is because it fluffs out its feathers when perching on a branch. Also known as the broad-billed roller. Generally a bluish green with a brown head and a thick red beak, it gets its name from the white spots under its wings that look like silver coins when it flies overhead. Somewhat smaller and less colourful than the common Indian roller (*Coracias benghalensis*).*

Two weeks later, on March 5, Fletcher found himself back in Kalimpong. Afridi was already there, staying at the officers' mess but spending most of his time at Montrose with Kesang. Using his old alias, Allan Swift, Fletcher checked into the Himalayan Hotel. The three of them got together that evening. Kesang seemed happy to see him, though it was clear that he was now the odd man out. Despite a residual ache of jealousy, Fletcher was reconciled to her relationship with Afridi and no longer felt a desire to compete for Kesang's affections.

The blackout curtains had been removed and they sat together on the glassed-in porch, with the lights of Kalimpong scattered over the ridge like a galaxy that had fallen to earth. Afridi offered him a drink and got one for himself. His arm was out of the sling but it was still weak. Fletcher noticed that Afridi did most things with his right hand, like pouring from the bottle of whisky and holding a glass, though once he was seated, he kept exercising his left hand by opening and closing his fingers into a fist.

'Is your arm still painful?' he asked.

'Not seriously,' Afridi replied. 'It's just that the muscles need strengthening and stretching after being immobilized for a couple of months.'

'Fortunately, he's not likely to do any mountaineering for a while,' said Kesang, putting a hand on his wrist.

'Who knows?' said Afridi. 'It sounds as if we might need to climb, wherever this place is that we're going.'

'Did you bring a map?' Fletcher asked, taking a sip of Scotch.

'Yes,' said Afridi, 'but first I want to know what you're planning.'

'I really don't have much of a plan,' Fletcher replied. 'The instructions I was given are simple, to team up with you and retrieve the antiquities.'

'Why is everyone so interested in these old idols and thangkas?' said Kesang. 'I don't understand it.'

Afridi looked at her and said, 'But it's part of your heritage.'

'No, it isn't. I don't believe in religion, you know that,' she said. 'It's just a lot of "mumbo jumbo", as Daddy used to say, and I've never trusted the lamas. They live an easy life and get fat by tricking their followers into believing nonsense.'

'"The opiate of the people",' said Afridi. 'I thought you weren't a communist any more.'

'I'm not,' said Kesang, 'but that doesn't mean I've replaced it with anything else. Certainly not religion.'

Fletcher listened with amusement as they bantered for a while; he was glad to see that Kesang's cynicism was still intact. After a few minutes, they returned to the subject of the antiquities.

'So, the sacred terma has been hidden for four years,' said Afridi. 'It came out of Tibet long before the young Rinpoche was smuggled into Sikkim.'

'That's what Temba says,' Fletcher confirmed. 'He claims that he and three other Khampas carried it across the mountains about a month before the Dalai Lama escaped from Tibet in March 1959.'

'Which route did they take?' Kesang asked.

'An unnamed pass into Bhutan, just to the west of Mount Jomolhari. Very high country. They lost one of their yaks on the way, when it fell down a cliff, and they had to carry its load themselves,' Fletcher repeated what Sullivan had told him of his conversation with Temba. 'The snow and glaciers were bad enough but the forests were even more difficult, so thick that they had to tunnel through the foliage and the terrain was very steep with no paths to follow. Eventually, the yaks couldn't go any further and they had to turn them loose. By then they were desperate and decided to hide the treasure in a cave and come back to recover it later. But after they nearly died getting out, none of them had the courage to return.'

'So, how are you going to retrieve it?' Kesang asked.

'We'll have to go in by helicopter,' said Afridi.

'Will you inform the Bhutanese government?' she asked.

Afridi shook his head. 'Hopefully, we can get in and out before anyone notices. It's a part of Bhutan where nobody lives.'

'And you're absolutely convinced that Temba is telling the truth?' Kesang wanted to know.

'As much as we can ever be convinced,' said Fletcher. 'He's given us specific landmarks and details. His story is the most promising lead we've had so far.'

'Why don't you take him with you?' said Kesang.

'We considered that option,' Afridi said, 'but the helicopter can only carry two passengers along with the pilot and a limited payload. If we take a bigger chopper, it's more likely to arouse suspicions. Besides, Temba's presence may complicate matters....'

'I still don't understand why the Americans,' said Kesang, looking at Fletcher, 'your people. Why are they so interested in these relics?'

Picking up Afridi's glass and his own, Fletcher went across to the bar and poured them each another drink. When he sat down, he looked at Afridi and Kesang with a serious expression.

'Okay. I've been authorized to tell you something that must not leave this room,' he said. 'The antiquities are valuable, certainly, but they also include the remains of two American pilots whose plane crashed in Tibet in the spring of 1957, as they were returning after parachuting a group of Tibetan guerrillas into Kham province. Nobody in India was aware of this flight because it took off from an airfield in East Pakistan.'

Fletcher went on to explain how bone fragments had been recovered from the crash site and hidden for safekeeping at Yangchen Gompa monastery.

'So, the CIA just wants the remains,' said Kesang. 'They don't really care about the rest of the terma?'

'From what I've been told,' said Fletcher, 'there's a dilemma. Originally, the treasure was going to be sold to support the Chushi Gangdruk guerrillas but now that the US is working with India to create the Special Frontier Force that's the primary focus of attention, and nobody wants to be seen supporting a group of exiled vigilantes who can't be controlled.'

'Are they no longer willing to pay the Khampas?' said Afridi, a note of irritation in his voice.

'Let's put it this way,' Fletcher responded. 'They're ready to honour their commitment as long as the money doesn't go toward arming insurgents who might antagonize the Chinese into starting another border conflict.'

'But then who will they pay?' said Kesang.

'We're still working on that. Perhaps an organization that can channel funds to the Khampas. I've been told it's a question of "plausible deniability",' said Fletcher. 'Now, let's take a look at your map and try to figure out where we're going.'

Afridi unfolded the map on the coffee table.

'How old is this?' Fletcher asked.

'1923. Survey of India. One inch to a mile. It's still the most reliable map of this region,' said Afridi. 'Though it covers mostly Sikkim and Darjeeling, it shows a corner of Bhutan, the area we're interested in, between Jomolhari and another mountain, Gipmochi. The main route from Paro to Yatung follows the Amo Chu river but to the east of that is a wild, uninhabited tract of several hundred square miles, heavily forested below 14,000 feet.'

Running his fingers over the contours of the map, Fletcher examined the topography.

'Temba said that when they came out, after hiding the treasure, they followed a tributary of the Amo Chu. It starts somewhere up in this region, immediately to the west of Jomolhari. According to him, one of the landmarks is a ridge with three rocky outcroppings, like natural chortens. The place where they hid the treasure is directly below the central crag, in a narrow valley with cliffs on either side. Another landmark is a large tree, either a hemlock or a fir, which has two main trunks that curve out and upward like the horns on a yak. From the base of that tree, the cave is visible on the cliffs across the valley.'

As they studied the map together, they came up with several possible locations, though the contours were a confusing maze of swirling lines. After staring at it for a while, Fletcher felt he was looking at an optical illusion in which hidden images appeared and disappeared.

Kesang had ordered in dinner from the Nanking and they served themselves out of pots on the stove after warming it up. She said that Eddie Lim and his family had returned from the internment camp three weeks ago. They were still traumatized by the experience but Eddie had got the restaurant started again.

As they began to eat, Kesang turned to Fletcher. 'You haven't congratulated Imtiaz, have you?' she said.

'For what?' he asked, looking across the table.

'He's been promoted,' she said. 'Major Imtiaz Afridi.'

◆

The engine on the Indian Air Force helicopter started up with a whine followed by the chugging sound of its pistons and the oscillating whirr of the rotor blades. The pilot of the Russian-made Mil Mi-1 had flown up from Bagdogra that morning. A helipad was located within the army compound, near the mess where Afridi was staying. Fletcher had been brought in surreptitiously, hidden in the back of a jeep. When the chopper took off, they circled out over the Teesta Valley, as if they were heading downriver but then the pilot veered northeast towards the higher mountains along the border of Sikkim and Bhutan.

This was a recce flight and, fortunately, the weather was clear. The pilot had mentioned that during the fighting with China he had been flying mostly over NEFA, picking up wounded soldiers and dropping supplies. He pointed out several bullet holes in the fuselage, as if to say they didn't have to face that danger any more. For the first ten minutes of the flight, they were over Indian territory but then they crossed a high ridge and entered Bhutanese airspace. Fletcher had memorized as much of the map as he could and spotted the Amo Chu river and one of the tributaries they had identified. Ahead of them, they could see the white pyramid of Jomolhari. Soon they were over high meadows where the pilot turned back, exploring a parallel valley. The air was calm and there was little turbulence, though the helicopter shuddered from engine vibration. They had enough fuel for an hour and a half of flying. Afridi was in the co-pilot's seat and could see out the windscreen but Fletcher had to unbuckle his seatbelt to get a clear view of the terrain. After an hour of flying, the pilot signalled that they would need to head back soon, as they circled over another valley and descended almost level with the treetops.

Moments later, Afridi pointed to their left and Fletcher saw the three outcroppings of rock that Temba had described. As they passed over them, the valley below was visible and they could see the cliffs facing each other. Just to be sure, they asked the pilot to make another pass and the helicopter circled slowly around, giving them a 360-degree view of the valley. All three of them kept an eye out for any kind of clearing or open space where the helicopter might touch down but the forest canopy was so thick there seemed to be nothing for miles around.

After they returned to the helipad in Kalimpong and could speak without shouting over the noise of the engine, the pilot shook his head discouragingly.

'The only place I could set down is somewhere above the treeline and that's almost fifteen miles beyond your location,' he said.

'Could you hover and lower us by ropes?' Afridi asked.

'Maybe further down the valley…but it's too constricted near those cliffs and you'd end up stranded in the treetops,' the pilot said. 'Even if I get you in, I certainly won't be able to get you out of there.'

◆

Despite the daunting terrain, they decided to set off two days later, on 10 March at 6 a.m. If they weren't able to find a landing spot closer to the cave, the pilot would drop them on a meadow at the head of the valley, from where they could cut through the forest to reach the site. Fletcher estimated that it would take them three days, while Afridi thought it was more likely to be four. They were equipped with 200 feet of rope, along with pitons and carabiners. Though they tried to keep their loads as light as possible, each of their packs weighed more than fifty pounds.

'How are you going to carry the treasure out?' Kesang asked. She had insisted on coming to the helipad to see them off.

'Let's find it first,' said Afridi. 'Then we can solve that problem later on.'

'How's your arm?' Fletcher asked.

'Better,' said Afridi, 'but certainly not a hundred per cent.'

As they waited for the helicopter to arrive, Fletcher noticed an unusual bird perched at the top of a horse chestnut tree nearby. He took his binoculars out of their case, which was tied to his pack.

'What is it?' Afridi asked.

'I'm not sure,' Fletcher replied. 'Looks like a roller.'

He could hear the distant rumble of the chopper approaching and the bird took flight. As it opened its wings, he could see the white spots underneath.

'A dollarbird,' he said. 'Some people say it brings rain.'

The pilot arrived exactly on time and kept the engine running while the two of them piled into the chopper. As they lifted off, Fletcher saw Kesang waving below but within a few seconds she was gone and there was nothing beneath them except for an undulating ocean of trees.

As they turned northward, away from the Teesta Valley, Fletcher could see several fires burning on the ridges, the smoke trailing up the slope and flames lapping at the green foliage.

'Is that a wildfire?' he shouted, pointing.

'No. It's villagers clearing the jungle,' Afridi answered. 'Some of them still practise slash and burn agriculture. They'll plant their crops in the ashes and harvest it after the monsoon.'

Passing over the fire and on to the next valley, they could smell the smoke. Now that they knew where they were going, it took only twenty minutes to reach the three crags. Today, the snow peaks were covered with thick layers of clouds and the flight was rougher than last time. Circling over the valley, they scanned the ridges for any sign of a place to land but it seemed hopeless until Afridi shouted, 'What's that over there? Below the second chorten.'

As the pilot descended a little lower, Fletcher could see what looked like a slab of rock at the base of the crag. A section was overgrown with creepers and plants but part of it was exposed, a relatively flat shelf of granite about thirty feet across. Afridi glanced over at the pilot, who looked doubtful but nudged his chopper forward, keeping the rocky outcropping safely to his left. As he dropped lower, the tops of the trees were blown about by gusts of air from the rotors. The landing site seemed too small and the slab tilted slightly but the pilot put up his thumb as he turned and swept out in an arc, to approach the rock from a different angle. Fletcher felt a wave of vertigo as the chopper swung around and swooped in like a raptor descending on its prey in slow motion, a sickening plunge that ended with a sudden thud, as the skids hit the rock.

Afridi shouted to the pilot again, asking him to pick them up in two days from this same rock. Hauling their packs out of the chopper, they had only a couple feet of the slab to stand on, beyond which lay a fifty-foot drop into the trees. Fletcher hoped there was a way to get off the ledge as the helicopter rose above them and headed back to Bagdogra. The pulsing sound of its engine diminished and the two men were aware of the silence and solitude surrounding them.

'Are you sure that two days is enough time?' Fletcher asked.

'It will have to be,' said Afridi, surveying the valley below them. 'I'm not sure I want to spend more than two nights out here.'

The granite slab on which they stood looked larger than it had from the air though Fletcher knew the pilot had taken a risk landing here. Fortunately, there was very little wind, even if it was exposed.

After casting about, they found a gully that funnelled down into the forest and they descended from the rock without using a rope. Once they were under the trees, the sky was blotted out and they were enveloped by green shadows. The slope of the mountain was about forty-five degrees and the ground was thick with decomposing leaves. Fortunately, the monsoon hadn't started yet and there were no leeches.

'According to Temba, we need to get to the bottom of this ridge,' said Fletcher. 'If we head straight down from here, we should hit the tree he described or get close enough to find it.'

Being inside the forest after the helicopter ride was disorienting but going downhill was relatively easy, for they could glissade through the leaf litter and soft soil. The only thing that worried Fletcher was the thought of hauling sacks full of brass and copper images up this slope. About halfway down, they came to a rhododendron jungle that slowed their progress. The trees were flowering, with bright pink and red blossoms but the cheerful colours belied a depressing tangle of limbs. They had to pick their way between the twisted branches and their bulky packs made it impossible to fit through the narrower gaps. For a while it felt as if they would never make it down but after two hours, the rhododendrons gave way to larger trees and a more open understory.

They could hear the sound of a stream below them and gaps in the branches revealed sections of the opposite slope. There was still no sign of the giant conifer until Afridi found an opening in the foliage which gave them a view up the valley. About 400 yards away, they spotted the landmark, its twin trunks like the horns on a yak.

Scrambling through bamboo thickets, they traversed the slope until they were able to haul themselves up to the foot of the tree. It was an enormous hemlock, with splayed roots that clutched the slope with an ancient grip. Out of breath from the exertion, the two men dropped their packs and sat down in the dappled sunlight that filtered through the spreading branches. Taking out his binoculars, Fletcher scanned the valley further up, where the forest parted to reveal two sheer walls of rock on either side of the stream.

Near the top of the cliffs on the far side of the valley, Fletcher spotted an opening in the rocks, about twenty feet below an overhang.

'There it is,' he said.

Afridi had seen it too with his naked eye.

'What's that on the overhang, just to the right of the cave?' he asked.

Fletcher focused his binoculars before letting out a whistle of dismay.

'Beehives,' he said.

38

Yellow-backed Honeyguide

Indicator xanthonotus

*A small, sparrow-like bird with a pinched beak. Mostly olive-grey
with a bright yellow rump and face. Found in close proximity to
the honeycombs of Himalayan rock bees, it feeds on wax and larvae.
Though little is recorded about this species' behaviour in the Himalayas,
honeyguides in Africa (*Indicator indicator*) are known to lead human
beings to wild hives. After the honeycombs have been harvested, the bird
feeds on the remains. It is believed to be a brood parasite that lays its
eggs in barbet nests.*

Descending to the bottom of the valley, Fletcher and Afridi followed the stream to the foot of the cliffs. This wasn't as simple as it looked because there were two waterfalls they had to circumvent. Eventually, however, they reached a spit of sand and gravel next to a pool of flowing water, a hundred feet below the cave. Moving cautiously, so as not to disturb the bees, they could see four large honeycombs suspended like stalactites from the overhang. Even without his binoculars, Fletcher was able to make out their seething surfaces, alive with hundreds of giant rock bees. Thupten Lepcha's warning from several months ago replayed itself in his mind: 'A swarm can kill a horse or a man.'

Afridi studied the cliff, trying to determine which line they should climb.

'Do you think you'll be able to make it?' he asked.

Fletcher nodded. 'I should be able to follow your lead. It's the bees I'm more worried about.'

'The first thirty feet will be easy,' said Afridi. 'But after that we'll have to use the crack on the right to reach the ledge below the cave.'

'How did the Khampas get up there?' Fletcher wondered aloud.

'I'm guessing they approached from above and there were no beehives four years ago,' said Afridi. 'They could have descended without ropes and crawled beneath the overhang. Unfortunately, we don't have that option.'

Staring up at the cave, Fletcher caught sight of a small, grey bird perched on the limb of a tree at the top of the cliff. It flitted back and forth a few times and then landed on an upper section of a hive where only a few bees had congregated. The flash of sulphurous yellow on its lower back was clearly visible. Salim Ali, in the *The Birds of Sikkim*, had noted that little was known about the honeyguide's distribution or behaviour, mentioning that further research was required. Under the present circumstance, however, Fletcher had no time for birdwatching.

Gathering dead wood from the forest, the two of them stacked it at the foot of the cliff, working as silently as possible to avoid agitating the bees. Fletcher also collected dry stems of bamboo for kindling. Before they set the fire alight, Afridi uncoiled the rope and sorted through the hardware for the climb, fitting pitons, carabiners, and a hammer into a mesh belt that he buckled around his waist.

'You're sure your arm is okay?' Fletcher asked.

'We'll find out soon enough,' Afridi replied, as he tied on a rope harness, wrapping it around each leg and securing it with bowline knots. He then attached a carabiner to the crosspiece. After rigging up the same kind of harness for Fletcher he tested it to make sure it would hold his weight. Satisfied that the knots were secure, Afridi signalled Fletcher to light the fire.

'Once the smoke drives off the bees, I'll start climbing,' said Afridi. 'You'll have to belay me and keep the fire going at the same time. After I reach the top, I'll take a look inside the cave. If I need you to come up, I'll let you know. Be sure to put plenty of wood on the fire before you head up, so it doesn't go out.'

Fletcher nodded and produced a box of matches. The fire started slowly but soon they had a blaze going and a column of smoke rose up to the hive. At the first hint of the flames below, the bees had grown restless and soon they began to swarm with an angry hum that sounded like a car engine being revved to full throttle. The two men had wrapped their sleeping bags around their heads and bodies, to protect themselves, crouching as close to the fire as they dared. A number of bees hovered around them but stayed away from the flames. As Fletcher reached out to put another stick on the fire he was stung on his hand. The pain was intense and the bite swelled up almost instantly.

After ten minutes, however, the bees began to disperse, as the smoke grew thicker. Looking up, they could see only a few stragglers circling above. Shrugging off his sleeping bag, Afridi started up the rocks. He moved swiftly and easily over the first pitch, which was more of a scramble than a climb. Thirty feet up, he pounded in the first piton. Fletcher tossed more brush on the fire and took up the slack on the rope, as Afridi moved higher. He was clearly favouring his left arm, as he jammed his right hand into the diagonal crack. After a second piton was hammered in, he ascended with the practised rhythm and grace of an experienced climber. Though he made it look easy, Fletcher already felt a knot in his stomach as he saw how exposed the last forty feet were. Flattening himself against the rocks, Afridi stretched out with his right foot to find purchase on the vertical surface. For a moment, it looked as if he might slip but he shifted his weight expertly and reached up to grab the ledge above. Only one obstacle remained, a protruding shard of rock that he would need to climb around. Most of his weight was now on his injured arm and Fletcher held his breath as Afridi struggled to drive another piton into the crack. As soon as he accomplished this, he was stung on the shoulder by a bee. Suddenly, Fletcher felt his partner's full weight on the end of the rope but he braced himself and was able to hold him steady. Afridi regained his composure and worked his way up and around the protrusion to reach the narrow ledge, three feet below the cave. Seconds later, he had disappeared inside.

Feeding the fire with more sticks, Fletcher looked up at the strip of sky overhead, between the ridges on either side. The clouds were almost as dark as the smoke and moments later, he heard a rumble of thunder.

After two or three minutes Afridi reappeared at the mouth of the cave and beckoned for Fletcher to come up. Stoking the fire with several armloads of wood, he made his way up to the first piton. The smoke stung his eyes and it was difficult to breathe but the few bees that were still hovering nearby kept their distance. His right hand was swollen and painful where he had been stung between his thumb and forefinger. Clipping onto the rope he began to climb while Afridi maintained the tension from above. When he reached the crack, he gripped the edge with his right hand before extending his left arm higher, jamming his fingers into a crevice. There was nothing elegant about his technique, and he floundered more than once, but the taut rope gave him enough confidence to finally reach the ledge. Afridi offered him a hand as he crawled up into the mouth of the cave.

Coughing from the smoke he'd inhaled, Fletcher kneeled for a minute to catch his breath before getting to his feet. The darkness closed in around them as they entered the cave. Afridi switched on a torch that penetrated the gloom with a bright yellow beam. After a couple of yards, the rocks opened out into a chamber ten feet high and about the same width. At the back, Fletcher saw a heap of six sacks, piled on top of each other. As they approached, he noticed that they were made of woven yak hair, like the tents that nomads used in Tibet. The coarse fabric was stronger than burlap, though it had been patched and darned.

'Do you want to take a look at what's inside?' Afridi asked.

'Not here,' said Fletcher. 'Let's get them outside before the bees come back. We can lower them using the rope.'

'But, what do we do after that?' said Afridi, as they retreated back to the cave's entrance. 'Each sack weighs about eighty pounds. That's a heavy load to haul back up to the landing site. We don't have the time.'

At that moment, it began to rain, a sudden cloudburst pelting down on the forest outside. Though they were sheltered inside the cave, they watched the downpour with alarm. The rain lasted only twenty minutes but it was long enough to put out the fire.

As soon as the storm had passed the bees came back like squadrons of fighter jets returning to their base. The cave was only thirty feet away from the hives. Crouching in the shadows they could hear the angry hum of hundreds of *Apis dorsata* reclaiming their domain after having been displaced by the smoke.

Retreating to the back of the rock chamber, they sat down in the dark.

Fletcher stated the obvious: 'There's no way out.'

'Unless we escape during the night,' said Afridi. 'But there's no possibility of taking the relics with us.'

'Do bees ever sleep?' Fletcher asked.

'Honestly, I don't know the answer to that question,' said Afridi with a frustrated laugh. 'But I imagine they must.'

'Do you think they dream?' Fletcher chuckled.

'Yes, I'm sure they dream of taking revenge on whoever it was that smoked them off their hives,' Afridi replied.

They remained silent for a while, leaving the torch off to save the batteries. Whatever food they'd brought with them was in their packs below. Neither of them had eaten since they'd had dinner with Kesang, the night before.

'This whole thing is a bit of a lost cause, isn't it?' said Fletcher.

'What is?' said Afridi. 'Our treasure hunt?'

'No, the liberation of Tibet,' he said. 'The communists will never give it up.'

'Perhaps,' Afridi mused, 'but that's not why I'm here. My job is simple. I have to ensure the security of our borders. Unlike you Americans, I'm not fighting for some intangible ideals, like "democracy" or "freedom".'

'Do you really think that arming and training a few hundred Khampa commandos will protect your frontier?' Fletcher asked.

'Not by itself,' said Afridi, 'but the next time the Chinese attack, we'll be better prepared and the SFF will be part of our response. Meanwhile, they can harass our enemy and infiltrate Tibet, providing us with conclusive intelligence.'

'Conclusive Intelligence!' Fletcher laughed. 'You're the one who told me, a year ago in Kashmir, that the truth is never black or white but always shades of grey.'

'Did I?' said Afridi, softly. 'Obviously, I wasn't thinking of this cave. It's definitely black.'

They kept their voices to a whisper.

'Are you still convinced that Kesang's plan will work?' Fletcher asked.

'I think so,' said Afridi. 'Of course, there's always the possibility of something going wrong but she seems committed to the idea.'

'It means she'll have to trust me,' Fletcher said.

'I think she does,' Afridi answered.

'And what do you get out of it?'

'Nothing,' said Afridi.

'Then why did you agree?' Fletcher asked.

'Because it's the right thing to do,' he said.

'Well, nothing's going to happen unless we get these antiquities back to Kalimpong,' said Fletcher. 'I want to take another look outside.'

The two of them returned to the mouth of the cave, from where they could look back down the valley to the massive hemlock tree with its twin trunks. It was surrounded by lesser trees, as well as a large swath of bamboo that grew on a knoll below, where the slope of the ridge levelled off before dropping to the stream. On their way down, they had skirted the bamboo thickets, which spread in a dense, feathery wave of foliage that extended for roughly a 100 yards.

'Here's an idea,' whispered Fletcher, as they peered out across the valley. 'Why don't we try to clear a landing spot for the helicopter tomorrow, on that knoll over there that's covered with bamboo?'

'Wishful thinking,' said Afridi. 'All we've got are pocketknives. Even if we had machetes, it would take us a week to hack out enough space.'

'Not necessarily,' Fletcher replied. 'What if we burn it?'

Afridi looked at him with a thoughtful expression.

'It's all very green,' he said. 'I'm not sure it will ignite.'

'But if we start four or five bonfires at the lower end, it should create enough of a blaze to work its way up to the knoll. The thickets contain a lot of dry stems and leaves that will help keep it going, just like the villagers slash and burn the forest.'

As the sun went down, they studied the contours of the opposite ridge and figured that if they cleared a space even fifty yards across, it might be possible for the chopper to land. By the time it was dark, they both agreed it was worth a try.

Once the bees had settled down for the night, a couple of hours after sunset, Afridi descended on the rope, moving as silently as he could. Once he was on the ground, Fletcher tied the first sack to the rope. Using a piton as an anchor, he eased it over the edge. Initially, the hives grew restless and he could hear an agitated hum but after waiting patiently for the bees to quiet down, he was able to lower all six of the sacks, one by one. By now, it was almost midnight and he looped the rope through the anchor, tying on a harness as best he could. Afridi gave the rope a tug to signal that he was ready and Fletcher stepped down onto the ledge. He dared not use the torch in his pocket. Fumbling about in the dark, he finally found the crack and began to descend, clutching at the rocks as his arms trembled from fear and strain. His feet kept slipping and several times Afridi had to hold him steady with the rope but eventually, he reached the lower end of the cliff, where he could crawl down the rocks and drop to the spit of sand by the water.

Exhausted, the two of them ate a box of biscuits and a packet of yak cheese. After that they each had a bar of chocolate. Dipping mugs into the flowing water, they drank from the stream. Their sleeping bags were still wet from the rain but they were able to lie down for a couple of hours before dawn. Fletcher remained awake, his mind racing as he imagined how easily their plans could fail.

As soon as there was enough light for them to see their way through the forest, he and Afridi crossed the stream and started to climb the ridge at an angle. Though the jungle was dense and full of creepers, they came to the lower edge of the bamboo within half an hour. From their supplies they'd brought two bottles of kerosene, which was fuel for their stove. Almost immediately, they set to work, gathering dead branches and kindling to stack at the base of the thickets. The bamboo stood about eight feet high and the stems were no larger than an inch in diameter. As Fletcher had hoped, there was a fair amount of dead growth amidst the green.

Five bonfires were spaced out at intervals of approximately ten yards. By the time they were ready it was nine in the morning. After dousing the wood with splashes of kerosene, they lit the fires in turn, making sure that each of the bamboo thickets ignited before they moved on to the next. Though the fire started slowly, with a lot of smoke, there was enough of a breeze to help fan the flames. As soon as the conflagration got going, it created a strong draught, sucking the smoke upward and across the knoll.

'I feel like an arsonist,' said Fletcher. 'I hate to think what we're destroying.'

'It's a bit late for regrets,' said Afridi, as the flames jumped from one clump of bamboo to the next, spreading upward.

Returning to the stream bed, they could hear the crackle and roar of the fire behind them. Eyeing the beehives nervously, they cut sections of the rope and each of them lashed one of the sacks to the outside of his empty pack. Even with a layer of padding, the sharp edges of the metal relics dug into their backs and the awkward weight made them stagger as they headed back uphill. Fletcher imagined the Khampas struggling under these loads as they crossed the mountains.

It took four hours for them to ferry all six of the sacks to the edge of the fire, by which time more than half of the bamboo had been burnt. The momentum of the blaze had cleared most of the lower slope and part of the knoll. The surrounding trees had not caught fire, though many of their leaves were scorched. The two of them made one last trip to the foot of the cliff and retrieved their gear.

By the time they returned, most of the bamboo had been reduced to ash but the stumps were still smouldering. The exposed ground was uneven, falling away at an angle of ten to twenty degrees, but near the top of the knoll, it looked as if there might be enough space for the helicopter to land if the pilot was willing to descend into the valley.

Before it grew dark, they opened a tin of sausages and heated them in the embers of the fire. Eating these with a box of soda crackers, they made a meal of it before Afridi set off. He had decided to spend the night on the slab of rock below the crag. The helicopter would arrive early the next morning and he would try to persuade the pilot of their plan.

Once he was gone, Fletcher surveyed the destruction caused by the fire and walked up through the ashes to the level patch on the knoll. The smell of smoke was harsh and acrid, as he stepped around the burnt stubble of bamboo. By now most of the fire had died out, though sections were still smoking and he could feel the heat radiating up from the ground. The charred area was about the size of a football field, though irregular in shape and spread out over the slope. At the centre, however, it was close enough to being horizontal to give him some hope.

Returning to the spot where they had piled the sacks and their gear, Fletcher wrapped himself in a damp sleeping bag. Before the strip of sky was completely dark, he was fast asleep. Having been awake for forty-eight hours and after hauling the antiquities up the hill, he was exhausted and did not wake up until the next morning, when he heard the drumming of the helicopter's engine echoing within the valley, as the blast of air from the rotor blades kicked up a whirlwind of ash.

39

Great Himalayan Barbet

Megalaima virens magnifica

An ungainly bird, slightly larger than a pigeon, with a prominent yellow beak and dark purple head, it has an olive green body, striated brown breast and underbelly, turquoise and emerald wings, and a bright red vent under its tail. Entirely arboreal, it nests in the hollows of tree trunks and often perches atop tall conifers or oaks, emitting a plaintive cry, from which it gets its onomatopoeic name in Nepali, Nyahul, as well as the Lepcha, Kun-nyong.

The wailing call of the great barbet echoed across the valley from one of the fir trees above Rumtek monastery. The bird sounded as if it was voicing a persistent complaint, though there was a musical rhythm to its repeated refrain that blended in with the slow beating of drums and the moaning of horns and conch shells. As Fletcher and Afridi entered the main courtyard, they were met by the two lamas who had accompanied the young tulku from Tibet. Instead of coming by helicopter, they had driven up from Kalimpong and the last three miles to the monastery were completed on foot. A train of mules followed after them, carrying the sacks of terma.

Their arrival had been announced only a few minutes earlier and they had requested no ceremonies or celebrations, not wanting to draw attention to the relics. The Karmapa, who was head of monastery, was away from Rumtek, attending a Buddhist conclave in Bodh Gaya, but the young Rinpoche was in residence. He received them in one of the smaller rooms adjacent to the main temple and presented them with white scarves. His mother was also there, though she sat apart in one corner and watched them enter with pensive eyes.

A number of other monks and acolytes pressed their way into the room out of curiosity. The muleteers carried in the sacks, two of them lifting each load. It appeared as if they were delivering a shipment of potatoes though the metal objects clattered as they were deposited on the floor in front of the boy. He looked no older than Fletcher remembered him from his last visit, though he seemed more content in his new surroundings and had an expression of benign innocence on his face as he watched the sacks arrive.

Stepping forward, Afridi explained in Hindi that this was the terma recovered from Yangchen monastery in Kham, which had been carried across the mountains by loyal defenders of the faith four years earlier. He said that he was honoured to be able to return the sacred relics to their rightful owners. As one of the monks translated for the others, expressions of astonishment and delight creased the faces of the two lamas from Yangchen. The young boy gestured impatiently for them to open the sacks, eager to see what they contained.

Fletcher took out his pocketknife and cut the threads that sewed up one end of the first sack. Then he and Afridi spilled the contents out onto a carpet in front of the Rinpoche. Dozens of idols and ritual objects were revealed, jumbled together like a heap of scrap metal. Most of the artefacts were badly tarnished and some had been damaged. After the second sack was emptied, the 'precious one' couldn't restrain himself any longer and got to his feet. Tripping over his robes, he ran forward to examine the artefacts as if they were toys delivered for his pleasure. Choosing a brass statuette of a fierce-looking figure that could have been either a demon or a deity, the boy ran his fingers over the fiery halo that surrounded its head, with a smile on his face. Glancing across at his mother, he held it up for her to see, then chose a prayer wheel and spun it around.

One of the two lamas spoke in Tibetan, his voice expressing awe. The monk who had translated Afridi's words now told them in Hindi, 'The Rinpoche recognizes the treasures from his monastery.'

The boy continued rummaging through the pile of ritual objects as Fletcher and Afridi opened the remaining sacks. One of them contained a bundle of thangka scrolls, which they placed on a low table to one side.

Many of them looked as if they had been damaged by water and some of the embroidery was torn but when one of the two lamas unrolled an image of a green goddess, both he and his companion seemed to recognize the thangka, folding their hands.

Collecting the empty sacks, Fletcher and Afridi retreated from the room, leaving the boy and his attendants to sort through their treasure. The terma had been restored to those who recognized its significance beyond any material value.

On the drive back to Kalimpong, Fletcher asked, 'Do you think we earned any merit today?'

'Just enough to wipe out the bad karma we brought on ourselves by setting the forest on fire,' said Afridi.

'That's the problem, isn't it?' said Fletcher. 'Our good deeds always get cancelled out because of the means by which they are achieved.'

Two hours later, they arrived back at Montrose just before dusk. The alpenglow on Kanchenjunga turned the snow peaks from gold to purple, then, finally, to leaden grey, in the reverse alchemy of evening light.

◆

The whole plan had been Kesang's idea.

Four nights ago, before they had gone in search of the terma, the three of them had been discussing what to do with the relics, if they were found. Kesang had listened to Fletcher and Afridi arguing over whether the treasure should be handed over to the Khampas or to the Americans. As Fletcher had explained, the CIA was still willing to buy the antiquities but no longer wanted the money to fund an armed insurgency in Tibet. A third option, that Afridi had proposed, was that it be given to the Indian authorities, though none of them was in favour of that. Interrupting their debate, Kesang had suggested that the relics be returned to the young tulku and his attendants at Rumtek. They were the rightful heirs to the treasure, since the boy had been recognized as a reincarnation of the Rinpoche of Yangchen. As for the remains of the American pilots, Fletcher could take custody of those and return them to the CIA, so they would be given a proper burial.

'That's all very well,' Afridi had said, 'but it means the Khampas get nothing for having risked their lives carrying it over the mountains.'

'The situation is different now than it was back then,' Kesang had reminded him. 'The war between India and China has changed the whole dynamic. When the Khampas brought the relics across they expected to sell them so they could buy arms. Now, India and the US are recruiting the Khampas for the Special Frontier Force. They'll be given weapons and training for free.'

'It's not the same thing,' Afridi had disagreed.

'Maybe we should just leave the terma where it is,' Fletcher had suggested in frustration. 'Sometimes it's better not to find what's hidden instead of digging up the past. It often leads to more disputes and conflict than it's worth.'

'That would save us a lot of trouble,' Afridi had acknowledged.

'Unfortunately, I committed to bringing back the pilots' remains,' Fletcher had said, 'which means we need to get to the cave.'

Kesang had asked, 'What was that expression you used, "plausible…?"'

'Deniability,' Fletcher had responded.

'So, the CIA is willing to pay the money to someone who will help the Khampas, as long as it isn't given to them directly?'

Fletcher had nodded. 'And preferably not to fund an armed resistance, which might stir up more trouble on the border.'

'Then why don't they give the money to the Tibetan Rehabilitation and Welfare Society, which runs a charitable centre in Gangtok for Tibetan refugees? Many of them are Khampas, and some of them are former Chushi Gangdruk guerillas who were wounded and disabled while fighting the Chinese,' Kesang had proposed. 'I'm one of the trustees of TRWS and I'll make sure the money gets used properly.'

Glancing across at Afridi, Fletcher had shrugged. 'I could give it a try.'

Kesang had then prodded Afridi. 'Come on, Imtiaz, what do you think?'

He'd shaken his head. 'It solves one problem, but not the other.'

'What do you mean?'

'The relics belong to the Yangchen Gompa monastery,' Afridi had explained. 'It just doesn't seem right, when we have an opportunity to give the terma back to the survivors of that monastery, that we should deny them that legacy.'

'But they *will* get their relics!' Kesang had insisted. 'You'll give them back. That's the plan!'

Both Fletcher and Afridi had looked at her, confused.

'Then there's nothing to sell to the CIA,' Afridi had pointed out.

'Yes, there is.' Kesang had laughed. 'We'll give the Americans all of the artefacts that Daddy collected. Emil Zorman said most of them were antiques and they were worth a lot of money. I don't want them any more and I think Daddy would have been delighted to think that all of the relics he bought from refugees were being used to fund the rehabilitation centre.'

'Are you sure?' Fletcher had asked.

'Absolutely,' she'd said. 'As long as you can get the CIA to agree.'

'And we won't tell them that the artefacts they're buying didn't come from Yangchen Gompa?' Afridi had looked at Kesang with bemused admiration.

'Nobody will know the difference,' she had replied. 'The only person who might have recognized where they came from was Zorman—and he's dead.'

◆

'Bait and switch,' said Fletcher, as he helped Kesang refill a sack with an assortment of brass figurines and votive lamps. 'It's an American expression.'

'You said, all they really cared about were the pilots' remains,' she replied.

'That's true,' said Fletcher. 'But I just hope nobody finds out I was part of this scam.'

As soon as he and Afridi had brought the relics back to Kalimpong, the day before, Fletcher had opened the sacks and found a canister containing bone fragments. It was a large, cylindrical tin that looked as if it might have originally been filled with flour or tsampa. The lid was tightly fitted and he'd had to use his pocketknife to pry it open. Inside were several cloth bundles in which the bones had been wrapped. Taking out one, he discovered a section of a human jawbone with several teeth intact. Though it was a grisly relic, Fletcher felt some satisfaction that they might be able to identify the dead man using his dental records. Carefully wrapping it up again, he resealed the tin, which weighed about eight or ten pounds. Meanwhile, Afridi had gone off to arrange a vehicle to take Fletcher to Bagdogra. By the time he returned, they had filled all of the sacks.

◆

The next morning, Afridi picked him up from the hotel in a jeep that looked identical to the one they had been ambushed in a year ago. Their driver was an older man this time, with a white moustache. After they collected the sacks of antiquities and the canister from Montrose, Fletcher gave Kesang a hug and shook hands with Afridi. They both came down to the gate to see him off and he felt a mild ache of regret as he drove away.

This time there was no checkpoint at the Teesta Bridge and riding in a military jeep, he wasn't stopped. The two-and-a-half hour drive was uneventful and at the airport they were waved through the security barrier, driving straight onto the tarmac where the Convair was parked. As they pulled up, Sullivan stepped out of the plane and came down the staircase, an unlit pipe in his mouth.

'Hey, you got to travel first class,' said Fletcher, as they greeted each other.

'The ambassador and his guests flew in this morning, so I hitched a ride,' said Sullivan. 'They've gone up to Gangtok to attend the Crown Prince and Hope Cooke's wedding.'

The pilot had opened the cargo hold and two of the airport staff helped unload the sacks from the back of the jeep and stow them in the plane. Fletcher handed the canister to Sullivan, who examined it with a sceptical eye.

'It's not the most elegant urn,' said Fletcher. 'But the remains are inside.'

'Any trouble finding them?' Sullivan asked.

'Some day I'll tell you the whole story,' Fletcher said. 'How about the payment? Were you able to work that out?'

'One point two million bucks,' said Sullivan, passing the canister to one of the men who was loading the plane and telling him to put it inside the cabin. 'After I got your message through Agatha, I had to pull a lot of strings. The money will be deposited in the Tibetan

Rehabilitation and Welfare Society's account with American Express in Calcutta, broken into two dozen payments from various sources, none of which leads back to us. I just hope you know what you're doing. I had to go all the way to the top for approval. It wasn't easy.'

'At least you didn't have to deal with giant bees,' said Fletcher, grinning.

'What do you mean?' Sullivan looked puzzled.

'Never mind, it's a long story,' Fletcher replied.

'Why don't you come back to Delhi with me?' Sullivan suggested, gesturing towards the Convair. 'You can tell me what happened on the way.'

'Not today, thanks.' Fletcher shook his head then pointed to the jeep. 'We're going to turn around and drive straight back up to Gangtok. I have an invitation to attend the royal wedding.'

Sullivan gave him a suspicious glance.

'You're not worried about the Intelligence Bureau?' he asked.

'No, we're all on the same side now…at least for the time being,' Fletcher assured him. 'Besides, Major Afridi has cleared Allan Swift's name.'

◆

After dropping his suitcase at the Blue Poppy guesthouse and changing into a fresh set of clothes, Fletcher asked the driver to drop him at the palace gate. He could hear music playing as they approached. The Sikkim Guards were dressed in ceremonial regalia—red jackets with black facing and woven bamboo helmets ornamented with cockades of peacock feathers. Dismissing the driver with thanks, he walked up to the palace, where he could see a crowd of guests on the lawns. It was late afternoon and the wedding ceremony had been held a few hours earlier in the royal chapel.

As Fletcher approached the colourful marquees set up for the reception, he spotted several of the people he'd met the year before in Gangtok, including the Political Officer. He also recognized a song by the Isley Brothers, 'Twistin' with Linda,' which was pouring out of the loudspeakers. A number of people were dancing. Amongst them was Ambassador Galbraith, manfully performing an arthritic twist with

Princess Coocoola. The Maharaj Kumar and his bride, dressed in brocade robes, were seated on a pair of thrones under one of the canopies, where photographers and courtiers hovered.

Fletcher stuck to the periphery of the party but he could not elude the Kazini, dressed in all her finery, including the red panda stole. As she rushed across to him, he tried to duck out of sight but there was nowhere to hide.

'Allan! Mr Swift!' she cried. 'I finally got to meet the ambassador, no thanks to you, but I'm afraid it's too late. The damage has been done!'

'I'm surprised you're here,' he said. 'I thought you disapproved of the wedding.'

'Of course, I had to be here!' she said, dramatically. 'Whether I like it or not.'

Across the lawns, he caught sight of Colonel Norton chatting with a group of Indian Army officers in uniform. As the music subsided, Fletcher was about to excuse himself, when he felt an arm slip through his.

Sage Carlyle had two Leicas dangling from her neck and the cameras clattered together as they kissed each other on the cheek.

'Gee! I've been looking for you all over,' she cried.

'I just arrived,' he said, as she kissed him again on the other cheek, while the Kazini watched with a censorious stare.

Fletcher began to introduce them but the Kazini stopped him.

'We've already met,' she said, coldly. 'There are far too many Americans here! Miss Carlyle was telling me that she also attended Sarah Loony College, like the blushing bride.'

Fletcher felt Sage's fingers entwine with his, as the Kazini turned and ploughed her way through the crowd.

'Why did she call you Allan?' Sage asked.

'I don't know,' he said. 'Forget about her.'

'So, you got my letter?' she said. 'I wasn't sure it would reach you.'

'Yeah,' he said. 'I'm afraid I couldn't reply.'

'I was worried you might not be in India,' said Sage, 'Maybe you'd finished your research and gone back home.'

'No, I've been here most of the time,' he said, glancing down at her cameras. 'So, have you got any good pictures?'

'Oh yeah!' she exclaimed, untangling her fingers from his before caressing the inside of his arm, just above his elbow. 'It's so spectacular here. The mountains. The colours. Totally exotic! I just hope I don't run out of film....'

'I can imagine the cover of Cosmo,' he said with a laugh. 'Romantic Royal Wedding in Shangri-La!'

'Well, you know how it is,' said Sage. 'Nothing like a good fairy tale!'

'Sure,' he said, looking at her with a sceptical smile, 'So long as everyone lives happily ever after....'

Epilogue

22 November 1963 – John F. Kennedy is assassinated.

2 December 1963 – Tashi Namgyal, eleventh Chogyal of Sikkim, dies of cancer.

27 May 1964 – Jawaharlal Nehru dies of heart failure.

4 April 1965 – Coronation of Palden Thondup Namgyal as twelfth Chogyal of Sikkim.

4 April 1973 – On the celebration of the Chogyal's fiftieth birthday, black flag demonstrations and riots break out, protesting against his rule.

15 August 1973 – With the growing agitation, Hope Cooke and her two children depart from Sikkim.

14 April 1975 – Sikkim's monarchy abolished and Sikkim annexed by India.

16 May 1975 – Kazi Lhendup Dorjee becomes the first Chief Minister of Sikkim.

9 September 1976 – Mao Tse-tung dies of multiple organ failure.

11 March 1978 – Crown Prince Tenzing Namgyal dies in a car crash.

1980 – Hope Cooke and Palden Thondup Namgyal divorce.

29 January 1982 – Palden Thondup Namgyal dies in New York City of cancer.

28 July 2007 – Kazi Lhendup Dorjee dies of heart failure.

16 June 2020 – A clash between India and China in Ladakh's Galwan Valley leads to hand-to-hand combat in which twenty Indian troops and an unknown number of Chinese soldiers are killed because of an unresolved border dispute.

Sources

Ali, Salim, *The Birds of Sikkim*, Bombay: Oxford University Press, 1962.

Bird, Kai, *The Good Spy: The Life and Death of Robert Ames*, New York: Crown, 2014.

Conboy, Kenneth and James Morrison, *The CIA's Secret War in Tibet*, Lawrence: University Press of Kansas, 2002.

Dalvi, J. P., *Himalayan Blunder*, Dehradun: Natraj (4th edn), 2010.

Duff, Andrew, *Sikkim*, London: Vintage, 2015.

Galbraith, John Kenneth, *Ambassador's Journal*, Boston: Houghton Mifflin, 1969.

Kennedy, Robert F., *Thirteen Days: A Memoir of the Cuban Missile Crisis*, New York: W. W. Norton Company, 1971.

Ray, Sunanda Datta, *Sikkim: Smash and Grab*, Delhi: Tranquebar (2nd edn), 2013.

Rustomji, Nari, *Enchanted Frontiers: Sikkim, Bhutan and India's North-Eastern Borderlands*, Bombay: Oxford University Press, 1971.

Thomas, Evan, *The Very Best Men: The Daring Early Years of the CIA*, New York: Simon and Schuster, 1995.

Verma, Shiv Kunal, *1962: The War that Wasn't*, New Delhi: Aleph Book Company, 2016.

Common and Latin names, for birds described in this book are, as much as possible, consistent with general usage during 1962. Many of these names have now been changed. In addition to drawing upon Salim Ali's books, I am extremely grateful to Robert Fleming Jr for reviewing my descriptions of birds and making corrections and suggesting additions. Bikram Grewal also kindly read the chapter headings. My thanks to Geoffrey Ward and his sister Helen Ward for providing details about the American community in Delhi during the 1950s. Prajwal Parajuly answered questions about Kalimpong and I am most grateful for his help. Tenzing Nima provided insights on Tibet. None of these individuals, however, should be held responsible for errors or exaggerations in a work of fiction.